Sophia rose ~~...~~ **came over to** ~~...~~ **, brushing his shoulder to reach for his plate.**

Her long tresses flowed onto his lap as she brought her face inches from his. He smelled of earth, raw-hide and musk, and her breathing quickened as their eyes met. He was a beautiful man who hated her, but right now, she saw desire darken his eyes. She whispered gently, blowing her breath over his lips, playing the vixen he thought she was, "I'll clean this up and then we'll get right to work so you won't have to stay any longer than necessary."

Logan stared at her, their gazes linked and then his hand touched the ribbon of exposed skin at her waist. Her breath caught in her throat and her senses heightened as he splayed his fingers along the rim of her shirt.

It was unexpected magic.

Dear Reader,

I'm beyond thrilled that *Sunset Surrender* is the first book in Mills & Boon®'s new RICH, RUGGED RANCHERS promotion. Rich and rugged (and gorgeous) describes my hero, Logan Slade, to the letter. He owns and operates Sunset Ranch, raising prized horses on land the Slade family has owned for generations.

In *Sunset Surrender,* you'll also meet Sophia Montrose, the beautiful Las Vegas showgirl turned hotel manager who has inherited half of Sunset Lodge located on Slade property. She's a thorn in Logan's backside and a woman who can hold her own against a man who bitterly opposes her return to the ranch. But Sophia isn't the woman he thinks she is—she's more—and she sets out to prove that Logan has always been wrong about her.

Sparks fly between Logan and Sophia and the sizzle is evident from page one. I hope you enjoy seeing Logan's ultimate "surrender" in the first installment of the SLADES OF SUNSET RANCH series. Luke's and Justin's stories are coming soon.

My motto: the bold, passionate, heart-stopping cowboy always gets the girl!

Happy reading!

Charlene Sands

SUNSET SURRENDER

BY
CHARLENE SANDS

All the characters in this book have no existence outside the imagination of the author, and have no relation whatsoever to anyone bearing the same name or names. They are not even distantly inspired by any individual known or unknown to the author, and all the incidents are pure invention.

All Rights Reserved including the right of reproduction in whole or in part in any form. This edition is published by arrangement with Harlequin Enterprises II B.V./S.à.r.l. The text of this publication or any part thereof may not be reproduced or transmitted in any form or by any means, electronic or mechanical, including photocopying, recording, storage in an information retrieval system, or otherwise, without the written permission of the publisher.

This book is sold subject to the condition that it shall not, by way of trade or otherwise, be lent, resold, hired out or otherwise circulated without the prior consent of the publisher in any form of binding or cover other than that in which it is published and without a similar condition including this condition being imposed on the subsequent purchaser.

® and ™ are trademarks owned and used by the trademark owner and/or its licensee. Trademarks marked with ® are registered with the United Kingdom Patent Office and/or the Office for Harmonisation in the Internal Market and in other countries.

Published in Great Britain 2013
by Mills & Boon, an imprint of Harlequin (UK) Limited,
Eton House, 18-24 Paradise Road, Richmond, Surrey TW9 1SR

© Charlene Swink 2013

ISBN: 978 0 263 90467 3
ebook ISBN: 978 1 472 00586 1

51-0313

Harlequin (UK) policy is to use papers that are natural, renewable and recyclable products and made from wood grown in sustainable forests. The logging and manufacturing processes conform to the legal environmental regulations of the country of origin.

Printed and bound in Spain
by Blackprint CPI, Barcelona

Charlene Sands is a *USA TODAY* bestselling author of thirty-five romance novels, writing sexy contemporary romances and stories of the Old West. Her books have been honored with the National Readers Choice Award, the *Cataromance* Reviewer's Choice Award and she's a double recipient of the Booksellers' Best Award. She belongs to the Orange County Chapter and the Los Angeles Chapter of RWA.

Charlene writes bold, passionate, heart-stopping cowboys *and always real good men!* She knows a little something about true romance—she married her high school sweetheart. When not writing, Charlene enjoys sunny Pacific beaches, great coffee, reading books from her favorite authors and spoiling her new baby granddaughters. You can find her on Facebook, Pinterest and Twitter. Charlene loves to hear from her readers. You can write her at PO Box 4883, West Hills, CA 91308, USA, or sign up for her newsletter for fun blog posts and ongoing contests at www.charlenesands.com.

With all my love to Everley Frances and Kyra Nicole.
You are my sweet little wonders!

One

Sophia Montrose stared into the cowboy's cold black eyes. His mouth was hard and a twitch away from a sneer.

"Couldn't wait to show up here, now could you?"

It was not a sunny welcome back to Sunset Ranch. Not that Sophia really expected one from Logan Slade. She'd decided long ago that she would stand her ground and refuse to let him intimidate her. But she hadn't crossed paths with him since she'd left Sunset Ranch as a girl of fifteen, and had forgotten how his rugged good looks could make her heartbeat speed up. Yet even though maturity had done him justice in a dangerously sinful way, she wouldn't lose sight of how Logan Slade resented her being here, just as much as he had when she'd lived on Slade land before.

"Is Luke home?" Standing on the doorstep of the ranch house, Sophia hoped to see the friendly face of Logan's younger brother soon.

"No. He'll be home tomorrow. You want to come back?"

She shook her head. She had nowhere else to go. She'd given up her small Las Vegas apartment and had driven for hours to reach the ranch this afternoon. She didn't want to take a room in Carson City. She was ready to start her new life, now. This minute. "I came for the keys to the cottage."

He leveled an unforgiving look at her. "You'll get them."

Logan had instructed his attorney not to give her the keys in advance. He'd wanted her to come for them personally. It was Logan's way. He wanted to see her squirm, or at the very least, make her feel uncomfortable the second she stepped foot on Slade property.

She put out her hand, palm up, and tried for civility. "Please. I'd like to get settled."

He assessed her for one moment, then whipped around and entered his house, tossing a command over his shoulder. "Follow me."

She was left on the threshold with her hand out. Quickly lowering it to her side, she tilted her chin up, and took a few steps inside the house.

The minute she entered, her throat tightened and good memories washed away Logan's attempt to ruin this homecoming. The place was as beautiful as she remembered. She'd loved the warmth of the Slade home, the pretty earth colors, the cozily arranged furniture that faced a wide stone fireplace that reached the ceiling. Antiques, bronze statues and expensive artwork decorated the room. Hard wood and contrasting soft hues made the Nevada ranch house perfectly welcoming.

How many times had she played here with Luke? How many birthday parties and private Sunset Lodge events had she attended here with her mother? A stream of good feelings settled into her bones.

She followed behind Logan, his shiny black boots clicking against polished wood. His tall muscular frame ate up space as he sauntered down the long hallway toward his late father

Randall Slade's office. Logan was neat as a pin, looking crisp in a blue plaid shirt and brand-new jeans. Broad-backed and slim-hipped, he had a fine way of filling out his clothes. He made no attempt to speak with her. She didn't expect small talk from him anyway.

Sophia could only imagine his tirade when the terms of his father's last will and testament had been read by the Slades' private attorney. It must have been a last-minute decision on Mr. Slade's part to include her in the will, because when Luke had called—a voice from her past—she'd noted his surprised tone. But he was encouraging. He couldn't wait to see her again after all these years, he'd said, despite the circumstances.

But no one could have been more surprised than Sophia when she'd learned she'd inherited half ownership of Sunset Lodge from Randall Slade. The only stipulation was that she had to manage the lodge for one year before she could sell her share.

It had been twelve years since she'd lived here. Her mother, as the manager of Sunset Lodge, had left abruptly, breaking all ties to the Slade family and asking Sophia to do the same. It meant losing Luke's friendship and many other things, when they'd left Sunset Ranch.

"It's for the best," her mother had said. But Sophia hadn't understood that, the way children couldn't understand sacrifice and hardship and doing the right thing. Sophia had been yanked out of high school in her first year without any warning. She'd left girlfriends behind—and all of her dreams—and had cried herself to sleep every night during those first few months.

Now, with her mother gone after fighting a two-year battle with cancer, Sophia was here to claim her unexpected inheritance. Randall Slade had always been kind to her, showing her compassion, and Sophia thought him a good man. He had treated Sophia like family, had been a father figure to her when her own father had abandoned her at the age of three.

"In here," Logan rasped, ducking into the office.

She followed him inside.

"Have a seat." He pointed to a crimson leather sofa that looked stiff and new. As she gazed around the room, she noted that the entire room had been updated.

Instead of the paneled walls and golden curtains she'd remembered, the walls were clean, textured and stately. Wide electronically controlled windows opened to the grounds outside. Above, rustic chandelier lamps had been replaced with track lights that pointed down at the desk like a row of dutiful soldiers. It was as if all evidence of Randall Slade and his reign at Sunset Ranch had been removed.

"No, thank you." Her decision to stand garnered a quick glance and then a grunt from Logan. Sophia smiled to herself. She'd cling to her small victories.

She wished Luke had been the one to greet her today. She would've liked him to be the first person she'd face upon her return to Sunset Ranch. But she'd moved up her arrival by a few days out of necessity, and maybe it was a good thing to get this confrontation with Logan over with first, rather than hold on to her dread. When she saw Luke again, there wouldn't be worries about his older brother overshadowing their reunion.

"I'm sorry about your father," Sophia said out of reverence to Randall Slade's memory. "He was a decent man. I'm sure you miss him very much."

From behind his long plank desk, Logan's stony expression didn't budge. "We're not here to discuss my relationship with my father."

"You won't even allow me to offer my condolences?" Sophia spoke softly, injured that Logan wouldn't grant her that much. "He was always kind to me."

Leather creaked as he lowered down in a swivel chair behind his desk. "He was kind to Montrose women at the expense of my family."

She stood five feet seven inches tall in bare feet and yet Logan, sitting behind his desk with penetrating eyes locked on her, appeared the more imposing. She swallowed past a lump in her throat. Her mother's death was still painfully raw to her. She knew Logan resented her mother. Maybe he hated her, but she wouldn't allow him to speak ill of her. "My mother died several months ago, Logan. I miss her, just as I'm sure you miss your father. I will ask you to keep your thoughts to yourself about what you think you know."

"I know the truth, Sophia. And there's no way to sugarcoat it." His voice held conviction. "Your mother had an affair with my father, right under my mother's nose. Louisa wanted his money and he was too blinded by her beauty to see what she was doing. Our family was never the same after that. It nearly destroyed us."

Sophia glanced out the window at the beautiful grounds and the stables where exquisite horses were raised to be sold to the highest bidder. The lodge beyond was a private resort designed to house elite guests who wanted a ranch-type experience with all the trimmings.

The Slade brothers—Justin, Luke and Logan—had endured their mother and father's deaths but they had each other, and they'd always have Sunset Ranch, whereas Sophia was completely alone. For whatever pain the Slades went through, she was truly sorry, but what had happened between her mother, Louisa and Randall Slade was complicated and not so easily explained.

"My mother saved your parents' marriage."

Logan shot back, "You've worn too many headdresses in your day, Sophia. All that strutting around half-naked on Las Vegas stages has gotten to you."

His triumphant gaze penetrated straight through her. She shouldn't have been surprised that he knew about her profession as a showgirl. She'd managed to keep under the radar for most of her adult life, but when her mother had taken ill Sophia had tough choices to make to provide for both of them and she wasn't ashamed of it. Nearly everyone within earshot in Nevada had learned about her scandalous marriage to an aging millionaire. What was to be a private union had ended up becoming fodder for the tabloids once the news of her marriage got out. Even in Las Vegas, a twenty-six-year-old showgirl marrying a seventy-one year old oil magnate on the sly was big news.

"So you know?"

"I read, Sophia."

"My marriage and my last profession aren't any of your business," she said softly. Her heart was full of grief and she had no room left for more. Not from Logan and not on her first day back here. There would be more battles to come, she was sure, but she didn't want to argue with him today.

He swept his eyes over her again, this time more precisely, as if he were ranking her on some kind of male scale. He scanned over the long wisps of black hair that had escaped from the severe knot at the back of her head and then his gaze traveled from her amber eyes to her full lips. He lingered there, and she wondered if he remembered the kiss they'd shared in high school. The one that had left Sophia breathless and wanting more. The one that Logan had used to humiliate her. She'd never gotten over her first real kiss or the pain that it had caused her.

"You're beautiful, Sophia," was all seventeen-year-old Logan had had to say as he'd taken her into his arms behind the gymnasium. He'd pressed his body close and kissed her lips as if he were born to do so. It had been glorious and sweet and passionate, all rolled up into one. Sophia had been taken by the sweeping, unexpected feelings stirring around in her belly. On instinct, she had wrapped her arms around his neck and he'd kept on kissing her, Sophia giving in to the older boy's practiced mouth until laughter, from the other side of the brick wall, interrupted them. Logan had abruptly broken off the kiss and stared solemnly into her eyes for a brief moment frozen in time, before he took off, leaving her standing there dumbfounded as he joined his friends.

News of Logan's bet with their three high school classmates—that Sophia wouldn't push him away if he kissed her—had been the buzz all around school the next day. Sophia was easy, just like her mother.

Now she angled her chin down to stare at him, combating the sensations swamping her and wishing she'd never been attracted to Luke's older brother in the first place. She hated that the heat of his gaze did things to her. Hated that she hadn't forgotten that one surprising kiss. It was as if Logan had stamped her for life.

He continued his visual assault with a gaze that traveled along the neckline of her conservative summer dress and lingered on her ample bustline. For as much as she tried, her clothes simply couldn't hide the fullness of her breasts. They were evident no matter what she wore, and she'd actually considered a reduction at one point in her life when putting food on the table and paying hospital bills hadn't yet been a priority. But her body and her exotic Spanish looks had paid the bills when it mattered most. She had to be grateful for that.

Logan's gaze finally scoured over her legs, which were almost in full view from his place behind the desk. She wished she'd sat down when he'd given her the opportunity, rather than be studied this way. Now, under his scrutiny, she tensed.

When he was through eyeing her, he said, "What'd you do, give the old guy heart failure in the bedroom?"

Sophia gasped at the notion and took the comment as an insult, because that's exactly how Logan had intended it. He'd rather think the worst of her than offer her even the slightest ounce of respect. "He's not dead, thank goodness. We're... divorced."

Logan contemplated her for a second. "Short marriage. Was Gordon Gregory smart enough to get a prenup?"

"Not that it's any of your business, but I was the one who demanded it."

Logan leaned back in his chair and laughed. "You don't fool me, Sophia. You're just like your mother."

"Thank you. I'll take that as a compliment. My mother was an amazing woman."

The smile left Logan's face. He came forward in his seat to brace his hands on the desk. Serious now, he stared straight into her eyes. "Look, I'll make you a deal. I'm willing to buy out your half of the lodge. You won't have to stay on and run the place for a year. I can have my attorney get around that stipulation somehow. I'm prepared to make you a mighty generous offer."

"No."

"You don't want to know the amount?" He had a pen in hand, ready to write down a sum.

"No amount of money will do."

Logan didn't seem convinced. He shrugged, and thought she was negotiating. "Let's cut to the chase, Sophia. I'll pay you twice what it's worth."

He took a knife and stabbed her in the heart with that offer. He wanted to get rid of her, and now she knew just how much. But she wouldn't allow that to stop her. She had legal rights to the lodge and no matter what he offered, Sophia wasn't going to leave. "No. I'm staying. I will run Sunset Lodge."

Sunset Ranch had been her home for twelve years. She'd loved living at the cottage next to the lodge. It was the only place she'd ever wanted to live. The only place she'd ever regarded as her home. And she wasn't about to let Logan Slade run her off.

She would stay.

And she would be as successful a manager as her mother had been.

"Now please, Logan. Hand over the keys."

* * *

Logan walked Sophia outside to her car. The old dented Camry looked the worse for wear with nearly bald tires and paint getting thin. The scrap of metal was fifteen years old if it was a day. Hardly the kind of wheels he expected a Las Vegas showgirl who'd been married to a loaded old geezer to drive.

He held on to the cottage keys, wishing his dang father hadn't seen fit to put Sophia in his will. She was too beautiful, too perfect. Every feature on her face was flawless. She had golden eyes, inky black hair and skin that glowed in the Nevada sunshine. She was the kind of woman that made men do stupid things. He didn't want to think about what kind of trouble she would stir up around here. His men would bend over backward for her, he was sure. They'd done the same for Louisa. All that woman had to do was smile pretty, and the ranch hands would do her bidding. She'd had them eating out of the palm of her hand.

Sophia had grown into the spitting image of her mother and then some. In fact, Logan hated to admit it but Sophia Montrose was even more stunning than her mother had been.

"So, refresh my memory. Why in hell do you want to live way out here with the dust and the flies and horse dung?"

Sophia rolled her eyes, and the deep breath she sucked in lifted her ample chest, stretching the material of her dress to its limit. Logan's groin tightened. He didn't like his immediate reaction to her one damn bit.

"Sunset Ranch was my home, too, Logan. For twelve years of my life. It was a happy time, and I loved working alongside my mother at the lodge, which—thanks to your father's kindness—is half mine now. So why would I not want to live here?"

Logan rubbed the back of his neck. He still didn't get why his father put Sophia Montrose in his will. "It's hardly an exciting life."

Sophia repeated his words. "It's hardly an exciting life."

Logan's brows lifted. "You telling me you didn't like living in Las Vegas? A woman like you?"

Sophia narrowed her eyes. "You have no idea who I am, Logan."

He knew she was the kind of woman who wasn't above sleeping with an old man to get her hands on his money. The old codger must have come to his senses before she cleaned him out, prenup or not.

"I can't change the past," she said. "But I'm here to make a life for myself."

"On Slade land."

"Yes, on Slade land. Now, are you going to keep jingling those keys in front of me or are you going to hand them over?"

Logan looked at the keys in his hand. "No one has lived there since you left."

Sophia's brows gathered. "Are you saying that the cottage is exactly the same?"

He nodded. "My father wouldn't allow anyone else to live there. Another victory for Louisa. You can bet that decision didn't set well with my mother. I used to hear them fighting about it late at night."

"That's hardly my mother's fault. Or mine, for that matter."

"You'll have to let the current manager at the lodge go."

Sophia met his smug stare. "Go? What do you mean?"

"I mean, she's out of a job now. The thing of it is, Sophia, you're going to replace her as manager. Last I checked the place can't have two full-time managers. Mrs. Polanski has to be notified."

"You don't honestly expect me to go in there and fire her, do you?"

"Well, if you don't want to, she can stay on and I'll buy you out. That'll solve your problem."

Sophia crossed her arms under her breasts and glared at him. "You go straight to hell."

Logan grinned. He couldn't help it. He'd succeeded in rankling her. Up until this point, she'd been a cool customer. But he'd be darned if the woman didn't just get prettier with her face heating up and her eyes shooting sparks. "I'm just telling you like it is, Sophia. Mrs. Polanski has managed the place going on eight years now. She's good and the guests like her."

"And you left it up to me to fire her. How sweet of you."

"Something has to give. It seems my father didn't think of everything when he gave away our lodge."

"I only have half ownership. He didn't give it all away."

"I bet you wish he had."

She lifted her perfectly sculpted chin and replied without pause. "Yes, sure. I wish I had full ownership."

Logan eyed her. He hadn't expected her to admit it.

"Maybe then I wouldn't have to deal with you…or fire an employee."

Now, Logan's blood boiled. "That lodge has been in the Slade family for generations. It was a little hole-in-the-wall inn for drifters and penniless soldiers after World War II, until my grandfather came along and built it into the fine establishment it is today. You tell me how you figure into that picture?"

Sophia raised her arms into the air, her temper flaring. "I don't know why your father was so generous with me, Logan. I don't know what you want me to say, but obviously your father had faith in me to do the job right. I'm here now and I am going to manage the lodge. If I have to let someone go, I'll do it. But," she said, pointing her finger at his chest, "I can assure you, I will not forget that you placed me in this position the very second I stepped onto the ranch."

"That's the way I want to be remembered, Sophia. As the guy who is going to test you, time and again. You don't belong here, but I won't stand in your way, either, if you do a good job. And don't worry, I'm relinquishing my duties at the lodge to Luke. You'll deal with him from now on." He dropped the keys into her hand. "Starting tomorrow."

She closed her hands around the keys. "I didn't want to start out like this, Logan."

He opened the car door for her and spoke with as much civility as he could muster. "Half a mile down the road. I'm sure you remember how to get there."

"Yes, I do remember," she said. As she squeezed past him to get into the car, her knockout breasts brushed his chest and the firm contact, along with the stirring scent of her erotic perfume, assaulted him like a blow to the gut.

He closed the car door, and watched her Camry vanish into the horizon as half a dozen curses slipped out of his mouth.

The second Logan was out of sight in her rearview mirror, Sophia slumped her shoulders and loosened the tight grip she had on the steering wheel. She eased her foot off the pedal a little and let the car amble along the road that led to Sunset Lodge. She simply would not think of Logan Slade again. He angered her, but he also thrilled her, and it was an emotion she didn't welcome—and one she tried to will away. Her mother had once told her that matters of the heart could not be explained or understood. They just were. Sophia would not be a fool in regard to Logan Slade. He'd offered her a small fortune just to be rid of her. How could she feel anything for him but disdain?

Certainly, she could avoid him while living here. Nestled between the grand Sierra Nevadas and Carson City, Sunset Ranch was vast, spanning miles in a diamond-shaped perimeter. Tomorrow, when Luke arrived home, she'd renew their friendship and she'd deal with him on matters involving her lodge duties. At least she had one friend on Sunset Ranch she could count on.

"Don't you worry about a thing, darlin'," he'd said. "I'll make sure you get a proper welcome home."

Snow from winter storms capped the tallest peaks of the mountain range, reminding her of vanilla ice cream on a waffle cone. The image made her smile. She'd almost forgotten how peaceful and beautiful the landscape was on Sunset Ranch in the spring, the indigo skies dotted with white marshmallow clouds. It was so different from the crowded marquee-laden noisy streets of Las Vegas.

The lodge stables came into view first, and her heart squeezed tight that her mother couldn't be here to see the grounds once again. Louisa had loved caring for the horses in her spare time. "So sorry, Mama."

Sophia blinked away a tear, taking a deep breath.

As she drove a little farther, the lodge filled her vision. It wasn't what one would expect to see on a Nevada ranch. The lodge was grand, made of natural, rounded gray stone mingled with cedar sidings in a glorious combination that spoke of elegance and grace. The surrounding land was fertile and filled with wispy wildflowers in bloom. And the immediate grounds were groomed impeccably.

It was considered a privilege by the employees to tend the property and work the stables. Not too many workers came and went at Sunset Lodge. The Slades had always maintained long-standing relationships with those on staff.

Sophia felt queasy about having to release Mrs. Polanski, and any thought she had of stopping in to see the lodge vanished in an instant. She couldn't face that hurdle right now. She would settle into the cottage first and get organized. She would wait until tomorrow to speak to Luke about the woman.

The cottage was tucked behind and out of view of the lodge. It afforded a good amount of privacy, which Sophia wanted now above all else. The media splash her secret marriage had created, along with watching her mother lose her struggle with cancer, had taken a giant toll on her. She needed to regroup and dive into work she would enjoy. More than anything else, Sophia had to prove something to herself.

All her life, she had gotten by on her looks. She'd never had the chance to go to college, but she'd never regretted the time she'd spent with her mother, helping her manage small motels and inns on the outskirts of Las Vegas. When her mother became ill, Sophia had honed her natural dance abilities to land ensemble roles for big-time casinos in Las Vegas. She'd made enough money to support the two of them as a showgirl, not so much because of her brains or talent, but because she looked the way she did.

Now was her chance to dig in, to give it her all and to shine doing something she loved.

"Ms. Montrose, hello!"

A rider on a gorgeous bay mare sidled up next to the car. She didn't realize how slowly she was actually driving. She rolled the window the rest of the way down.

"It's Ward Halliday. Remember me?"

She glanced at the Slade's head horse wrangler. "Oh, Mr. Halliday. Yes, I do recognize you. How have you been?"

He grinned crookedly. "Getting old and grouchy," he said as he rode along beside her car. "But seeing you here sure brightened my day."

"Well, thank you. It's good be ho—here. I've missed it."

His grin faded and he gave her a solemn nod. "Sure am sorry to hear about your mama, girl."

She put her foot on the brake and the car rolled to a stop. "Thank you. It was a hard time."

"Yeah, I'm sure that it was," he said, pulling up on the mare's reins. "She was a nice woman. She made cookies a time or two for my boy, Hunter. Gosh, he was a little cuss then."

"I remember. I helped her, Mr. Ward."

A sweet smile wrinkled his face. "Heck, you're not fifteen anymore. You can call me Ward. Here comes Hunter now."

He turned in his saddle just as a younger man approached on a horse. "He was just a kid when you left the ranch. He's working here with me now and planning on going to Texas A & M in the fall."

Sophia turned off the engine, and stepped out of the car. The sun beamed down with early afternoon intensity and she shielded her eyes as she gazed up to greet the young man. "So you're little Hunter. It's good to see you again."

He took no offense yet straightened her out good-naturedly. "Not so little anymore, miss."

No, he wasn't. Hunter Halliday was taller than his dad and broader in the shoulders. "I can see that."

"Are you fixin' on moving in right now?" he asked.

"Yes, I was just on my way to the cottage."

Ward looked at the boxes in the backseat of her car. "You need help? Hunter will help you unload."

"Oh, well…I could use a hand, but if you're busy—"

"I'm not busy at all," Hunter said. "Mr. Slade sent me out to see if I can help."

He did? Logan hadn't seemed to care one bit that Sophia had to move all of her things into the cottage by herself. He hadn't offered to help, the way a gentleman would, but then she really hadn't expected much from him. "Then yes. I would appreciate your help."

Ward tipped his hat. "Welcome home, Ms. Montrose."

"Call me Sophia," she said just before he turned his horse around.

"Will do," he called over his shoulder.

Sophia smiled and got back into her car. "I'll meet you at the cottage," she said to Hunter.

Hunter took off and somehow managed to beat her there. He ground-tethered his horse and came forward to open the car door for her.

"You got here fast."

He grinned. "I know a shortcut, miss."

"Of course." She was reminded of all the shortcuts she'd taken on horseback when she lived here. The paved roads weren't always the quickest way from point A to point B. "And please, call me Sophia, too."

He was already reaching into her backseat for a box.

"Sure thing."

He came up with three boxes, stacking them and managing to keep them balanced as he walked to the door. Sophia put the key into the lock. Her heart hammered against her chest, and Hunter beat her to the words that were just forming on her lips.

"I bet it's just the way you remembered it."

She breathed out. "I hope so."

She opened the door without fanfare and moved quietly into the cozy three-bedroom cottage. She glanced around, taking everything in with a quick scan. "It is just as I remembered it."

Hunter glanced around. "I've always wondered what the place looked like on the inside. It's sorta nice. Homey."

"Yes," Sophia agreed. She honestly hadn't known what to expect after Logan informed her no one else had lived here since she and her mother left. Somewhere in the back of her mind, she'd wondered if he would deliberately let the place fall to ruin out of bitterness.

"Where would you like the boxes?" Hunter asked.

She walked into the master bedroom that was once her mother's and forced away her sentimentality for Hunter's sake. She didn't want to cry in front of him. "In here, I think."

He followed her, and then set the boxes on the floor by the long three-drawer dresser. Sunlight streamed inside and cast a golden glow on the room. "Wow, looks like a daisy patch in here."

Sophia smiled. "My mother loved daisies. They were her favorite flower." And the room, decorated with white eyelet curtains covered with teensy daisies and a bedspread of creams and buttercup yellows, depicted that love. "My mama liked things bright. That's how she viewed the world."

Hunter didn't say anything about that. He finished unloading her car and she thanked him for his help. Once she was alone, she sat down on the bed. The curtains were crisp, the bedspread fluffy. There wasn't a speck of dust anywhere. Everything was in good condition—too good to have been left uncared for all this time. Someone had made sure these things were well preserved. And she had a feeling that some-one had been Randall Slade.

He was still taking care of her, even from the grave.

After half an hour of unpacking, the doorbell chimed. It was the same singsong melody that she'd remembered. Cu-rious, she walked to the door and looked through the peep-hole. An older woman stood on the cottage threshold holding a lovely vase of pink roses and greenery.

Sophia opened the door.

"Ms. Montrose?"

She nodded slowly. "Yes, I'm Sophia Montrose."

"I'm Ruth Polanski. I've come to welcome you to Sun-set Lodge."

Sophia shuddered. Ruth Polanski, the manager of the lodge? This was the woman she would have to let go. She wasn't ready for this. She hadn't had time to figure out a way to give the woman the bad news. If Logan sent her over here…

"Would you like to come inside?"

"Just for a minute," the silver-haired woman said. "I'm off duty now and don't want to impose. But I wanted to meet you and give you something to warm your home." She handed Sophia the lovely flower-filled vase. "Welcome," she said, her kind eyes crinkling with her smile.

Sophia held the vase in one hand and gestured for her to enter with the other. Her heart raced. She didn't know if she could do this. And she wondered why Luke hadn't mentioned having to fire an elderly woman in order to take her position as manager. Surely, her friend would have known the delicate position this placed her in. "Thank you. They are beautiful."

"I hope you don't mind me coming over here so quickly.

Hunter stopped by and gave me the news and I was very anxious to meet you. I've managed the lodge for eight years now."

"Oh, uh, yes. Logan informed me of that today."

"I can't tell you how happy I am. I mean, I am sad that Mr. Slade passed on. He was a good man—tough but good—and I promised him something when his heart started failing last year."

"Oh?"

Ruth Polanski stood in the middle of the parlor, looking slightly relieved to be sharing this. "Well, he made me promise to stay on as manager until you came to take over."

"He made you promise to stay?"

"That's right. I've been itching to retire. Everybody on the ranch knows it, too. I've got three grandchildren and a husband who retired last year. But I wouldn't go back on my promise and I never told a soul about our agreement. It's the way he wanted it. Mr. Slade's been good to me, and Logan, well, he's a saint in man's clothing."

Had she been sipping a drink, Sophia would have choked hearing those last words.

"Are you saying you want to quit your position as manager?" Sophia was catching on, and her anger was kicking up steam faster than a whistling tea kettle.

"Why, yes. Didn't Logan tell you? I've been waiting for you to arrive. Of course, I won't leave you high and dry. I'll stick around until you get the hang of our operation here."

"Th-thank you."

"Very welcome. It's not too much different than when you were living here. The lodge still has a great reputation for service and accommodations, and we have the same festivities and trail rides in the spring and summer months that we've always had. I'm sure you know all of this. Whenever you're ready, I'll be happy to show you the ropes. And once I'm gone, Logan will be able to answer any questions you have."

Sophia smiled sweetly. The sainted man would soon get

an earful from her. Sophia wasn't good at playing the victim. She would find a way to get even with Logan Slade for deliberately misleading her. From now on, she would keep her guard up around him. "Yes, Mrs. Polanski, once you're gone, I'm certain Logan will be answering to me."

Two

Morning sunlight beamed in through the daisy-print curtains in a cheerful greeting Sophia wasn't quite ready for. Waking up in her mother's old room, her hazy disorientation didn't last long as her eyes focused and she remembered where she was and that today was the start of her new life. The sun's warmth soaked into her bones and helped soothe away her anger at Logan Slade. Thanks to him, she'd had a hard time falling asleep last night. He'd made sure her homecoming wasn't a thing of dreams. Wouldn't he love to know that Sophia had had her own doubts about moving back here. That she feared that her old surroundings would cause her pain. That maybe she couldn't handle this big a job as well as her mother had. If determination had anything to do with success, then Sophia wouldn't have a worry, because above all else, she would see this through. But doubts still had a way of creeping in after all the mental pep talks faded away.

Six weeks ago, she wouldn't have pictured herself back on Slade land, living at the cottage where she'd grown up and being part owner of glorious Sunset Lodge. The elder Slade and her mother had left this earth just a few months apart and somewhere in the back of her mind, she believed that Louisa and Randall were together now, bonded by love and reunited in spirit. That thought comforted Sophia as she lifted her arms through the sleeves of her flowery silk robe and padded from the soft bedside carpeting onto the stone floor that led to the kitchen.

Sophia had always loved the open-air feel to the kitchen, the large picture window, wood-beam ceilings and textured archways that separated the room from the parlor. The countertops were not built of modern stone, but made with small tiles in varying soft shades of tans and creams. The cabinets were buttercup yellow and the appliances were pristine with analog controls that suited Sophia just fine. She knew every drawer, every cabinet. Everything had been preserved as it once was.

It was too easy to slip back into a time when she'd been happy, when her mother was alive, and when she'd felt free of danger.

A shudder tingled along her spine and thoughts popped into her head of her showgirl days in Las Vegas when she had reason not to feel safe. Just then, she glanced out the window and saw a black-and-white Border collie racing by the cottage. The dog clenched a wooden spatula dripping with something she hoped was lemon batter in his mouth. A dark-haired boy chased him, calling out, "Blackie, come back!"

Sophia chuckled at the scene straight out of a Saturday-morning cartoon. She went to the front door and stepped onto her porch. She spotted the back end of Blackie as he raced around the cottage, tail wagging, seeming to enjoy the sport. The little boy, on the other hand, red-faced from exertion and slowing down, looked ready for the game to end.

Sophia went down the steps and hid behind the front wall, listening for the patter of four paws hitting the ground. Just as the dog turned the corner, Sophia crouched down, surprising the animal. But Blackie was too quick for her. As she lunged, he did a last-second side shuffle and maneuvered away, trotting past her. "Blackie, you stop right now!"

The dog immediately froze, the lemon batter dripping from his mouth, his big brown eyes—dark and innocent—watching her with a curious stare. His little game was over.

The boy rounded the corner next and came to a halt several feet away. His chest heaved up and down rapidly. He had an I'm-not-supposed-to-speak-to-strangers look on his face.

"It's okay," she said softly. "I'm Sophia Montrose. I live here now. I'll be working at Sunset Lodge."

The boy nodded, then shot the dog a quick glance. Blackie had decided to sit his bottom down ten feet away to watch them, with the spatula still clenched between his teeth. Every so often, his tongue would come out to lap up some batter.

"What's your name?" she asked the boy.

He paused for a split second. When he spoke, Sophia knew from the innocence in his voice, he was younger than he appeared. "Edward."

"Hi, Edward. How old are you?"

"T-ten," he said. "H-how—how old are you?"

The boy stuttered, and Sophia hoped it wasn't because she had frightened him in any way. "I'm almost twenty-eight. Looks as if little Blackie has something of yours that you want back."

"Y-yes, ma'am. Only, the s-spatula's not mine. B-Blackie s-stole it from Nana's kitchen at the lodge. And she's gonna be m-mad. He's not s-supposed to go in the k-kitchen."

"I see. Well, I bet that if we talk for a minute and ignore him, Blackie will wander over here, and then we'll get it back."

The boy shifted his gaze to the dog, sunken down to the ground on all fours holding the spatula between his front paws, happily licking away. Edward faced her again with a dubious expression.

"Do you live around here?" she asked.

Shaggy brown hair fell into his eyes when he nodded. "I live with my nana at the l-lodge. She's the c-cook."

Sophia was sure now that she wasn't the cause of the boy's stutter. He seemed comfortable with the fact that the words weren't coming out smoothly, as though his manner of speech was something he'd gotten used to. "Well, then I'm sure I'll be meeting her soon. I'll be starting work at the lodge today."

"Yes, ma'am."

"Is Blackie your dog?"

The boy shook his head. "He belongs to Mr. S-Slade. I feed him and walk him and stuff. It's my j-job."

"I see. Does Blackie belong to Luke or Logan?"

The boy had to think about that a second. "Logan Slade." His dark eyes blinked several times as if a light just dawned inside his head. "You w-won't tell h-him, will you?"

"That Blackie got into the kitchen?"

He nodded.

"No, I won't tell him," she assured him with a smile. "But maybe you should tell your grandmother what happened."

"I l-left the back door open and B-Blackie snuck inside to have b-breakfast with me."

"He did, did he?"

"Nana wasn't there at f-first, but when she came back, she y-yelled at Blackie and that's when he grabbed her s-spatula right outta the b-bowl and took off."

The culprit dog stealing right under Nana's nose made Sophia smile. "I think Blackie likes lemon batter. I can't blame him. I used to sneak a lick or two from the bowl when my mama made lemon chiffon cake."

"Nana lets me l-lick the bowl s-sometimes, too."

The dog finally left the spatula on the ground and trotted

over to Edward. "There, you see," Sophia said. "He came to you."

Edward fluffed the top of the collie's head several times and then lifted his dark-eyed gaze to Sophia. "He's a good dog, u-usually."

"Oh, I can see that he is." Sophia bent down to stroke his rumpled coat and the dog gave her a long grateful look, tongue hanging out. She was no longer the enemy trying to take his treat, but an admirer willing to pet him.

"He's quite a mess," she noted. "I'll get something to wash him down. Wait here."

She walked inside the cottage and seconds later came out with a cloth soaked with hot water. "Go ahead and remove the evidence."

She handed Edward the washcloth, and then strode to where the dog had abandoned the spatula. Bending down, she lifted the dirt-smeared utensil gingerly with two fingers dangling it by the wooden end that was the less filthy. "Your nana might want to retire this one."

"Yes, ma'am." Edward's face crumpled. "She w-won't be h-happy about that."

"I wouldn't think so. Maybe you could make it up to her."

"H-how?"

"There sure are a lot of gorgeous purple wildflowers growing this time of year. Does your nana like flowers?"

He shrugged. "Don't know."

"Most women love flowers. I bet your nana does. A handful of those purple wildflowers and a promise that Blackie won't steal from the kitchen again might make her happy."

The boy pondered that idea with a nod. She set the spatula in his hand and his gaze lingered on her.

"Maybe I'll see you at the lodge later, Edward."

"Okay."

The youngster walked away with the dog at his heels. Just

as Sophia was about to enter the house, he turned around one last time, giving her a long thoughtful stare.

She waved and walked inside.

Sophia showered and picked her clothes carefully for her first day on the job. She'd learned from her mother that the lodge guests wanted the flavor of the Old West, along with their luxuries. Dress professionally, but always keep in mind that this is a ranch establishment. A coral silk dress, cinched at the waist with a wide suede belt, along with a lightweight jacket rolled up at the sleeves and a pair of tan leather boots, gave just the right impression of professional and Western. After dressing, Sophia gobbled up a bowlful of cereal and slurped down coffee, ready and eager to start her day.

She had something to prove.

To Logan Slade.

But mostly to herself.

Half an hour later, Sophia walked into Sunset Lodge. She banked her feelings of nostalgia and disbelief that half of this glorious establishment was actually hers now and crossed the beautifully appointed lobby. Walking past a massive stone fireplace, cozy seating areas and cedar pillars, she turned to the left and headed straight toward the manager's office. She found it in the exact location she'd remembered. The door was open, and she paused for a second at the threshold, her hand fisted and ready for a courtesy knock when Ruth Polanski's voice stopped her in midmotion.

"Welcome, Sophia. Come in, please." Ruth rose from her desk and came forward with a smile. Instead of putting out her hand in greeting, the older woman wrapped both arms around Sophia's shoulders, brought her close and gave her a warm, loving hug. Sophia's heart rang out. She hadn't been held or embraced like this since her mother had passed and now this kindhearted woman—whom she wouldn't have to fire—welcomed her with genuine affection. Sensations of loss enveloped her, making her miss her mother even more.

"Good morning," she said, holding back her emotions.

"I'm glad you're here," Ruth said. "How was your first night back on Sunset Ranch?"

Sophia opted to fib. Ruth didn't need to know how Logan had ruined her sleep last night. "Fine. The cottage is just as I remembered it. I did well."

"Good, my dear. Well, we can get started in here soon enough, but at the moment, I think it's important to show you around the lodge and introduce you to our staff. You may even remember a few of our employees."

"I just might," Sophia said.

"Shall we?"

"That sounds wonderful."

Sophia loved touring the grounds and seeing familiar faces. Many of the employees remembered her as a child and offered condolences regarding her mother. It was a trip down memory lane, but Sophia also focused on what was new, and what might need changing. She'd taken a clipboard with her to jot down notes and when she arrived back in Ruth's office—her office now—she went over the notes with Ruth to get her take on them.

Learning the lodge's new computer system was a breeze. Ruth showed her the basics, and Sophia picked up on it from there. She'd worked alongside her mother at inns and motels for years. There wasn't a program she couldn't figure out. Often her mother had relied on her to navigate new technology.

Poor Ruth. Sophia sensed the woman's eagerness to retire in every anxious glance the lady gave her. When Sophia grasped a new concept easily, the worry lines around the older woman's mouth eased into a small smile. Sophia was all about making a smooth transition and, now that she'd gotten to know Ruth a little better, she was glad that she couldn't foresee any obstacles that would hinder her taking over the reins.

You're not the hired help anymore, Sophia. You own half of the lodge now.

Sophia had a hard time wrapping her mind around that. She'd never owned anything of value in her life. So the transition from employee to owner might just be the hardest of all for her to grasp.

By the end of the day, Ruth bid her goodbye. "These are yours now." She placed a set of keys in Sophia's hand. "You can lock up the office whenever you'd like."

When Sophia blinked her surprise, Ruth shook her head. "I'm not abandoning you, so don't you worry. I'll be here until the end of next week to conclude some business I need to tend to. If you need me to stay on longer, I surely will, but I'm impressed at how quickly you've caught on."

"Thank you," Sophia said. "You've made my first day enjoyable."

"I worked you hard," Ruth said honestly, before her lips lifted gently. "I almost feel guilty about it, but I think you're capable and I'll be sure to tell Logan that."

"You mean, Luke, right? I was told I'll be dealing with Luke from now on."

"Oh, yes, that's right. Though neither one of those boys would ever steer you wrong."

Sophia could argue, but kept her lips buttoned tight.

She walked home in a daze, thinking of what she'd accomplished today, what she was expected to do and how it would all work. Within minutes, she found herself inside the cottage, her boots off, her jacket tossed across the parlor sofa, holding a glass of passion-fruit iced tea in her hand. She plopped onto the sofa, closed her eyes and sipped her tea. When her stomach complained, she remembered she hadn't eaten much today. Excitement mixed with uncertainty had killed her appetite.

She sat in silence and enjoyed the peace but for another growl coming up from the depth of her belly. Then, a few seconds later, she heard a car pull up in front of the cottage. The engine shut off and a door slammed. She rose from her seat so quickly tea splattered onto her dress over her right breast. Wonderful. There was no time to wipe it dry. Her Las Vegas showgirl friends would always tease that she had a natural stop for spillage, and while Sophia had laughed along with them, she'd never really found it too amusing.

She heard footsteps approaching the porch and when the knock came, Sophia was ready, setting her hand on the knob and twisting. She pulled the door open and stared into the incredibly handsome face of a mature Luke Slade.

"Hey, there," he said. "I thought you could use a friend about now."

"So how are you *really* doing, Soph?" Luke asked ten minutes later, after they'd exchanged condolences for the parents they'd lost.

Soph?

He was back to calling her that. Sophia had forgotten how Luke liked to shorten her name. The familiar ring and the slight twang in Luke's voice brought back good memories of the times they'd shared. Any awkwardness Sophia thought that they might encounter in their first meeting never developed. Luke was still Luke. It was a big relief to her to find that the pal she could always rely on hadn't changed too much except to become a confident, gorgeous hunk of a man. She was happy to spend this time with him and Sophia let down her guard to converse with him easily.

Now he sat on the far end of the parlor sofa at an angle facing her, with the heel of one boot resting across his knee, sipping iced tea. He wore faded Wrangler jeans and a blue chambray shirt that was equally faded. His smile and the warmth in his eyes were still the same, though clearly Luke had grown out of his gangly, awkward stage.

"I miss Mama so much, Luke. For so many years it was us against the world. And now that she's gone, I'm a little lost."

"Consider yourself *found,* honey. Sunset Ranch is your home now."

Luke leaned forward and as his work-hardened hands covered hers, she glanced down at their entwined fingers, thankful for his friendship. Luke had always understood her. He'd always had her back. He'd been a good friend, even when they were younger and it wasn't considered cool to have a girl as a friend. Luke had held his own. And as Sophia gave his hand a deliberate squeeze, returning the solace, she waited for a spark to ignite between them. She waited for her palms to sweat. She waited for a tingle.

Seconds ticked by.

Nothing. Not a twinge. No fire.

She'd always wondered whether she'd feel differently about Luke if she were to return to Sunset Ranch. She'd wondered if there would be something more.

She released his hand and lifted her lashes slowly to meet his gaze. Luke had a grin plastered on his face. Clearly he had read her thoughts and had been wondering the same thing. Even though warmth crept up her neck, there was no tension between them. And that was the problem.

"You are a knockout, Sophia, that's for sure."

"You're cowboy eye candy, Luke."

Dubious, he gave a shake of his head, and then each of them threw their heads back and laughed.

Just like when they were kids.

They were friends, period. That much was reestablished and Sophia was glad of that. There was no reason to complicate her life right now anyway. She'd been put through the wringer these past few years, marrying an older man who'd offered to help provide for her mother's medical treatments and praying for a miracle to save her mother's life. She hadn't come out of it unscathed, either. She'd paid a dear price for her high hopes and naïveté.

"Thank you, Luke. You always know how to make me feel better."

He gave her a wink. "Glad to oblige. So what's your game plan?"

"Well," she said, leaning back against the sofa. The chintz material gave underneath her, the cushions fitting her bottom as she curled her legs under her dress and got comfortable. "I hope to make a smooth transition with Ruth Polanski and take over the reins soon. Ruth thinks I'll be ready by the end of next week. I have my doubts." She tilted her head to one side, keeping accusation out of her tone. "And thanks for the heads-up, by the way, buster. You didn't mention that I'd be replacing her as manager."

Luke's beautiful blue eyes rounded innocently. "I didn't think it would be a problem. She's been itching to retire."

"Yes, I found that out the hard way. Your brother led me to believe I'd have to fire Ruth in order to take my position at the lodge."

Luke stared at her for a full five seconds, then rubbed the back of his neck. "Ah, hell."

Sophia let go a heavy sigh.

"Logan was messing with you," Luke said.

"But it wasn't done in jest."

Luke leaned forward to put his glass of tea down on the stone cocktail table. "Don't let him get to you, Sophia. He's got a burr up his butt about what happened in the past. He'll come around soon enough."

"Do you really believe that?" Sophia heard the hope in her own voice. All she wanted to do was live peacefully at Sunset Ranch. She didn't expect Logan to welcome her with open arms, but if he would simply not stand in her way, or better yet, just ignore her, she'd consider it a victory.

Small lines around Luke's eyes crinkled as he winced. "Honestly? Not really. At least not anytime soon. He's more stubborn than I am."

She remembered the arguments she'd had with Luke when they were growing up. He rarely backed down from anything if he thought he had right on his side. "That's saying something," Sophia muttered.

"Hey!"

She smiled. "Just speaking from memory. I'm sure you're more reasonable now."

"Damn straight I am. I mean, I wasn't stubborn so much as I was right and I've always been reasonable."

Sophia nodded, not to belabor the point. It felt good bantering with Luke again.

"So what else did you and my brother talk about yesterday?"

"He tried to…" she began, but then thought better of it.

"Go on." Luke nodded his encouragement. "What did he try to do?"

Sophia didn't want to get between Luke and his brother. There had been enough of that when they were kids. Logan would be rude to her or worse yet, pretend she didn't exist, and Luke would come to her rescue. As a result, the two brothers had been at odds with each other, at least when it had come to her. She didn't want to rekindle that bad blood. "Nothing."

"He did something, Soph. If you don't tell me, I'll go straight to the source. I'll find out."

"Don't bully me, Luke."

"I'm not bullying you, for heaven's sake. But you need to tell me."

Sophia sat silently.

Luke rose slowly from the sofa, battling his reluctance to leave. "All right, I'll go ask my brother if you—"

"Okay, fine. I'll tell you."

He took his seat again.

"You have to promise not to interfere. I don't want to come between the two of you."

Luke's lips tightened and twisted back and forth for so long, Sophia thought he wouldn't agree. "Fine, you have my word."

Sophia took a swallow, sorry now that she'd brought the subject up. "Well, not only did Logan lead me to believe that I'd have to relieve Ruth of her duties, but he tried to buy me out of the inheritance. He said he'd have his lawyer find a way around the stipulation that I stay on for a year to run the place. He offered me a huge sum of money."

"Aw, crap." Luke took to rubbing the back of his neck again. "That guy beats a dead horse, doesn't he?"

Sophia drew back and gasped.

"Sorry. Bad choice of words."

Yes, it was, considering that Sunset Ranch was all about raising and nurturing the finest horses in the country. "He doesn't want me here. Logan's got piss for brains sometimes. He knows damn well he can't buy you out."

"Exactly, but he sure drove his point home about wanting to be rid of me."

"I'm sorrier than you can imagine that I wasn't here to greet you yesterday."

"It's not your fault, Luke. I'll admit that ever since you called me, I've been dying to see you again, but you can't reschedule *your* life around my comings and goings. I'm a big girl now, and Logan doesn't scare me."

"He may not scare you, Sophia, but he hurt you. And that's just plain wrong if you ask me."

Sophia didn't want the reminder of how Logan had made her feel yesterday. It seemed that for the majority of her life, she'd been on the outside looking in. She'd never gotten over that feeling. That's why coming back to Sunset Ranch, the one place she'd ever felt as though she'd belonged, was so important to her.

"You know what," she said, with a wave of the hand, "let's change the subject. Tell me about yourself, Luke. You mentioned you were in the rodeo for a while. What was that like?"

Sophia settled back and listened to her friend tell her about his life after she'd left Sunset Ranch. And when he offered to take her to dinner for the spiciest chili in the West, her stomach grumbled quietly at the mention of food.

"Yes. I'd love to have dinner with you."

The only thing louder than The Kickin' Kitchen's piped in honky-tonk music was the Red Savina habaneros they put in the chili. The hot stuff made Logan's insides sing like a hillbilly band and required a generous dowsing of cold beer to wash away the flames. After a morning of schmoozing with prospective clients and an afternoon of pencil pushing in his office, he couldn't think of anything better to do tonight than eating a bowlful of chili with a friend.

"You want another go round?" Ward Halliday asked, after slurping up the last spoonful of chili on his plate. Ward had a stomach of iron, which served him well on all-you-can-suffer chili night at Kickin'.

Logan glanced at the empty bowl sitting in front of him. "Nope. I haven't put out the last blaze catching fire in my stomach yet. But you go ahead." He caught the new waitress's eye and crooked his finger.

She sauntered over, giving him a big smile as she approached. "Hi, boys, you ready for more?"

"My friend here will tempt fate once again. You can bring him some," Logan said. "You don't sell antacids for dessert, do you, darlin'?"

She acted as if she hadn't heard that question a thousand times before. As a matter of fact, maybe she hadn't. From what he could recall, being a semiregular and all, the young blonde hadn't worked at Kickin' all that long. Her name tag said she was Shelby from California.

"Hey, not a bad idea. I could start a side business and re-tire before I'm thirty."

"And what would you do if you retired?" Logan asked, not-ing how attractive she was in a cute-as-a-button sort of way.

She stared off into the distance for a few beats, before fo-cusing on him with an honest-to-goodness look. "I could tell you what I wouldn't do. I wouldn't be working two jobs and struggling to take care of my grandfather in his tiny house by the interstate. Poor man would have a nice place to live and a real good nurse to care for him in his last days."

"Sorry to hear your grandpa's not well," Logan said.

"I appreciate that. He's a dear man and I'm doing my best." She shrugged a shoulder. "I'm afraid I'm all he's got right now."

Logan eyed the pretty woman with admiration. It was re-freshing to hear how loyalty and devotion still meant some-thing to some folks. "Well, then I think he's got a hell of a lot."

The girl's smile returned, beaming on Logan like shining stadium lights. "Thanks, I needed to hear that today. What else can I get for you?"

"You're welcome. And if you could bring us another round of beers, too, I would appreciate it."

"You got it," she said, and turned to take an order from the next table.

Ward shook his head when the waitress was out of ear-shot. "Man, oh, man."

"What?" Logan didn't wait for Ward to answer before he tipped his head back and guzzled down the remaining drops of his beer.

"You sure know how to sweet-talk a woman."

"That's all it is, is talk, Halliday. Besides, she was real nice." Logan leaned way back in his chair, tipping it on end, stretching out his legs. He hadn't had a date with a woman in a long while. And Shelby from California had piqued his inter-est enough for him to consider breaking his three-month-long streak of being dateless. But Shelby seemed to have enough on her plate, without dating a man who had no interest in permanence. He chose his women wisely and when he did, it was a just-for-laughs, without-any-strings-attached kind of thing. Whether it lasted one week or a few months, he made sure the women he dated weren't the home-and-hearth kind.

"Well, if Molly could've seen you flirting with that blonde, she would've pestered you until you asked the girl out."

Logan leaned back in his seat. "Your wife's been itching to marry me off."

"Don't I know it? She's forever going on and on about you three Slade boys not getting hitched. I can only imagine the pestering she'll give my boy when Hunter gets of age."

"Hunter doesn't have a girl?"

"No, sir. Right about now, he's focused on attending college in the fall. Saving his money, too."

"That's always a good thing," Logan said. He'd known Hunter since birth, but the big strapping boy wasn't much of a talker. Logan knew he loved horses, though. He'd taken after his father that way. Ward had taught Hunter the value in treating an animal with respect.

A few minutes later, Shelby came by with Ward's second bowl of chili and two more beers. She set everything down on the table. "Here you go, boys."

"Thanks, miss," Ward said, lifting his spoon, ready to dive in.

"You're very welcome," she said, giving Ward her attention before sending Logan another big smile. "If you need anything else, just let me know."

When she turned to help another customer, Logan watched the gentle sway of her hips in her short navy blue waitress uniform.

"Truth is, I haven't had a date in a long while," he muttered.

Ward didn't seem to hear him. He was too busy looking

straight past him and waving his hand with a come-here gesture. Logan craned his head toward Kickin's front door and a vile curse slipped from his lips.

"Well now, would you look at who's just come in," Ward was saying. "It's Luke and Ms. Sophia. They're heading this way."

"Damn it, Ward. Put your hand down, and stop waving them over."

Baffled by Logan's tone, the older man drew his brows together. "Why, oh… Oh, right." He shrugged his shoulders in sheepish apology.

Ward's lightbulb moment was too little too late. The Slades had always tried to keep their private lives just that—*private*. But back in the day, news of Louisa Montrose's illicit affair with his father had leaked out faster than a sledgehammer to a water pipe, and Logan figured pretty much everyone at Sunset Ranch knew that he wasn't keen on any of the Montrose women. Especially now. Especially since Randall Slade had decided to give away half ownership of the lodge to his mistress's daughter.

Logan hadn't been discreet in his disdain. When he first heard the news of her inheritance, he slammed his fist into the barn wall. His damn hand had been bruised for days and, even though it had healed, every so often the pain would come back just enough to annoy him.

Very much like Sophia.

Three

Sophia hadn't expected to see Logan in the chili place. She'd been looking forward to sharing the meal with Luke, without any fuss or anxiety. All-you-can-suffer chili sounded like a great plan, but all-you-can-suffer Logan—not so good.

Luke whispered in Sophia's ear as they approached the table. "I swear I didn't know he was going to be here."

"I know," she assured him. In the short time since she'd been reacquainted with Luke, she was sure that he wouldn't have set her up like this.

"We won't stay. Just say hello."

"No, Luke," she said, "I won't have you avoiding your brother because of me."

"Logan won't care if we find another table."

"But I do."

Sophia feared she'd caused a rift between the brothers already. One way or another, she would have to find a way to be civil around Logan, for everyone's sake.

"Hello to both of you," Ward said once they arrived at his

and Logan's booth. "I see you're introducing Ms. Sophia to the fine dining in town."

"I am. Doesn't get finer than Kickin'," Luke said to Ward with a smile, before turning his attention to Logan.

He sipped his beer, and then nodded an acknowledgment to his brother.

She wouldn't allow Logan to ignore her and opted to be the bigger person. "It's good to see you again, Ward. And you, too, Logan."

Logan slanted a look her way, his gaze landing on the bodice of her coral dress. He refused to make eye contact with her, as if she wasn't worthy of any more of his attention than that. "Sophia."

Idiot.

"I'm having me a second bowl of Number Three," Ward said, in an attempt to ease the tension at the table. "The higher the number, the higher the heat level. Only goes up to five. But I'm not that brave."

"I think three's pretty brave," Sophia said. Kickin' Kitchen wasn't around when she lived here, and now her interest was piqued. Her Spanish ancestry and mother's heavy hand with spices gave her a taste for daring foods.

"Beginner's start at Number One and pretty much stay there for a few years," Logan said smugly, eyeing her with a challenge in his eyes. "Some can't even handle that."

Sophia straightened to her full height. Mr. High and Mighty actually volunteered something more than a grunt. She shot her chin out, and took the bait. But she planned for him to be the one eating crow. "I bet I could handle Number Three."

Logan stopped drinking his beer long enough to say, "That I'd like to see."

"Whoa, Sophia," Luke said with a shake of the head. "I just graduated to Three a few months ago."

Ward gave her a skeptical look.

Sophia took Logan's challenge. "I'd be happy to prove you wrong."

The waitress came sprinting by to deliver a round of drinks to the booth. "You folks need a table?" she asked Luke. "'Cause we're getting slammed. It's a twenty-minute wait."

"That's fine. We'll wait," Luke said with a firm nod, clearly protecting Sophia. "Slade. Table for two."

Logan set his beer bottle down with a thud and his dark eyes sharpened on her. "Chickening out?"

Luke shook his head at Sophia, his eyes darkening with caution, but it was too late for his warning. Her mind was made up. For one, she wouldn't let Luke baby her and, two, Logan needed to be put in his place. When Ward rose to offer her a seat, she lowered down and slid across the booth, making room for him to sit beside her.

"I'm not chickening out," she said triumphantly to Logan, and then turned to flash Ward a generous smile. "Thank you, kind sir."

Ward nodded, color rising up on his neck. "Welcome."

Logan's mouth twitched, and he sighed with resignation as he made room for his brother in the booth. "Yeah, sure. Why not."

"Cancel that table for two," Luke said to the waitress as he took a seat beside Logan. "Looks like we'll be joining them."

"Sure thing. I'll be back in a sec with menus."

Before the waitress turned away, Luke stopped her with a gentle command. "No need. We know what we want." Luke met with Sophia's eyes once again. She nodded, giving the waitress her order. "I'll have a Number Three."

"Make that two Number Threes," Luke said with a sigh, "and two beers."

"No beer for me," Sophia said. "I'll have water."

The waitress made a mental note.

"You'd best bring three glasses of ice water then, for starters," Ward said, looking a bit concerned. "Those habaneros will drain the last ounce of moisture from your mouth."

"Sure, I'll be back with waters, beer and two Number Threes." The waitress moved on and Sophia found herself facing Logan directly across the booth.

It wasn't a hard picture, seeing the two Slade cowboys sitting side by side. They had similar good looks. The biggest difference was that Luke's eyes were blue, like his mother's, and his hair was a sandy color, rather than Logan's dark brown. But the men were worlds apart in personality traits.

Luke inclined his head toward Sophia. "Beer might have quenched your thirst better."

"I don't drink."

"Ever?" Luke asked, looking a little astonished. "I'm sorry. I didn't know."

"You couldn't possibly know," she said quietly, holding in her anguish. Luke didn't know everything there was to know about the grown-up woman she'd become, unlike Logan, who *thought* he knew everything about her. "My father was an alcoholic," she explained, "and I've never found a taste for the stuff. It's my way of rebelling."

Not that she felt obligated to give a reason, but her father's story was a constant reminder of the pitfalls and fragile nature of the human spirit and she especially wanted Logan to understand that her life hadn't been all peaches and cream. His family didn't have a monopoly on heartache. Despite being married to a loving beautiful woman, Sophia's father had left her mother with a three-year-old child to raise. As an adult it was still pretty hard for her to rationalize his actions, though she'd tried hard to work through being fatherless most of her life. Alberto Montrose chose a love affair with liquor that ultimately ruined him. The last Sophia had heard, which was more than ten years ago, her father had been seen wandering the streets of San Francisco, ragged and homeless. Liquor *was* his wife, child, addiction and downfall, all rolled up into one.

"Enough said," Luke announced, wearing a compassionate expression. "Water is underrated anyway."

"Yeah, you can't live without it," Ward offered needlessly.

Logan chuckled, and sipped his beer, watching her as if she were a spectacle. "Your stomach's gonna rebel in a few minutes."

This time Luke wasn't disagreeing. "You're in for it, Sophia. But you always were a daredevil. That much I do know."

"Me? What about wrestling bucking broncos for five years of your life?"

"Six," Ward and Luke said in unison.

"And I wasn't wrestling with them, darlin'. I rode them for nine seconds at a time."

"Most times, it was five seconds in the saddle, and the rest of the time on the ground, eating the horse's dust," Logan offered, happy to give Luke a bad time.

"Eating dust may be easier than eating Number Threes."

Sophia gave the men an eye-roll and shook her head. "I will consider myself properly warned by all three of you. I promise you I'll hold my own."

She moved her long hair to one shoulder and shuffled in her seat, adjusting to the booth's cushion to get more comfortable. Logan watched her movements, his gaze flicking over her body until their eyes finally met in a daring stare. A hot sprinkle of desire spread through her belly like warm sugar. For the slightest pinch of time, Sophia spotted a glimmer of admiration in his eyes for what she was about to do. Which, in her estimation, wasn't all that admirable. She would eat a bowl of Kickin' chili. How hard would that be?

And in that moment, no matter how much she hated to admit it, she saw Logan in a different light. She saw him as someone who could match her spirit, someone she might enjoy being around and someone who could fill the gaping void threatening to swallow her up. A shell that no one, not even a wonderful man like Luke, could ever fill.

"What the hell?" Ward jerked in his seat and all heads turned his way. "Pardon me, miss." Apology touched his eyes as he briefly glanced at her, before pulling his cell phone out of his pocket. "Darn vibrating thing. Always shocks the vinegar outta me."

Logan's short laugh flashed a smile that cut deep ridges into each side of his mouth. Sophia took a quick breath and focused on Ward rather than allow that warm-sugar sensation to spread any further. She reminded herself that Logan hated her.

Ward glanced at the phone's screen. "It's a call from Hunter. He wouldn't be calling if it weren't important."

Logan said, "Go ahead and answer it, Ward."

Ward spoke to his son, nodding his head and saying "uh-huh, uh-huh," about half a dozen times. He finished his conversation with, "Okay, I'll be right there."

Ward set the phone back into his pocket as he spoke. "My boy needs help at the ranch. Skylar is foaling early. He's thinking it's gonna be a difficult delivery. Luke, she's your favorite mare. You coming with me?"

Ward rose from his seat. Luke did, too, blinking away the fear on his face. "Yeah, I'd better see to her."

From what Sophia gathered, no one on the ranch knew more about horses than Luke. He had a natural way with them. Even Ward, Sunset Ranch's head wrangler, seemed to look to Luke for help.

"Sorry, Soph. I've got to go. We almost lost her last time she foaled."

"Okay, I understand," Sophia said, grabbing her clutch purse, "I'll go with you."

"No," Luke said. "You stay and eat your dinner. I know you're hungry. Your meal is coming."

"But I, uh—" Sophia looked from Logan's unreadable expression to Luke. "I don't have to—"

"For Pete's sake, woman," Logan said with a shake of the

head. "I won't bite. Ward can drive to the ranch with Luke. I'll take you home later. After you eat your Number Three."

"But—"

"Are you chickening out again?"

"No!"

"Okay, then." Logan slid his brother a reassuring look. "You go on. Don't worry about anything but saving Skylar and her foal."

"Play nice," Luke said, pointing his finger at Logan.

"Get outta here," Logan said, grabbing for his beer with a casual shrug, as if to say he didn't have anything to worry about.

Luke didn't budge. "Logan."

"Damn it, you have my word."

Finally satisfied, Luke nodded. "Fair enough. I'm sorry, Sophia," Luke said. "But Logan will get you home safely. I've really gotta run."

Ward had already excused himself and was waiting for Luke by the entranceway. "I'll be fine. Don't worry about me. I only hope it goes well for the mare." Luke met up with Ward and the two men exited the café in a hurry. And just like that, Sophia found herself alone with Logan Slade.

He was stuck with Sophia for the rest of the night. Hell, a man could do much worse than entertaining a gorgeous woman with a killer body for the evening. She was a damn sight better to look at than the antique cast-iron pots and pans hanging on the wall. A damn sight more appealing than rusted tricycles and red wagons that littered the shelves circling the perimeter of the café. She sure had every man in the joint giving her the eye and giving him a solid way-to-go look as they scanned the booth. Logan would be on his best behavior tonight. Not because he'd eased up on his thinking about Sophia, but because he'd given his brother his word. For Luke's sake, Logan would treat Sophia kindly.

After a long minute of silence, she asked, "Do you think the mare will be okay?"

He blew out a breath. "Don't know. Birthing can be tricky at times. Skylar is a trouper though. She's strong and if anyone can help her, it'd be Luke."

"That's what I've heard. Luke knows a lot about horses."

"He does," Logan said, keeping his tone light. If the woman wanted to praise his brother to high heaven tonight, he wouldn't stop her. He wouldn't like it much, but he wouldn't stop her. The two of them were already thick as thieves again.

His brother's relationship with Sophia had always irked him. Logan was the oldest of the three boys—Justin being the youngest. Logan had been very close to Luke until Sophia had gotten in the way. Ever since their friendship had developed, Logan felt like he'd been left out in the cold. Montrose women had managed to shred Slade family loyalty. It shouldn't be so, but Luke couldn't see it any more than his father had. Their blindness left a bitter taste in Logan's mouth, sharper than the chili he'd just polished off. His only consolation was that Shelby was heading toward the table with Sophia's burn-as-it-goes-down chili on her tray. "Your chili's coming up."

The waitress set the bowl in front of Sophia. Spicy aromatic scents of peppers, onions and cilantro drifted to his side of the table. "Thanks, Shelby."

"You got it." She shot him another sweet smile before walking away.

Sophia took her time, opening her cloth napkin and placing it on her lap. Then she lifted her lashes and those brilliant amber eyes surrounded with flecks of gold fell on him. "Smells delicious," she said.

"That's why we're here."

The second he said "we," his pulse pounded in his ears and images popped into his head of the two of them, really playing nice. For anyone in the café watching, it might appear that they were on a date.

It'd be a cold day in hell, he thought, yet he couldn't take his eyes off her.

Sophia dipped into the chili and came up with a rounded spoonful with cheese dripping off the sides. Steam shot straight up for half a yard then disappeared into the air. Sophia pursed her lips and blew gently, her mouth forming a small *O* to whisper away the heat.

Logan's Adam's apple bobbed in his throat. His damn body pinched tight, and he sat mesmerized as Sophia prepared to take her first bite of ass-kicking chili. Logan had never thought of chili and sex together, but now, that's all he could think about. Watching her take her first bite, swallow, then gaze up at him, looking satisfied and accomplished, gave him a sexual thrill that he'd never experienced before. It was beyond crazy and like a fool, he grinned.

So did she.

The light in her eyes matched the way he was feeling inside, most likely for entirely different reasons. "Piece of cake," she said.

Piece of something, he thought, grateful the lower half of him was covered by the table. It hadn't escaped him that *he* was the one suffering as Sophia ate from her bowl of all-you-can-suffer Kickin' chili.

He watched her eat three more spoonfuls without even a slight flinch. The woman was good at spicy.

"You know," she began, stirring the chili with the stainless-steel spoon, "it was nice of you to ask Hunter to help me move in yesterday."

"Who said I asked him?" he shot back.

"So you didn't?" Her almond-shaped eyes rounded in surprise.

He shrugged. "Maybe I did."

"I didn't think you'd given it a thought. You didn't personally offer to help."

"Did you expect me to?"

"I had hoped you'd be a gentleman. I didn't want to start off at Sunset Ranch with bad feelings."

Logan ignored that last part of her statement. He wasn't in the mood to get into it with her tonight. "I'm not the welcoming committee. I have a ranch to run. Hunter helped you. Isn't that good enough?"

"Yes, I suppose. I was beginning to feel good about that, and you, until you set me up with Ruth Polanski. It was a low blow, even coming from you, Logan. You led me to believe I had to fire the woman."

Logan scrubbed his jaw. It wasn't his proudest moment, but he'd been angry and wanted to lash out at her when she'd first arrived. She'd called it correctly. It had been a low blow. Logan didn't play dirty. Not usually. Yet he wasn't ready to apologize. "You must have been pleasantly surprised when you learned you didn't have to let her go."

"I worried about it all night."

He put himself in a no-guilt zone and hung tight. "I'm sure you slept well enough."

Sophia shook her head and her long wavy hair, caressing one side of her shoulder, flowed over her breast. "You need to let go of the past, Logan. You'd be a happier man."

A lecture, coming from her? "What makes you think I'm not happy? I'm sitting here, watching you pretend to stomach that chili. Tell the truth, Sophia. It's burning like hell now."

To his surprise, she put her hand just under her breasts, spread her fingers out over her stomach and delivered a low rumble of laughter. "You'd love to believe that."

"You won't admit it?"

"Maybe it's more fun to keep you guessing. When's the last time you've had fun, Logan?"

"What do you care?"

"That long?" Sophia asked, shaking her head as she lifted another spoonful to her mouth.

The woman was getting to him and damn if he wasn't enjoying himself. Not because he thought Sophia was suffering with the chili, but because she was a woman who stood up to a challenge and managed to keep him guessing.

"You're forgetting who's driving you home."

"Oh, no. I am very well aware," she said, her amber eyes blazing with warmth enough to make heat crawl up his belly *and* put a lump in his throat.

He swigged the last ounce of his beer with a quick gulp.

Sophia, on the other hand, had yet to reach for her glass of water.

Sophia sank into the comfy, forgiving seat cushion of Logan's black pickup truck. The luxury four-wheel drive sported a polished wood and beige leather interior with a dashboard full of digital controls an airline pilot would envy. She fastened her seat belt and watched the scenery go by as they exited the café's parking lot and took to the open road. An hour ago, the golden sunset had faded and now lights from the town they left behind sparkled like tiny diamonds in her side rearview mirror.

Sophia eyed Logan as he drove with one hand on top of the steering wheel. Country music played softly. The lack of conversation was actually comforting. They'd extinguished their small talk while in the café. She couldn't think of anything else she wanted to say to him that didn't involve business, and Sophia wasn't in the mood to spar with him about that right now.

Logan was used to comfort, style and the finer things in life. Even though he lived on a ranch, everything he owned, from his classic felt Stetson hat and expensive tooled-leather boots to the exquisite sprawling ranch home, was top-notch. She hadn't missed the one-hundred-dollar tip he'd laid on the table for the waitress just minutes ago. She had gushed and tried to give it back, but Logan had insisted on her keeping it. Apparently, he had money to burn. Sophia would bet her last dollar that the designer watch he wore on his wrist cost more than her mother's yearly salary when she'd worked at the Desert Breeze Motor Inn.

They'd spent three years working in that dive, before Louisa had finally landed a job more suitable for her managerial skills. In many respects though, the life Sophia had with her mother was richer and worth more than any of the material possessions she could ever hope to own.

Sophia had gotten a small taste of the good life when she'd married. Though many believed she'd married the older man for his money, Sophia had convinced her mother that she'd married for the promise of love. When in truth, neither had been true *exactly*.

A sharp jolting pain twitched in her stomach. She gasped silently, holding her hands firmly in place when her initial reaction was to rub her belly. The pain was fleeting, and then it was gone. Sophia released the breath caught in her throat. She'd be okay. The chili had gone down smoothly earlier and at the time, she hadn't had any doubts about it.

Another jolt hit her. This time, the pain spiraled up, burning toward her rib cage. "Oh," she breathed out as slowly and as quietly as she could, slanting a look at Logan, who was listening to the country music playing on the radio, his focus on the dark road ahead.

The next pang hit and her body tightened up. She grabbed her clutch purse and set it onto her stomach, then slid her hand underneath it. Her fingers dug in and she tried to smooth away the rebellion going on inside.

"Ohh." The pain gripped her hard this time and she leaned forward and hugged her stomach with both arms. Beads of sweat moistened her forehead.

Logan shot a glance at her. "It finally hit you?"

She bit her lip and nodded helplessly.

"Is it bad?"

Again, she nodded. Perspiration trickled down the back of her neck, sticking to her hair.

"Hang on. I'll get you home fast."

Logan revved the engine and the truck roared down the highway. Minutes later they reached the gates of Sunset Ranch and Logan slowed the truck. "My house or the cottage?"

"Take me home," she said, wanting the comfort of her own surroundings, new as they were, but also familiar.

The truck roared to life again and after a short time, the dimmed lamppost lights in front of the stone house came into view. Sophia thanked all things holy that she was finally home.

Logan brought the truck to an abrupt halt. He got out, and she heard his boots on the gravel path as he approached the passenger's side. Doubled over now, she pressed both arms against her belly, attempting to make the aching go away. Logan opened her door and when their eyes met, the stern set of his jaw softened and he cursed. "I'll get you out."

Before she could protest, he bent down to unfasten her seat belt, removing her arms from around her belly first to get them out of his way.

"It's not necessary to carry me," she whispered.

Her statement fell on deaf ears. He scooped her from the seat, one hand lifting under her knees, the other at her shoulders. As if this weren't humiliating enough, her dress slid to her upper thighs. Logan's gaze locked onto her legs shamelessly as he brought her out of the truck. His hip shoved the door closed.

As he strode purposefully toward her front door, Sophia clung to his neck, giving in to the power and strength of his arms. Cradled this way, she felt safe and protected, though she knew in her head she should be wary of him. She shouldn't let down her guard. Once they reached the porch, he set her legs down, reached into his pocket and came out with a set of keys. He inserted one into the lock and kicked open the front door. Then he picked her back up.

Moonlight streamed inside, illuminating the front room just enough to guide the way. Logan moved with the grace of a cat into the house, finding the parlor sofa easily. He lowered her gently onto her backside. With her arms still locked around his neck, Logan's face came within inches of hers and their gazes met through the darkness. A brief moment passed between them. The dark coolness in his eyes blazed now with heat so strong, memories flooded Sophia's mind of the one blissful, wonderful, sizzling kiss they'd shared so long ago. Her stomach stopped aching for a short time and she became mesmerized by the possibility that was Logan Slade. But just as her mind wrapped around the idea, the heat in Logan's eyes offering that possibility died away, replaced again by a cold, unreadable stare. Sophia swallowed hard, relinquishing the moment to foolishness.

Logan unlocked her arms from around his neck and rose to full height. "I'll be right back."

She lay her head down on the arm of the sofa and listened as he went to his truck. When he returned, he flipped on a lamp on the end table. Soft light flowed into the room. Standing over her, he lifted her hand in his and plopped two round pink tablets down in her palm. "Take these first," he said.

She stared at them.

"They will help," he offered, his voice gruff.

They might be poison for all she knew, but she was pretty sure they were antacids, and though she was certain they wouldn't help, she lifted them to her lips, opened her mouth and chewed. They went down like chalk and made her mouth dry.

"Now," Logan said, "Take a swig of this."

He bent onto his knees by the sofa. With a gentle hand, he lifted her head and guided a pink bottle to her lips.

She shook her head. Mixing medications wasn't wise. "I don't think so."

He leaned back a little, holding the bottle away from her. "Trust me on this, it works. I've been where you are now. Why do you suppose I carry this stuff in my truck on Kickin' days?"

Sophia closed her eyes to the look of concern on Logan's face. It didn't make sense that he would try to help her. He detested her and wanted her gone *yesterday*. How could she trust him?

Another cutting pain seized her stomach. "Oh."

His hand, still nestled in her hair, lifted her head up a little more. "C'mon, Sophia. Just drink it."

She bit the bullet and gave him her trust, craning her neck forward. He tipped the bottle, and she sipped from it a few times.

"That's good," he said. "Give it a few minutes."

She lay her head down after swallowing the awful liquid. "You don't have to stay."

Once again, he ignored her comment. He rose and walked off. She listened for the front door to close, hoping that he'd leave, but instead she heard him fidgeting around in the kitchen. He turned on the microwave. The thought of food of any sort made her queasy.

Her eyes drifted closed and only when she felt something warm being placed on her belly, did she open them again. The warmed dishtowel acted much like a heating pad and soon, between the meds and the heat, the gripping pain in her stomach began to ease.

"You should take a warm bath later," he said.

She lifted her gaze to Logan's face.

"Of course, I'd offer to do that with you, too," he said, the momentary flicker of heat once again in his eyes, "but I've got a feeling that wouldn't go over too well."

It hurt to smile, but Sophia managed to anyway. "You'll never know."

"The way I didn't know you were going to be sick?"

Humiliation mixed with anger and Sophia hinged her body forward to get up from the sofa. "Is that why you're here? To rub my nose in it?"

He laid a hand on her shoulder, easing her back down. "Lay back. Don't get riled."

"Don't rile me then." Her head plopped down on the arm of the sofa again.

"You don't like being wrong."

"Why are you helping me?" She turned her head to face him.

"You don't know my compassionate side."

"Do you have one?"

"Are you feeling better yet?"

Sophia stopped arguing with Logan long enough to realize she was feeling better. Almost as quickly as her stomach had become unsettled, it began to feel remarkably normal again. "Yes, I am." She glanced into his eyes. They were so intense and stubborn one minute, and then so kind and caring the next. "I do feel better."

Logan nodded. "I don't kick a person when they're down."

"You mean you want a level playing field for when you destroy me?"

"I never said I wanted to destroy you, *Soph*."

Soph?

And then it all became clear. Just when she'd thought Logan might have come around and wanted to be civil to her, just when she thought the past was forgiven and they could start anew, she caught on to what he was doing. She still owed him her thanks for helping her recover from her suffering tonight, but now she knew the reason why. "It's because of Luke, isn't it? You promised to see me home safely and you're a man of your word. You're doing this for Luke. Not for me."

His eyebrows dented into his forehead. "You have a strange way of thanking a man."

Sophia's ire sparked. Logan ran hot and cold with her and she never knew where she stood with him. Her frustration echoed in a shrewish raised voice. "How would you like me to thank you?"

Instantly, his gaze swept over her as she lay on the couch. "Let me give you that bath and we can call it even."

The idea of bathing with Logan brought a different kind of queasiness to her belly. Images danced in her head. But she was weak where Logan Slade was concerned. He didn't deserve her passionate thoughts.

But then another thought entered her mind, an uncomfortable memory that had nothing to do with Logan at all. *Don't go there, Sophia,* she reminded herself. You don't have to be afraid anymore. But the image from her Las Vegas days wouldn't leave her.

She had been sitting in front of her dressing-room mirror backstage before her performance when she discovered the first note tucked under her makeup case. Bone-chilling fear had traveled along her spine when she read the words.

You are too beautiful, Sophia. You will be mine one day.

She'd received five similar notes, all with the same strange sentiment. What had freaked her out most was that the person sending the notes had known a lot about her. She'd found envelopes printed with her name on the front windshield of her car or left for her at the motel where her mother worked. The actual words weren't threatening, so she'd never gone to the police, and she'd never worried her mother about them, either. But Sophia had been frightened on more than one occasion when she'd sensed that someone had been watching her.

After a while, Sophia started really looking at the faces of the men who would come to her shows. She began wondering if the note writer was among them, studying her.

"Thinking about it?" Logan asked, taunting her to answer.

Sophia returned her attention to the man who had rescued her this evening, the man who had invited himself to bathe with her. He had known what her answer would be before he suggested it. He wasn't serious. Perhaps, if she had an inkling that he was, she might be persuaded to change her mind. *Yes, join me in a bath, Logan.*

But Sophia was through playing his games tonight. She had enough bad memories to battle and now a queasy stomach to deal with. He'd been kind earlier and she'd wanted to believe that they could get along. She'd relished being in his arms while he carried her inside. She'd appreciated him staying to make sure she would recover. But had she only imagined his concern?

"You should go now."

He looked at her sprawled out on the sofa and inhaled sharply, as if the idea of bathing with her hadn't been a joke. "Yeah, I was thinking that same thing."

"Th-thank you for driving me home," she said through tight lips that didn't want to form the words. "And for…for helping me tonight."

He gave her a quick nod.

Sophia turned away from him then, feeling mixed up inside. She closed her eyes to the sound of Logan's footsteps fading away. There was no fond farewell from him. No "I hope you feel better," and no "Call me if you need my help again." It was a chilling reminder for her not to let down her guard with Logan. He would fool her time and time again, if she allowed it.

The front door opened and closed, and then he was gone.

Only then did Sophia realize that Logan Slade had his own key to the cottage.

He could barge in on her anytime he wanted.

Four

Constance Branford offered Sophia a lemon poppy seed muffin with strawberry filling. She'd briefly met the lodge's head cook yesterday on her tour with Ruth, and now Sophia sat beside her at a long country oak table, the only piece of furniture in the lodge's spotless stainless-steel kitchen that wasn't updated and brand-new. "Oh, no thanks, Constance. I couldn't possibly."

Edward's nana withdrew the basket. To avoid insulting the chef, Sophia quickly explained, "I had my first encounter with Kickin's chili last night. My stomach is still touchy."

Constance made a tsking sound. "That's not food," she said with a shake of her head. "I don't know why the men go there. Edward's been hounding me to let him eat there, but it's not for a young one's stomach. He'll just have to wait."

Sophia smiled. The head chef certainly had her ideas about what constituted a good meal. "Apparently, it's not for my stomach, either. I should stick to the lodge's food." She took in the broad range of pastries, biscuits and muffins set out and ready to be served. Behind them, two sous chefs were busy chopping up vegetables and preparing batters. She thought about how Blackie had made off with the spatula right under Constance's nose and how Edward had offered her his apology. The boy had taken Sophia's advice. Right in the middle of the table in a clear mason jar sat a small bouquet of wildflowers, picked straight from the fields outside the lodge.

"Your grandson is a nice boy," Sophia said.

"He's mischievous, like any ten-year-old, but yes, a good boy. He's had a rough time without his parents." Constance, whose eyes brightened when speaking of Edward, didn't fit the mold of a white-haired, rocking-chair nana at all. The astute, intelligent woman who ran the lodge's kitchen was quite capable, but there was an underlying current of sadness in her expression, too.

"I know something about losing a parent. It's never easy, but with a child…"

Constance shook her head. "Edward's parents aren't dead." Sophia blinked.

"My son and his wife have drug addictions. It got really bad and the first seven years of Edward's life were tumultuous. They left Edward with me, and I have legal custody."

"Oh. I'm sorry to hear that." Sophia had experience with her father's addiction but poor Edward had to live through that turmoil with both of his parents. At least for Sophia, she'd been blessed with a loving mother to raise her, but the boy hadn't been so lucky. Perhaps the resulting trauma was responsible for his speech problems.

"The best thing those two ever did was to hand over his custody to me without putting up a fight. They knew Edward would be better off with me. I'm doing the best I can to give him a stable home."

"Sunset Ranch is the best place for that. I grew up on the ranch and loved living here as a child."

"I agree. And Logan has been kind to Edward, giving

him responsibilities on the ranch to make my grandson feel needed. Letting him take care of Blackie was a very good idea."

Logan again? Why did everyone think the man a saint? But in this case, Sophia couldn't begrudge his kindness to the boy. "Boys and dogs go hand in hand."

Constance glanced at her watch. "He should be back from walking the dog soon. He gets up early on school days to feed and walk Blackie."

"Shall we go over this month's menus now, before he gets here?"

"Certainly. Can you handle coffee?"

"It smells delicious." She stroked her tender stomach that was begging for something warm and comforting. "I would love some."

Constance poured them both a cup and they got down to business. Sophia had some ideas for a summery theme for next month's menu. But she had to be delicate about making suggestions. Stepping into Ruth's shoes, and trying to make changes this early on, could ruffle feathers. Even so, Sophia was determined to have a hand in everything going on at Sunset Ranch. She remembered her mother's prowess and how involved she'd been with every aspect of the lodge.

Ten minutes later after a productive conversation with Constance, Edward walked through the kitchen doors, wearing a backpack and a shy smile. Sophia waved at him as he shuffled his way over to his nana.

"Edward," Constance said, "have you fed and walked Blackie already?"

He nodded and slipped Sophia a guilty glance. She reassured him with a friendly smile that said their little secret was safe, not that she'd ever tattle on the boy to Logan about their encounter yesterday, or anything for that matter. "Hello, Edward. Good to see you again."

"Hi."

"Is your lunch in your backpack?" Constance asked.

Again, he nodded.

"Okay then, off you go. You don't want to be late for the bus." Constance took his hand and walked him to the door. He reached up to give his nana a big hug, Constance squeezing him tight and kissing his forehead before letting him go. "Have a good day at school, sweetie."

Right before he strode out the door, he turned to Sophia and gave her a wide smile. "G-goodbye."

Touched by the boy's consideration, she tipped her head. "Bye, Edward."

Sophia finished her coffee and concluded her business with Constance, bidding her farewell and walking away from the kitchen's savory scents. In the well-designed lobby, her heels clicked on the stone floors as she headed toward her office. She still had difficulty believing that she owned any part of these elegantly rustic surroundings, yet each morning before she got out of bed, she reminded herself that half of the lodge belonged to her.

Luke appeared, seemingly out of nowhere, and walked alongside her. "Mornin'. Hey, can I speak with you a sec?"

"Good morning, Luke. I was going to call you this morning. How did your horse do last night?"

"She's gonna be okay. It was a tough delivery, but she managed. Her foal is real fine. You have to come see her."

"I will. You must be relieved."

"Surely am, but I think the mare might've struggled *less* than you did last night. I heard you had it rough after I left Kickin'."

"Oh," she said, her shoulders slumping. She wasn't thrilled she'd been the topic of discussion between the two brothers. Logan must have spilled all the beans with glee. "I see your brother told you I didn't handle the Number Three well."

Luke's face twisted with self-recrimination. "I should have never brought you there."

"Oh, no. It's not your fault. I should've known better. This has been a trying week for me, coming back here and dealing with all the changes in my life. Next time I'll do better."

"*Next* time? Honey, if you think I'm taking you back anytime soon—"

"I'm going back, Luke. One day."

His shoulders lifted in a dismissive shrug. "I'm just grateful that Logan was there to help you."

"Yes, your brother is my knight in shining armor," she grumbled quietly.

Luke threw his head back and laughed. Then she found humor in it, too, and laughed along with him. He took her arm and steered her out the front door. They strode along the length of the veranda and stood with the morning light to their backs as late spring sunshine warmed the air on a blue-sky day. Luke looked left then right, as if making sure they were alone. Whatever was on his mind today, he wanted a private conversation.

"I have an idea," he began. "Ruth's official last day of work is coming up. I'd like to throw her a surprise retirement party."

"That's nice of you, Luke. I'm sure she'd appreciate it."

"I'd like to do it at the house rather than the lodge. You know, get her out of the work environment. I was thinking out back, in our yard. Logan's thinking it's a good idea, too. The weather's been really nice at night."

"Go on." Sophia suspected that Luke was hinting that she be a part of his scheme, somehow.

"The thing is, Ruth usually coordinated our parties at the lodge, and well…I can't really ask her to do it. What I know about throwing a party can fit in my pinkie finger." He raised a work-roughened, rodeo-injured little finger.

So that was it. "You want my help?"

He fixed his gaze on her and shrugged. "I would *love* your help."

Sophia didn't have to think twice. "Of course."

Luke sighed with relief. "Great. You don't know how much I appreciate it. Funny, but I trust you more than the event planner we've used in the past. I want to make this special for Ruth."

"I'll do my best."

"It's not too much for you? You did just arrive. You have a new home and new job to settle into." Concern washed over his features as if he'd just realized what he was asking of her.

"I'm sure I can handle it. How many guests are we talking about here?"

"Probably sixty? We'd invite all the employees, although some will have to split shifts in order to stop by. There's several loyal patrons who have known Ruth from the beginning, and then there's her family. I'd like her grandkids to be invited, too."

"Okay. I could probably put that together. You want this to be a surprise?"

He glanced away for a second toward the pasture. "Yeah, I think so. Ruth wouldn't let us go to any fuss if she knew about it."

"I understand."

"Are you available tonight to go over the details? I'll bring dinner. No spice, no chili peppers, I promise."

Sophia was available every night. She had no hot dates, no friends other than Luke to hang out with, and putting together a party for Ruth would help her get to know the employees better, anyway. It was win-win. "Seven o'clock?"

"I'll be there."

Luke released a sigh of relief. "Thanks, Soph." He leaned forward to kiss her cheek chastely then smiled at her. "You're a lifesaver."

The knock came precisely at seven o'clock. Sophia's appetite had surged back to life this afternoon, and she was ready to share a delicious *bland* meal with a good friend. She had the table set for two and her laptop ready for the work they'd do on the retirement party. Sophia padded barefoot to the door, dressed comfortably in black capri pants and a white tank top tied at the side of her waist.

She opened the door with flair, eager for the company, and did an immediate double take, shaking her head and blinking.

"You're eyes aren't deceiving you." The comment spilled from Logan's tight lips. "It's not your pal Luke."

Sophia stared at the man standing on her doorstep. Her heart did a little flip. Her initial reaction to him still baffled her. Why was she so susceptible to him? He wasn't anything special, she reasoned. But then again, Sophia couldn't lie to herself. He was special in the ways that mattered to most women—smart, handsome, capable, kind to almost everyone else on the planet but her. And he was standing on her threshold with enough confidence to fill an arena. "What are you doing here?"

It wasn't the most mannerly greeting in the world. Even though her body reacted to Logan, she wasn't ready for another round of sparring. She'd looked forward to being with her friend this evening.

"There's been an accident. Luke's in the hospital."

Shocked, she gasped noisily as her hand flew to her chest. "Oh, my God. What happened?"

"A feisty stallion got loose this afternoon at the barn and Luke lost his footing trying to contain him. He was knocked down, and Trib nailed him good with both front hooves."

"Oh, no! How is he?"

"He's got three broken ribs, one broken arm and a concussion."

"I'm so sorry. Oh, poor Luke." Sophia's heart ached hearing the news about her friend.

"Luke's pretty tough, but all those rodeo injuries are surfacing again. He got hit pretty hard."

"Where is he?"

"Carson City Memorial."

"Can I see him?"

He shook his head. "The doctors sent me home. I've been with him all afternoon. He can't have any visitors tonight. They want him to rest. Someone will be observing him during the night for the concussion. With luck, they'll send him home tomorrow or the next day. He's going to be laid up for a while though."

Sophia realized she'd kept Logan out on the front porch. "Come in." She turned around and took a few steps into the parlor. "I'm so surprised." She'd wished Logan had called her from the hospital. She would've dropped everything to see Luke, but wishing for Logan to do anything for her was futile.

Logan followed her inside, his boot heels scraping against the floor. "Trib's a hard case and may be just as hardheaded as Luke. He's called Tribute in front of prospective buyers, but when they're out of hearing range we call him Tribulation. He's a grief maker. Of course, Luke's not blaming the dang horse. He blames himself for getting in the way."

Sophia turned to Logan, noticing for the first time that he held a white take-out bag.

"I feel terrible," she said.

"Your stomach aching again?"

"No, my stomach's fine. I feel bad for Luke. He doesn't deserve this."

"It was a freakish thing. Luke never lets a horse get the best of him. Nothing like this has happened before on the ranch."

"But he's going to be all right?" The thought of Luke in pain saddened her but she held back tears and told herself that Luke was strong and would probably heal quickly. At least, that was her rationalization. It was a small wonder that Logan hadn't blamed her for bringing Luke bad luck. And a small part of her wondered if that weren't truly the case. Luke befriends her and he winds up in the hospital. It was crazy to even consider it, yet Sophia couldn't deny the flash of guilt forcing its way into her thoughts.

"Yeah, eventually. He should make a full recovery."

"That's good news," she blurted. She couldn't hide her feelings. She cared about Luke.

Logan glanced at her with narrowed eyes, his mouth twitching, but whatever he was about to say to her he let drop. He strode past her and entered the kitchen. She followed him and watched as he removed items from the bag, placing them on the counter. "What's that?"

"Our dinner."

Any fool could see *and* smell the food he was arranging in the kitchen, but she never expected Logan to make the delivery and offer to eat with her. "Excuse me?"

"Don't be surprised. Was I supposed to argue with my brother about this?" He turned to her with recrimination in his eyes. "He made me promise to bring you dinner and work with you on Ruth's retirement party."

The air bottled up inside her lungs drained out. She was speechless.

"In fact, you and I are gonna have to pick up the slack at the lodge. Luke will be out of commission for a good long time."

Sophia walked to the counter, looking at the two dishes of pasta primavera Logan had taken out of the bag. Crusty Italian bread and a salad were also sitting on the counter.

"Meaning, we're going to have to work together from now on?"

Logan nodded, not looking happy about the prospect.

"He made you promise to be civil to me?"

Logan shrugged a shoulder. "Like I said, I'm not arguing with my brother when he's laid up."

"If you don't pull any more Ruth Polanskis on me, we might just manage working together."

Logan held back a devilish grin, but she saw the triumph in his eyes.

"Do we have a deal? For Luke's sake?" she asked, her hand on one tilted hip. She did not approve of Logan's smug look, no matter how hard he tried to conceal it.

Once again, Logan narrowed his eyes and gave her body a long leisurely sweeping appraisal. When he did that, Sophia felt as if he were devouring her whole. It took him a few seconds, but he finally agreed with a sharp nod. "For Luke's sake."

Sophia stared at him for a moment and sighed silently. They needed to eat quickly and get to work but she couldn't resist asking, "Did he also tell you what food to bring?"

Logan's mouth twitched again. This time she might have actually insulted him, but he took it in stride.

"No, I thought it up all by myself."

Okay, she thought, *I'll play nice.* She was hungry and ready for food that wouldn't knock her socks off. "Looks delicious."

Logan gave her the once-over again, his gaze fastening on the three inch-strip of exposed skin at her waist. "Yep, can't argue with that."

Sophia bit her tongue, holding back from giving him a piece of her mind. She had a better way of getting even with him. She wasn't forgetting about his ploy regarding Ruth Polanski. His scorching-hot gaze aside, she would have to show him that she wasn't easy prey.

They sat eating quietly in her small alcove off the kitchen. The linens were soft and white, the flowers wild from the pasture, the glasses sparkling under the fading light. Sophia was well aware of the handsome, uncompromising man sitting across the table from her. He'd brought a lovely meal seasoned mildly so that it went down easily and soothed her tender tummy. He'd also brought his underlying anger with him. It was a given, but Sophia wouldn't let that stop her from gobbling up everything on her plate. She'd played it safe and hadn't put food in her stomach for nearly twenty-four hours and now she was looking for seconds.

Logan rose from the table and brought over the container of food. She scooped a few more spoonfuls onto her own plate, watching him as he held it. This was strangely nice.

Maybe Logan had the need to control every situation. Coming here to tell her about the accident had been done on his terms, not hers. He could have called her to explain about Luke. He could have alerted her that he would be coming by for dinner. Instead he chose to show up at her door unannounced.

As if reading her mind, he set down his fork and commented, "I never thought I'd be sitting in this kitchen, having dinner with you."

"Boggles the mind. Our second meal together in two nights." Sophia gave him a sweet smile, refusing to be intimidated.

"Let's not make a habit of this." He surveyed the rooms in his line of vision—the kitchen, parlor and hallway that led to the bedrooms. "I don't care for this place."

"The place is wonderful. It's me you don't care for. So just be honest about it."

Logan sipped water from his glass, and then eyed her carefully. "My brother kissed you today."

Sophia's radar went up. She'd promised herself she would be on guard around Logan, but now he'd dropped another bomb on her that she hadn't expected. "Did he tell you that?"

Logan glanced at her lips, and then lifted his lids to look her squarely in the eyes. "I was at the lodge this morning."

"So you saw Luke give me an innocent kiss and what?"

"Maybe I don't think anything about you is innocent."

Sophia's stomach began to ache, not from the food but from the conversation. Darn him for creating more turmoil in her belly. Logan liked playing judge and jury. In his mind, he'd already convicted her of a half-dozen crimes. "And why is that?"

"The apple doesn't fall far from the tree."

"So now I'm a cliché to you, Logan? I've already told you if you're comparing me to my mother, it's a compliment. She was a wonderful woman. I only wish I could be more like her."

"Yeah, well, I used to want to be like my father. Blind worship doesn't work. Sooner or later, you find out that the person you thought you knew wasn't that person at all."

It was pointless to argue with him. Sophia didn't want to spend her time defending herself or her mother. Logan's mind was made up and nothing she could say would change that. Even though she knew the truth about her mother and his father, he would never believe her. He didn't trust her, and she was through trying to gain that trust from him. Through trying to prove herself to him. The only thing she cared about was doing a good job at the lodge and proving to *herself* that she was worthy of Randall Slade's generosity.

"I'm sorry, Logan. It must have been a big blow for you to learn your father wasn't perfect. Most of us aren't, you know."

She rose from her seat and came over to his side of the table, brushing his shoulder to reach for his plate. Her long tresses flowed onto his lap as she brought her face inches from his. He smelled of earth, rawhide and musk, and her breathing quickened as their eyes met. He was a beautiful man who hated her, but right now, she saw desire darken his eyes and that did amazing, warm things to her sensitive belly. She was close enough that if she stumbled, she'd be lap dancing with Logan. The image didn't amuse her as much as it made her lust. She whispered gently, blowing her breath over his lips, playing the vixen he thought she was, "I'll clean this up, and then we'll get right to work so you won't have to stay any longer than necessary."

He stared at her, their gazes locked and then his hand

touched the ribbon of exposed skin at her waist. Her breath caught in her throat and her senses heightened as he splayed his fingers along the hem of her shirt. It was unexpected magic. Sophia relished the feel of him touching her. She didn't flinch or budge a muscle when Logan moved his hand in a soft caress that traveled back and forth over her midriff. She closed her eyes, mental goose bumps erupting in her mind. There was a connection between them, something raw and elemental and basic that defied logic or scrutiny. When he touched her, she reacted.

He made the tug that landed her on his lap and now the lap dance didn't seem so far off, didn't seem so outlandish in her mind. She felt the strength of his legs beneath her, the power of the hand that held her in place, while the other hand continued to make her body tingle.

She knew she shouldn't allow him this touch. She shouldn't allow him to get the upper hand again, but she was powerless to stop him. She craved the warmth and the thrill of Logan's caress. He managed to loosen the knotted fabric at her waist and she waited, filled with unabashed desire. He took a big swallow, his throat working while his hand slid underneath her top. Inch by inch, he moved his palm up her torso. Her nipples puckered in anticipation. The pulse between her legs throbbed. It was exquisite and sensual. She hadn't been with a man in years, not like this. The idea of Logan taking liberties with her body shocked her mind, but her body gave him all he wanted.

She arched her back, and wiggled slightly on his lap. His fingers pushed her bra down and her ample breasts spilled out. They were full, sensitized, and she waited for his touch. When it finally came she jerked slightly from the beautiful sensation. He palmed one breast, then the other, and a groan escaped from the depths of his throat. She murmured with pleasure, and squeezed her legs tight when his thumb rubbed over her nipple.

The pleasure was ripe and fresh and so greatly welcomed, but Sophia had to put a stop to this. She wouldn't give in to Logan. She couldn't give in to what they both craved. He would only turn it against her and make her life at Sunset Ranch unbearable. She didn't trust him. And she owed him for hurting her all those years ago.

Her breaths coming as heavy as his, she brought her hands to his face and leaned in close. This had to be her idea. When he tried to meet her lips, she pulled back a little, making sure he knew kissing him was her idea. This had to be her choice, her decision and on her terms.

She waited, and he backed off, then she brought her lips to his to sip first, and then draw out the moment. It was just as good as she'd remembered as an innocent girl of fifteen. Memories rushed forth of the glory and newness of Logan's kiss. His mouth accommodated hers now, just as before, but this time she was initiating the kiss. She pressed her mouth fully over his lips and deepened the connection. The world went a little fuzzy then. Logan's breath rushed out and he removed his hand from her breast. The loss was keenly felt. He wrapped his arm around her waist, and brought her up tight against his chest. Sophia took control again. She parted her lips, and slipped her tongue inside his mouth. She tasted him with a sweeping exploration and he joined in, their tongues mating.

Satisfied that Logan had relinquished control, Sophia couldn't let things go too far. Up until today, Logan had called all the shots. But putting a stop to Logan Slade's passion wasn't as easy as she thought it would be. He was a man who thrilled her and made her dizzy with desire. He, and only he, brought out an incredible, nearly insatiable hunger in her. Ever since the day that he'd first kissed her behind the gym, Sophia had dreamed of him and hated him at the same time for turning a beautiful memory into something sordid and obscene.

Summoning her willpower and abandoning the innate pleasure, she inched back, slowly pulling away from him until their lips were no longer locked.

Logan felt the loss, his gaze darting to her lips immediately. His expression changed from desire to determination. He reached for her, pulling her into a tight embrace. Crushing her to his chest, he slid his chair back; the jarring noise echoed against the stone floor. He stood, bringing her up with him. They faced each other now. A blaze of hunger lit his eyes, telling her he would take her here, right now.

A shocking thrill coursed through her body. Suddenly the battle lines got blurry, and she wondered if she was making a mistake in backing away. Everything fluid and tingling in her body said Yes to this man. Yet her mind told her to resist and not give Logan what he wanted. What *she* wanted. It would never be right between them.

"No, Logan," she whispered, nearly breathless. She put her hands firmly against him and pushed. The solid wall of his chest didn't budge. Frustrated, she took a step back, needing to create space between them. "We're not doing this. We can't."

He blinked and looked at her, the fire in his eyes replaced by an intense stare.

This had been a bad idea from the start. She was a ravaged mess with her shirt askew, her hair mussed and her lips bruised from his kiss. She realized too late that she'd played with fire. And she would get burned, too. Yet she couldn't relent. She had to stand her ground. It was the only way.

"Let me guess," he said with a rasp. "This is about getting even with me for high school and Ruth Polanski?"

Sophia closed her eyes. Her little payback plan had backfired. She refused to give him an answer. Instead, when her eyes opened, it was to look at his beautiful mouth wishing for things that would never be. Tension crackled in the air.

"Two brothers in one day, Sophia. Is that your style now?"

"Luke kissed me as a friend," she shot back quickly. "To

thank me for helping with Ruth's party." Why did it always come back to Luke? "It was a peck on the cheek and nothing more."

Logan frowned and his eyes filled with disgust. "And you kissed me, why? To prove a point? To get back at me for something stupid I did as a kid in high school?"

It was the first time she'd heard Logan refer to that time with regret. She nodded. "Yes, yes. I admit it, Logan. You needed a dose of your own medicine. You needed to come down off your throne and not pass judgment on me unfairly. I wanted to prove a point. You don't like it when the roles are reversed, do you? When you're the one being played?"

He heaved a breath, as if trying to temper his impatience. "Sweetheart, if you think I was being played," he said, pointing at her disheveled appearance, "then take a good look in the mirror. You enjoyed every second of my hands on you."

Shaking, Sophia fumbled to tie up her T-shirt and thread her fingers through her mussed hair. As she straightened herself out, she was aware of Logan's eyes on her. His statement was true—she'd nearly been ravaged by him before she'd come to her senses. Slowly, she lifted her lashes to look at him. "I...know."

He flinched. Her honesty surprised him and she witnessed a debate going on in the depths of his dark eyes. It was as if he were being pulled in two directions—either to take her back into his arms and finish what they'd started or to take his leave.

Moments ticked by.

Sophia watched him carefully, her body immobile. What she'd just admitted to him was ludicrous and yet it was the truth.

"Hell, I need some air," he said finally. He grabbed his hat, plunked it on his head and took a few steps toward the door. Then he pivoted to face her one last time. "We have to work together, Sophia. Meet me in my office tomorrow afternoon. We'll go over the plans then."

She gave him a brisk nod.

And then he was gone.

Five

With morning sunlight at his back, Logan gunned his truck, heading for Carson Memorial Hospital. He turned up the volume on the radio, trying to focus on the words of a Tim Mc-Graw song. But the lyrics didn't sink in. Instead, an image of Sophia Montrose sprawled across his lap, arching toward him, giving him access to her body, flashed into his mind. He couldn't drown those memories out with loud music. He couldn't concentrate on business ventures. No matter how much he'd tried, the recollection of Sophia's velvet-soft mouth brushing his, her firm flesh under his fingertips, the swell of her full, beautiful breasts in his palms continued to plague his thoughts.

Last night after leaving the cottage, he'd drowned out those images with a bottle of Jack Daniels. But today he'd hoped to hell he could fight the mental battles on his own. He refused to fall victim to Sophia Montrose, beautiful and desirable as she was, because he knew better. He'd seen what his father's love for a Montrose had done to his family.

When he'd been in high school he wanted to teach Sophia a lesson. He'd wanted to put her in her place. He'd wanted to lash out at her. He'd kissed her, never expecting that he'd be the one to learn a lesson. That kiss had startled him, and he'd been surprised at his own reaction to her. He'd never expected it to be so good. Sophia had made him feel as if he could conquer the world. And damn it, last night, and as much as he'd fought it, that same feeling had returned.

He reached the hospital, and pulled into a parking space, hoping a visit with Luke would clear his mind. He was concerned for his brother. Luke would heal from his injuries, but he'd be a bear to live with during his recovery.

Logan got out of his truck and strode purposefully through the front doors. He walked through the lobby, and took the elevator up. The doors opened to the third floor and, as he marched past a row of rooms, he kept his eyes trained straight ahead. He didn't like looking in on people in their sickbeds. His brother was too young to be laid up in a hospital. Though Luke had taken his share of tumbles while in the rodeo, he'd usually wound up getting patched up in the emergency room and sent on his way.

Logan reached his brother's room and stopped by the door to steal a look inside.

Luke had a smile on his weary face, a brighter expression than yesterday. It was a relief to see him looking a little better until Logan noticed that he wasn't alone. There was a reason for his brother's good mood.

Sophia was in the room.

She smiled at Luke, her gaze focused only on him as she moved toward his bed with a ribbon-tied bouquet of flowers in her hand. She stopped by the window next to his bed, standing at his shoulder, and gently moved a stray lock of hair from his forehead. Her soft melodic laughter wafted through the room.

Logan winced at the scene they made together. An image

of holding Sophia in his arms returned, and in that instant emotions he wouldn't name streamed into his consciousness.

He cursed aloud and both heads turned his way.

"Logan," his brother said in a weak voice. He managed a quick smile. "Come in."

As he walked into the room, Sophia made herself busy putting the flowers in a plastic water pitcher.

"How you doing?" he asked his brother.

"Pretty good today. Considering."

"You feel dizzy?" Logan asked. "The doc said you might for a few days."

"Not too much anymore. Wait, are there two of you standing there?"

"You're not funny," Logan said, though he was relieved to see Luke hadn't lost his sense of humor. He hated seeing his strong, good-natured brother reduced to wearing a tie-at-the-back hospital gown, lying on a remote-controlled sickbed. His right arm was in a cast, and three broken ribs didn't allow him to move much.

"Sophia says I am."

Logan shot Sophia a quick glance. She made eye contact with him for one second before focusing back on the flowers she was arranging. "Well, then it's gospel. You are."

"My brother is in full agreement with me? Doesn't happen every day."

"You're not laid up every day."

"Don't remind me. Once the meds wear off, I won't be smiling much."

"I hear you." Logan took a swallow. "You need anything?"

Luke shot him a pointed look. "Can you get me out of here today?"

"I take it your doc already told you no."

"Flat-out no. Thought you could pull some strings."

Logan put his hands out, palms up. "I didn't bring a rope."

"Now you're not funny." Luke closed his eyes then. Clearly,

the conversation was a strain on him, which only proved that Luke wasn't ready to come home. Knowing Luke, he wouldn't get much rest at the ranch. As much as he hated to admit it, Luke was better off in the hospital right now.

Sophia gave Luke a sympathetic look, her amber eyes forlorn. God, she was gorgeous, and so wrong for any of the Slade men that Logan felt the truth of it deep down in his bones. She was forbidden fruit, sure to poison any man who dared to take a bite. He wasn't entirely convinced she'd come to the hospital out of friendship and concern for his brother. He didn't trust her motives and it wasn't *just* because of his father's indiscretion with her mother. Sophia herself had married a rich old codger for his money. That fact couldn't be disputed.

Carefully, she put her hand on Luke's arm and he opened his eyes to look at her. "I'd better go now," she said. "I don't want to tax your strength."

He nodded. "I'm glad you stopped by. Thanks for the flowers."

She smiled warmly and bent to kiss his cheek. "I'll check on you later."

She picked up her purse, and gave Logan a cursory glance as she walked out of the room.

With his eyes closed again, Luke murmured, "What's up with the two of you anyway?"

Logan pulled a chair over to the bed and took a seat. He didn't pretend not to know what his brother was talking about. "Nothing's up. Why?"

"I'm injured, not blind." He snapped his eyes open. "You two looked...*guilty* about something."

"I hardly noticed her."

Luke's eyes drifted closed again. "Exactly. Sophia is hard *not* to notice. Did you have another fight?"

Just the opposite, he thought. They had...lust. And it'd been eating at Logan since their encounter last night. If Sophia had wanted retribution, she'd gotten her wish. "No. We didn't fight."

Luke took a long labored breath. His ribs must hurt like hell. Logan had broken a rib once as a kid, jumping out of a tree and hitting solid ground hard. He remembered breathing being really difficult for days.

"You working together okay?"

"Yeah, yeah," Logan said. "As a matter of fact, we're gonna work on Ruth's party later in the day."

"Just don't give her a hard time, okay?"

It was a good thing Luke's eyes were closed. He couldn't see Logan's mouth twist with annoyance. "Sure thing. We'll be right as rain. You just concentrate on getting some rest. I'll come by later on."

Luke turned his head to the side and slowly nodded. "I'm coming home tomorrow, doctor or no doctor."

Logan knew he meant business. Nothing much kept his brother down.

Sophia spent the morning going over upcoming events at the lodge with Ruth. There was the annual Memorial Day barbecue, marking the beginning of the summer season, as well as a wedding planned in the first week of June. Sophia took notes, reviewed the ledgers and read the week's guest surveys to see if there was anything they could improve on. She made her daily rounds inside the lodge, checking on the staff, and then strolled outside to meet with sunshine and warm fresh air.

So far, so good, she thought as she stood on the veranda, looking out at the newly blossoming garden, the green pastures and beyond. Everywhere her eyes touched belonged to the Slades but for the dazzling Sierra Nevadas. Now she was a small part of that empire. Being half owner of the lodge brought her a fuller range of responsibilities than managerial duties and although it was a bit daunting, Sophia had geared herself up for the challenge.

She strode past the gates and headed for the stables. One of the services of the lodge was to offer guided horse rides on the property, and Sophia held a revised schedule on her clipboard.

Just as she arrived, Hunter Halliday rounded the barn wall, and stopped three inches short of bowling her over. Stunned, she leaned way back, the clipboard flying out of her hands as she lost her balance. Hunter reached for her, his hands firm and steady on her shoulders to right her.

"Oh, Ms. Sophia. Didn't see you coming."

He was taller than her by five inches and broad-shouldered for a boy of seventeen. She had to look up at him. "It's all right. I didn't see you, either."

"As long as you're okay," he said, giving her body a quick scan. Once he realized his hands were still on her, he removed them quickly, and blushed red under his tanned skin.

She straightened herself out, took a breath and thought to ease Hunter's mind by getting right down to business. "I'm fine, really. I need to run something by your dad." She bent to retrieve the clipboard off the ground. When she came up holding it, Hunter appeared perplexed that he hadn't thought to pick it up himself.

He blinked. "Sorry."

"No problem. Is your dad here by any chance?"

"Nope," he said. "Dad's at the ranch today."

"Actually, maybe you can help me. Will you check over this new schedule, and tell me if it looks okay? I made some changes." She handed him the clipboard.

Hunter seemed relieved that she'd moved on to business. "Sure, I can do that."

"No hurry. If you want to bring it by the office tomorrow morning, that's soon enough."

"I'll do that."

"Thank you. Oh, and Hunter…good catch. I might have fallen on my butt if you hadn't caught me."

Hunter smiled shyly. "I wouldn't have let that happen."

Sophia walked away from the barn thinking that Ward Halliday had raised a well-mannered boy.

Her mood brightened even more when she spotted Edward across the yard with Blackie at his heels. The boy tossed a ball and Blackie took off running.

Sophia came up just as Blackie returned. "Hello, Edward."

"Hi," he said.

"No school today?"

He shook his head. "It's p-parent's day."

Sophia immediately ached for Edward. Neither one of his parents would show up for the parents' conference today. His teacher wouldn't share with them his strengths and weaknesses in the classroom. They wouldn't hear about his behavior and his homework habits. They wouldn't come home feeling proud of his accomplishments. Sophia hid her sorrow for the boy. She reminded herself that he had Constance. His grandmother was determined to make sure Edward knew he was loved. "That means it's really kids' day."

The boy grinned, and Blackie jumped up against Edward's lanky frame, pleading for another ball toss. Edward didn't disappoint. He threw the ball and the dog went running again. "I g-get to play with B-Blackie and then go o-on a h-hike with Mr. Slade."

Sophia winced inwardly. Logan was compassionate with the boy. She was glad of it, but seeing that side of Logan only confused her more. "Where do you hike?"

Edward pointed to a low rise on the mountains. "Up th-there."

"And does Blackie get to go?"

"Yep."

"Sounds like fun."

Edward gave her a thoughtful look. "W-want to come?"

Sophia was touched by the invitation. "Oh, uh…"

"Ms. Montrose has work to do."

Sophia whirled around, startled by the sound of Logan's voice. It was the second time today she'd been nearly bowled over. "Logan, where did you come from?"

He grinned. "Same place as everybody else."

She wanted to slap the crooked smile off his face, until he looked at Edward with warmth in his eyes, and ruffled the boy's hair.

"Hi there. You enjoying your day off from school?" Logan asked.

"Yes, sir." The dog jaunted back and Edward pulled the ball from his mouth.

"Good. You get your chores done, and I'll come get you in three hours. We'll go on that hike, okay?"

"Okay," he said.

Edward tossed the ball toward the barn, and then ran as fast as he could to catch up to the dog that had dashed after it. Once he'd gotten a good thirty feet away, he turned and waved to Sophia.

Sophia waved back, and watched him until he entered the barn.

"You're good with the boy," Sophia said, not realizing she'd spoken the words aloud.

Logan clucked his tongue. "As opposed to being down-right mean and rotten?"

Sophia snapped her head up, annoyed at Logan for sucking the joy out of a purely innocent comment. "It's a wonder you can stand up straight with that giant chip on your shoulder."

He put his head down, stared at his boots and sighed heavily. "Yeah, I suppose you're right. You paid me a com-pliment and—"

"You found something sinister in an honest observation."

Logan's dark brows lifted, creasing his forehead. "You make me sound like a devil."

Since when did Logan care *what* she thought of him? She searched his eyes and with a shake of her head admitted, "I don't think you're mean."

He looked away, unwilling to share a poignant moment with her, unwilling to realize that she didn't hold harsh feelings for him the way he did for her. "Edward has had a rough childhood. His parents have made bad choices, and the boy shouldn't have to pay for that."

As he spoke, she noted the pain in Logan's voice. For a brief moment, she wondered if Logan related to Edward because he'd had pain in his life, too. Pain she was certain he attributed to her mother's relationship with his dad. "Life isn't always fair," Sophia said.

He stared at her. "No, it isn't."

Sophia balked at his negative tone. This conversation was going nowhere. "I'd better get back to work."

She brushed by him, but before she was out of his reach, he took hold of her arm, his fingertips gently digging into the flesh. His touch stirred her senses. She paused for a second, sensations rippling through her body. On a silent sigh, she turned to face him. "What?"

"I've got appointments all afternoon, and the hike with Edward later. We have to talk about Ruth's party sometime."

"Your schedule is busier than mine. Tell me when, and I'll be there."

"First thing tomorrow morning. Come to my office at 8:00 a.m. sharp."

Logan's home office was private, so there'd be no chance of Ruth catching on. She'd never suspect a thing and that was the whole point of the surprise. Sophia dreaded being alone with Logan, yet what choice did she have—they were partners. "I'll be there."

He released his gentle hold on her and she walked away. But the impact of Logan's touch stayed with her for the remainder of the workday.

Well past seven o'clock, she closed up her office and left the lodge as the sun made one last blazing hurrah on the horizon. She enjoyed the glorious sunset on the walk home. But when she climbed the steps leading up to her front door, just as she put her key into the lock, a rustling sound from behind her interrupted her peace. She felt a presence. Someone was in the bushes. She turned sharply to see who it was. "Is someone there?" she called out.

No one appeared. There was no response. In the fading light she scanned the area, searching the garden, shrubs and thicket of trees and then farther, past the yard. Had she imagined it? With her back turned, she'd been so certain that someone was approaching from behind. An eerie sensation crept up her spine.

For a moment, she stood perfectly still, listening. A lump formed in her throat and before she allowed butterflies to take flight in her stomach, she gave herself a mental talking to. *Don't let your imagination go wild. No one is out there. It was probably the wind.*

Though at the moment, not so much as a breeze blew by.

Sophia shook off the feeling of déjà vu, turned the doorknob and flipped on the light switch as she entered the house, making sure to lock the front door. She moved carefully through the rooms, looking around, and finally decided she was being silly. She was safe on Sunset Ranch. There were security gates, and the property was well guarded.

But just in case, Sophia slept with the lamp on that night.

The next morning, Sophia stood at the cottage's entranceway, staring at a plain piece of folded, white computer paper she'd lifted from the welcome mat outside her door. Curious, she glanced out to the yard, looking to find someone who might have left her a note. Coming up empty in her search, she unfolded the paper quickly and read four words typed above the crease.

She blinked, and reread the note.

Her shoulders slumped, and her breath came in shortened bursts. "Oh…no."

Slight tremors coursed through her body, and she fought the sensations, trying to make sense of what she'd found. The words were not threatening—should not instill panic. And yet she couldn't tamp down her fear. She couldn't believe this was happening to her…again.

You are very beautiful.

Last night, she'd been certain someone had been watching her. And today, as she'd slipped into her brown slacks and sleeveless cream blouse after her morning shower, she'd realized how foolish she'd been.

"Don't be paranoid, Sophia," she'd said into the bathroom mirror, tying her long hair back into a loose braid. "You heard a frightened animal dash from the yard or a bird flitting through the branches of the tall pines." She had herself convinced it was nothing. But after seeing those four words, Sophia feared her world could very well tip upside down. She wasn't convinced or sure of anything anymore. There was only one conclusion she could come to.

Someone *had* been outside her cottage last night.

Someone was watching her.

Sophia squinted against the morning sunshine, looked around the yard once again and then shut the door. Her legs wobbly, she made her way to the sofa and lowered herself onto it.

She closed her eyes.

She had to get a grip.

Yet she couldn't move or summon up the energy to start her busy day. Her mind flashed to two years ago and that very frightening time in her life.

Shortly after her mother's cancer treatments had begun, she'd landed a position on the chorus line for the Las Vegas Fantasy Follies. Hospital bills had piled up faster than she could work them off. She'd been scared and worried about a mother who was in major denial about the severity of her illness. Out of necessity, Sophia had become both a worried, doting daughter and the only breadwinner for their little family.

When the first note had arrived to her dressing room, Sophia hadn't thought much of it. Her mind was on her mother's chemo treatments…and kicking her legs high enough and in sync with the other dancers in order to keep her job. Two more notes had followed. After she'd received the third note delivered to the dressing room, her closest friend in the follies remarked, "Oh, wow, Sophia. You have yourself a stalker."

It was then that Sophia had learned that propositions usually came to showgirls in face-to-face encounters with gentlemen backstage after the show. They weren't typed out on unadorned, *untraceable* white computer paper.

The notes kept coming sporadically; there was no rhyme or reason to them. Sophia had gotten spooked on several occasions when she was sure there was one particular pair of eyes in her audience with deeper, more observant, more sinister motives than watching pretty girls dance, jiggle and tease on a glitzy stage. There were other times when she felt as if she were being followed home, although she'd never seen a soul. Her life had been one great big ball of fear. Fear for her mother, fear for her job, fear for her safety. She'd called the police once, and they'd taken a report noting her complaint, but they said no crime had been committed and Sophia figured she was pretty much on her own.

Until Gordon Gregory had come to her rescue, her grey-haired knight in shining armor.

Gordon felt he owed the Montrose women a great debt for saving his granddaughter's life. Months prior, Louisa had taken in a wayward girl who had run away from her parents' home in Northern California. She'd shown up in the alley behind the motel Louisa managed, high on drugs and beaten pretty severely from a mugging. The girl had been a runaway for certain and might have died on the backstreets of Las Vegas if Louisa and Sophia hadn't taken her in and nursed her back to health. The frightened girl threatened to run again if they called the police. They hadn't. Instead they'd talked to her for three days straight and gained her trust, making her see that she had hit rock bottom. But she still had a chance to save herself, and once she agreed to go home and make a fresh start, they'd learned that the misguided teenager was Amanda Gregory, granddaughter to Gordon Gregory, a wealthy oil magnate who had a home in Las Vegas.

Gordon was so grateful to Louisa and Sophia for saving Amanda that he'd offered to give them anything they wanted. The sky was the limit.

"We shouldn't be rewarded for doing the right thing," her ailing mother had told him.

After that, Gordon had become a friend. And when things got bad and the two Montrose women had really needed help, Gordon had intervened with his offer to take Sophia away from the Follies and any danger she might have been in, marry her and give Louisa the best possible health care. The older gentleman had principles and old-fashioned notions about marriage, despite his four failed unions and the big age difference. He'd insisted there would be no strings attached initially if Sophia was in agreement. He'd offered her time to adjust to the marriage and a safe haven from all her worries. At the time, with skyrocketing medical bills, a would-be stalker and an ill mother on her hands, Sophia had had no choice. Basically, Gordon had been the answer to her prayers. Sophia had even managed to convince her mother that she'd be happy with Gordon, but in truth, she'd wanted to give her mother peace of mind that her daughter would be well cared for if anything happened to her.

The marriage was to be a quiet affair. But the details of

her marriage had been leaked to the tabloids, which naturally resulted in splashy front-page headlines. Sophia was not painted in a good light—the twentysomething gold-digging showgirl married to the aging oil magnate. At the time, Sophia had been out of options and her mother's health had been foremost in her mind.

Sophia wasn't always proud of her decisions. There were times when deep remorse set in. Her choices may not have always been wise, but she'd done what she'd had to do, out of necessity.

She would not go back to living in fear.

Slowly, methodically Sophia squeezed the note in her palm, her fingers digging in until the paper curled into an abstract form. She watched the words crumple away as she tightened her fist and then gave a final squeeze. The wrinkled lump in her hand couldn't hurt her anymore. It couldn't cause her any anguish now.

She would have to forget about this and hope it was a fluke. A mere coincidence. After all, it had been the other sentence absent from this note that had changed a compliment into a threat. Today's note didn't say "You will be mine one day."

Sophia clung to that notion.

Still shaken, she rose from the sofa and moved to the kitchen, where she pressed her toe to the foot pedal of the stainless-steel garbage can. The note belonged in the past. She wouldn't allow it to terrify her. She wouldn't give it credence. Not here, not now. She was trying to rebuild her life on Sunset Ranch. With one forceful toss, the note was history. The lid of the garbage can slammed shut, and Sophia put the ordeal out of her mind. She grabbed her purse, slung it over her shoulder and walked out of the cottage on legs that moved solely by steely, stubborn conviction.

She would not allow that note to destroy her day.

Ten minutes later she couldn't say the same thing about Logan Slade.

* * *

"You're late, Sophia. What part of eight sharp don't you understand?"

Sophia winced at Logan's demeaning tone. He was lecturing her as if she were a student in his classroom, sounding uncannily like Mr. Anderson in ninth-grade history.

Tardiness will only get you detention for the day. You make me wait, and I make you wait.

"You're right," she said, taking a seat to face him from across his office desk. "I'm sorry. It won't happen again." Sophia set her shoulder bag down on the seat next to her and opened up her valise, drawing out a clipboard.

Logan's angry tone ebbed. "You look pale. Didn't you sleep last night?"

Sophia straightened in her seat. The darn note had rattled her more than she'd have thought. On the short drive to Logan's house, she'd been reliving the past—thinking of her mother, her life and her bad choices. Her nerves were almost shot and she had to put on a good front for Logan not to see her distress. For all her bravado, Sophia felt things stronger than she let on and it manifested in a trembling body and a distracted mind. "I slept wonderfully, thank you."

"*Sorry* and *thank you,* all in the thirty seconds since you've been here, Sophia?"

Her chin went up. "Would you rather that I tell you how rude you were to me when I walked in?"

Logan grinned as if he'd coaxed the response he'd wanted from her. "I expect promptness."

"In a perfect world, maybe you should."

"What's not so perfect about your world?"

Sophia gazed down at the floor. She wouldn't answer Logan's question, but she was tempted to. She would love to tell him the truth about her imperfect life, and make him see that she was not the sordid, calculating woman he thought her to be. Not that he'd believe her. His mind was made up. "We don't have enough time in the day."

"Good point," he said, studying her for a moment before glancing at his watch. "Let's get down to business. I have another meeting in an hour."

Glad the focus was off her, Sophia discussed her ideas about the surprise party, how she thought they could pull it off without Ruth knowing and her plans for the menu and decorations. Uncharacteristically, Logan agreed with her about everything. She was pleased that he chose not to argue the details. When it came to throwing a party, Logan didn't have a clue. He was smart enough to defer to her. Yet she had a hard time focusing one hundred percent of her attention on the task at hand when her thoughts today were on the past.

She missed her mother. She still couldn't believe she was gone. Oftentimes, she'd wanted to pick up the phone to call her.

Hey, Mama, I finally got your chili recipe right.

Hey, Mama, the daisies are in full bloom outside your bedroom window.

Hey, Mama, I just wanted to say good morning.

The loss was so keen that it always took Sophia a few seconds to realize that she would never be able to call her mother again.

"Sophia?" Logan's voice broke through her thoughts.

She snapped her head up. "Oh, uh… Yes?"

His brows gathered as he aimed a pointed question at her. "Something's up with you today. What's going on?"

Sophia stared into Logan's deep, dark eyes. For half a second, she wanted to confide in him about the mysterious note and how it had stirred bad memories for her. "I, uh—"

His gaze drifted down to her hand holding the pen. She'd forgotten to bring her laptop, something Logan had probably noticed but hadn't mentioned. She took notes the old-fashioned way today, and her hand trembled as she jotted things down.

"Nothing. I missed breakfast. I guess I'm a little shaky." That was the truth. She hadn't eaten this morning and it was a good enough reason to give him.

Although he gave her a nod of understanding, the entire time they spoke, she felt Logan's gaze penetrating her, watching and waiting for a hint to indicate why she was acting so out of character. He was, by nature, suspicious of her. And no amount of explanation would convince him to be otherwise.

Once the plans were set for the party, they moved the discussion to her progress with the lodge. Sophia forced herself to concentrate on details for the next fifteen minutes, and they concluded their business within the hour.

Logan rose from his desk, hawklike eyes watching her every move. She rose, too. Thankfully, her legs were stronger now, and her nerves not quite so raw. She had a full day of work ahead of her and a party to plan.

"I'll call you tonight to check on the progress," he said.

Sophia slipped her purse strap over her shoulder. "Fine." He came around his desk to meet her, and walked her toward the door. "How is Luke this morning?" she asked.

"Better, from what the doctors tell me."

"Is he coming home today?" Sophia couldn't keep hope out of her voice, which garnered a tight-lipped response from Logan. "If he has anything to say about it, he will."

"Give him my best when you see him."

"Will do," he said as they reached the office door. "Oh, and Sophia."

"Hmm?"

"Eat something. Can't have Sunset Lodge's manager faint dead away in the middle of the lobby."

Sophia sent him a sugary-sweet smile. "Thanks for your concern."

"Anytime."

Sophia had the distinct feeling that Logan Slade had his eyes trained on her backside as she walked out of his office and down the hall.

"I'll go crazy if I stick around here much longer." Luke's frustrated words issued from his mouth in a whisper.

Poor guy, Sophia thought. He couldn't move too much in his bed without feeling tremendous pain. Yet he stubbornly refused to take the meds the doctor had prescribed for him.

"You have to give yourself some time, Luke," Sophia said. "You've been home only a few days."

"Can't do a damn thing on the ranch, either. With my cracked ribs and this here busted-up arm."

Sophia glanced at the cumbersome cast that went more than halfway up his right arm and couldn't argue the point. Luke wasn't one to sit still, yet what option did he have? He'd ridden the rodeo circuit and from what she'd gathered he'd never suffered an injury like this before. "What you need is something to take your mind off your troubles." Sophia leaned toward him to bring a freshly baked butter cookie dusted with powdered sugar near his mouth. "Here, try one of these," she said. "I made them early this morning for you."

Luke's gaze lowered to the cookie hovering by his lips. "Smells delicious. Lay it on me."

He opened his mouth, and she inserted the cookie. He took a bite and chewed thoughtfully, then swallowed and sighed with appreciation, laying his head back against the bed pillow. "You're an angel, Sophia."

Too bad his brother didn't think so. She was an angel to Luke, and the devil's spawn to Logan. One wouldn't think the two men had the same blood running through their veins.

"That cookie melted in my mouth. Gotta be the best cookie I've ever had." Then he added, "Don't be telling Constance I said so."

She put the rest of the cookie into his mouth. Her mother's

recipe never failed to make people smile. "I made two dozen," she said, gesturing with a head tilt toward the plate on his nightstand, sitting next to the bouquet of flowers she'd brought him when he first arrived from the hospital. "You can thank me later, after you've finished all of them."

Luke's left hand came out to take hers. "I can thank you now—"

"No problem, I love to bake—"

"For coming to see me twice already since I've been home," he rasped out. "And for listening to me moan and groan."

"That's what friends are for."

Morning sunshine streamed in through the shuttered windows facing east. But the beautiful day didn't have an effect on Luke's sour mood. He was a man accustomed to being on the move. "There'll be a hell of a lot more moaning and groaning," he confessed.

"I know. I can't blame you. But you'll heal. You have to be patient." Sophia moved from the chair to the side of his bed, carefully lowering down so as not to disturb him. "Here," she said, leaning forward and offering him a second cookie. "Have another."

He bit down, and closed his eyes while he chewed. "How are things at the lodge?" he asked quietly.

A pipe had burst, leaking water into the rooms on the second floor, the smoke alarm had gone off for no apparent reason in the kitchen and one of the guests had slipped and sprained an ankle while stepping down from their saddle since Luke's accident. Business as usual, she mused. "It's coming along."

"Glad to hear it. You fit right in on Sunset Ranch."

Sophia sighed. "I love it here."

"And I love that you're here, feeding me cookies."

She laughed and Luke cracked a smile, but a second later,

he paid for the movement with a grimace of pain. Sophia grimaced, too, sympathizing with him.

"Is there anything I can do for you before I go to work?" she asked.

Luke shook his head. "Nope. You go on. Thanks for the visit and the cookies."

"I spoiled your breakfast."

"You spoiled me, period."

"I'll come back again soon."

"I might not be here."

Sophia thought he was kidding until she saw a spark of determination in his eyes. "Where would you be?"

"An old rodeo buddy of mine is recovering from a bad injury. Broke his back a while ago. He's got a cabin on the north shore of Tahoe and is itching for a drinking partner. I'm thinking on it. I'm gonna be pretty darn useless around here for the next couple of weeks."

"Can you travel?"

"I can if I take those dang pills. It's not a far trip. Logan offered to drive me if I decide to go. He thinks it's a good idea. Wants me outta his hair, from all the complaining I've been doing."

Sophia shook her head. "I'm sure your brother wants what's best for you. Will you let me know if you decide to go? I'd want to say goodbye."

"Sure thing."

Sophia rose from the bed gingerly, and gave him one last look before exiting the room. She moved through the house with familiarity, as if it was only yesterday that she'd played in these stately paneled rooms and raced down the hallways on her way out the kitchen to a backyard that had doubled as an amusement park in her childhood.

The Slades had a tree house that looked like a Western fort with a steep slide and rubber swings. They had bicycles and wagons and a giant fenced-off pool. They owned horses and had been taught from an early age to respect animals, and all of their other possessions, as well. Sophia had often heard Mr. Slade instruct his boys, "Take care of things, or be prepared to lose them."

The boys took it strictly as a warning then, but later in life Sophia realized how smart Randall Slade had been. He'd meant it as a life lesson.

Sophia had almost reached the front door when Logan's deep voice stopped her cold. "Sophia, I'd like a word with you. Got a second?"

His words echoed in the entryway as Sophia slowly pivoted on her three-inch heels. She found Logan striding toward her, his face a mask of indifference but for a jaw that twitched as he approached.

Her heart skipped a beat at the sight of him. She asked herself, why him? Why did she find him so darn attractive when clearly the two of them would never happen? Logan had a perfectly gorgeous, fun-loving sibling whom Sophia adored, but Luke didn't make butterflies take flight in her belly or make her nerves jump and her body tingle the way Logan did.

He'd touched her intimately the other night.

And she'd wanted more.

Irritated at her train of thought, she gave him a terse response. "I'm on my way to the lodge."

"Busy?"

"I have some issues that need tending. Yes, I'm very busy."

His mouth curved up in a casual smile that belied his words. "But not too busy to hand-feed my brother your cookies."

Sophia blinked, surprised that Logan had known about that. "Were you spying on me?"

He took her question matter-of-factly. "I'd hardly call it spying. It's my house. I passed by Luke's room and saw the two of you in there. Cozy little picture you made."

Sophia closed her eyes briefly, praying for patience. Damn

him. She would not let Logan get the best of her. "Luke enjoyed my cookies. You should try one. They are delicious."

His eyes moved over her, gently caressing each curve of her body. The dress she wore today was clingy and cranberry-red and Logan could hardly miss the fact that Sophia had forgotten to wear her usual matching jacket that concealed her cleavage somewhat. She felt exposed to his gaze. He touched every inch of her with eyes that devoured, eyes that held a thrilling promise. "Maybe I want my own batch, Sophia."

The underlying sensuality of his comment fascinated her. She put her head down, her gaze catching the shiny polished tips of his black snakeskin boots. Rugged, rough-edged and appealing, Logan Slade made mincemeat of her resolve. She raised her head slightly, not quite able to meet his eyes. Instead she stared at the tanned skin exposed by the opened collar of his chambray shirt. She replied in a broken, quiet whisper. "Maybe...one day, Logan."

He put his hand under her chin. With the tips of his fingers, he lifted her face a fraction of an inch until she was forced to look into his eyes. They smoldered like dark coals and sent a warm shot of heat through her body. It wasn't fair that Logan could do her so much damage with a mere look, a single tender touch.

He bent his head and Sophia pleaded with him. "Don't... don't kiss me."

He inched closer. "You want me to."

She did. She wanted him to kiss her. She wanted him to make her feel the way he had the other night.

The lap dance night.

"Logan, you out there?" Luke's strained voice broke through their moment like a cold splash of water.

Logan cursed quietly.

Sophia swallowed down hard.

Both looked in the direction of Luke's bedroom.

"Yeah, I'm here," Logan called back to him. "I'm coming."

Sophia stepped away from Logan, turning her back on him to reach for the doorknob. Before she gave it a turn, Logan's husky voice resonated in her soul. "Looks like Luke saved you again."

Sophia put her head down, taking a moment to absorb the sensations rushing around inside her. Something was happening between them, but she didn't know if she could trust what she was feeling. She didn't know if she could trust Logan, period. "Maybe I don't want to be saved."

The sound of his receding footsteps faded on the plank floors. He'd walked away to see to his brother and hadn't heard her. It was just as well. There were too many "maybes" involved with Logan. Sophia opened the door and stepped outside. The Nevada sun warmed her cheeks and the clear sky above brightened her outlook.

She had repaired pipes that needed her approval, a lodge guest's temper to soothe and a meeting with her staff this morning.

She loved every crazy minute of it.

She wouldn't have time to think about Logan Slade any more today.

Six

Sophia never had the chance to say goodbye to Luke. He left the night after her visit to deliver the cookies. Logan had thought it best for Luke to travel late at night so that he could sleep during the trip to Tahoe. Apparently, from what she could gather, his host, Casey Thomas, was a good guy, wild in his younger rodeo days, but now a big fan of the simple life. The two would drink and shoot the breeze at Casey's lakeside cabin.

But as Sophia gazed out the window of her cottage this evening, dressed and ready for Ruth's surprise party, she felt Luke's absence in the pit of her stomach. He'd been gone for five days and she'd spoken to him twice in that time, but she hadn't confided in him. Since he'd left, she'd received two more notes on her doorstep.

You are very beautiful.

The notes were always folded neatly and always typed on plain white computer paper. While receiving one note might have been a fluke and something she could ignore, receiving two more meant that whoever was out there, whoever was sending these notes was persistent. She feared they would continue to torment her. She'd been sleeping with the lights on lately. She'd been listening intently for out-of-the-ordinary sounds in and around the cottage.

Sophia let go a deep breath to steady her nerves. Tonight, she would play an integral role in getting Ruth to her surprise party. Sophia had worked her buns off this week, making arrangements, hiding a drastic change in employees' schedules from Ruth and working with Logan and his staff to get the Slade home ready for the party.

The cover story was that Ruth and Sophia were to meet one of Randall Slade's high-profile friends who was interested in using Sunset Lodge as a summer retreat for the entire staff of a private college. Sophia had explained that Logan would first host a special dinner at the Slade ranch house to impress the client, then one of Ruth's last duties would be to help Sophia put him up for the night at the lodge and give him the royal treatment tomorrow.

Ruth bought the entire concept and Sophia was certain she didn't have a clue what was really going on. Sophia was on pins and needles, though. Without Luke here for support, being secretive with Ruth all week and receiving another one of those notes made her jumpy.

Before exiting the cottage, Sophia scanned the property thoroughly, just like she'd been doing all week long. She grabbed her wrap and her purse and looked around one last time before locking up the cottage and getting into her car. She had no proof or evidence to back her feeling of being watched, other than that one night when she heard a disturbance in her yard, yet Sophia felt the sensation deep down in her bones.

Thirty minutes later, after picking up Ruth, who was dressed very elegantly in a cobalt-blue and silver dress, Sophia delivered Ruth to the Slade home.

Logan answered the door personally, dressed in a dark Western suit and string tie—a handsome maverick with a charming smile. Upon spotting Ruth, he gave her a welcoming kiss on the cheek, and then gave Sophia a quick approving nod as his razor-sharp gaze raked over her upswept hair, shimmery sequined cocktail dress and sandaled feet.

"Our guest is outside. He is anxious to meet with you both." Logan stepped between them, offering the ladies his arm. With Ruth chatting amiably on his right and Sophia on his left, the three of them walked through the wide parlor double doors to be greeted by the sight of twinkling lights, grandly decorated tables and about sixty of Ruth's friends and coworkers.

"Surprise!" the gathered crowd shouted in unison, stunning Ruth into silence. Tears filled her eyes. With her hand to her chest, she truly appeared surprised.

Logan and Sophia looked at each other. For a brief moment in time they shared the triumph. They'd pulled it off.

The festivities got under way quickly. Ruth was swarmed by guests giving their congratulations, kisses and loving hugs. She was the center of attention, as she should be, with her husband, her children and grandchildren by her side.

Sophia took a minute for herself. She strolled to the edge of the beautifully landscaped yard. Beyond the whitewashed wooden fences illuminated by strings of tiny lights was pasture land that stretched for miles. It was so vast and remote, so steeped in eerily quiet darkness that a chill ran down her spine. She shivered in the warm night and rubbed her hands up and down her arms, attempting to bank her feelings of uncertainty. Those anonymous notes were weighing on her and affecting her daily routine. She couldn't get them off her mind.

"Need some quiet time?"

The voice from behind made her jump.

She whirled around. "Oh!"

Logan's face was cast in shadows, making him look sinister, but oddly enough his comment had been soft and calming. "Apparently not, since you're here now."

Logan flashed a smile. His expression wasn't one of battle. He offered her one of the two crystal champagne flutes he held in his hand. "Here, have a drink."

Sophia shook her head. "I don't…drink."

"It's sparkling cider."

Thoughtful, Sophia mused.

As he handed her a glass, his fingers caressed hers, and she felt the impact of his touch down to her toes. "Thank you."

"To Ruth," he said, and then added, "and to you. You pulled off a great surprise party."

Warmed by the compliment, she brought her glass to his with a gentle clink. "Thank you. But you helped."

"Very little."

He was being magnanimous tonight. Sophia welcomed it, but as she brought the drink to her mouth, her hand trembled. She still hadn't gotten over her initial bout of nerves. Or was it Logan making her nervous?

"What's wrong with you, Sophia? You've been jumpy for days."

Logan had noticed.

Sophia turned to face the bleakness of the distant pasture. She couldn't look at Logan now. She was weak and vulnerable at the moment, and tears welled in her eyes. It was ridiculous that a little kindness shown by Logan Slade could bring on so much sentiment. "It's nothing that concerns you."

He moved closer. His presence surrounded her from behind. "You admit there is something?" His warm breath caressed her earlobe.

Sophia squeezed her eyes closed.

"Answer me, Sophia," Logan said.

He made her believe he cared about her. Why else would he question her? But Sophia couldn't place much faith in Logan's motives. She'd learned that lesson long ago. If the notes persisted, then Sophia would confide in a Slade, but the man she would tell would be Luke.

Sophia spun around to face Logan. "We should get back to the par—"

"Miss S-Sophia, Mr. Logan." Edward came running toward them, his face animated. The night's breeze fluffed the wisps of his hair as he approached. "L-look what just came. It's a g-giant f-flower horse! Y-you have to s-see it!"

When he reached her, Sophia crouched down to his level. His eyes, lit with excitement, lightened Sophia's heavy mood. "Hi, Edward. So what is this we have to see?"

"A h-horse made of f-flowers. It's as b-big as a real h-horse. Mr. Luke sent it for the p-party. Y-you have to s-see it."

Sophia glanced at Logan. His lips twisted, but he didn't let on to Edward that he'd interrupted a private conversation.

"Would you like to show it to me?" Sophia asked.

Edward's head bobbed up and down.

Sophia chuckled and put out her hand. Edward looked into her eyes first, then shyly took her hand. "Lead the way, my friend."

Edward took off at a fast pace, with Sophia running on the tips of her toes to keep up.

She assumed Logan was somewhere behind them, making his way back to the festivities.

Secretly, Sophia was grateful for the interruption.

Or should she call it an escape?

Logan swirled bourbon and soda in a tumbler, his shoulder braced against the patio pillar, his gaze keenly fastened on Sophia. She swayed her hips in time with the music on the dance floor and caught the attention of every male at the party, married or not. Even the damn disc jockey was eyeing her. How could he blame them? She was a stunner in a black-sequined dress that shimmered under the festive party lights. At this time, in that dress, Sophia couldn't conceal her luscious form. She didn't try to cover herself up with a jacket or sweater. She was a curvy glamour queen with her hair up in a tangle, held together by rhinestone clips.

Gorgeous.

Hunter had her in his arms now. Every so often, she would smile at him, making mush of the poor kid. She'd already danced with Ward, Ruth's husband and young Edward. She appeared to be having a great time, but there was something underlying, something not quite right about her tonight.

When she wasn't in the limelight, her expression held tension. He'd seen her dart cautious glances around, as if watching for something or someone.

Lately, every time he'd approached her she'd just about jumped out of her skin. It wasn't his concern, unless what was troubling her had something to do with Sunset Ranch.

Then it mattered to him.

Ward walked over to him, drink in hand. They drank together for a while in silence, keeping their eyes trained on the dance floor. When the song ended and the DJ announced a fifteen-minute break, the hum of lively conversation and laughter reached their ears. Sophia made quiet work of seeing that everyone was accommodated and having a good time. The food had been served and things were going smoothly.

"Ruth is sure having a good time," Ward said. "Your father would have been pleased to see this."

For once, Logan had to agree about his father. He'd been a fair and decent employer—that much he would grant him, and he would have approved of honoring Ruth's service to Sunset Lodge like this. "She sure was surprised."

"You pulled it off," Ward said, taking a sip of whiskey.

"Not me so much. Sophia."

Logan's gaze landed on her again. She was never far from his scope of vision. He'd been deliberately watching her all night. Truth be told, even if he tried, he wouldn't be able to keep his eyes off her.

"She's a hard worker. Real nice, too," Ward said. "I think my boy is smitten."

Restrained laughter slipped from Logan's mouth. "Yeah. Him and all the rest of the crew. She's no different than her mother in that regard."

Ward shot Logan a sideways glance. "Maybe the two women should be judged on their own merits. Or better yet, maybe they shouldn't be judged at all."

Ward's little lecture was getting on his nerves. Sure the man had status on the ranch. He and his father had been close, and Ward looked upon the Slade boys as kin, but Logan wasn't going to change his mind about Sophia Montrose, no matter how many people came to her defense.

"Just being cautious, Ward."

"That why she's been in your line of vision all night?"

Logan eyed him with a sour look. "You keeping track?"

"I'm thinking you should go over there and ask her to dance when the music starts up again."

"And I'm thinking she's got no room on her dance card."

Ward let out a hearty laugh. "I bet she'd make room for you."

Logan shook his head slowly. "Doubtful. I'm the devil to her."

Ward finished off his drink and set it down on a nearby table. "Maybe you should stop acting like one. Give the lady a chance." With that, Ward walked toward his son and started up a conversation with him.

Logan frowned and marched over to the bar to get another drink.

Before dinner, Logan walked up the steps to the deck and offered up a toast and tribute to Ruth. Everyone stood and raised their glasses. His speech was short but filled with gratitude for her outstanding service, especially during these past few trying months after his father's death. He managed to get a few laughs with anecdotes about Ruth's first days on the job and he wished her well in her retirement.

When the speech was over, Ruth was summoned up to say a few words. Her heartfelt goodbye and vow to get even with Logan for conning her with this surprise party brought some misty-eyed laughter from the gathering.

After dinner, dessert and coffee were served, the music mellowed out and one by one the guests began taking their leave. Sophia walked many of them outside. Logan didn't miss the way she stood on his doorstep with a proprietary hand on the door as she thanked the guests for coming and wished them a safe drive home. She said all the right things. She was the perfect hostess.

Logan was just about to pay her the compliment when his phone buzzed. It was late and he didn't want to take any calls tonight but when the caller ID popped up on the screen, Logan immediately answered the call from his youngest brother.

"Hey, Justin. How're the marines treating you these days?"

Logan walked into his office to speak with his brother about when he was coming home. His brother loved the military, but Logan sensed a longing for Sunset Ranch in him lately. Twenty minutes later, when he strode to the backyard, he found all the guests gone. The housekeeping staff was folding up the tablecloths, breaking down the tables and stacking the chairs. They were an efficient machine that didn't need any help from him, so he pivoted and went in search of Sophia.

"Where is Ms, Montrose?" he asked one of the waiters in the kitchen.

"She left with Mrs. Polanski ten minutes ago," he said. "She said to tell you good-night."

Logan waited until the last of his staff had cleaned up and taken off before he plopped down on the sofa, letting go a weary sigh. He knew how to pick good horseflesh. He knew what stallions would produce the best offspring. He knew how to keep his farm running smoothly and in the black, but what he knew about throwing a surprise party would fit in a shot glass with room to spare.

Ruth had been pleased and had thanked him half a dozen times. Her service had been recognized. His father *would* have been proud of how it all went down.

His father.

Logan had idolized him. Growing up as the eldest son, he'd wanted to be just like Randall Slade one day: fair, decent, honest, hardworking. He'd thought the sun rose and set on that man's shoulders. Until one day, his faith in his father had been destroyed.

It was past midnight on a school night when Logan woke from a bad dream. Sweat beaded on his forehead and his body trembled as his eyes opened to the darkness of his bedroom. Too keyed up to sleep, Logan rose and knew what would calm him. Logan had gotten only a glimpse of him when he'd first arrived today. Champion, the purebred Arabian stallion.

Logan tiptoed out of the house to keep from waking his parents. His father would not approve of an unsupervised visit to a horse new to the farm. Stallions were known for erratic behavior, especially in new environments. So Logan was careful not to make a peep as he walked toward the barn and the special stall designated for Champion.

He'd gotten ten feet into the huge barn when he'd heard whispers in the dark.

How he'd wished he'd turned around and run home.

But instead, he'd hidden outside of the tack room and listened.

"I need you in my life, Louisa. You're the only woman I've ever loved."

It was his father's voice.

Panicked now, Logan couldn't move. Curiosity and disbelief kept him glued in place.

His father was talking to Louisa Montrose, the manager of Sunset Lodge.

"I love you, too, mi amor," Lousia whispered. "I want you with me always."

Logan's ears burned as he heard their soft sighs and passionate moans. It wasn't so dark that Logan couldn't peer through the slits in the wood and see his father sprawled over Louisa on the tack room cot, kissing her, making little sounds of pleasure whisper from her lips.

"You know why I married her, Louisa. It was a merger of our families' land," he said. "And she was pregnant with Logan."

"It doesn't matter," Louisa said on a breath. "It doesn't matter."

Logan snapped his eyes opened. Reliving that memory never brought him any peace. Why would it? That night, Logan had been shocked and felt a keen overwhelming sense of loss. Everything he'd believed about his life was a lie. His father had been a scoundrel. He'd married for business reasons. He'd married because he'd gotten a woman pregnant. With that notion came great heartache. Logan's birth had been an accident. They hadn't wanted him. But even more than that, the man Logan had come to love, admire and idolize wasn't who he thought him to be.

Logan had caught his father in the act of adultery fifty yards from where his mother slept.

Not a pretty sight for a boy on the threshold of manhood.

That memory put him on edge. Why in hell did Ward have to mention his father tonight? Logan rose from his seat and roamed aimlessly around the house. His restlessness unnerved him as the images of his father and Louisa Montrose played over and over in his mind.

He spotted Sophia's black-sequined wrap lying across the entryway table. She'd left the party without it. On impulse, he picked it up and brought it to his nose, taking in the exotic scent that was uniquely hers. Logan closed his eyes for a moment, savoring the fragrance. Then, without hesitation and with her wrap clutched in his hand, he strode out the front door.

Tonight, not even Logan's sharpest sense of warning could stop him from seeking Sophia out.

Sophia parked her car in the driveway and breathed a big sigh of relief. She was finally home. She'd had a long, tiring day and she was glad it was over. The party had gone as planned. Ruth's husband had driven the grandkids home and Sophia had offered to drop Ruth back off at her house. On the way, Ruth had gushed again at how much she'd appreciated the party and how grateful she was to Sophia for all the work she'd put into it.

Sophia appreciated being appreciated and she was also glad to have made a dear friend in Ruth. After this weekend, Sophia would be managing Sunset Lodge by herself. Luckily, as her friend had reminded her, Ruth was only a phone call away if she needed advice.

With her body dragging, Sophia exited her car. She was ready for a hot shower and a good night's sleep. She'd earned it this week.

Stepping from the pavement onto the flowery path toward her front door, she heard a noise. Footsteps crunching on spring leaves. She whipped around. Knotted in fear, she focused her attention on the source of the sound. It was coming from behind a row of pink azalea bushes on the side of the cottage. Straining her eyes to see beyond the porch lamp's circle of light, she couldn't make out anything in the dark. Her heart beat wildly. Crazy thoughts entered her head. She imagined someone darting out from the bushes to attack her.

A madman was after her. He'd followed her from Las Vegas. He knew her every move.

Sophia couldn't get inside the house fast enough. She fumbled with the key. It fell from her shaky hands and pinged onto the brick porch. "Oh, no."

She scrambled to pick it up and out of the corner of her eye she saw another movement, a tall shadow that crossed into the lamplit path from the opposite direction of the azalea bushes. Fear immobilized her as she struggled to make sense of it. Fleeting questions rushed through her mind. Were they coming at her from two different directions? Steeling her nerves, she vowed she wouldn't be a helpless victim. She whirled around, ready to take a swing, ready to defend herself, ready to scream. She opened her mouth, her arm raised for a fight.

"Sophia?" Logan's questioning voice broke through her panic. She saw his Stetson first, as he approached from out of the shadows and into the light.

A dire gasp of relief escaped her throat. "Logan?" Slowly, she slumped against the front door, her legs shaking so badly she could barely stand. The door did a good job of keeping her upright. "Thank God, it's you."

"You look white as a sheet," he said softly, as if she were a child. "What's got you so scared?"

Tears welled in her eyes. She put her hand to her mouth and shook her head.

"Did someone hurt you?"

She continued to shake her head. "I'm f-fine. I, uh… What are you doing here?"

He held out the sequined wrap she'd worn to the party. "You left this."

"I didn't hear your car pull up."

"I walked over."

Sophia didn't respond.

"You're shaking like a leaf." He took the key she was gripping for dear life out of her hand and inserted it into the lock. "Let's get you inside the house."

Sophia managed to step out of his way, and once he opened the door he put his hand to her back and guided her to the parlor sofa. "Have a seat."

Sophia obeyed him automatically. She was still trembling as she sank into the cushions. She closed her eyes and inhaled a quiet breath to calm down. She was safe. Logan was here. The cushions gave way when he took a seat on the opposite end of the sofa.

"What happened out there?"

Sophia snapped her eyes open at his serious tone. All softness was gone from his voice. Leaning forward with elbows braced on his knees, he turned his head to face her.

"I want the truth."

Despite her distracted mind, the insult registered. He believed that she was accustomed to lying to him and *this* time he demanded she speak with honesty. But she couldn't do battle with him tonight over his remark. She was comforted to have him here. "The *truth* is, I thought someone was out there. I heard a noise by the azaleas."

"Go on."

Sophia looked away from him.

"There's got to be more than that. You've lived on this ranch before. You know there's dozens of species of animals that could make noises in the bushes before scurrying away. When I arrived, you said, 'Thank God, it's you.' Has someone been bothering you?"

"Besides you?" She smiled sweetly but his frown said he didn't find any humor in her statement. "Sorry. I was actually relieved that you showed up when you did."

"Now I know something's wrong. You're never glad to see me. Tell me."

Sophia sighed. She didn't want to get into this with Logan, but her fear was very real tonight and judging by the look on his face, he wasn't going anywhere without an explanation. "I've received three notes on my doorstep," she began, and then recounted the incidents that had happened since she'd moved to the cottage. When Logan questioned her further, Sophia had no choice but to explain about the similar incidents in Las Vegas.

Logan sat quietly listening to her, asking a probing question here and there, and once all was out in the open about her would-be Fantasy Follies stalker, Logan made an announcement. "We need to go to the sheriff."

"No," Sophia said. "I won't do that."

"Why the hell not?"

"I've been through this before. The notes aren't threatening and there's nothing they can do anyway. And…I don't want to bring negative attention to Sunset Lodge. Monday is my first day as a full-fledged manager."

"You were scared out of your mind a minute ago."

"It could be nothing. I have a secret admirer, maybe." Sophia was grasping at straws.

"I'm sure you have more than a few of those, but if someone is putting notes on your doorstep and *watching* you…you don't want to mess with that."

"I don't know that for sure. Maybe my imagination got the best of me. Maybe it was a wild animal in the bushes."

"You don't believe that," Logan said, "and now I don't, either. Not after hearing about the notes. Are you refusing to speak with the sheriff?"

She gave him a nod. "Yes, I am refusing."

Logan's eyes narrowed on her, but she wasn't going to back down. She'd had enough bad press and negative attention when she married Gordon Gregory. She didn't want a media circus here at Sunset Lodge. It was a place of serenity and beauty. She wouldn't mar that perception with the law snooping around, questioning staff and guests. She loved Sunset Lodge too much for that.

Logan rubbed his jaw as he considered her from across the sofa. "You know we have a good security system on the ranch and at the lodge. Now I'm thinking that might have been breached. Someone on the ranch may be out for no good. That makes it my business, Sophia. And, frankly, it worries me. You won't go to the law, and I can't have you living here alone anymore."

"Meaning what?" Sophia didn't like the way he was steering this conversation.

"Meaning, you're moving into the main house with me. And it's not up for discussion."

Seven

Every bone in her body was well aware that she was living alone with Logan Slade. The house was big, but not big enough to miss seeing him saunter into the kitchen in the morning with an unshaven face and sexy, mussed hair. Or notice him unbutton his shirt, exposing a sliver of bronzed skin as he headed to his bedroom for a shower. With Luke gone, Sophia didn't have the buffer she needed to keep up the facade that somehow Logan hadn't begun to wedge his way into her heart.

He checked in on her in the morning at breakfast and insisted that she have dinner at the house every night. When Sophia's eyes would light up over his concern, his expression would turn to stone and he'd remind her that safety on the ranch was the key issue.

Sophia should have been exhausted. Putting in long hours at the lodge during the day was enough to fatigue an Olympic athlete, much less a woman of her size and stature. But the truth was, Sophia had restless energy. Seeing Logan coming in and out of the house every day, made her jumpy and anxious. They'd have brief, stilted conversations at meals, and before he rose from the table, Logan would gaze at her with yearning in his eyes. It was fleeting and reluctant, but Sophia saw it. He wasn't as immune to her as he let on. Maybe the wall of defense he'd built up against her was beginning to crumble a little bit.

Now, three days into her stay at his home, Sophia watched him rise from the dinner table as usual, the moment the last bite on his plate was gone. "I'm going to turn in early," he said, stretching his arms over his head. He looked a little weary with a five-o'clock shadow on his face and reddened eyes.

Sophia nodded. "Good night," she said politely, then blurted what was on her mind. "I think I'll take a ride."

"Where? The stores will be closing soon."

Sophia smiled. "Not that kind of ride. I'm not interested in shopping. I need some air. I thought I'd ask Hunter to saddle up a mare and ride out with me."

"I sent Hunter home an hour ago."

Sophia shrugged a shoulder. "That's okay. I'll find someone else." Sophia rose from the table, grabbing his empty plate along with hers.

He reached out to touch her upper arm. "Just about everyone's gone home for the night. Why don't you turn in and do it another time?"

"I'm not a prisoner here, am I? I can saddle up a horse and take a ride."

His hand wound around her arm, gently, but only to make his point. "It'll be dark in less than an hour, Sophia."

His penetrating gaze bored into her and they stared at each other for a long while. Finally, he released his hold on her. "Fine, suit yourself."

Sophia didn't get any satisfaction in upsetting Logan. She didn't set out to annoy him, but she did need an outlet for her pent-up energy. And a ride along the paths of Sunset Ranch would do the trick. She wasn't fool enough to go by herself. She should be able to find a riding partner, if not here at the ranch, then at the lodge.

Twenty minutes later, after changing into her riding clothes, Sophia walked into the barn. Horses whinnied in their stalls. Some kicked and others brought their heads up to greet her with a snort as she walked by. She stopped to stroke the face of a good-natured aging palomino. "Hello, Buttercup."

Buttercup wasn't a star of pure-breeding stock that would be sold off to clients. She and half a dozen other horses were kept on the premises to take prospective clients for rides in the pasture and, more important, to lend a mellow tone to the more spirited animals in the barn.

Sophia gave each of the horses a little attention as she headed to the tack room to pick up her gear. There wasn't a soul around to help her saddle up and just as she was going to take Logan's advice and turn back, changing her mind about the ride, he appeared in the doorway.

"You still want that ride?" he asked.

Startled by his appearance, Sophia tamped down her initial gut reaction. But Logan noticed the momentary fear she couldn't hide from her expression. "Oh, uh…yes. I'd like to take a ride."

"You're still jumpy, aren't you?"

"No."

The sound of his boots echoed against the walls as he strode farther into the small room until his face was inches from hers. "You are."

"Not now. I have you here. And there haven't been any more notes or incidents."

"You knew I wouldn't let you take a ride alone. Or go with anyone else."

Sophia stared at him. "Is that what you thought? I was hinting for you to take me?"

"Weren't you?"

"No, I just wanted to get out of the house."

"I'd think you'd want some peace after working all day."

"The house is…"

"Is what, Sophia?" Logan whispered her name.

"Lonely," she said, confessing one of her vulnerabilities.

His expression changed, softened. His gaze traveled up and down her body until she was so excited that her breathing grew ragged and heavy. Her chest heaving now, Logan stared at the top button on her blouse that prevented her breasts from spilling out.

"Without Luke in the house, and you barely speaking to me—"

"Luke?" Something flickered in his eyes. "You don't want Luke."

Sophia's heart raced. The conversation had switched direction. And Logan's powerful gaze destroyed her rational sense. "Luke's my fri—"

Logan pulled her into his arms. He smelled of earth and musk, so strong, so powerful. His breath warmed her throat and his words made her mouth go dry. "We're not gonna talk about my brother tonight, darlin'."

His determination made her go limp. Her voice lowered until she could barely hear the words she spoke, "Wh-what are we going to talk about?"

He brought her body tight against his. "Your loneliness." Then he smiled, a flash against a stark, handsome face, the gleam brightening his eyes. "Then again, we don't have to do much talking at all."

His lips touched hers tenderly as if he wanted to draw out all of her fears, all of her loneliness. The kiss was sweetly gentle, and Sophia had to remind herself that it was Logan who was kissing her, Logan who held her in his arms.

He brought his hands to her face and cupped her cheeks, murmuring sweet nothings as he kissed her. Sophia surrendered herself to the compassion Logan was showing her. He suckled her lips, tasting from her, his firm delicious mouth giving her time to adjust to what was happening between them. "You're safe with me," he whispered over her lips.

She felt protected and cared for but then in the back of her mind, coming from a very dark place, a warning bell sounded.

This was Logan Slade. He hated her.

So why did he make her feel as if she were floating on a cloud?

She ignored her misgivings and dove into the sensations he stirred in her. She'd always been attracted to Logan and now, with his kisses heating her through and through, she thought she could be a little bit in love with him. She told herself that and stopped trying to analyze the pleasure he offered her. It felt too good having him strip away her loneliness.

Sophia placed her hands on his chest, her fingers spreading across rough cotton as she stroked him eagerly. A groan emanated from his throat and Sophia continued to touch him, to explore the strong washboard across his ribs.

He slipped off her ponytail holder and in the faint, fading sunlight watched her hair flow freely to frame her face. Appreciation shone in the glint of his eyes and he released a relenting sound that came from the depths of his throat. "You make me forget who I am," he murmured.

Sophia put her arms around his neck and rose up to kiss him soundly on the lips. Softly, she whispered, "You're Logan Slade and you don't like me very much."

Logan wove his hands through her long hair, letting the tresses slip between his fingers. He released a deep sigh. "There are things I like about you, Sophia. More than I've liked about any other woman."

He pressed his mouth to hers again. Sophia relished the kiss and the words behind the kiss. She whispered over his lips, "What do you like about me?"

"Kissing you is right up there," he said softly.

He paused to gaze at the strands of hair framing her face. "You've got the prettiest hair."

A soft whimper escaped her throat. His compliments were a heady elixir.

He slid his hands over her shoulders and stroked down her arms. Tingles erupted from his soft caress. "Your body is perfect. It's been killing me living with you. Knowing you're lying just steps away in another bedroom."

Fiery heat arrowed down her belly. "Logan," she breathed out.

There was no stopping this now. They were caught up in a game that had only one outcome. He pulled her taut against his rock-hard chest. Jeans to jeans, their legs touched, denim rubbing together. His hand rested on the soft material of her white blouse and with two nimble fingers he stroked her exposed skin just above the buttons.

Sophia's breath caught. She closed her eyes, savoring the sensual touch that brought goose bumps. He toyed with her there, making her ache, making her lean back and give him reign to do what he pleased.

She heard a snap and then a tear as her blouse split apart, two buttons flying onto the floor. Her eyes popped open. He watched her, waited for her approval.

She smiled and a little bubble of laughter rose from her throat.

Logan pulled the blouse out of her jeans and off her shoulders, discarding it with a flick of his wrist. Then he touched the top of her breasts, the flat of his palms against her plump ripe skin spilling from her bra. "I like touching you. I can't get enough."

He unhooked her bra and with a reverent groan watched her breasts fall free of their restraints. The look on his face made her body ache for more. He cupped her, weighed the globes in his hands as he kissed her again and again. Their mouths opened and the kisses grew hotter and more frenzied.

After a minute, Logan slid his lips to her ear, his words clipped and ragged. "In another second, I'm not gonna be able to stop."

Sophia understood him. She was already at the point of no return. But Logan wasn't a brute—he gave her the choice.

"I don't want you to."

"Don't move," he said.

And she stood there, waiting while Logan set a quilt on a weathered leather sofa that was banked against the tack room wall. He came back to lift her into his arms, and then lowered her down gently. He removed her boots and the rest of her clothes.

Then he stared at her for a few seconds.

She felt exposed. Naked and lying in wait for him to make love to her.

"I like the way your eyes darken when you look at me," he said, and then added, "I knew you were beautiful, but Sophia, honey, you take my breath away."

And suddenly she didn't feel ashamed or embarrassed anymore. She didn't feel vulnerable. She wanted this. She wanted Logan. There wasn't a doubt in her mind.

Next, he removed his shirt and a glow lit her eyes when everything else came off.

"Mercy," Sophia uttered, gazing at him.

"I'll take that as a compliment, darlin'."

But Logan didn't cover her with his body right away. Instead he came up beside her to kiss her again. "Close your eyes," he ordered.

She obeyed.

His touch was soft and gentle as he stroked her between her thighs. And when his ministrations grew more bold, more forceful, she shuddered and let go a tiny moan of pleasure. Logan was relentless and worked her body, tormenting her until her moans were continuous and in tune with the throbbing heat pulsating at her core.

Her body jerked and splintered. Her breaths short and quick, she experienced a powerful release.

"Sophia," Logan murmured, as she came down to earth. Gently, he stroked her hair and kissed her cheeks. "You have no idea what a turn-on it is seeing you go wild like that."

The room was darker now. The sun had almost set and Sophia could barely make out Logan's shadow as he brought himself down on top of her. She reached out, desperately wanting to be joined with him.

He spoke with urgency, his voice a rasp that thrilled her. "I've waited a long time for this. For you."

Twenty minutes later, cocooned in the warmth of Logan's strong arms, Sophia opened her eyes to darkness. The air inside the tack room was Nevada-dry and cool yet both of their bodies glistened with hot, sticky sweat.

Sophia sighed at the completion she felt. A soft purr hummed through her body. Every ounce of her flesh felt pleasantly devoured. Logan was an expert lover and he'd brought out her wilder side with his whispered words of encouragement, his powerful thrusts and his strong body covering hers.

Their releases had come out of sync with each other, but Sophia hadn't minded. She liked going first. Then she watched Logan's face twist with pleasure as he groaned from his inner depths until one last potent plunge brought him over the edge.

After that, they'd both fallen in a heap of exhaustion.

Quietly stunned.

And when Sophia's thoughts traveled once again to that dark place of uncertainty, Logan was there, stroking her arm and kissing her forehead. She relished his touch and the soothing way he treated her in the aftermath of lovemaking. The few lovers she'd had before hadn't been nearly as attentive after the deed was done. Sophia had made mistakes with men, but she'd never kept a man around if he wasn't respectful.

Where would she and Logan go from here? She had no idea what he was thinking. He'd said all the right things. He'd *done* all the right things and her body sang from the sweetest pleasure a man could give a woman. Now Sophia was at a crossroads in her life.

She'd been wary of Logan Slade for as long as she could remember. Tonight, she'd let down her guard and allowed him entrance not only to her body, but to her heart.

She loved Logan.

She was sure of it now.

She couldn't have given to him what she'd denied even the most persuasive of men who had come in and out of her life, without feeling great emotion. She'd given him her trust and hadn't regretted it for a second.

"How you doing, darlin'?"

The endearments he'd been using with her tonight made her smile inside. She assumed that he thought of her as a brat, a bitch and a hussy so to hear him come full circle gave her joy. "I'm pretty good."

"I won't argue there." He turned on his side to face her and she curled around to look him in the eyes. "You cold?" he asked.

"A little bit."

He slid his hand up and down along the curve of her hip, and each inch of naked skin warmed under his touch. "We should probably get out of here. Someone might walk in."

Sophia's eyes rounded. She hadn't thought of that. She'd lost all sense of time and place when Logan had seduced her. "We probably should."

Logan gave her a reluctant look, and then rose first. In the dark, he found her clothes strewn across the floor and handed them to her. She sat up to put them on and watched him in the shadows, a sense of pride swelling in her heart. How could she feel this way about a man who had injured her so often?

Once they were dressed—Sophia had a dickens of a time securing her blouse without the buttons, so Logan gave her his shirt to put on—they walked quietly out of the room and through the barn. Horses whinnied and snickered as they strode by, but they didn't take the time to give them attention. When they reached the wide double doors, Logan peered out, looking right, then left.

"Do you think someone's out there?" she asked, not worried about her would-be stalker so much as an employee wandering the grounds and catching them half dressed.

"Don't know."

"Should we walk out separately?"

Logan grinned and shook his head. "Honey, you moved into my house three days ago. You think any man on my ranch is thinking we're baking cookies inside?"

Sophia's brows lifted. "But that's not true! We weren't doing anything."

His grin slipped into a small smile. He gazed out the barn door again. "Not up until about an hour ago. Doesn't matter now. You want to make a run for it?" He put out his hand and stared at her.

Sophia saw the adventure in that. They had to travel the length of half a football field to make it to the house. She tucked her hand in his and they made a mad dash across the yard.

Sophia's soft laughter bubbled over. She hadn't felt this carefree in years. She ran a step behind Logan, who tugged her along, and she could have sworn she heard the beautiful sound of his laughter, too.

Tonight, Logan wanted dessert. And he wanted Sophia. The two went hand in hand in his mind. Both would satisfy his craving. "Let's have some ice cream," he said as they came to a halt inside his house.

Sophia's topaz eyes brilliant and her breaths labored, she smiled at him as if he were a child. "Let me guess. You want strawberry?"

He blinked. "How did you know?"

"It's your favorite. I remember from birthday parties here. I like vanilla, Luke likes chocolate and you love strawberry."

"Observant. Add that to the list of things I like about Sophia Montrose. Come on," he said, stifling his frustration. He wouldn't let the fact that Sophia always had Luke's name on her lips bother him tonight. His brother was a part of their equation and he always had been. Luke and Sophia were friends, and he would make sure that's all they ever would be.

Luke had a weak spot when it came to Sophia.

Logan wouldn't be so naive.

He hadn't meant to bed Sophia but now that he had, he wasn't fool enough to let her go until he was good and ready. No man in his right mind would let a luscious beauty like Sophia slip through his fingers. But he still didn't trust her motives. He knew enough to be wary of her, even as he held her hand in his as he led her to the kitchen. "C'mon. I'm sure we can scrounge up some vanilla ice cream for you."

Dressed in his shirt that was three sizes too big for her, her hair wild about her face, Sophia followed him into the kitchen. Moonlight streamed in through a window and the wide, double-paneled back door. Logan decided to keep the lights off. He liked seeing Sophia by the light of the moon. "Have a seat while I dish it up." He pulled out a stool for her behind the rectangular island countertop and she sat down.

"Logan Slade serving me?" She leaned forward, bracing her elbows on the granite with her fists under her chin. "Hell *must* have frozen over."

He grinned. "It's a night for firsts. The fat lady sang *and* pigs flew in the barn a few minutes ago."

Immediate color rushed to her face, painting her olive skin rosy. "Maybe there is such a thing as miracles."

Logan opened the freezer door with a big smile on his face. Sparring with Sophia kept him on his toes. "It was sorta like an out-of-body experience, honey."

"Yes. Who would have believed?"

"Not me and sure as anything, not you, I'd venture to guess."

"I wanted a ride."

Logan brought out two half gallons of ice cream and set them on the counter in front of her. Wiggling his eyebrows, he said, "Be careful what you wish for."

"I'll try to remember that."

He came up with a scoop and began dishing vanilla and strawberry ice cream into two bowls. He slid one over to her.

"Are we going to eat this in the dark?" she asked.

"You mind?"

She thought about it a moment and then shook her head. "Not at all, but why?"

"Things taste better in the dark."

"Really?"

"Think about it…what do you do when you really want to savor something?"

Sophia's lips curved up. "You close your eyes."

"Exactly."

She nodded. "I never thought about it, but it makes sense."

Logan plopped down on the stool next to her and dove into his ice cream, taking a big bite. Then he closed his eyes. Strawberry ice cream and Sophia all in one night *was* something to savor. He didn't know what compelled him to divulge the truth, but before he could hold it back, he blurted, "Until a second ago, I didn't know that, either. The honest truth is that you look dazzling in moonlight and I couldn't see spoiling the mood with artificial lighting. The other stuff I said is a load of horse manure."

Sophia put her head down, her eyes downcast. She stared at her ice cream then began shaking her head. Logan wasn't sure what to make of it—he'd never admitted to feeding baloney to anyone before.

When Sophia finally lifted her head, amusement lit her eyes and she laughed right in his face, giggling so hard she put her spoon down to contain the laughter with a hand to the stomach.

"What? I pay you a compliment and you laugh." Logan's ears rang from the contagious sound of her sweet giggles. He spooned another chunk of ice cream into his mouth and swallowed, unable to keep from grinning along with her.

"Oh, Logan," she said between chuckles, "you always amaze me."

It seemed to be a night of amazements. He jammed another spoonful of ice cream into his mouth and then pointed to her bowl scooped high with vanilla ice cream. "Eat up, darlin'. You're lagging."

She dipped her spoon in and gave it a taste. Her dark-lashed eyes slowly closed as she swallowed. A lump formed in Logan's throat. Watching Sophia relish anything was like watching an artist apply the first strokes of paint to a fresh canvas.

And tonight, Sophia had been hard to resist. Besides her beautiful face and knockout body, she made him smile. They'd had incredible sex less than an hour ago. Why shouldn't he laugh along with her and allow himself a night of indulgence?

"Here," he said after watching Sophia take two more delicate bites of her ice cream. "Let me help."

He took the spoon from her hand and scooped up a good-sized amount of vanilla ice cream from the bowl. Sophia's lips eagerly parted for him with a sensual curve upward as he inserted the spoon into her mouth. This wasn't like feeding a baby, Logan mused. It was erotic as hell. Her mouth moved up and down and her eyelids closed as she tasted the dessert he fed her. He leaned closer, whispering, "I want more, Sophia."

Her eyes snapped open and without hesitation, she replied softly, "So do I."

Logan brought his mouth to hers, brushing a gentle kiss over her chilled lips. He tasted the sweet vanilla cream that lingered there. "I'm not talking about ice cream."

She nodded and whispered, "I'm not hungry for ice cream, either."

Logan's heart hammered in his chest. The woman was a temptation that could destroy a weaker man. Logan pushed his seat out and stood, taking Sophia by her arms and lifting her up against him. She wrapped both arms around his neck and he bent his head to take her in a fiery kiss that got all of his juices flowing. He pulled her closer, melding their bodies, fitting her against him like a tailor-made suit. He curved his hands on the slope of her buttocks and rocked her against the erection straining his jeans.

Sophia moaned at the deliberate contact, giving him a little cry of anticipation that matched his own desperate desire.

He swept her up and carried her out of the kitchen and down the long hallway. Her eyes gleaming, her body nearly weightless in his arms, he kissed her several times as he strode into his master bedroom. When he reached his large bed, he turned down his bedspread and then lowered Sophia onto silky sheets. Her luxurious hair fanned out against the pillow and he stripped her bare within seconds, needing to see her naked on his bed.

His fantasies, the secret ones he'd kept hidden from the world, came to fruition, seeing her here now, waiting for him with lust in her eyes. He'd bedded her once tonight, quickly, on a worn-out sofa in the barn, but this was where Sophia needed to be. Cast in moonlight, her body accommodated on a luxurious bed—his bed—and now Logan would take his time with her. He would savor her like she was a sweet bowl of strawberry ice cream. And he would lick every last creamy inch of her, until they were both satisfied.

"As much as I like you in my shirt, taking it off is definitely an improvement."

Sophia wasn't coy or timid; she was bold as she lay there allowing him to study her. She was a rare find, a woman who could easily grace the cover of the *Sports Illustrated* swimsuit issue. She was perfect in her naked form.

"I'm a little lonely in this big bed," she whispered, rolling to her side and patting the area next to her.

"I told you I'd take care of your loneliness."

He unhooked his belt, kicked off his boots and then lowered himself down onto the bed. He reached for her, just as she came up over him to straddle his thighs. He'd kept his jeans on, and now he wished he hadn't.

"You're lonely, too, Logan," she said softly. "You simply don't realize it."

There was truth to that, he admitted to himself, but now was not the time for that conversation. "Then keep me company for a while."

"I intend to," she whispered.

Her breasts were round and full, overflowing in his hands. A man could die happy like this. He brought one rosy-tipped peak into his mouth and Sophia uttered a little cry of pleasure. Logan paid proper attention to both of her breasts, cupping and weighing them, kissing and suckling. Sophia was lost, writhing with uncontrolled passion.

She was beautiful atop him. Her hands flat on his chest, her body fluid and primed for sex, Logan's control was ready to snap. It was too much and not enough. He wanted to own her, to take possession and never let go. It was strange to feel that way about any woman, but with Sophia it felt right.

He made love to every ounce of her with heated kisses and strokes of his tongue until he could barely breathe from the fire building in his system. His hands wove through her long thick hair and he bruised her lips with hot crushing kisses.

He made sure Sophia was well loved in every way. It pleased him to please her.

His mind briefly went to his father and how he'd lusted after Louisa Montrose. The only difference being that Logan wasn't married to another woman. He hadn't spoken vows or pledged his love to one woman and then bedded another. He would never fall in love with a Montrose. Sophia wouldn't break him. Not in that way.

He wanted her in his bed.

He'd never fall into the same trap his father had.

Nothing had changed in that regard.

Sophia's soft, labored moans were frantic. She unzipped his jeans, and all thoughts of his father went out the window. The gorgeous woman slipped her hand around his swollen member and he'd barely had time to put a condom on before she sought an end to their mutual torment.

He guided her down and with one slow, earth-shattering thrust they were joined.

Sophia tossed her head back, taking him inside her. The arch of her back, the sheet of dark hair tossing from side to side as she slid her sweet body over his, were a thing of beauty.

Logan seared those images into his memory as they rode the waves of glory together.

I love you, Logan, Sophia thought as she glanced at him. Though he was normally well-groomed, this morning, short, thick strands of his hair stuck out in several directions and a day-old beard darkened his handsome features.

Sophia wasn't going to cry. She wasn't going to make a scene. She would be strong. Like her mother. She wouldn't let Logan know how much she loved him. Not now. She couldn't trust him with those feelings. She couldn't tell him truths that he wasn't ready to hear. She knew it would take time, but Sophia had never been in love before. She'd never felt the full force of the emotion and the power it wielded might cause her great injury. She knew she would have to step carefully to avoid the land mines of her own making.

Sophia lay there with a lump in her throat. Logan had made love to her thoroughly last night. She still ached in private places from his ruthless pursuit of satisfying her. He had made his mark on her. She would never forget her first night with Logan Slade. She hoped there were many more to come. She would not give up on her love.

Was she being a fool?

Her mother's words rang out clearly in Sophia's mind. She had never forgotten them. "Loving Randall Slade was a waste of love."

Because it had ended in heartache. Sophia wouldn't allow that to happen with Logan. Her love would not be wasted. It couldn't be. She'd given everything she'd had to give to him. Would he be so cruel as to throw it all away?

Dawn peeked out on the horizon, the first glimmering rays of light sneaking into the room. Sophia gave Logan one last glance, and then rose from the bed. Her feet landed quietly on the floor and she tiptoed away hoping not to wake him.

She grabbed Logan's shirt she'd worn last night, along with her pants, and dressed before she exited the room. The Slades' household staff did not live at the house, but they would arrive shortly.

Logan's remark about how his men knew they weren't just baking cookies together came to mind.

Sophia cringed at the notion. She'd never wanted a reputation as a gold-digger, but it seemed to follow her every move. She would have fallen in love with Logan Slade even if he were penniless. Money wasn't the issue but who would believe that about her now? On paper, and from what people perceived about her, she appeared guilty.

And then there was Luke. What was she going to say to

him? When he arrived home, would he understand her motives? Would he hate that she'd fallen in love with his brother?

Sophia entered her room, quietly shutting the door behind her. She wasn't ready to start the day, but doubted she could fall back to sleep. She stripped off her clothes, walked into the bathroom and turned on the shower faucet. She stepped inside and let the warm water slide over her skin. She stood there for a long time in the steamy hot spray, deep in thought.

The night she shared with Logan had been remarkable. The earth had moved and the stars had aligned. She sighed at the memories—the taste of his mouth, the scratch of his stubble bruising her skin, his strong hands gentle on her, all rushed through her mind. It had been ecstasy and Sophia wouldn't allow herself to think of it as a one-night stand.

But she had no clue what Logan was thinking. She wondered if he'd set out to seduce her or if they'd been caught up in something powerful that both of them couldn't deny. Last night, their relationship had changed forever.

Sophia washed her hair and scrubbed her body with lavender-scented soap. The pleasing fragrance had always soothed her nerves and made her feel better. When she stepped out of the shower and dried off, most of her pressing doubts were banished.

Someone knocked on her bedroom door. Sophia took a quick breath, wrapped herself in a plush towel and shook out her wet hair before going to the door. "Who is it?"

"It's me, Sophia."

The sound of Logan's voice gave her tingles. She opened the door slowly. His cool dark eyes blazed with warmth when he looked at her draped in the towel. "Tempting."

He was dressed in business clothes, dark slacks and a white shirt. Seeing him again took her breath away. "Good morning."

"Mornin'. You're up early," he said.

"I, uh, woke up and couldn't fall back to sleep."

"You wanted to skip out of my room before the house-keeper arrived."

"Yes," she admitted, her face flaming. "Do you blame me?"

His smile was seductive, his voice a rasp of desire. "Don't run away from me, Sophia."

She nibbled on her lower lip, unsure what to say.

He stepped into the room with a gleam in his eyes. He reached for the top of her towel. Her throat tightened and she just stood there rooted to the spot with his big hand on her chest. When she thought he'd undo the towel, his fingers stayed on her skin just above the cotton. The intimate touch made goose bumps erupt on her arms.

He bent his head and kissed her, whispering over her lips, "You know I have a shower in my room. Big enough for two. Next time, we'll do it together."

An immediate image rushed into her mind and Logan smiled knowingly. But his automatic assumption that there would be a next time flashed in her head like a lightbulb moment.

Sophia surprised herself by saying, "We can't..." She hesitated, knowing in her heart this was the right thing to say. Even so, it pained her to draw a line in the sand. "We can't have an affair."

Logan didn't flinch, but she noted a quick flicker in his eyes. "Because we don't like each other?"

Because I've fallen in love with you and need more than that.

But Sophia couldn't tell him that. She couldn't trust him with her love. He was still the same man, with the same prejudices and opinions. "I never said I didn't like you."

The corner of his mouth crooked up. "Last night was good, Sophia. You can't deny it." He brushed her hair to one side, touching her shoulder in a soft caress. She trembled from his touch and the blazing warmth in his eyes. "We could have more nights like the one we just had."

She summoned her courage and asked him the question that would define this new relationship. "Have you changed your mind about my mother? About me? Do you still resent me and my presence here?"

The warmth in his eyes evaporated. He dropped his hand from her hair. "Don't go there, Sophia. It'll only ruin things."

Sophia closed her eyes. She had her answer and her heart ached with the brutal truth. Last night hadn't been about fondness, caring or love. It had been about lust and sex. Logan didn't have to say the words, but she knew now that she'd been a fool to think he'd change his mind so easily. He still thought her mother was a calculating home wrecker. He'd probably thought worse of Sophia. He still took exception to her inheritance. She couldn't forget that he'd tried to buy out her share of Sunset Lodge when she'd first arrived just to get rid of her.

Yet her love for him didn't diminish. It didn't fade, not even a tiny bit, knowing what he thought about her. Sophia loved him from the bottom of her heart. And unfortunately, it would take a lot more heartache before she stopped loving him. But she wouldn't give any more of herself until he could make her believe there was some hope.

She tilted her chin, thinking haughtiness worked better with clothes on, but a towel and wet hair would have to do in this circumstance. "Then we have nothing to talk about."

Boldly, she searched his eyes, daring him to say something. To plead his case or try to convince her otherwise. But Logan didn't say a word.

Instead, he reached out and slowly unwrapped the towel from around her body. The material dropped to the floor in a lush heap. She stood bared to him, her skin freshly cleaned and perfumed.

He raked his gaze over her naked form and then inhaled

a sharp clipped breath. His mouth moved and she listened to words that would stay with her until the end of time. "This isn't over, Sophia. You'll see that soon enough."

Eight

Sophia sat in the office she no longer shared with Ruth Polanski, her desk the only one in the room now. She'd turned it around to face the window and the verdant grounds of the lodge with the regal Sierra Nevada Mountains in the background. She could be happy here. No, she amended that. She *would* be happy here. Living a peaceful life at Sunset Ranch was what she truly wanted now.

All of the managerial duties at Sunset Lodge were on her shoulders. She relished the challenge, and dove into her work. This morning she had to make phone calls to vendors and deal with a stable boy who'd been rude to one of the guests. In the afternoon, she had a luncheon planned with a local landscaper. Sophia had a few changes in mind that would enhance the overall property. And she had to go over Logan's budget for the year.

She heard footsteps approaching, and turned to find Hunter Halliday standing behind her half-closed door. In his arms, he held an exquisite arrangement of lilies. "Ms. Montrose?"

Technically, she was Mrs. Gregory, but she'd never used her legal name. She wondered what prompted her to think about that now. "Come in, Hunter."

The strapping boy sauntered into the room and stood in front of her desk, looking uncomfortable with the feminine flowers in his hands. Sophia stared at the stargazers tinted with a touch of pink on the petals. "They are lovely," she said when Hunter didn't volunteer any information.

He'd been staring at her.

"Oh, um… Mr. Slade sent me over with these."

"They're from Mr. Slade?" Sophia's mouth dropped open. For an instant, when she'd seen Hunter bringing them in, she'd thought the flowers had come from Hanson Landscapers. It wasn't unusual for vendors to send managers perks, thank-yous or deal sweeteners to butter them up.

"Yes, ma'am. And he said to read the note in *private*."

She felt her face turning three shades of pink. "Okay."

A small white envelope appeared in her line of vision as Hunter set the flowers down on the only cleared-off space on her desk. "All right to put these here?"

"Uh, yes. That's fine." The arrival of these amazingly beautiful flowers put a major roadblock in thinking that she could ignore what had happened between her and Logan last night.

This isn't over.

Those three words Logan had spoken echoed in her heart. She didn't want it to be over between her and Logan, either. Heavens, it had barely just begun. But Sophia's pride wasn't a small thing. She couldn't face herself in the mirror every morning, knowing that Logan hadn't changed his mind about her. How could she possibly give herself to him, love or no love, without expecting him to make some concessions, without him willing to hear her explanations and tell her side of the story?

He still thought of her mother as a wicked woman, and thought of her as a gold-digger.

She sighed aloud and Hunter's eyes snapped to hers. "Oh, uh, thanks for delivering the flowers, Hunter."

"You're welcome."

Hunter didn't budge an inch. He hovered by her desk, watching her.

She smiled.

He sent her a troubled look. There seemed to be something on the boy's mind.

"Is there anything else?" she asked.

"Yep. But I don't know if it's appropriate for me to say."

Sophia wanted to reassure the boy. His unease was practically tangible. "If something's bothering you, you can tell me what it is. Why don't you sit down?"

"Okay." He took a seat across the desk and didn't look any more comfortable in it than he did while he was standing. He rubbed his hands back and forth and Sophia waited for him to speak.

"It's about Gabriel Strongbow."

Sophia's brow rose at the name. He was the stable boy Sophia had received a complaint about. "What about him?"

"I guess you could say we're friends. I'd like to put in a good word for him, ma'am. If I might."

"I haven't spoken to him yet. But I'll listen to what he has to say."

"He thinks he's gonna be fired, and he really can't afford it. He's helping his mother out by working this job and trying to stay in school. And I just want to say that he wasn't rude to the guest."

"So, you're vouching for him?"

"Well, I wasn't there actually. But I've seen Gabe with Rebecca Wagner and he's been nice and polite to her. Rebecca has been flirting with him all week. They like each other is all. Rebecca handed him her phone number yesterday and

Mrs. Wagner found out about it and accused him of all sorts of things. Gabe hasn't done anything wrong."

Sophia knew of the Wagner family. Rebecca was a pretty sixteen-year-old girl. Ruth had told her the three Wagners were regulars at the lodge. They'd been coming twice a year for over a decade. "Sounds like Mrs. Wagner is overprotective of her daughter. But you know that we have strict rules about employees and guests. It's not a line but a wall that we've constructed at Sunset Lodge and it isn't to be breached."

"Yes, I know." Hunter took a deep breath. "Just had to say my piece."

"And I've heard you." Sophia sent him a smile. "You're a good friend to Gabe."

"Just want what's fair."

"I'll be fair with him," she said.

Hunter relaxed somewhat, his eyes filled with appreciation. "Thanks."

Sophia braced her arms on the desk and leaned forward. "Tell me about Gabriel Strongbow."

Hunter shrugged and contemplated briefly before he began. "He's a senior in high school. Working at the stables part-time. He's got a little sister. His dad passed about three years ago and now they're struggling to hang on to their house."

"I see." Sophia could relate to living from paycheck to paycheck, trying to keep from drowning in a sea of debt and hoping that her fate wasn't solely based on the whim of an employer. "Well, Gabe's been with us for over a year and up until this point," she said, fanning through the boy's file, "he's been a good employee. That's all I can tell you, Hunter. I really shouldn't have discussed this with you at all, so please keep this conversation to yourself."

"Yes, ma'am."

Hunter rose, gave her one last parting look and then took his leave.

Sophia got up and walked to the door, closing it while deep

in thought. Sometimes a manager had to be judge and jury. She had to determine what was best for the establishment without infringing on the employee's rights. It was a balancing act, but in this case unless the complaints proved true and there was a blatant miscarriage of rules, she was pretty sure Gabriel Strongbow's job wouldn't be in jeopardy.

Sophia had never fired anyone in her life.

Putting those thoughts aside, she walked over to the lily arrangement and stared at the flowers a moment. They were truly perfect. Logan couldn't have picked anything she would have liked more. It was uncanny how sometimes the two of them were on the same wavelength. Then there were the *other* times when they butted heads and saw things very differently.

Sophia braced herself. She didn't know what to expect from Logan Slade anymore but she was dying of curiosity to see what Logan had to say that was to be read in private. She lifted the white envelope from its plastic holder and slipped the small piece of paper out. Unfolding it, she read the handwritten note silently.

Sophia,
Can't get the image of how I left you this morning out
of my head.
Have dinner with me tonight. 8:00 p.m.
It'll be our first date.
Change my mind.
Logan

Sophia's hand shook so much, the words she'd just read and then reread became fuzzy. She moved on wobbly legs to her chair and lowered down slowly, her fingers gripping the edges for balance. The world seemed to tilt off-kilter at the moment. She couldn't believe what Logan had written. He told her in those few sentences that he was willing to try.

Could it be possible?

Change my mind.

Moisture stung her eyes and one sole tear rolled down her cheek. Emotions welled up and a soft cautious beam of hope began to glow inside her. Was the indomitable man finally softening to her? Would he be willing to listen and really hear what she had to say?

Maybe one day soon. Sophia wouldn't press her luck tonight, but she would meet with him. They would go on their first date, and she would see where that would take them.

There was hope now, that her love would not be wasted.

Logan hadn't been to the cemetery since his father's funeral. But today he found himself standing over his parents' graves with a bouquet of roses in his hands. He stared at the headstones, wondering about his father and mother's relationship. To a boy who only saw what was right in front of him, Logan had thought his parents loved each other. He had thought that their family was as strong and as sturdy as the Ponderosa pines. He had thought his father was the fairest, most honest man in the world.

It was all a facade to conceal the truth. His father had lied and had conspired to destroy the family by abandoning his mother and bringing Louisa Montrose into the picture.

New anger rose up now as he gazed at their graves. The only crime his mother had committed in all of this was to love Randall Slade and expect his loyalty in return. After his mother found out about the affair, she'd protected her family by firing Louisa Montrose and banishing her and Sophia from the ranch. Ivy had forged on, raising her sons and loving a man who didn't love her in return. In Logan's mind, Ivy Slade was a hero—a woman who'd born great injury living in a house with a man who had betrayed and humiliated her.

"I'm sorry, Mom," he said, his voice nearly breaking. He bent on one knee to brush away dried blades of grass and fallen leaves from her headstone. And then he laid the dozen buttercup roses down—her favorite—keeping the flat of his hand on the headstone. This was his time with his mother. Every couple of months, he spent just a few minutes here where he could feel a connection to her.

It was the second time today Logan had offered up flowers. He'd sent Sophia flowers this morning, and she'd sent him a message that she would be ready tonight at eight o'clock for their first date.

Logan wondered if he was a hypocrite to lay tremendous blame on his father, when Logan himself had been lured in by a Montrose. Yet he understood a man's weakness when mind and body were involved. Sophia had gotten under his skin. She was like an addiction. He had to have her, but he'd taken his father's failures to heart. He'd learned a valuable lesson and he'd vowed to never let himself become vulnerable to Sophia.

He could make the distinction, between lust and love.

With that notion in mind, Logan pivoted on his heels and got into his truck. As he drove out of the cemetery, he turned on the radio. Brad Paisley's voice carried over the airwaves with lyrics that touted the joys of fishing. Logan sang along with him, his mood lighter and anticipation stirring in his gut. Tonight, he had a date with a beautiful woman.

Four hours later, Logan rapped on Sophia's bedroom door, hat in hand. He hadn't seen her since this morning. A classic oil-painting image of her had stayed in his head all day— Sophia standing nude, one hip elevated, the curve of her feminine body inviting and the look in her eyes enticing. It had taken every ounce of his willpower to walk away from her. But he couldn't lie to her. He couldn't tell her the things she wanted to hear, so he'd done what he had to do.

She opened the door and gave him a small smile. "Hi." One large gold hoop dangled from her ear. "Come in," she said, turning and walking toward her dressing mirror.

Logan followed behind her.

"Sorry, I'm running late," she said, putting on the other earring as she faced the mirror.

"No problem." Logan stood beside her. Watching Sophia put the finishing touches on her outfit wasn't a hardship.

"We had a last-minute emergency at the lodge. The sprinkler system went off right in the middle of our barbecue dinner. Everyone went scrambling and we—"

Logan cut her off with a brief kiss. "Let's not talk about work tonight," he said.

He took a step back as the delicious taste of her mouth got his juices flowing. He couldn't imagine concentrating on irritated guests or broken sprinkler systems with the way Sophia looked tonight. Her hair was up in some sort of pretty curly twist at the top of her head. Her short gold dress glimmered and draped in soft folds over her chest. It was cinched at her slender waist, accentuating her female curves and hugging her thighs. Jeweled sandals encased her feet.

"O-okay," she said, touching the back of her hair nervously. "No business tonight then."

"You look amazing, Sophia."

Her scent perfumed the air. It was the same tempting fragrance she'd worn last night when they'd been dueling between the sheets. It wasn't a smell he would soon forget.

"Thank you. I wasn't sure how to dress. Your note didn't say where we were going."

He rubbed the back of his neck. "Yeah, well…I wasn't sure you'd accept my invitation."

Her tawny eyes lifted to study his face. "You sent lovely flowers, but it was what you wrote that made me agree."

Logan winced inwardly. He shouldn't have written what he had. He wasn't sure he would ever follow through and change his mind. But this morning after the hot erotic night they'd shared, he'd been thinking with a brain located south of his belt buckle.

He'd made no promises to Sophia though. And he clung to that reasoning as he put his hand to the luscious curve of her back, leading her from the bedroom and out of the house.

"You're not working tomorrow," he said after he helped her slip into the passenger's side of his car.

"I don't have to go in until the afternoon. But, Logan," she said, with a warning in her voice.

"We're taking a drive and we'll be out late. That's all I meant, little Ms. Suspicious."

Sophia chuckled and the sweet sound filled his head.

"I want to show you something."

"Is it a secret?" she asked.

"Sorta."

Sophia's voice got higher. "Really?"

Logan nodded. He wasn't quite sure why he'd decided to bring Sophia to the spot he had in mind except that it was important that he impress her. "It's a special place."

"For all of your first dates?"

Sophia was fishing for clues, but he didn't mind answering her truthfully. "You're the first woman I'm taking there."

Sophia opened her mouth to say something, but then those full lips clamped down and she shot him a skeptical look.

He shrugged. "You don't have to believe me. But it's true."

"Does this place have a name?"

He gave her a nod. "The Hideaway."

Her brows gathered. "I've never heard of it."

"Exactly my point, darlin'. Now sit back and relax. It's an hour's drive from here."

Carved out of a mountainside, The Hideaway was a chateau overlooking a vast sea of sugar pine trees with bulky trunks and branches lifting skyward like regal green giants. Beyond the forest, the still waters of Lake Tahoe glistened in the distance under starry moonlight. Lights wrapped around garden posts twinkled near where Sophia stood on the terrace outside the restaurant. She leaned against a square column, looking out. Peace and contentment filled her.

Logan walked up and handed her a glass of sparkling water.

"Thank you," she said, gazing out. She took a sip of her drink. The cool lime-flavored liquid bubbled and popped on the way down her throat.

"I thought you might like it here." He held a glass in his hand. She was pretty sure it was scotch.

"You own The Hideaway, don't you?" she asked.

Logan had driven up a narrow mountain road to get here and when they'd arrived, Sophia had been surprised by what she'd found—a restaurant designed with a European rustic flare nestled in the woods. Porcelain tile work lay beneath her feet and textured walls surrounded her. The dining room had private seating areas with tufted embroidered sofas and love seats. Atop a travertine fireplace mantel half a dozen pillar candles burned, casting soft shadows on the walls.

"You catch on fast." His teasing smile was so genuine and rare that Sophia found herself staring at his mouth. He looked handsome in a three-piece Western suit with a brocade vest, but when he flashed his pearly whites her heart raced.

"The empty restaurant and the little tour you gave introducing me to the chef and his staff were dead giveaways."

He grinned. "I can't fool you. The food's pretty good. The place is quiet. And the view is…"

"Magnificent," she whispered in awe. Her gaze wandered over the trees to the shimmering silver lake as she took in the natural splendor.

"Yeah, it is." His tone made her turn away from the sugar pines to face him.

He stared at her a long moment, his eyes piercing her soul. He took a sip of his scotch and shook his head as if trying to clear out his thoughts.

"What is it?" she asked softly.

He drew a deep breath. "Nothing."

But it was something. He'd looked tormented for a second. The amused gleam in his eyes evaporated—he'd gone to some distant place—and regret marred his handsome expression.

"We can eat anytime you want," he said, transforming his expression to produce a charming smile. "The chef has prepared something special for us."

Sophia wouldn't question Logan further. She refused to let her mind go to a dark place of doubt and uncertainty. Maybe she'd only imagined the tortured look on his face. "I would love to try the chef's specialty."

Logan showed her to a table that was in the prettiest corner of the room. She was well aware that he had closed down the restaurant for a private meal with her. She couldn't say she wasn't impressed and flattered. "Do you go to such trouble for all your first dates?"

"I can honestly tell you, no, I don't."

His declaration made Sophia extremely happy. "More like a Kickin' Kitchen kind of thing then?"

"Don't disparage Kickin'. The food's great when you know your limits."

Sophia raised her brows but she let Logan get away with that jibe. She was glad to see his mood lighten. "So how long have you owned this place?"

"Six months."

"I think it's a wonderful chateau but I'm a little surprised."

"Because I'm a rancher and this isn't really in my wheelhouse?"

Sophia didn't want to pry but she was curious, so she gave him a slight nod.

"My friend owned the place, but he couldn't make it work. His managerial skills were not up to snuff. He was losing business, about to go into foreclosure." Logan shrugged as if buying a business was an everyday occurrence for him. "I don't like to see beautiful things fall to ruin, and in this case,

I could do something about it. I saved my friend's ass and bought it at a fair price."

Sophia glanced around the entire restaurant. It was cozy and warm and elegant. "Your friend is very lucky."

"It was business."

"Maybe," Sophia said. "Or maybe you're more softhearted than you think."

"Definitely...*not*."

Logan finished off the last ounce of his scotch. He could be a hard-ass at times, but Sophia knew there was a softer side to Logan Slade, whether or not he wanted to admit it. When his guard was down, Sophia figured him to be a pretty decent man. Then a thought struck. "Isn't Luke staying somewhere close by?"

Logan studied her for a few long moments. "He's on the other side of the lake, some twenty miles of winding road from here." In a clipped voice, he asked, "Why? You want to stop by for a visit?"

She heard masked resentment in his tone. Logan and Luke were at odds lately and it was best for her not to interfere. Though she missed Luke and hoped he was doing well, she didn't know how he would take the news about her being in love with Logan. She'd avoided calling him and felt like a heel about it, but she didn't know how to broach the subject about her and Logan. Everything was up in the air anyway. Sophia had no clue what the future held for them. What could she say to Luke?

I've moved into your house and slept with your brother.

"What I want is to be right here with you," she said honestly.

Logan seemed satisfied with her reply. He gave a quick nod. "My brother's doing okay."

"I'm happy to hear that."

The subject was dropped and dinner was served. It was the most exquisite melt-in-your-mouth meal Sophia had ever

eaten—a dish with tender herb-infused sirloin strips and shi-
take mushrooms along with delicately grilled then lightly
fried vegetables. Summoning her bravado, she broached a
question that had been on her mind. "What was your relationship like with your father after my mother and I left Sunset Ranch?"

Logan's lips tightened and he moved his empty plate away
a little more forcefully than necessary. "Why do you want
to know?"

Sophia toyed with her hair, curling a loose strand around
her finger. "I always wondered what happened after we left."

Logan rubbed the underside of his chin, contemplating for
a second, then gave a sigh before responding. "I hated him."

His admission wasn't a surprise. She'd come to understand a boy's disillusionment over a man he'd once idolized.
She could sympathize with Logan now, and feel the pain he
must have endured. Her situation hadn't been all that different in terms of the pain she'd felt over her father, although
Sophia hadn't known him. She'd been too young, but his betrayal had affected her life regardless. He'd hurt her mother
and had abandoned his family. Growing up fatherless, Sophia had lived with the hurt and hatred inside for many years.
"I'm sorry."

"I'm thinking you really are," he said, but before their eyes
could hold a connection, Logan looked away.

"Do you still hate him?" Sophia spoke in a hushed tone,
hoping to keep this conversation going.

Logan winced. "What difference does it make now? He's
gone."

"Forgiveness heals."

Logan began shaking his head. "I'm not there yet, Sophia.
Let's not be spoiling our date with this kind of talk."

Sophia didn't mean to push him, but she was falling deeper
and deeper in love with him. She wanted everything out in
the open, so they could cut a clear path together without any

obstacles getting in their way. He'd asked her to change his mind, but she couldn't do that unless he was willing to discuss painful memories. But it was obvious, tonight was not the night. "You're right. We'll talk of other things."

Logan rose from his seat and announced, "We'll have dessert out on the terrace, if that's all right with you."

Sophia stood. "Yes, I'd like that."

"Good. I'm in need of fresh air."

Logan put a hand to her waist just as she pivoted and their bodies brushed intimately. She stood inches from him, her face lifted to his. "I'm sorry, Logan. I didn't mean to upset you."

He moved even closer and something intense flared in his eyes. "The only thing upsetting me is not being able to touch you."

"You've touched me," she whispered.

His head angled down and he murmured softly, blowing warm breath over her ear. "Not the way I want. I'm on first-date best behavior."

Sophia sucked oxygen into her lungs. "You get an A for effort and a big, gold star."

His mouth hovered near hers and their breaths mingled. "I'd rather have a kiss."

Surprised, she smiled softly but Logan didn't wait for her permission. He took her in a leisurely kiss filled with enough delicious promise to break down all of her defenses, all of her firm resolutions.

Dessert was abandoned and they drove home quietly holding hands and sharing heated glances in the car.

When Logan escorted her into the house, there wasn't a doubt in her mind where she would sleep tonight. Whatever this was between them, whatever Logan thought of her and however she was supposed to change his mind, she couldn't stop the compelling magnetism that linked her to him. She couldn't deny what seemed like her destiny.

She placed her faith in him, depending on his sense of fairness and decency. Judging by their personal history it was a giant leap for her to make.

Logan wouldn't betray her trust, would he?

Nine

Sophia had never slept with a man on a first date, and with wry amusement she decided that waking up in Logan's bed this morning after an incredible bout of lovemaking was worth the distinction. Making love in the tack room the other night didn't count. At least in her sleep-groggy mind it didn't. She rationalized that that had been an impulse born of desire and lust with no promise of the future. She'd been seduced by something far greater than her own willpower. But ever since Logan had sent her flowers and written a note claiming he was going to try, asking her out on a genuine, pull-out-all-stops kind of date, Sophia had come to conclusions that meant lowering her guard and taking a risk.

The evening had been magical for her. And when Logan actually gave her a chaste good-night kiss, attempting to keep his promise of best first-date behavior, Sophia had put a halt to the charade. She'd taken Logan's hand and together they walked into his bedroom with no words spoken.

Now, Sophia lay sprawled out on his bed, a soft cotton sheet covering her naked body and a smile on her lips.

Logan walked into the room and whipped off her covers. "Wake up, sleepyhead."

"Mmm," she said, grabbing for the covers. "I'm being lazy before I have to go into work."

"What? And leave all this?" Logan shook his head. "You're not going into work today, honey," he announced. "I have it all arranged."

"I wish you weren't kidding."

"I'm not." He winked and spoke with smug satisfaction. "Your meetings are postponed and Lois Benson will cover for you today. She's in line for assistant manager and she's eager to prove herself. Besides, I have the day planned for us."

Sophia was beside herself with joy. She didn't have anything pressing on her schedule today and the idea of spending the entire day with Logan was beyond appealing. "Does it involve more sleeping in this big comfy bed?"

Logan bent to land a solid kiss on her mouth. "It does involve this bed, sweetheart, I will damn well guarantee you that."

Sophia chuckled and laid back on the mattress. But her rest was short-lived before Logan whisked her up into his arms. "First I think you need to try out my shower."

"Are you joining me?" she asked, intrigued with the notion, kicking her legs playfully as he carried her toward the bathroom.

"Sure am. I have to show you what buttons and knobs to turn on."

Sophia giggled and just minutes later they were soapy and steamy and covered with moisture. Logan loved her with his mouth until she was adequately tortured and fully spent. Sophia coaxed a similar response from him when she put her lips around the silky skin sheathing his manhood. The intense sound of three showerheads raining down couldn't drown out

Logan's groans of completion. He held her tight in his arms as the water continued to cleanse them.

"You're an amazing man," Sophia said, her heart bursting. She'd almost told him how much she loved him then but at the last moment she held back, too unsure of his reaction.

"We are good together, Sophia," he murmured, sprinkling kisses over her throat, her chin and her lips. She closed her eyes and held on for dear life, her emotions threatening to overwhelm her.

The rest of the day was spent riding mares along a stream that ran through the backwoods of Slade property, stopping for a picnic lunch near the trickling waters and making lazy, crazy love in the middle of nowhere on a blanket by the stream's bank. It was the perfect day and later that evening when they'd returned to Sunset Ranch, they got comfortable in Logan's bed and watched old classic Westerns. Sophia fell asleep in Logan's arms never feeling more content.

The next week was blissful heaven. Sophia shared her mornings and nights with Logan Slade. She'd wake to kisses drizzled on her cheek from a man who was seriously dangerous to her equilibrium. They'd shower and dress, and then eat a light breakfast together before going their separate ways. Sophia poured her concentration into Sunset Lodge, working as hard as she could to prove to herself and Logan that she was capable and deserved the inheritance Randall Slade had bestowed upon her. She beamed inside and that spark kept a smile on her face through every task, every duty she took on.

Logan seemed happy, too, for the most part. But every once in a while she'd catch him in a moment when his expression would falter, as if something cold and foreboding had wrestled itself into his mind. When that happened, dreadful shivers crept up her spine.

If there was any buzz about her relationship with Logan at the ranch or Sunset Lodge, it hadn't reached Sophia's ears.

There wasn't much she could do about it if there was. She wasn't going to let gossip stand in the way of what she wanted.

She never had.

On Thursday afternoon, Sophia sat at her office desk and typed in a text message to Luke. How is my friend doing today?

A couple of days ago, Sophia had decided the best way to avoid a conversation she didn't want to have with Logan's brother was to text him. She could use a minimum of words to ask how he was doing and those brand-new audio texting applications allowed him to answer. For a man with a broken arm and healing ribs, voice-activated texting couldn't be beat.

She received an immediate message back. I'm healing. Feeling better every day. Miss you and the ranch.

I miss you, too, but all is well here. She punched in three smiley faces and decided that was over the top. She erased two of them, and then hit Send. Conversation over.

She was a coward. She admitted it. Logan wouldn't tell Luke what was going on between them. It landed on Sophia's shoulders, but it was an awkward situation to say the least. So she'd avoided the subject altogether. She was concerned for Luke, but yet her lack of courage kept her from having a real conversation with him.

The sound of Blackie's sharp barks took her out of her deep thoughts. She got up from her desk and walked out of her office in search of the dog. She exited through the lobby doors and walked along the path toward the side of the lodge. She chuckled when she spotted Blackie jumping off the ground, all four legs in midair at once as Edward teased him with a rib bone. The dog nearly toppled the boy over trying to get to the bone.

Edward cackled with laughter and Sophia's mood lightened. She walked up to them, and both boy and dog stopped playing.

"Hello, Edward. I see you have something Blackie wants."

Edward looked at her shyly. She hadn't seen the boy around for a while. "Y-yes, ma'am."

"And hello to you, too, Blackie."

The dog forgot about the bone, and with tail wagging, came over to her. She bent down to stroke his coat and Blackie's head tilted to one side, his tongue hanging out in a true doggie smile. "Are you behaving yourself?"

His tail wagged faster.

"He is. He h-hasn't come into N-Nana's kitchen a-again ever." Edward, always ready to come to Blackie's defense, stuck the bone into his back pocket, out of sight of the dog for now.

"That's good." Sophia gave Blackie a last pat and, rising, turned her attention to the boy. "How have you been, Edward?"

He looked at her and then glanced down. "F-fine."

"I haven't seen you too much lately."

"I d-don't have any h-homework today."

"Oh, that's explains it, you've been busy studying. I used to love those days best when the teacher gave us a day off. Do you still like to hike, Edward?"

He nodded. "I go with Mr. S-Slade some-t-times."

"I would love to hike with you, too, when school is out. Would that be all right?"

His face turned crimson and a small smile emerged. He was a sweet boy. Sophia tried her best to put him at ease and let him know she was his friend. He darted a glance toward the cottage, his eyes wide with curiosity and an unspoken question on his lips. He had to be curious why she wasn't living there anymore. It wasn't an easy thing to explain to a ten-year-old boy. "We'll make plans for that hike as soon as summer starts, okay?"

"Okay."

"Well, you and Blackie have a nice day. I just wanted to say hello to both of you. I'll see you again soon."

The rib bone reappeared and Edward gave it a toss. Sophia put her hand over her brows, shadowing her eyes from the blazing sunlight as she watched Blackie digging in, outrunning Edward in a race for his treat.

Seeing the boy was a nice diversion, a break in the long day she'd needed. She had two hours left of work before she would see Logan again and she would count the minutes.

As she made her way along the flowery path to the lodge's entrance she stopped short when a black stretch limousine caught her eye. It pulled to stop under the portico and a chauffeur dressed in a tan uniform got out.

A gasp escaped her as memories rushed through her mind. She recognized that limo with the famous script *G* emblazoned on the side doors. The driver opened the passenger door and two men exited. One was the deadly handsome cowboy she loved and the other was her older, distinguished, wealthy ex-husband, Gordon Gregory. He was medium height, blue-eyed and not bad-looking for an older man, wrinkles and all. He dressed impeccably and had a full head of silver hair.

Seeing the two men together made her heart pound. One man might be her future—the other was her past. She took a big swallow and stood there immobilized, looking to Logan first. His expression was unreadable. Gordon, on the other hand, smiled.

Darn, this was the last thing she needed. She and Logan were working things out and becoming closer. How would he react seeing her ex-husband and being reminded of the worst thing he'd thought about her?

"Hello, my beautiful Sophia." Gordon's possessive tone made her uneasy.

Logan slid him a disapproving look.

"Hello, Gordon. What are you doing here?"

"He came to buy a stallion," Logan said through tight lips. "We've just had a good talk."

Sophia's face flamed and she cringed inside. Had they

been talking about her? When she'd married Gordon it had
been out of desperate need. He'd been wonderful and kind in
the beginning and so grateful about his granddaughter that
she'd thought she was doing the right thing for her mother
when she'd married him. She'd fooled herself into thinking
she could come to love him in time. He'd promised her a
marriage with no strings attached. Maybe she'd been a little
naive to actually believe that, but at the time, Sophia hadn't
been looking to the future. She'd been focused on the present
and the best way to help her mother. Shortly after her mother
passed away, Gordon's expectations had changed and so had
his attitude. He'd come on strong in the guise of helping her
grieve for Louisa. And one night he'd blurted that his debt
to her had been paid in full. They were on even ground now
and it was time for Sophia to start acting like a wife to him.
He'd boxed her into a corner and there was only one way out
that she could see. She'd ended the marriage.

"I couldn't stop by Sunset Ranch and not come by for a
visit," he went on. "Logan here was kind enough to show me
to the lodge. I'd like a private word with you, my dear. Now
would be a good time."

She felt Logan's eyes on her as he spoke firmly to Gordon.
"*Only* if it's a good time for Sophia. Is it?"

The older man's brows flew up and he chuckled. "I see.
She's got you under her spell already. I can't really blame you.
She's quite a woman. You should have seen her on that cho-
rus line. She was a standout, destined to become a headliner."

Sophia's stomach began to ache. Gordon's appearance here
threatened to undermine the reputation she'd tried to live
down with Logan. "I have a few minutes, Gordon."

"Fine, fine." When Gordon reached for Sophia's arm,
Logan stepped between them and faced her, turning his back
on the older man. "Are you sure you have time for this guy?"
he asked her. "I could care less about the sale of the stallion."

Sophia wanted to kiss him for intervening, for making

sure Gordon didn't lay a hand on her. Especially since, for all Logan knew, Sophia had been intimate with the older man. "I'm sure."

Logan nodded, and for a second she noted a hint of accusation in his eyes. "I'll see you later."

"I'll be there," she whispered softly before turning to Gordon. "We can talk in my office."

She led the way, keeping one step ahead of him. Once she climbed the steps to the entrance, she opened the door and turned. Logan stood grounded to the spot, his gaze keen and sharp, missing nothing.

There's nothing to see, Logan. No great conspiracy. No gold-digging.

Sophia walked with her chin high and her mind reeling. Why on earth was Gordon here? She entered her office and settled behind her desk, pointing to a chair. "Please have a seat."

The elderly man lowered himself with regal authority. "You've moved on, Sophia. I take it you've snagged that rich cowboy and convinced him to let you run this place."

"Actually, you and I both know I inherited half ownership of Sunset Lodge. I'm sure you've done your homework, Gordon. And I doubt a man like Logan Slade would allow anyone to *snag* him," she added.

"Ah, but if a woman could do it, it would be you," he said.

That just showed how little Gordon really knew about the situation. Logan had tried to bribe her to get her to leave the ranch just weeks ago.

"How is Amanda?"

He seemed pleased that she'd asked. "My granddaughter is doing very well. She lost a year of high school during that crazy time, but she's on the right road now. She'll be starting college in the fall."

Sophia's heart warmed. Amanda had been a mixed-up kid who'd needed guidance in her life and some professional counseling. Sophia was glad to have helped her see that her life was worth salvaging. "I'm glad to hear it. Please give her my best."

"I will."

"What can I help you with?" She tilted her head, still curious why he'd shown up here. She knew darn well buying a horse wasn't the only reason. That had been the excuse.

He smiled again, his eyes crinkling heavily at the corners. "I came to buy a stallion and I have, but I'm also here to honor a promise I made to Louisa."

At the mention of her mother's name, Sophia's shoulders slumped and she was struck with immediate sadness. All of the brassiness she'd summoned to deal with Gordon disappeared. "Wh-what promise?"

"To make sure you were all right. To make sure you were safe. You see, your mother may have pretended not to know how sick she was, but she knew. We would have candid talks about it. Louisa and I had actually become very close in the end. She never wanted you to worry. She knew you had enough to deal with. You marrying me gave your mother peace of mind."

She'd hoped so. With her whole heart, she had truly hoped so. Sophia closed her eyes, momentarily absorbing the truth of his words. Her mother always pretended to feel better than she actually felt to ease Sophia's mind. She'd been a trouper about her treatments and always tried to put a smile on her face even when her health had begun to decline. Sophia wished she could be as strong and capable and caring a woman as her mother had been.

"I think she would've liked you to stay married to me," Gordon said.

"I might have, if you hadn't pressured me."

"I was very patient with you, Sophia. I was good to you."

"Yes, I can't deny that. You were very good to my mother and me."

"So can you blame me for wanting a real wife? Your mother was gone, God rest her soul, and you were safe, away from a stalker's threats. I figured—"

"I'd owe you?"

"No, Sophia. I had hoped you'd have real affection for me."

"I appreciate everything you did for me, but contrary to what some might believe, I can't be bought. You put pressure on me shortly after my mother died and made me very uncomfortable. Gordon, you're not a man who takes no lightly. You pressed me until I had no choice but to walk away."

Gordon actually looked contrite. "I'm sorry. It was a mistake on my part to pressure you. I'm a bit spoiled. I usually get what I want and, beautiful Sophia, you were my wife."

Sophia had walked away without a dime of Gordon's great wealth. She'd insisted on a prenup that said exactly that. She'd never wanted his money. She'd never wanted to be beholden to Gordon. "I know," she whispered, "but I couldn't give you what you wanted."

Gordon put his head down. He steepled his fingers and spoke quietly. "You may think me a silly old man for saying so, but I fell in love with you, Sophia."

Sophia was touched and she believed him, but Gordon Gregory fell in love a lot. He'd been married and divorced five times in his seventy-one years. "And you deserve a woman in your life who will give you love back."

"I see that now." A shrug rolled off his shoulder. "Well… I've done my part, Sophia. I've checked on you for Louisa's sake. I see you've made a life for yourself here. Are you happy?"

Sophia didn't have to think twice. "Yes."

He nodded and gave her a thoughtful look. "Then I'd venture to guess Logan Slade is a very lucky man."

After Sophia bid farewell to Gordon, she sat in her office staring at the paperwork on her desk. The numbers on the

account sheets made no sense. She wouldn't even try to turn
on her computer. She couldn't concentrate. She couldn't seem
to think of much else but Gordon Gregory's appearance here
today. She'd never expected him to seek her out. That part of
her life, a trying, difficult part of her life, was over. Seeing
Logan drive up in the limo with Gordon had really rattled her.

While she'd silently grieved for her mother all these
months, speaking with Gordon today and hashing over their
lives had brought fresh pain to her heart. From her grave, her
mother was still trying to look out for her—still trying to protect her. It served to make Sophia miss her mother even more.

She'd married a man for what he could give her, yes. But
it wasn't a selfish money-grubbing move. It had been for her
mother's sake. Gordon had provided safe haven in his man-
sion for both the Montrose women and hopefully now that
she'd grown closer to Logan, he would believe her.

With that resolved in her mind, Sophia managed to struggle through her work. Apprehension gripped her stomach
tight. Logan had been a wonderful lover and they'd shared so
much with each other, but the one thing that Sophia needed
from him now was his willingness to see her in a different
light. It mattered now. So much. She wanted his trust. She
wanted him to believe in her.

The brim on his hat cocked low, Hunter Halliday gave a
light rap at her opened office door. "It's that time," he said,
stepping one foot into the office.

For the past week, Hunter had come in the late afternoon
to alert her it was time to feed the horses. Aside from her
time spent with Logan, hand-feeding the horses with Hunter
was the best part of her day. "Thank goodness. I am so ready
to call it a day."

Hunter waited for her to straighten her desk and lock up
the office. They walked out the side door that led toward the
lodge stables, making pleasant small talk. Several of the lodge
guests were about, the scent of horse dung and straw giving

them the full ranch-type experience. She waved to them and walked farther down to where Hunter kept a jumbo-sized bag of carrots.

At the corral, five horses trotted over and nudged each other out of the way trying to get their fair share of food. Sophia let each horse take a carrot out of her palm and then patted their foreheads, one right after the other. Hunter took a few carrots over to an elderly couple who stood watching from several feet away. He gave them each a turn feeding the horses.

Sophia walked over to them. "They love getting extra treats."

The woman smiled. "Well, then we'll have to come by to-morrow at this time, too."

Hunter agreed and started up a conversation with the two of them while Sophia bid them farewell. Her mood lighter, she felt a little better about talking to Logan tonight.

"Ms. Montrose?" Hunter called as she approached her car. "You heading over to the main house?"

"Yes, I am."

"Will you say hello to Luke for me?"

Confused, Sophia gave Hunter a shake of the head. *"Luke?"*

"Yes, ma'am. I saw him going into the house an hour ago. Luke's back."

Ten

A knot formed in Sophia's stomach as she parked her Camry by the ranch house garage. She sat in the car a minute, still unsure what to do about Luke. If Logan was home, maybe he'd already had a conversation with him. Or maybe he'd left that privilege for her. Sophia had wanted a little more time with Logan. And after her visit from Gordon today, she'd hoped she could be honest and up-front about things he didn't want to talk about. She'd hoped she could make headway with him. It would require faith and trust on both their parts.

Sadly, she still didn't have a clear definition of her relationship with Logan. And she still didn't know what she would say to Luke. She got out of the car and made her way toward the house, wondering if she could find the right words. Deep in thought, she climbed the steps and entered the house, closing the door behind her.

Instantly, two booming male voices resounding from the long hallway stopped her cold. She couldn't make out the words, but she certainly knew harsh tones when she heard them. And it was clear that Logan and Luke were butting heads again. When she heard her name mentioned, Sophia moved down the hallway, compelled by a force stronger than good etiquette allowed to secretly listen to the two men she cared most about. She leaned against the outside wall of Logan's office, out of sight.

"You're telling me that Sophia has moved into the house?" Luke's voice was full of his displeasure.

Logan's impatient words rang out. "I told you about the threats at the cottage."

"So she's here for her own safety?"

"There's more. We're not going to tiptoe around now that you're home."

"Meaning what?"

Logan's voice carried a distinct certainty. "Meaning she's with me now."

There was a long pause, and Sophia squeezed her eyes shut. She didn't know what to expect from this conversation. Logan hadn't been subtle or taken the time to ease Luke into the idea.

"You son of a bitch." Disbelief reverberated off the walls. "You're sleeping with her."

"That's right, Luke. It's a mutual arrangement."

Again there was a long pause as Luke absorbed that for a minute. Sophia didn't know if she should make her presence known, but his next words made her rethink revealing herself until she'd heard Logan's answer.

"So then you've forgiven her of all crimes? You don't think she's out for our money?"

"I didn't say that."

"You're not cutting her any slack, are you?" Luke asked angrily.

"I'm watching our backs, Luke."

"You're going to hurt her and if you do, I'll—"

"I'm making damn well sure you don't hook up with her.

You'd be foolish enough to fall in love with her. At least with me, I know that'll never happen. I'm protecting our interests."

"You're a bastard, Logan." Luke's words were sharp, cutting. "Sophia deserves better than that."

Logan lashed back, "Yeah, what do you know? You didn't wake up one night and wander into the barn as a kid to find our father, the esteemed Randall Slade, sprawled over her mother in the tack room. The two of them were going at it—"

Sophia gasped. Stunned, she moved on shaky legs into the office doorway. The Slade men both looked up at the same time, shocked to see her standing there in full view.

She felt the blood drain from her face. Her body went limp as she faced Logan. She'd overheard everything. Logan had never cared for her. He'd never fall in love with her. She took a swallow, having to look deep into his eyes and hear him repeat the one thing that brought it all together. The one thing that proved his wicked deception.

"The t-tack room, Logan?"

Logan's hard eyes softened. "Sophia."

Luke let out a curse. "Don't listen to him, Sophia. He's an—"

"Answer me, Logan," she demanded, raising her voice. Luke wouldn't understand why this was so devastating to her. "You saw our parents together in the *tack* room?"

Logan blinked and began shaking his head. "You weren't meant to hear this conversation."

Sophia couldn't breathe. Her chest pounded and her stomach twisted in agony. She'd never felt so completely betrayed. This was all a game to Logan—and a way to keep her away from Luke. He must have had a good long laugh over it when he seduced her in the very place he'd found his father making love to her mother. She was at a loss so profound a cold wave wrapped around her body and threatened to freeze her out. It was as if the light beaming inside her died. She was numb and brokenhearted, but forces from deep within would not allow her to walk out of here until Logan heard the truth.

"First of all, Luke is right. You're a bastard."

Logan flinched, which gave her a measure of satisfaction. The man wasn't made entirely of stone. If her words cut him, they were only a tiny tear, unlike the way she'd been ripped apart.

"You've never wanted to hear the truth about your parents. I've wanted to tell you but I thought I should wait until I had your trust. But I see now I'll never have that. Luke, you should know this, too. When your mother and father married it was more an arrangement to bring two powerful ranching families together. There was never great passion between them. Randall married because she'd gotten pregnant with you. He didn't love her the way she wanted to be loved though. The way every woman deserves to be loved. But your mother and father did merge the ranches and did build a family together."

Sophia put her head down. She couldn't bear to see the look of pain in Logan's expression. After a few seconds, she forged on. He needed to hear this. Even if he didn't believe her, she owed this to her mother and to herself. She faced Logan again, looking him straight in the eyes, holding back her tears. "When we came to live at the ranch, there was nothing between my mother and your father but mutual respect. Over the years, they grew closer and fought the attraction with everything they had but eventually they fell deeply in love. My mother was tormented. I would hear her crying during the night. Often she'd speak of leaving the ranch, of finding another job somewhere else. But I loved living here. I loved it so much and I couldn't understand at the time why my mother wanted to leave. I pleaded with her to stay on. I couldn't bear the thought of not living at the cottage or on Sunset Ranch. So we stayed."

Early memories of her mother's sadness were fresh in her mind. Sophia remembered her mother crying and the defeat in her voice in those brief moments when she'd let her guard down. It had been a painful time for her. "Your father was set to divorce Ivy. It wasn't an easy decision for him but he'd been determined. My mother stopped him. She wouldn't allow Randall to break up his family for her. Everyone thought that Ivy found out about their affair and fired my mother. But the truth was that my mother went to Ivy to apologize. She offered to move away so that she and Randall could patch up their relationship and keep the family together. Mama always told me she'd done the right thing. She couldn't have lived with herself if she'd broken up your family. She never took a penny of Randall's money and she made him promise to never follow her. To my knowledge he never did."

"But he did provide for you in his will," Luke pointed out.

The room got quiet. Logan's face masked his emotions.

"My mother loved Randall Slade with her whole heart and she gave him up. It was the hardest thing she ever had to do." Sophia choked up then and tears spilled from her eyes when she looked at Logan one last time. "Mama…always said…it was a waste of love."

His dark eyes flickered and he moved toward her. But Sophia backed away, putting out a hand warning him not to come closer. "I'm moving back into the cottage. I want to be left alone. I hope both of you will respect my wishes."

"Sophia, me?" Luke asked.

Warmth filled her heart for the man who was her friend. It was a blessing to see Luke looking so fit, regardless of the cast on his arm. She could barely breathe, barely talk. Her words were soft, a quiet plea for Luke's understanding. "I'm sorry, but I need to be alone right now."

She turned then, and walked out the door. She'd never had hope torn from her body this way before. She'd never had such devastating disillusionment.

She missed her mother more now than ever before.

And she knew that she would miss loving Logan Slade almost as much.

Logan lowered down into his chair and squeezed his eyes shut. But the image of Sophia appeared in his head anyway. Her fiery spirit gone, she'd looked broken and beat down. Accusation and betrayal had marred her beautiful face.

The tack room, Logan?

Logan winced. It hadn't been planned. He hadn't set out to seduce her that night. It had been an ironic twist, a coincidence that Logan hadn't thought about until after the deed was done. When he realized he made love to her there, he hadn't put much significance in it. Until now. Until the angry words had slipped from his mouth during his argument with his brother and Sophia had overheard. He'd said brutal, harsh things about keeping Luke away from her, about how he would never fall in love with her. She'd heard it all.

Luke walked over to him, his voice menacing. "Stand up, so I can knock you on your ass."

Logan didn't bother to look at him. "With your left hand?"

"Jerk."

Logan's love/hate relationship with his brother was getting on his nerves. He wanted to be left alone with his miserable thoughts. "Get outta here, Luke."

"Sophia shouldn't be alone at the cottage."

"I know that," he snapped.

"I'll go over there tonight. She'll let me in. She *likes* me."

Logan stood now, and got directly in his brother's face. He felt the veins in his neck popping. "Don't go near her. If anyone's gonna protect her, it'll be me. You understand that?"

Luke opened his big mouth, but nothing came out. They stared at each other, practically nose to nose, and then Luke's eyes widened and he burst out laughing. Logan balled his fists.

"This is rich," Luke said when his laughter died down. "You love her. You have fallen head over heels in love with Sophia, and now she can't stand you. She'd rather risk a stalker's threats than be under the same roof as you."

"You're delusional, bro."

"All this time you've been convincing yourself that Sophia is just like her mother. And it would serve you right to find that she *was* exactly like Louisa—a goodhearted, kind woman who deserved a break in life. A woman who made our father happy for a short time. Hell, Logan. I knew Mom and Dad weren't happy for years. They were partners in business and they had kids to raise so they stuck it out. Their marriage wasn't what you thought it was."

"You know this because you're the sensitive one and all."

"I didn't see Dad as a god. He was mortal and had human flaws, just like the rest of us. I don't say what he did was right and I know Dad did love Mom in his own way. They raised us and managed to keep the family together. But maybe our folks shouldn't have stayed together. Maybe they'd have both been happier apart. Maybe you got it all wrong, Logan. Ever think of that?"

Logan's nostrils flared. "I don't have it wrong."

"Okay, then fine. Let Sophia walk out of your life."

"She just did and I didn't go after her, did I?"

A look of disgust spread over Luke's face. "Your loss."

Logan watched his pain-the-ass brother turn around and walk out of his office with slower than usual steps. The trip home had taxed his strength but at least he did look stronger than when he'd left. And the accident sure hadn't changed his stubborn nature.

Once Logan was alone in his office, he made a call to add extra security to the premises. He would drive by the cottage tonight as well to check up on the place.

No one on Slade property would be in danger. He'd see to that.

Sophia included.

"I need your signatures here, here and here," Logan said, leaning over her desk pointing to three lines on a contract necessary for a revamping of the stables. The winters were harsh and the old barns needed new heating.

Logan had made it his business to stop by her office every day for the past five days for some reason or another. Every time he'd walked in she'd turned away, unwilling to meet him eye to eye. She knew he was checking up on her. She'd seen his car by the cottage on several occasions, but she also knew that Logan wasn't so much concerned about her welfare as he was about protecting his ranch from an intruder. He couldn't fool her any longer with a look or a smile. She knew his black heart now and even though the pain was still there, hovering like stormy gray clouds, Sophia was coping.

"Leave them and I'll read them over later." She used her very best business voice.

"I've had our attorney look them over. They are good to go."

Sophia nodded and signed on the dotted lines, shoving the papers back across the desk. She quickly withdrew her hands so their fingers wouldn't brush. She stepped back so she didn't have to breathe in his subtle earthy aftershave and be reminded of the nights they'd spent together.

"You're still not talking to me?" he asked.

"I talk to you every day." She was cool and dismissive on the outside, but inside her blood boiled. She prayed it would get easier seeing Logan each day. That he would leave her alone and let her go on with her life. Even when she was aloof with him, she sensed his eyes constantly on her, watching her movements.

Hands on hips, he stood over her desk and let out a frustrated sigh. "I never made false promises to you."

"Yes, you're right," she said. "You didn't." She wasn't going to go there. She wouldn't argue. She wouldn't defend. Her indifference was her only protection. "Now, is there anything else?"

"We can't go on working like this."

Sophia shut down her computer screen, still unwilling to look at him. "We won't have to. Luke's well enough to take over the lodge duties again. You're free as of today."

She heard Blackie's high-pitched barks from outside. Edward was probably on the grounds playing fetch with the dog. It was late afternoon and her work was finished for the day. She straightened the papers on her desk and rose. This time she cast a look at Logan. It was hard not to notice the way his clothes fit his body so perfectly, the stretch of soft cotton over his broad chest and jeans hugging his hips. There was a sexy five-o'clock shadow on his face and a tick went to town on his jaw. All of it made her heart do crazy things. It was dangerous to look at Logan. Dangerous to be so near.

"I have to go," she said quietly.

He spoke through tight lips. "Talk to me, Sophia."

"I can't. I have a…an appointment."

Logan's brows dented his forehead. "With who?"

She lifted her chin and kept her voice steady. "I'm having dinner with your brother."

Logan's face pinched tight. "Luke? Why in hell does it always come back to Luke?"

Sophia closed her eyes briefly, hoping to tamp down her emotions. Five minutes alone with Logan Slade was five minutes of torture. Heaven help her, she still loved him. "Because he's something to me that you never were, Logan. He's my friend. And right now I really need a friend."

As Sophia brushed by him, her nostrils drank in his scent. Leather and musk would be forever imprinted on her brain.

She had almost escaped the room when Logan spoke up. "What if I told you I'm green with jealousy over your friendship with my brother."

Sophia didn't move a muscle. She stood half in, half out of her office, her throat constricting. His admission had stunned her.

As a child, Logan had been the outsider, but purely of his own making. She and Luke would have welcomed him into their little friendship ring with open arms. But he'd never seen it that way. Logan had had a chip on his shoulder when it came to her. She'd always suspected Logan had thought she'd usurped his brother's attention.

She kept her back to him and spoke softly. "And what if I told you you could've been a part of our friendship? Luke adored his older brother and I would've accepted you as a friend."

She scurried out the door, fearing her own gentle heart. She couldn't bear to see Logan's expression now. A part of her hated him and a part of her felt sorry for the boy who'd been disillusioned so long ago.

Dinner at Dusty's Steakhouse was delicious and *safe*, Luke and Sophia having decided to leave the fire-alarm chili at Kickin' for another night. Her friend had been true to form, charming and fun-loving, and they'd had a few laughs. It was good to see Luke's health improve each day. But Sophia had been distracted all evening, struggling to keep her mind from jumping back to her conversation with Logan.

"What's wrong, Soph? Still can't get my brother out of your system?" Luke put his good arm around her shoulder in the friendly way he had as they walked up the cottage path.

"It's not that...exactly."

"Then what is it?"

She shrugged. She didn't want to ruin the peace of the night by talking about her problems with Logan. "Nothing. Sorry if I haven't been good company tonight."

"Don't be putting words in my mouth, Sophia. The company's fine. You've got something on your mind and I'd like to hear it."

Sophia stopped when she reached the entrance to the cottage. She turned to look into Luke's sky-blue eyes, wondering if she should be discussing Logan with his younger brother. The two men hardly got along, but she knew they loved each other. She didn't want to add fuel to the fire.

"Okay, if you're not going to tell me, let me guess. Logan said some other bonehead thing to you that's got you upset."

Sophia sighed and shook her head. "Not really...this is different."

"I'm surprised you're talking to him at all."

"You know I have to. Sunset Lodge is important to me. I can't let my personal life get in the way of my work."

His eyes lit with mischief. "Honey, I'm amazed you haven't slugged him yet, or kicked him in the—"

"Seriously, Luke," she said cutting him off. She'd never admit that the thought had crossed her mind to do both of those things to Logan in crazy fleeting moments of despair.

"Seriously, Sophia." Luke's voice grew softer, a plea from one friend to another. "You gonna tell me what my brother said to you?"

She looked away for a moment, nibbled on her lower lip and then finally answered Luke. "Logan admitted he was jealous of us when we were kids. I wasn't going to bring it up but—"

Disbelief and surprise crossed Luke's expression as his voice rose in pitch. "He thought you and I were—"

"No, no. Not in that way. He was jealous of our friendship. Did you know that?"

Luke's blond brows furrowed and he shook his head. "No, I never thought he gave a damn. Son of a gun. I thought we were too immature for him. He was always going on and on about how stupid we were, playing games, whispering secrets to each other. Doing things good friends do."

"Maybe he wanted to join us."

"Nah...I don't think so." Then Luke thought about it a moment. "But maybe."

Sophia nodded. "Yeah, maybe."

"If it was true, I'm kinda shocked he'd admit it to you now. It's not like Logan to confess something like that. Maybe the hard-hearted guy is finally softening up a bit. Even King Kong had a soft spot for a beautiful woman."

Sophia smiled at the reference comparing Logan to a giant ape.

"At least I made you smile."

She was grateful for Luke's company, but the stresses of the past week had taken their toll on her stamina. She tried to cover up a yawn and failed.

"You're beat," Luke said, stating the obvious.

She was. "Dinner was delicious."

"And this time you didn't wind up with a bellyache afterward."

"True."

She opened the front door and Luke stepped in behind her. She sent him an eye-roll and he just shrugged. "I'm outta here as soon as I find out where you hide the good stuff."

They'd had this disagreement in the restaurant, but in the end, Sophia agreed to let Luke inspect the cottage before he went home.

He moved down the hallway. The sound of doors opening and closing made her shake her head. There hadn't been any suspicious behavior or any more notes in days, thank goodness. Sophia was ready to put it all behind her. When Luke walked back into her parlor, he had a smile on his face. "Apparently you really don't drink. Couldn't even find a can of near beer."

"Thank you for checking. Now, let me get some sleep. I

have a big day of meetings tomorrow and they start first thing in the morning." Sophia rose on tiptoe. She touched her lips to his cheek in a chaste kiss. "Thanks for dinner."

Luke walked out the door and waited until he heard the click of the lock before bidding her farewell from her doorstep. "Sleep tight, Sophia."

"Good night, Luke."

It's hard not to love Sophia.

Gordon Gregory's parting shot had stuck in Logan's mind days after he'd sold Storm to the old geezer. Logan's response to the man's declaration had been an unintelligible grunt. He wasn't going to discuss Sophia with him. He'd believed that Gregory had come to the ranch to stir up trouble, and when he'd left that day Logan had done an internet search regarding his marriage to Sophia. He found that at one point, *Revealed* magazine had splashed Sophia's name across the front cover with a picture of her in full titillating Fantasy Follies costume. Logan had ground his teeth seeing her decked out in sequins barely covering her body with the old codger groping her waist.

Now as he stared at that cover shot on his office computer, he saw something he hadn't noticed before. When he'd looked at the picture, his focus had been on her body, shrink-wrapped into a showgirl's costume. Hell, any man would go there. She was perfect in all ways that mattered to men and it was natural to look at her full breasts, small waist and slender, smooth legs. But what he hadn't noticed before was the look in her eyes.

He studied those amber eyes now. They gave her away. There wasn't joy or contentment or even satisfaction on nabbing a rich man in those tawny depths. The photo revealed something entirely different. And for the first time since Sophia had come to Sunset Ranch, a shiver of cold dread worked its way down Logan's spine.

Logan had once made Sophia's eyes beam with joy. He'd made her eyes glow with contentment. He'd seen a look of sheer satisfaction spread across her beautiful face.

Marrying Gregory hadn't done any of those things for her.

Instead, the look in her eyes spoke of desperation and regret.

The phone rang, interrupting his thoughts. He picked it up and growled, "What?"

"Mr. Slade? It's Peggy Coswell from Human Resources at the lodge. I was wondering if...well, if you knew where Ms. Montrose is? She's late for our eight-o'clock meeting."

Logan glanced at the computer clock at the corner of his screen. "That was forty-five minutes ago."

"Yes, sir. She hasn't come into her office today."

Logan's heart beat faster. "Where else have you checked?"

"No one has seen her on the hotel grounds this morning. She's not answering her phone."

Fear gripped Logan's gut and twisted it like a pretzel. His mind turned to Luke. He'd had dinner with her last night. If he'd spent the night with Sophia... Logan's mind wouldn't go there. She wouldn't do that. Sophia just wouldn't sleep with his brother. And in that instant he knew two things. Sophia wasn't the kind of woman he'd made her out to be. She wasn't a gold-digging opportunist bent on getting rich any way she could. She wasn't out to take over Sunset Ranch or make a mockery of the Slade family. The other thing he knew would have to wait. He could deal with only one thing right now: finding Sophia. Making sure she was safe.

"Call security and have them comb the area for her. Call me back on my cell if you hear anything."

Logan rose from his desk, his breathing rapid and his strides long and efficient. He made it to Luke's room on the other side of the house in seconds. Pushing open the door, he found Luke still in bed. Alone. Relief registered that he hadn't been wrong about his brother's relationship with Sophia. He wouldn't have to beat the stuffing out of him.

"Logan, man…don't you believe in knocking?"

"Sophia missed a meeting with the staff today. No one's seen her all morning. She's not answering her cell phone. When's the last time you saw her?"

Luke came out of his haze. Since his accident, he'd been sleeping longer than usual in the mornings, making up for uncomfortable nights. "Uh, about nine last night. I checked out her place after dinner and then came home."

"Stay here and make some calls. See what you can find out. I'm going to the cottage."

Still hazy, Luke sat up straighter in the bed, running a hand through his hair. "Will do. Find her, Logan."

"Planning on it."

Logan fired up the truck's engine and sped down the road. Half a mile never seemed so long a drive. He arrived at the cottage and saw that Sophia's car was parked outside. Hope pulled through his fear and he bounded out of the truck, not bothering to knock on the door. He inserted the key he'd kept with him and pushed through the door. "Sophia? Sophia?"

Clearly, she wasn't in the parlor or kitchen. With stealthy steps, Logan moved down the short hallway, wishing he'd taken his gun on the way out. He'd never had cause to use it on the ranch except once when a snake spooked his horse while on a perimeter ride along the property. He'd been thrown within three feet of the irritated rattler. Damn thing had been ready to attack and Logan took aim and shot him dead with that Glock.

Logan didn't know what to make of Sophia's disappearance. She wasn't in the house, but her clothes were still hanging in the closet and her car was parked outside. When he put a hand to the coffeepot, it was lukewarm. She'd used it this morning.

After scanning the kitchen area he searched the parlor. Something caught his eye. He'd almost missed it because the sole thin-stemmed purple wildflower blended in so well with the floral cushions of the sofa. He didn't think much of it. Sophia liked flowers, but as he picked it up and moved pillows around searching for clues, he found something tucked under one square pillow that made his breath catch in his throat.

A note.

Typed on plain paper and folded neatly.

You are very beautiful.

"Son of a bitch!" Logan's mind raced. He'd hoped to high heaven that Sophia's disappearance had been something innocent, a miscommunication that could be cleared up and explained easily enough. He'd hoped she would come waltzing through that front door and find him standing there, worried sick over her.

He took his hat off and stared at the tan leather band, plaguing his mind for a clue. For guidance. The sheriff should be alerted, although the law wouldn't put much credence in a report of a missing woman who'd been gone only an hour. Still, he'd make the call. He'd do anything to make sure Sophia was safe.

Before he could punch the buttons, his cell phone buzzed. He answered his brother's call before it rang again. "Did you find her?"

"Not exactly," Luke said. "Constance said Edward is missing, too. He took Blackie for a walk an hour ago and hasn't returned. He missed his school bus."

"Okay, could be a coincidence. The boy could have lost track of time. Constance have any idea where he might have gone?"

"He likes to walk the dog up by the stream over by the old feed shed. She's mighty worried, Logan."

"I'm on it. I'll check it out and call you—"

Logan stopped midsentence. An unmistakable black-and-white blur raced past the cottage. Logan pushed through the front door and shouted for the dog. "Blackie!"

The dog stopped when he saw him and trotted over with his tail down, completely out of breath. Logan knelt to his level. "Where you going, boy? To the lodge? Where's Edward? Does he need help?"

The dog turned his head in the direction he'd just come from. It didn't take a detective to figure out that Blackie was looking for help. Logan grabbed the dog in his arms and deposited him in the cab of the truck as he finished his conversation with Luke.

"I'm not that far away from the stream. I'm heading there now. I've got the dog. Hopefully, he can lead me to both of them."

Logan drove the truck off-road for three quarters of a mile over gopher holes and rough pasture lands that had been played out. He was headed to the old feed shack that faced a rocky stream that flowed into a pond. It was a perfect place for a young boy to play. Logan and his brothers used to go there after school to look for worms and water snakes.

When he spotted the shed, Logan shut down the engine and parked. He opened the door and the dog scurried over his lap and bounded from the cab racing toward the stream. Logan followed him.

Sophia came into his line of vision first. She sat on a big granite boulder, her leg elevated and her right shoe off. Something squeezed tight in Logan's heart. He shook with profound relief. He'd never been so glad to see anyone in his life. He'd never experienced the kind of fear that threatened to swallow a man up whole and spit him out in small chunks. He'd never been so sure of anything in his life now, looking at Sophia Montrose and realizing that he'd almost let her slip through his fingers.

Edward approached him, his head downcast, a guilty look on his face.

"What happened, Edward?" he asked, still moving toward the boulder where Sophia sat immobilized.

"Ms. Sophia t-twisted her foot. She c-can't walk."

Logan made eye contact with Sophia. Her hair was a mess, her blouse was hanging loose around her skirt and her ankle was twice the size it should be. Raw deep emotion lodged in his throat.

"Why are you out here?" he asked the boy.

Edward shoved his head down again.

"It's okay, Edward. Tell Logan about the notes," Sophia said.

Logan blinked and his voice came out gruff and demanding. "Yeah, tell me about the notes."

Edward stared at the ground. "I t-typed them t-to Ms. Sophia."

Logan's deep voice rose from his throat like a big boom. *You did what?"*

Edward's body visibly shook.

"It's okay, Logan," Sophia rushed out, putting silent warning in her tone. "Edward explained it to me. He wasn't trying to scare me. Just the opposite. He was feeling a little shy about wanting to be my friend. We've had a long talk this morning. I put two and two together today when I found another note along with the same purple wildflowers that he'd given his grandmother once. I decided to follow Edward out here so we could talk. But I didn't expect to step into a gopher hole and twist my foot along the way."

"Your grandmother is worried sick." Logan tamped down his fury at the boy. It was clear that Sophia wanted to go easy on Edward. Her expression called for mercy and Logan would take heed. Even youngsters like Edward were smitten with Sophia. The rich old coot had it right.

It was hard not to love Sophia.

He was about to call Luke when his brother's Chevy Silverado pulled up next to his truck. Luke and Constance got out and Constance ran over to Edward. The boy was nearly squeezed to death with a big grandmotherly hug. Edward gave her his explanation of what had happened and how he'd sent Blackie for help because he didn't want to leave Sophia alone.

"Luke, take the boy and Constance back to the ranch, will you?" Logan said after all the apologies were made. Sophia made sure Edward's actions were painted in a better light than he deserved, in Logan's opinion. And Constance was happy enough to have her grandson back safely. She promised to make sure Edward understood the consequences of what he'd done. Logan thought the boy skated, but his concern now was for Sophia. "And call off the search."

"Will do." Luke glanced at Sophia's injured foot and took a step toward her.

"Luke." Logan gave his brother a firm warning. "I've got this."

Luke's gaze darted to Sophia. She sat regally on that boulder, doing a good job of concealing her physical pain with her arms crossed over her body and displeasure curling her mouth. "Sure thing, bro. You just let me know how that works out for you."

Logan waited for Luke's engine to roar to life, and the three of them were well on the road before he walked over to Sophia. She eyed him suspiciously and flinched a little when he leaned close to inspect her injured leg. He took it as a good sign that he still made her nervous and at this point; he'd take any crumb she offered.

He pushed his hat back on his head and lifted her ankle gently.

"Ow!"

"Did you hear a snap when you stepped in that gopher hole?" he asked.

"No."

"Probably just sprained, then."

She looked away. "Great."

Logan finished his inspection of her leg and set it down with care.

"You were too easy on the boy."

"It wasn't his fault. He honestly had no idea that I'd be frightened by the notes he sent. He's a shy boy who's had a rough life and I think he wanted us to be friends."

"The boy is smitten with you." He rubbed the back of his neck and sighed. "I get that. You have that effect on most men."

"That's not true."

She was being argumentative, and considering that he was her ride back to the ranch, Logan had to give her credit for her feisty attitude. "Let's say that you're right and I'm wrong."

"I am right," she said with a curt nod as if the subject was closed.

Logan sat his butt down next to her on the boulder. He stretched out his long legs, his boots digging into the earth. The soft purr of the lazy stream flowing by and a few birds flitting from tree to tree filled the silence. "Okay, then it's just me who thinks you're a beautiful, smart, kindhearted, hardworking woman with a body that makes me want to cry, and those big—"

"Logan!"

Logan chuckled and the movement knocked his shoulder against hers. "Eyes, Sophia. I was going to say big eyes."

Sophia didn't crack a smile. Her face crumpled with confusion. "You're not making any sense. You don't think those things about me. You've let me know exactly what you think of me, and it doesn't bear repeating."

"I know I was scared half out of my mind when I thought you were missing. Horrible thoughts entered my head of a stalker getting to you. I was going a little crazy until I pulled up and saw you on this boulder. I know I wouldn't have survived if anything had happened to you. I was wrong about you, Sophia."

"You were cruel to me. Those things you said."

"I didn't know you were listening. I said those things to Luke, because…I've always been a little jealous of your friendship. And I knew then what I was afraid to admit to myself up until today. I love you, Sophia. I love you so much, it scares me silly."

Sophia's ankle throbbed and she thought for certain the pain had gone to her head. She was sure she was hearing things. "You *love* me?"

"I've never said those words to a woman before. I've never wanted to. I've never believed in true love. Until now."

"So you don't believe all those awful things about me?"

"If you explain it to me, I'm ready to listen. I'll believe you, no matter what."

Sophia didn't hesitate. She'd wanted to clear the air for a long time. She'd wanted Logan to hear the truth and really have him hear her. "I didn't marry Gordon for his money, you have to know that. He was a friend and I needed his help."

Sophia spent the next few minutes explaining about Gordon Gregory and his granddaughter Amanda. She told Logan about the friendship that had developed afterward and how Gordon had offered to help both Louisa and Sophia when they'd had nowhere else to turn.

"I didn't ask for anything else from Gordon. And I never slept with him, Logan. I never did. That's why we divorced. After my mother passed, he put pressure on me. He claims he fell in love with me, but I didn't love him. I never felt that way about him." She repeated, "I never slept with him."

"But you slept with me."

Sophia closed her eyes briefly, taking a leap of faith again because there was nothing left for her to lose. Because everything she wanted was right here in front of her. She placed her faith and trust in Logan one last time. "Yes, I slept with you. I fell in love. Don't ask me why, Logan. I have no idea why I love you. By all rights I should have fallen in love with

Luke. But I don't feel that way about your brother. He and I are friends. Period."

Logan turned his body to fully face Sophia. She saw a look in his eyes, the same look Randall Slade had for her mother. The same look that every woman deserved to see in the eyes of the man she loved. "You love me?"

She nodded.

His lips rose in a quick smile and he took her hand, applying sweet pressure. He spoke in a voice steeped with determination. "I don't want our love to go to waste, Sophia. Not the way our parents' did. I can't deny what I feel for you anymore. Ever since that kiss in high school, I think I've always known there was something special between us. Something undeniable."

"I felt it, too," she whispered. "And I don't want our love to go to waste, either."

"Forgive me for being hard on you. I was a fool."

Hearing Logan admit his past mistakes and ask for her forgiveness was an intoxicating gift from the man she loved. "I think I can forgive you."

Logan's arms came around her. Gently he lifted her from the rock and cradled her, taking care with her swollen ankle. He brought his mouth ever so close. "Kiss me, Sophia."

She smiled. "You won't think I'm easy?"

"Nothing about you and me is easy, sweetheart."

She brought her mouth close and brushed her lips over his softly. Tension released from his body, his stance no longer rigidly defensive. The walls of mistrust and suspicion he'd built to protect himself came tumbling down around her until what remained was the rightness of their love.

It was Logan's ultimate surrender.

The battle was over. The kiss they shared was their beacon, a bright glow of light guiding their way out of the darkness. He loved her and she loved him. It had been complicated

between them for most of their lives. But now it was just...
simple.

"I love you, Logan Slade."

He kissed her tenderly and when he spoke his voice was
husky and rich with reverence. "Marry me, Sophia. Live with
me on Sunset Ranch. Be my partner, my friend, my wife."

Sophia set her palm on the sharp handsome plane of his
cheekbone and gazed deeply into his eyes. "I was never any
of those things before, but I want to be everything to you now.
Yes, Logan. I'll marry you."

Logan smiled, love shining in his eyes. "I'm a lucky man."

"And I'm a happy woman."

He took off his Stetson and in one smooth move, placed it
on her head, giving it a tug to secure the fit. "I can't wait to
make you a Slade. My father always said you were a woman
who'd make a fine wife."

They were words Sophia never thought she'd hear from
Logan.

"Do you think your father set this up?"

Logan contemplated for a moment. "From his grave?"

"No, but maybe before he died? I could never figure out
why he was so generous with me in his will. Do you think
he wanted me to find love on Sunset Ranch?"

Logan gave the notion some thought. "It's possible. My dad
loved you like a daughter and, Lord above, everyone knew
how much he loved the ranch."

Sophia's eyes misted with tears. "And his boys. He loved
his sons, Logan. Don't forget that."

Logan nodded and clear understanding filled his eyes.
"Maybe it was his secret wish that you marry a Slade, sweetheart."

"It would be nice to think so. Can you ever forgive your
father, Logan?"

"If he brought you to me I can surely forgive him."

Sophia smiled and he wiped a tear from her cheek. "Then let's just believe it as truth."

"I can do that."

Something good and long-lasting would come from Randall's love for Louisa.

And perhaps their love hadn't been wasted after all.

Sophia clung to that notion as hard and as tight as she held on to her cowboy.

With Logan's love surrounding her, she could finally call Sunset Ranch…home.

* * * * *

"I never had any intention of bullying you, Miss Sullivan."

Tori tried not to watch the soft curve of his lips as he spoke to her, but he was so close she had little choice. She remembered how she'd once fantasized about kissing those lips. Of course, that was before he turned on her and threw her out of his company onto her rear end. The surge of anger doused the old memories as her gaze met his.

"What then?" she asked, her voice laced with sarcasm. "Were you going to take your friend's suggestion and seduce me? Certainly you're so masterful in the bedroom that one good romp would change my mind, right?"

Wade moved a fraction of an inch closer to her. For a moment, Tori tensed, thinking he might be leaning in to kiss her. She wanted him to, and she didn't. She pressed a gentle hand to his chest. She could feel his heart racing just as quickly as her own. He was not immune to his own game.

They were both playing with fire.

Dear Reader,

I'm so excited to share this book with you. *Undeniable Demands* kicks off my very first series—SECRETS OF EDEN. When I first started writing for Mills & Boon® Desire™, I immersed myself in the world of wealthy, powerful alpha males. My first two heroes had family money to help them start their business empires, so this time I wanted to write some self-made heroes. I wanted a group of men who had defied the odds, overcome tragedy and made themselves into the sexy alpha heroes that Desire readers know and love.

But everyone has some baggage from their past, and the heroes of SECRETS OF EDEN are no exception. The foster brothers share a dark secret that threatens not only their family and their livelihood but their chance to find love. At the same time, their secret is what brings Wade and Victoria together. And boy, do the sparks fly! The spunky environmental architect isn't about to make anything easy for Wade, and it was fun to write about their tempestuous relationship.

I can't wait for you to fall in love with the whole Eden family, as I have. If you enjoy Wade and Tori's story, tell me by visiting my website at www.andrealaurence.com, like my fan page on Facebook or follow me on Twitter. I love to hear from my readers!

Enjoy!

Andrea

UNDENIABLE
DEMANDS

BY
ANDREA LAURENCE

MILLS & BOON

All the characters in this book have no existence outside the imagination of the author, and have no relation whatsoever to anyone bearing the same name or names. They are not even distantly inspired by any individual known or unknown to the author, and all the incidents are pure invention.

All Rights Reserved including the right of reproduction in whole or in part in any form. This edition is published by arrangement with Harlequin Enterprises II B.V./S.à.r.l. The text of this publication or any part thereof may not be reproduced or transmitted in any form or by any means, electronic or mechanical, including photocopying, recording, storage in an information retrieval system, or otherwise, without the written permission of the publisher.

This book is sold subject to the condition that it shall not, by way of trade or otherwise, be lent, resold, hired out or otherwise circulated without the prior consent of the publisher in any form of binding or cover other than that in which it is published and without a similar condition including this condition being imposed on the subsequent purchaser.

® and ™ are trademarks owned and used by the trademark owner and/or its licensee. Trademarks marked with ® are registered with the United Kingdom Patent Office and/or the Office for Harmonisation in the Internal Market and in other countries.

Published in Great Britain 2013
by Mills & Boon, an imprint of Harlequin (UK) Limited,
Eton House, 18-24 Paradise Road, Richmond, Surrey TW9 1SR

© Andrea Laurence 2013

ISBN: 978 0 263 90467 3
ebook ISBN: 978 1 472 00587 8

51-0313

Harlequin (UK) policy is to use papers that are natural, renewable and recyclable products and made from wood grown in sustainable forests. The logging and manufacturing processes conform to the legal environmental regulations of the country of origin.

Printed and bound in Spain
by Blackprint CPI, Barcelona

Andrea Laurence has been a lover of reading and writing stories since she learned her ABCs. She always dreamed of seeing her work in print and is thrilled to finally be able to share her books with the world. A dedicated West Coast girl transplanted to the Deep South, she's working on her own "happily ever after" with her boyfriend and their collection of animals that shed like nobody's business. You can contact Andrea at her website, www.andrealaurence.com.

To Vicki Lewis Thompson, Rhonda Nelson
and Kira Sinclair

You're the best plotting partners a girl could have.
You helped me take the smallest kernel of an idea
and develop it into a great multibook series.
I look forward to many more years of creativity,
laughter and good food with my ladies.

One

Wade hated the snow. Always had. You'd think a man born and raised in New England would feel differently or leave, but he'd done neither. Every November when the first few flakes started falling, a part of his soul would shrivel up until spring. That was why he'd booked himself a trip to Jamaica for the week before Christmas. He'd planned to return to the Edens', as always, for the holiday, but the frantic call he'd received from his foster sister, Julianne, had changed everything.

He had been loath to tell his assistant to cancel the trip, but perhaps if all went well, he could use the reservation after Christmas. He could ring in the New Year on a beach, drinking something frothy, with thoughts of his troubles buried deep.

Interesting choice of words.

The BMW SUV wound its way down the two-lane

road that led to the Garden of Eden Christmas Tree Farm. Wade preferred to drive his roadster, but rural Connecticut in winter was just not the place for it, so he'd left it in Manhattan. The SUV had snow tires, chains in the back and enough clearance not to scrape on chunks of ice in poorly cleared areas.

Spying the large red apple-shaped sign that marked the entrance to his foster parents' Christmas tree farm, Wade breathed a sigh of relief. He hadn't realized until that moment that he'd been holding his breath. Even under the less-than-ideal circumstances, returning home always made him feel better.

The farm was the only home he'd ever really had. None of the other foster homes had felt like one. He had no warm memories of living with his great-aunt before that, nor of his early years with his mother. But the Garden of Eden was just that: paradise. Especially for an abandoned young boy who could just as easily have become a career criminal as a millionaire in real estate.

The Edens changed everything. For him and every other child who had come to live there. He owed that couple his life. They were his parents, without question. Wade didn't know who his father was and had only seen his mother once since she dropped him at her aunt's doorstep as a toddler. When he thought of home and family, he thought of the farm and the family the Edens had pulled together.

They were able to have only one child of their own, their daughter, Julianne. For a time it seemed that their dreams of a house bustling with children who would help on the farm and one day take over the family business had been dashed. But then they decided to renovate an old barn into a bunkhouse perfect for rowdy boys and started taking in foster children.

Wade had been the first. Julianne had been in pig-tails when he arrived, dragging her favorite doll behind her. Wade had been in his share of foster homes, and this time just felt different. He was not a burden. Not a way to get a check from the state. He was their son.

Which is why he wished he was visiting them for another reason. In his own mind, disappointing his parents would be the greatest sin he could commit. Even worse than the one he'd committed fifteen years ago that got him into this mess.

Wade turned the SUV into the driveway, then by-passed the parking lot and took the small road behind their large Federal-style house to where the family kept their cars. It was nearing the middle of the afternoon on a Friday, but even so, there were at least ten customer cars in the lot. It was December 21—only a few days until Christmas. His mother, Molly, would be in the gift shop, pushing sugar cookies, cider and hot choco-late on folks while they waited for Ken or one of the employees to haul and bag their new tree.

Wade felt the sudden, familiar urge to start trimming trees and hauling them out to people's cars. He'd done it for all of his teenage years and every Christmas break from Yale. It came naturally to want to jump back into the work. But first things first. He had to take care of the business that had brought him here instead of the warm beaches of Jamaica.

Julianne's call had been unexpected. None of the kids were very good about calling or visiting their par-ents or each other like they should. They were all busy, all successful, the way the Edens had wanted them to be. But their success also made it easy to forget to make time for the important people in their lives.

When Julianne had shown up at the farm for Thanksgiving with little warning, she'd been in for quite the surprise. Their father, Ken, was recovering from a heart attack. They hadn't called any of the kids because they didn't want them worrying about it or the crippling hospital bills.

Wade, Heath, Xander, Brody—any of the boys could've written a check and taken care of their problems, but Ken and Molly insisted they had it under control. Unfortunately, their solution was to sell a few plots of land they couldn't use for growing trees. They couldn't understand why the kids were so upset. And of course, the kids couldn't tell their parents the truth. That secret needed to remain buried in the past. And Wade was here to make sure it stayed that way.

If he was lucky, he could take one of the four-wheelers out to the property, buy the land back from the new owner and return before Molly could start wondering what he was up to. He wouldn't keep the purchase a secret from his parents, but he'd certainly rather they not fret over the whole situation until it was done.

Wade found the house empty, as expected. He left a note on the worn kitchen table, slipped into his heavy coat and boots and went out to grab one of the four-wheelers. He could've driven his SUV, but he didn't want to pull up in an expensive car and start waving money around at people.

Heath and Brody had both made visits to the farm since Julianne broke the news. Digging up as much information as they could, they found out that the person who had bought the smallest parcel of land was already living out there in some kind of camper. That sounded positive to him. They might need the money more than the land. But if they thought some rich guy was bullying them to sell it, they'd clamp down. Or jack up the price.

Wade took the four-wheeler down the well-worn path that went through the center of the farm. After selling eighty-five acres, the Edens still had two hundred acres left. Almost all of it was populated with balsam and Fraser fir trees. The northeastern portion of the property was sloped and rocky. They'd never had much success planting trees out there, so he'd understood why Ken had opted to sell it. He just wished his father hadn't.

By the time he rounded a corner on the trail and neared the border of the Edens' property, it was a little after two-thirty. The sky was clear and blue and the sun's rays pounded down on the snow, making it nearly blinding despite his sunglasses. He slowed and pulled out the new surveyor's map Brody had downloaded. The eighty-five acres that his parents had sold were split into two large tracts and one small one. Comparing the map to the GPS location on his phone, he could tell that just over the rise was the smallest, a ten-acre residential property. He was fairly certain this was the one he was after.

Wade refolded the map and looked around for any familiar landmarks. He'd deliberately chosen a spot he would remember. There had been a crooked maple tree and a rock that looked like a giant turtle. He scanned the landscape, but it appeared to him as though all the trees were crooked, and all the rocks were buried under a foot of snow. It was impossible to know for sure if this chunk of the property was the right one.

Damn. He'd thought for certain that he would know the spot when he saw it. That night fifteen years ago remained etched in his memory no matter how hard he tried to forget it. It was one of those moments that changes your whole life. Where you make a decision, right or wrong, and have to live with it forever.

Still, Wade was certain this was the right area. He didn't remember traveling far enough to reach the other plots. He'd been in too big a hurry to roam around the property all night trying to find the perfect spot. He eyed another maple tree, this one more crooked than the others. That had to be the one. He'd just have to buy the land back and hope that once spring came around, he would find the turtle rock at its base and know he'd bought the right plot.

Surging forward through the snow, he continued up to the rise and then started descending into the clearing toward what looked like some sort of shimmering silver mirage.

He pulled closer and realized it was the midafternoon sun reflecting off the superbly polished aluminum siding of an old Airstream trailer. You could have got a suntan from the rays coming off that thing. Parked beside it was an old Ford pickup truck with dually tires to haul the twenty-foot monster of a camper.

Wade stopped and killed the engine on the four-wheeler. There was no sign of life from inside the camper yet. Brody had searched online for the property sale records and found the new owner was V. A. Sullivan. Cornwall was a fairly small town, and he didn't remember any Sullivans when he went to school, so they must be new to the area. That was just as well. He didn't need to deal with anyone who remembered his troublesome days before the Edens and might give him grief.

His boots crunched through the snow until he reached the rounded doorway. It had a small window in it that he watched for movement when he knocked. Nothing. No sound of people inside, either.

Just great. He'd come all the way out here for nothing.

Wade was about to turn and head back home when he heard the telltale click of a shotgun safety. His head spun to the left, following the sound, and he found himself in the sights. The woman was standing about twenty feet away, bundled just as heavily as he was in a winter coat with a knit cap and sunglasses hiding most of her features. Long strands of fiery red hair peeked out from her hat and blew in the chilly wind. The distinctive color immediately caught his eye. He'd known a woman with hair that color a long time ago. It had been beautiful, like liquid flames. Appropriate, since he was playing with fire now.

On reflex, his hands went up. Getting shot by some overprotective, rural militia type was not on his agenda for the day. "Hey, there," he called out, trying to sound as friendly and nonthreatening as he could.

The woman hesitated, and then the shotgun dropped slightly. "Can I help you?"

"Are you Mrs. Sullivan?" Hopefully Mr. Sullivan wasn't out in the woods with a shotgun of his own.

"*Miss* Sullivan," she corrected. "What's it to you?"

A single female. Even better. Wade had a certain charm about him that served him well with the fairer sex. He smiled widely. "My name is Wade Mitchell. I wanted to talk to you about possibly—"

"Arrogant, pigheaded real-estate developer Wade Mitchell?" The woman took a few steps forward.

Wade frowned. She didn't seem to care for him at all. He wished to God the woman wasn't so bundled up so he could see who she was. Maybe then he could figure out why the mention of his name seemed to agitate her. Of course, he was wearing just as much winter gear as she was. "Yes, ma'am, although I wouldn't go so far as to use those adjectives. I wanted to see if you would be interested in…"

His words dropped off as the shotgun rose again. "Aw, hell," she lamented. "I thought it looked kinda like you under all those layers, but I thought, why would Wade Mitchell be in Cornwall making my life hell again after all this time?"

Wade's eyes widened behind his dark sunglasses. "I have no intention of making your life hell, Miss Sullivan."

"Get off my land."

"I'm sorry, have I done something to you?" He scanned his brain. Had he dated a Sullivan? Beaten up her brother? He had no memory of what he could've done to piss this woman off so badly.

The woman stomped across the snow, closing the gap between them with the gun still pointed directly at him. She pulled off her sunglasses to study him more closely, revealing a lovely heart-shaped face and pale eyes. Her skin was creamy, the perfect backdrop to the fiery strands of hair framing her face. When her blue eyes met his, he noticed a challenge there, as though she was daring him not to remember her.

Fortunately, Wade had an excellent memory. One good enough to know that he was in trouble. The fiery redhead glaring at him was a hard woman to forget. He'd certainly tried over the years, but from time to time, she'd slipped into his subconscious and haunted his dreams with her piercing, ice-blue gaze. A gaze that reflected the hurt of betrayal that he couldn't understand.

Property owner V. A. Sullivan was none other than Victoria Sullivan: green architect, eco-warrior and the employee he'd fired from his company seven years ago.

His stomach instantly sank. Of all the people who could've bought this property, it had to be her. Victoria Sullivan. The first person he'd ever fired from his company. It had pained him at the time, but he'd really had no choice. He had a strict policy on ethics violations. She hadn't taken the news well. And judging by her stiff posture and tightly gripped firearm, she was still upset about it.

"Victoria!" he said with a wide smile, trying to sound pleasantly surprised to see her after all this time. "I had no idea you were living out here now."

"Miss Sullivan," she corrected.

Wade nodded. "Of course. Could you please drop the gun? I'm unarmed."

"You won't be when the cops come." Her words were as icy cold as the snow, but eventually the gun disengaged and dropped to her side.

She pushed past him to the front door of the Airstream, pulling it open and climbing the stairs. "What do you want, Mr. Mitchell?"

As she hung at the top of the steps, looking back at him, Wade realized he needed to change his tactic, and fast. His original plan had been to tell the owner that he wanted the property for one of his development projects. If he told her that, she'd refuse him just to ruin his plans.

He'd have to appeal to a different side of her. That is, if he could explain himself before she started shooting.

"Miss Sullivan, I'd like to buy back this property from you."

* * *

Tori hung on the steps, the rage slowly uncoiling in her belly. This man was determined to ruin everything she held dear. He had taken away her reputation and very nearly her career. His turning on her suddenly had also damaged her ability to trust men. Out of the blue, he'd accused her of terrible things and tossed her out. She'd lost her first real apartment after he fired her.

And now that she was trying to settle down and establish herself again, he wanted to destroy her plans for her dream home. She just knew it. Her jaw set firmly, she made her decision before he even asked the question. If he were on fire, she wouldn't bother to spit on him.

"It's not for sale." She slipped inside and let the door slam behind her.

She was pulling off her coat, about to toss it onto the foldout bed, when she heard the door of the trailer open behind her. Tori spun on her heel and found the bastard standing in her tiny kitchen. He'd slipped out of his winter coat and tugged off his hat as he entered. He stood there now in a pair of dress pants and a plaid button-down shirt. The hunter-green of the top made his own green eyes seem even darker and more intriguing than she remembered. Because of the stocking cap he'd worn, his short, dark brown hair was messier than she'd ever seen it.

Without his slick suits and perfect hair, he looked nothing like the real-estate giant who had ruled over his company from the top floor. But he still had a commanding presence. She'd forgotten how tall he was: at least six foot two, with a powerful build. The large man seemed to take up all the space in her trailer, which had always had the perfect amount of room for her. It was as though he'd sucked up all the air, making her oddly warm and her camper uncomfortably small.

And she hated that about him.

Without hesitating, she picked up her shotgun again. Truthfully, it was loaded with shells full of recycled rubber pellets. She carried it with her to the compost bin in case she needed to scare off any foraging critters. She'd caught a black bear in the bin last week. The rubber pellets would send animals scurrying without seriously hurting them. Hopefully it would do the same with Wade Mitchell.

"Do you mind stepping back outside? I spent a lot of money to renovate this trailer and I'm not going to ruin it by shooting you in here."

Wade had only a momentary flash of alarm in his eyes before he smiled at her in a way that made her cheeks flush and her knees weaken. She remembered feeling that way whenever he would walk down the hallway past her cubicle and greet her with "good morning." She'd been fresh out of college and in awe of the two young mavericks with their up-and-coming real-estate development company. Alex Stanton was the golden playboy, but she was instantly drawn to the darker, more serious Wade. Then and now, his wide grin and strong, aristocratic features usually got him his way.

If she wasn't careful, she might fall prey to them again. She knew better than to trust a guy like him.

"Miss Sullivan, can we please talk about this without you constantly threatening to shoot me?"

"There's nothing to talk about." Tori kept the gun in one hand while she pulled off her hat and scarf with the other. She was burning up, and it had nothing to do with her new propane heating system. It was Wade and her overheated and long-ignored libido. She hated that the man who'd betrayed and fired her could still send her pulse racing after all this time. "And it's rude to come inside uninvited, so you deserve to be shot."

"I apologize," he said, laying his coat across the bench seat of her dining table. "But it is imperative that I discuss this with you today."

Oh, she was sure it was. No doubt he had bought the forty-acre property beside her and wanted her additional ten to add to whatever ridiculous project he was developing out here. There might be an army of backhoes and land movers over the horizon just waiting for her to sign off so they could start their work. But she wasn't giving up this land. This purchase had been years in the making. Her genealogy research had been what lured her up here, but from the first time she'd set foot in the area, she knew this was where she wanted to build her home.

Finding out the Edens were selling some property had been the chance of a lifetime. The lot was perfect. It sloped down, slightly, but would allow her to design a stilted, multistory home that had a living room with a wide vista of windows overlooking the valley below. Being surrounded by two hundred acres of tree farm on two sides guaranteed she wouldn't have a strip mall out her back door anytime soon.

She had a couple months in between projects to start designing and building her house. It was the perfect opportunity just when she had the time and money to jump on it. And he couldn't have it.

"I know that you're used to getting your way, Mr. Mitchell, but I'm afraid it isn't going to happen this time."

On cue, her electric teapot began to chirp on the

counter and spit out steam. She'd turned it on before she'd stepped out to put some trash in her compost bin, and now it was ready for her to extend some unintended hospitality. When she turned to look at Wade again, he had seated himself at her dining-table booth, a look of smug expectation in his eyes.

With a sigh, she set down the shotgun. It was hard to make tea when you were holding a heavy, loaded firearm.

"May I ask how much you paid for the land?"

"You may not, although I'm sure it's public record somewhere if you take the time to have one of the corporate minions you haven't fired look for it." She pulled out two teacups from her bamboo plywood cabinet above the sink. She shook her loose leaf tea into two infusers, put them in the cups and poured the hot water over them.

"My guess would be about a hundred and twenty-five thousand. There're no utilities run out here yet."

Tori refused to look at him. Of course the real estate guy could nail the price within a few thousand dollars. "What's your point?"

"My point is that I'll offer you double what you paid for it."

At that, Tori fumbled the jar of organic honey and sent it crashing to the Marmoleum floor. Fortunately, it didn't shatter. She quickly crouched down to grab it, but he had reached out for it as well and beat her to it. He held out the jar to her. Tori looked down at him, only inches away, and felt a familiar and unwelcome tingle deep in her belly. When she took the jar from his hand, her fingers brushed his and the tingle turned into a surge right to her core.

Jerking upright as though she'd been burned by his

touch, she quickly recovered and removed the infusers, then added a dollop of the honey to each cup. She plunked his tea down in front of him and took a seat on the opposite side of the table.

"That's ridiculous." She said the words knowing she meant both her reaction to him and his offer for her land. Tori knew better than to let herself fall for Wade's good looks or his seemingly good offer.

"Maybe. But that's what I'm offering."

"You're hiding something," she accused. "You're the guy who built your business buying cheap buildings and flipping them for a fortune. No way you'd pay one penny more than is necessary to turn a profit on whatever project you're wanting to build out here."

Wade turned to look her in the eye. A lock of brown hair had fallen into his face, giving him a boyish charm she had to steel her resolve against. "I'm not building anything out here. This isn't about money."

Tori scoffed. "You don't get to be a millionaire before you're thirty unless you're born into money or driven by it. Either way, everything is about money."

Wade watched her. He took a sip of his tea before he answered. "This is about family. That's more important to me than even money. This property belonged to my parents. They sold it without telling me or my other siblings. We never would've let them do that if we'd known. They worked too hard their whole lives for this land. We grew up here. Our childhood was here. If we'd known they were having financial problems, I would've taken care of things before they resorted to this."

Tori felt herself being sucked in by his story. The expression on his handsome face was one of sincere concern. The words sounded so convincing. But this was the same man who had praised her potential and work ethic, then fired her the next day. Ryan had also seemed sincere, and nearly every word out of his mouth over the past two years had been a lie.

She had been raised with a naive spirit by hippies who wanted only to experience life and culture. They didn't have a malicious bone in their bodies and never thought other people did, either.

Life had taught Tori differently. Wade had taught her differently. He had heard her pleas of innocence and turned his back on them. He hadn't believed her. So why should she believe him now?

The people who had sold her this land—Molly and Ken Eden—were a very sweet older couple. No way they'd spawned a son like Mitchell. They didn't even have the same last name. It wasn't even a well-planned lie. She wanted to be insulted by his lack of faith in her ability to see through his crap. Did he think she would just melt into a puddle at his feet the minute he knocked on the door and flashed those deep green eyes at her? Or started waving cash?

She didn't need Wade's money. She'd paid cash for this property. She was one of the most highly sought after green architects in America. She'd traveled thousands of miles in this Airstream to build environmentally friendly buildings, homes and businesses. Tori had several large and successful projects in Seattle, Santa Fe and San Francisco. She was wrapping up one in Philadelphia just after the first of the year. She did well enough that she could laugh at his offer. But it couldn't hurt to push him and see how far he was willing to take this.

"What if I said I would sell it back to you for half a million?" There was no way the land was worth that much unless there was oil, gold or diamonds hidden beneath her feet. She doubted it, though. She'd never heard of Wade Mitchell being interested in any of those things. The only thing about land he cared for was what he could build on top of it.

Wade didn't even flinch. "I would get out my checkbook and sign on the dotted line so you could find an even better piece of land and everyone would be happy. Let me assure you that nothing is more important than preserving my family and my history."

Wow. He was certainly desperate for this land. She almost felt bad for him. Any other person might have immediately given in and made his day. Four times the value was a great offer. A crazy offer. One that she was probably crazy to turn down. Even with her success, half a million was quite a lump of cash. Tori could certainly do a lot with it: buy new land, build her dream house without a mortgage attached to it, get a new hybrid pickup truck. She had to admit, if it were any other person sitting across the table from her, she'd probably take the money and tow her trailer off into the sunset.

But it wasn't any other person. It was Wade Mitchell. And she wasn't about to sell him this land. Not for any price. Just because it was worth it to watch him squirm. This would be as close to payback as she would ever get. It was his bad luck that he wanted *her* land.

"You're really quite good," she said, nodding and watching her tea instead of his handsome face. She wouldn't let herself get pulled in and swayed by his mesmerizing eyes and fabricated sob story. She'd already caught herself being a sucker once this year, and that was enough. Maybe if he came around in a few weeks, she'd let him be her dumb mistake of the New

Year. "Did you practice that speech long or was that off the cuff?"

Wade stiffened, pushing the half-empty cup of tea aside and shelving the charm. "Is all this animosity over your termination years ago?"

Now it was Tori's turn to stiffen in her chair. He made her seem petty for holding that over him all these years later. "Absolutely. I don't take affronts to my reputation lightly."

"You weren't worried about your reputation when you slept with one of our suppliers and put my company in jeopardy."

"I didn't sleep with anybody. I told you then that I didn't do any of the things you accused me of. Nothing has changed. Just because you didn't believe me doesn't mean I wasn't telling the truth."

"They were serious charges, and I needed to deal with them as such. I did what I had to do."

"And I'm doing what I have to do. I'm keeping this land. It's mine. Whether or not I like you or resent what you did is irrelevant."

"This isn't about me or you and your damaged pride. This is about Ken and Molly Eden and everything they worked for. I want to give them back what's rightfully theirs."

Tori straightened and shot him as lethal a gaze as she could manage. "You mean, *mine*. I signed those papers at the lawyer's office two months ago. I didn't hold a gun to their heads and make them sell me this land."

"Wouldn't have surprised me if you did," he said bitterly, glancing over at the shotgun sitting on the counter.

"They sold it all on their own. I paid them full asking price and covered all my own closing expenses, so it's not like I cheated them, either. I don't know whether you're their son or not, Mr. *Mitchell,* but let me just tell you that if you *are* their son, you're a crappy one. They told me about Ken's heart attack and all their medical expenses. Where have you been? In Manhattan? Worrying about making money?"

"You think I don't know that?" he challenged. Wade's eyes flashed with a touch of a temper she'd seen years before. "I'm not proud of it, but I can fix it."

Tori stood up from her seat. "You're just going to have to find another way to soothe your conscience. Send them on a cruise or something, because you aren't going to browbeat me into selling this land. And that's final. Please leave."

Wade stood, bringing his head a hairbreadth away from scraping the top of her camper. He took a step toward her, and his body loomed large and intimidating in such close proximity.

Tori couldn't help the surge of awareness that ran through her body as he came near. Apparently it was far easier to despise him from a distance. It had been a long time since she'd been in the same room as Wade, and she'd certainly never been this close to him, but her body remembered him. With him inches away, looking down at her with a focused, penetrating intensity, her spine wanted to turn to jelly. His warm scent, a familiar mix of spicy cologne and salty skin, swirled around her with every breath she drew into her lungs.

She finally took a step back, pressing herself against the kitchen counter. She didn't like being this close to Wade. It messed with her focus, and that just made her even more irritated. Tori couldn't let him use his size or sexuality to intimidate her.

"This isn't over," he said, pinning her with his dark green eyes before grabbing his coat and walking out into the cold.

Two

Wade remembered Victoria Sullivan as being smart and beautiful. Apparently she was also the most infuriating and stubborn woman he'd ever encountered.

Wade stomped back to his four-wheeler and stood there a moment, letting the cold sink in and douse the aggravating mix of anger and attraction surging through his veins. When he was back in control, he shrugged into his coat, jumped on the ATV and peeled out of her yard in a doughnut as he used to do as a teenager. The back tires sent a sheet of snow flying against the side of her trailer. It was juvenile, but she seemed to bring out the worst in him.

He was fuming as he plowed through the snow. It should be illegal for a woman that gorgeous to have a mouth that irritating. Honestly, once she'd peeled out of her jacket and revealed a snug pair of jeans and a fitted, long-sleeved T-shirt, he'd almost forgotten why he was there. It wasn't until she picked up her shotgun again that he realized he'd followed her inside without her permission.

Victoria had been one of his best and brightest architects. He'd hired her straight out of college when the company he and Alex had started was still small and spending more than it earned. She'd contributed quite a bit to making their first few big projects a success. He'd even considered asking her out to dinner. But then his assistant had come to him with concerns about seeing Victoria at a restaurant looking a little too cozy with one of their potential suppliers. She had been quite vocal about giving the man an upcoming contract, and the implication was clear. He fired her on the spot. Part of him regretted that. And not just because she had knockout curves, flawless skin and long, fiery red hair that made him warm under the collar.

He had wanted to believe her when she said she didn't do it. The thought of her with another man nearly made him crazy. But the logical part of his brain was infuriated by her audacious attempt to influence corporate contracts like that. Sleeping with a potential contractor was just as bad as taking bribes from one. Both compromised a person's objectivity and put the ethics of his company in question.

He would not have it, so he terminated her. He never dreamed the decision would come back to haunt him.

If she were any other woman, he would've asked her to dinner to talk over his offer and kissed her to keep the inflammatory words from flying out of her mouth. Her temper, as spicy as her hair, was a massive turn-on. He had a weakness for redheads.

But she wasn't another woman. She was holding on to seven years of bitterness along with the key to something more important to him than anything else. Protecting his family was his number one priority. Toying with Victoria like a cat with a mouse could cost him dearly. He needed her to sell him this land. He couldn't fail. As much as he'd like to resolve their differences between the sheets, it wasn't the answer in this situation. He doubted it would sway her, and she'd probably shoot him if he tried to kiss her.

"Arrogant and pigheaded," Wade grumbled, turning to steer the four-wheeler down the center aisle of trees toward the entrance. She thought she knew so much. Well, she forgot rich, powerful, ruthless and determined Wade Mitchell came in the same package. He would secure that land and protect his family one way or another.

Wade came to an abrupt stop as an old pickup truck, draped in Christmas lights and garland, pulled in front of him. Piled into the trailer it towed was a crowd of bundled-up people sitting on bales of hay and singing Christmas carols. The driver, Owen, threw a hand up at Wade, then continued back toward the house.

Hayrides, Santa visits, sugar cookies and hot chocolate. Picking out a tree at the Garden of Eden wasn't just a shopping trip. It was an experience. On the weekends in December, the farm was a madhouse. And it had to be. A good portion of their income came from just this one month. Sure, they did other things throughout the year, but Christmas tree farms depended on a good Christmas to stay afloat.

And lately, it hadn't been enough.

Wade blamed himself for that. When the boys grew up and moved away, the Edens had to hire in help. Owen had always worked on the farm, but as each year went by, more staff was added and their expenses went up. Throw in a mountain of hospital bills and competition from increasingly more realistic fake trees, and the Edens were lucky they'd survived this long.

Wade followed the truck to the house and then veered off to park the ATV back under the awning where they kept it. The farm would be closing soon, so he skipped the house and headed around to the tree-processing area. Heart attack be damned, he found his dad out there with a couple of teenage boys. They were leveling, drilling, shaking and net-bagging all the trees selected by the last round of customers.

As though he'd never left, Wade grabbed a tree and put it on the shaker to remove any loose needles. When it was done, Ken laid the tree out to drill. They carried special stands in the gift shop that ensured a perfectly straight tree.

Wade held it still while Ken drilled.

"You haven't lost your touch, kid. Need a job?"

Wade smiled. "I could work for about a week. Then I've got to get back to town."

"That's fine, fine. We'll be closed by then, anyway." Ken lifted the tree and gave it to one of the boys to run through the netter. When he turned back, he gave Wade a big welcome hug. "Good to see you, son."

"Good to see you, too, Dad. Is that the last of the trees for tonight?"

"Yep. With perfect timing, you've shown up just when all the hard work is finished. Come help me haul these trees out to the parking lot and we'll go see your mother."

Wade grasped a tree in each hand and followed his father through the snow to the parking lot where the last few cars waited for their trees. He watched his father carefully for signs of ill health as he hauled around the trees and helped families tie them into trunks and onto roofs. The man wasn't quite sixty yet and had always appeared to be at the peak of health. His brown hair was mostly gray now, but his blue eyes were still bright and alert, and he didn't hesitate in his physical work. Ken had always been a lean man, but a strong man. If nothing else, he looked a little leaner than usual.

"There's nothing wrong with me, so quit looking for it." Ken snatched the last tree from Wade and hauled it down to the pickup truck waiting for it.

Wade followed him, then stood quietly until the truck pulled away. "I wasn't looking for anything."

"Liar. Everyone has been doing it since your mother told Julianne about that damned attack I had. It was no big deal. I'm fine. They gave me a pill to take. End of story. Don't be sitting around waiting for me to drop dead so you can inherit this place."

Both men chuckled, knowing Wade could buy and sell the farm ten times over and had no interest in getting his claws on any inheritance. "You're looking good to me, Dad."

"Yeah." He slapped Wade on the back and started walking toward the gift shop. "Most days I feel okay. I'm slowing down a little. Feeling my age. But that's just reality. The attack threw me for a loop—just came out of the blue. But between the pills and your mother's dogged determination to feed me oatmeal and vegetables, I should be fine. What are you doing up here so early, Wade? You kids don't usually show up until Christmas Eve."

"I had some time in my schedule, so I thought I'd spend it with you guys. Help out. I know I don't visit enough."

"Well, that's a nice lie. Be sure to tell your mother

that. She'll eat it up. All of you boys are in a panic since you found out we sold that land."

"I wouldn't call it a panic."

"Wouldn't you, now? Four out of the five of you kids have been here in the past month, just randomly checking in. I'm sure Xander would've come, too, if congress wasn't in session fighting over the stupid budget."

Wade shrugged. "Well, what do you expect, Dad? You kept your heart attack a secret. You're having financial trouble and you don't tell any of us. You know we all make good money. There was no need to start selling off the farm."

"I didn't sell off the farm. I sold off some useless rocks and dirt that were costing more money than they earned. And yes, you make a good living. I haven't made a good living in quite a few years. One doesn't make up for the other."

"Dad—"

Ken stopped in front of the gift shop, his hand on the doorknob. "I don't want any of your money, Wade. I don't want a dime from any of you kids. The unexpected medical bills just sucked up our savings. The past few years had been lean and we'd cut back on things, including our insurance, to weather the rough patch. Selling off the extra land let us pay off all the bills, buy a new insurance plan and stick some money away. Less land means less taxes and less for me to worry about. Everything will be just fine."

He pushed open the door to the gift store, ending the conversation. Wade had no choice but to let the subject drop and follow him in. They were instantly bombarded with lights and sounds straight from Santa's workshop. Jingling bells chimed from the door; Christmas music played from overhead speakers. A television in the back was showing holiday cartoons on a constant loop near the area where children could write letters to Santa and play with toys while Mommy shopped and Daddy loaded the tree.

Multicolored lights draped from the ceiling. The scent of pine and mulling spices permeated the room. The fireplace crackled on one wall, inviting customers to sit in rocking chairs and drink the hot chocolate Molly provided free.

"Wade!" The tiny and pleasantly plump woman behind the counter came rushing out to wrap her arms around her oldest boy.

He leaned down to hug her as he'd always had to do, accepting the fussing as she straightened his hair and inspected him for signs of stress or fatigue. She always accused him of working too much. She was probably right, but he'd learned his work ethic from them. "Hey, Mama."

"What a surprise to have you here so soon. Is this just a visit or are you here for the holiday?"

"For the duration."

"That's wonderful," she said, her eyes twinkling with happiness and Christmas lights. "But wait." She paused. "I thought Heath told me you were in Jamaica this week."

"Plans changed. I'm here instead."

"He's checking up on us," Ken called from the counter where he was pouring himself a cup of cider.

"I don't care," she called back. "I'll take him however I can get him." Molly hugged him again, then frowned at her son. "I don't have anything prepared for dinner," she said, aghast at the idea. "I wish I'd known you were coming. I was just going to feed your father a sandwich."

"Whole wheat, fat-free turkey, no mayo, no flavor," Ken grumbled.

"Don't worry about feeding me, Mama. I was going to run into Cornwall to meet a couple of the guys at the Wet Hen and grab a few things from the store. I'll get something to eat at the diner when I'm done."

"All right. But I'm going to the store first thing in the morning, and I'll get stocked up on everything I need to feed a household of boys for the holiday!"

Wade smiled. His mother looked absolutely giddy at the idea of slaving over a stove for five hungry men. He recalled times from his youth when he and the other boys were hitting growth spurts all at once. They couldn't get enough food into their stomachs. Hopefully now they would be easier to take care of.

"Why don't you just give me a list and I'll pick it up while I'm out."

"We don't need your money," Ken called from the rocking chair by the fire, though he didn't turn to face them.

Molly frowned at her husband, and Wade could see she was torn. They did need the money, but Ken was being stubborn. "That would be very nice of you, Wade. I'll write up a few things." She returned to the counter and made out a short list. "This should get us through a few days. I'll go into town for a fresh turkey on Monday morning."

"Okay," he said, leaning down to kiss her cheek. "I'll be back soon. Maybe I'll bring home one of those coconut cream pies from Daisy's."

"That would be lovely. Drive safely in the snow."

Wade stepped through the jingling door and headed

out into the newly darkened night in search of pie, a dozen eggs, a sack of potatoes and some information on Victoria Sullivan.

When Tori got into her truck, she had every intention of going to Daisy's to get something to eat. Maybe swing by the store for some quick and easy-to-prepare food to get her through the holidays when the diner was closed. And yet before she could help herself, her truck pulled into the parking lot of the Wet Hen, the local bar.

"Let's face it," she lamented to her dashboard. "I need a drink."

Just one. Just enough to take the edge off the nerves Wade had agitated. And if it helped suppress the attraction that was buzzing through her veins, all the better.

Tori slid from the cab of her truck, slammed the heavy door behind her and slipped through the door of the Wet Hen. The sign outside claimed the bar had been in business since 1897. Truthfully, it looked as if it had. A renovation wouldn't hurt, but she supposed that was part of its charm. The bar was dark, with old, worn wood on the walls, the floors and the tables. The photos on the walls of various local heroes and the sports memorabilia from the high school seemed to be there more to camouflage cracks in the plaster than anything else. The amber lights did little to illuminate the place, but she supposed a bright light would not only ruin the atmosphere but force the local fire department to condemn it.

The place was pretty quiet for six on a Friday. She imagined business would pick up later unless people were tied up in last-minute holiday activities. She made her way to the empty bar and pulled up a stool. It was from her perch that she heard the laughter of a group of men in the back corner. When she turned, Tori quickly amended her plans. She needed two drinks. Especially with that cocky bastard watching her from the back of the bar.

What was Wade doing here? It was a small town, but wasn't there somewhere else he should be? At home with his all-important family, perhaps? But no, he was throwing back a couple with an odd assortment of old and young men from around town. She recognized her lawyer, Randy Miller, and the old bald sheriff from one of the local television advertisements about the dangers of holiday drinking and driving. There were a couple others there she didn't recognize.

And at the moment, every one of them was looking at her.

Had Wade been talking to them about her? The arrogant curl of his smile and the laughter in the eyes of the other men left no doubt. The irritation pressed up Tori's spine until she was sitting bolt upright in her seat.

She wanted to leave. Not just the bar, but the town. Maybe even the state. In an hour she could have the trailer hooked up and ready to go. Part of the beauty of being nomadic was that you could leave whenever things got uncomfortable. That's what her parents had always done. Hung around somewhere until it got boring or awkward and then moved on to someplace else. Tori had always had trouble imagining living in one community her entire life. There was no place to go when things blew up in your face.

But there were also advantages to being settled: longtime friends and neighbors. People you could count on. Stability. Roots. A place to call home and raise a family. After toying with the idea of having that kind of life with Ryan and then having it all collapse around her, Tori had decided she was tired of running. She might not have the life and family she'd dreamed about with Ryan, but she could have it with someone else if she sat still long enough to have a meaningful relationship.

Cornwall spoke to her. This was where her family had come from and this was where she wanted to stay. But if she was going to build her dream home here, she'd better learn how to tough it out. There was no towing off a house. Being the new girl in a small town was hard enough. Lacking in coping skills wasn't going to help the situation.

If Wade thought he could bully her into selling by turning the town against her, he was in for a surprise. She wasn't going to play along with his charade. If he could play dirty, so could she.

"What can I get you?" The bartender had finally made his way over to her end of the bar. He looked like the kind of guy you'd find at a 115-year-old bar named the Wet Hen. Thin, leathery and gray-haired with an ancient, blurry anchor tattooed on his forearm. The tag pinned to his apron said his name was Skippy. She'd never seen anyone less like a Skippy in her life.

"Gin and tonic with lime." Strong and to the point without stooping to shots. She was tempted to just chug a few big gulps of tequila so she'd no longer care about Wade and his cronies. But she couldn't lose control of her inhibitions, either. Lord knew what kind of trouble she'd get into.

Skippy placed a bowl of peanuts and a napkin on the counter for the drink he quickly poured. He looked as though he had a solid fifty years of experience mixing drinks. When the lowball glass plopped down in front of her, she took a large, quick sip. Damned if that wasn't the best gin and tonic she'd ever had.

Go Skippy.

The alcohol surged straight into her veins. She'd been too agitated to eat anything since Wade left, and her empty stomach gladly soaked up the wicked brew. Three sips into her drink, her worries from earlier had dulled into distant concerns that could be drowned out, along with the loud bursts of male laughter coming from the corner. Thank goodness.

It wasn't until she'd finished her drink and half a bowl of peanuts that she bothered to look in their direction again. Wade was still watching her, although this time the amusement on his face was gone. As the other men around the table chatted, he seemed to have narrowed his focus to her. The expression on his face was quite serious. And openly appreciative of whatever he was seeing.

When their gazes met, Tori felt a jolt of electricity that ran down her spine and prickled across her skin like delicate flames licking at her. It was almost as though his look caressed her physically and drew her into him. It was the same feeling she'd had when he touched her today, handing her the honey jar. Sudden. Unexpected. Powerful.

And totally and completely unwanted.

The clunk of a glass on the bar in front of her startled Tori out of Wade's tractor beam. When she turned, she saw a fresh glass, courtesy of Skippy.

"This one's on the oldest Eden boy."

It took Tori a minute to figure out that probably meant Wade. "You mean the dark-headed one in the green shirt with the smug expression on his face?"

Skippy leaned onto the bar and turned toward the men in the back. "Yep."

"I thought his last name was Mitchell."

"It is."

"Then why'd you call him an Eden boy?"

Skippy shrugged. "'Cause that's what he is."

Tori frowned. Wade's family tree seemed to be a touch more complicated than she'd anticipated. "Tell him I don't want it."

Skippy snorted and shook his head. "He's sitting with the mayor, the sheriff, the best lawyer in town and the city councilman who granted my liquor license. Sorry, kiddo, but I'm not getting involved. You'll have to tell him that yourself."

"Fine," Tori said. The drink was making her feel brave anyway. Scooping up the full glass, she slid off the stool a little too fluidly and made her way across the bar to the table of men in the back.

All five of them halted their conversation and turned to look at her when she approached.

"You're welcome, Miss Sullivan," Wade said with a smile that made her stomach flutter and pissed her off at the same time. He was too cocky for his own good.

"Actually, I wasn't coming to thank you. I'm re-turning it."

"Is something wrong with the drink?" Wade challenged.

"Nothing aside from it being purchased by you." She set it down on the edge of the table in front of him. "No thanks."

A couple of the men chuckled softly and another shifted uncomfortably in his seat. Wade ignored them all, his gaze laser-focused on her. "Oh, come on, now.

Don't be that way. It was a 'Welcome to Cornwall' drink. A taste of some local hospitality."

"I've lived here for two months and only four people have bothered to speak to me the entire time. It's a little late for a warm welcome. Especially coming from the man who's trying to run me out of town."

"That's harsh. You can stay in town. Just not on that particular spot. Maybe Randy here can help you buy a new place." Wade slapped the younger man beside him on the shoulder. "He tells me he handled the sale of my parents' property."

"*My* property," she emphasized. "What else did he tell you, Wade? Are there any loopholes you can use to nullify the sale? Or are you just snooping around town trying to find some dirt on me you can use for blackmail?"

Wade shrugged casually, and Tori could feel her blood nearly boil in her veins with anger. "Not everything is about you, Miss Sullivan. I'm visiting my friends while I'm in town. If they just so happen to have information about you, then great. I like to be well-informed. Especially when going up against a worthy adversary."

"Don't flatter me. You can dig all you want, but you're not going to find any dirt, because I haven't done anything wrong. I'm not selling you my property, Mr. Mitchell. And that's final." Tori spun on her heel and took two big steps away before she heard the sound of muffled snickers behind her and a poorly masked whisper that suggested Wade's skills in the bedroom might improve her attitude.

That was the last straw. Snapping her head around, she caught Wade smirking at her backside as though he agreed with his uncouth companion's assessment.

She returned to their table. "I'm sorry, what was that? I can assure you my attitude was just fine until you started bullying me around. You may live in a world where you always get your way, but it's not going to happen this time. And neither your money nor your penis is going to change that. I'm not interested in either of them."

With that, she picked up her drink, watching as Wade assessed her with curious eyes. He'd had the good sense to shelve the smirk. "On second thought," she said with a sickeningly sweet smile, "I think I will take this drink. You could use a little cooling off." With a flick of her wrist Tori emptied the glass into Wade's lap.

The icy cold drink shocked him upright out of the chair, sending ice cubes scattering across the floor. Tori turned and walked back to the bar, ignoring his stream of profanity muffled by his friends' howls of laughter. She paid her bill, leaving a nice tip for Skippy, and headed for the door.

Curiosity was nagging at her, but she wouldn't allow herself to turn around and see what Wade was doing. She would give anything to see that smug look wiped off his face, and she was pretty sure that would do it. But looking back meant that she cared. She didn't want to give Wade that satisfaction. Instead, she marched out the front door and headed to her truck. She was nearly to the corner of the building when she heard rapid, heavy footsteps coming up behind her.

"What is your problem?" Wade snarled over her shoulder.

As calmly as she could, Tori turned to look at him. Even with a tight jaw and an angry red flush tainting his perfect, aristocratic features, he was the most hand-

some man she'd ever seen in person. And she hated
that that was her first thought when she looked at him.
Those kinds of thoughts weren't helpful when dealing
with the enemy. And that's what he was, despite the
facade he put up to play nice and the way her body reacted when he was close by.

Judging by the snarl that had replaced his cajoling
smile and the giant wet spot sprawled across his pants,
she was pretty sure he was done playing nice. And that
was fine by her. It would be much easier to deal with
Wade when he wasn't trying to be charming. It just
crossed the wires in her brain and made her think unproductive thoughts.

"My problem?" Tori said coolly. "I don't have a
problem. You're the one who needs something, not me."

"And dumping a drink in my lap is the solution?"

Now it was Tori's turn to shrug dismissively, as he
had. "It seemed like a good idea at the time. You all
were having too much fun at my expense. Just because
you have drinks with the mayor doesn't mean you can
bully me."

Wade narrowed his green gaze at her, slowly stepping forward until she found herself backed up against
the crumbling brick wall of the Hen. With one hand
planted on the wall on each side of her, he'd made sure
there was nowhere for her to go. Tori straightened her
spine and looked defiantly at him as he closed in.

"I never had any intention of bullying you, Miss
Sullivan."

Tori tried not to watch the soft curve of his lips as he
spoke to her, but he was so close she had little choice.
She remembered how she'd once fantasized about kissing those lips. Of course, that was before he turned on
her and threw her out of his company on her rear end.

The surge of anger doused the old memories, and her gaze met his.

"What then?" she asked, her voice laced with sarcasm. "Were you going to take your friend's suggestion and seduce me? Certainly you're so masterful in the bedroom that one good romp would change my mind, right?"

Wade moved a fraction of an inch closer to her. For a moment Tori tensed, thinking he might be leaning in to kiss her. She wanted him to, and she didn't. She'd probably thoroughly enjoy it and then slap him when it was over. It was hard to think with him this close. He stopped short of touching his lips to hers. She could feel his warm breath on her skin.

"I've never had a woman offer me real estate after sex, but it wouldn't be the first time one of my lovers felt the need to repay me for a fantastically pleasurable night together."

Just the words *fantastically pleasurable* wrought a hard throb of need. She fought the urge to lean in to him. To discover what it would feel like to have his hard angles pressing into her soft curves. It had been a long time since she'd even let herself think of something like that. Not since things blew up with Ryan. She didn't trust herself to make the right choices, even with the right kind of man.

And this was the absolute wrong man to light up her libido. He was too smooth. Too charming and certain of himself. It didn't matter what he said or did, for every move he made was a strategic one. But that didn't mean her every move couldn't be a tactical one, as well. He already believed she could be manipulated through sex, or he never would've fired her. Let him think he was getting to her. Let him think he was winning.

Tori pressed a gentle hand to his chest. Her lips parted in invitation; a ragged breath of arousal escaped from her lungs. It wasn't hard to play along: she just gave in to her impulses. She could feel his heart racing just as quickly as her own. He was not immune to his own game. They were both playing with fire.

"What makes you think I want you?" she whispered.

Granting her silent wish, he leaned in and pressed himself against her. The warmth of his hard body radiated through his clothing. The salty scent of male skin mingled with pine. Wade let his lips graze, nestling touches light as feathers along her jaw to her earlobe. The sensitive hollow of her neck sizzled with a touch that tempted and teased without giving her what she really wanted: his mouth against her skin and his hands beneath her shirt.

"Oh, you want me," he whispered confidently into her ear. "Of that I'm certain." Pulling away and taking all the night's warmth with him, he met her gaze and smiled widely. "Good night, Miss Sullivan."

She watched him stroll confidently down the sidewalk and disappear around the corner. She waited until the night was silent and still before she let the air out of her lungs. That man had managed to build a fire in her she hadn't expected, especially considering how much she despised him. This was a dangerous game, but if he was trying to seduce her into selling, it would at least be more pleasurable than fighting. Especially when he lost.

A smile of amusement curled her lips. "Oh, you only think you won this round, Wade Mitchell. But the fun is just beginning."

Three

By the time Wade returned to the farm that night, the lights in the big house were all out except for the front porch and the kitchen. His parents had always been early to bed, early to rise, as most farmers were. Thank goodness for the bunkhouse.

The renovated barn referred to as "the bunkhouse" had been where all the boys slept and played as kids. The historic Federal-style house that came with the farm was large, but old in style and design, never renovated to have enough bedrooms and bathrooms to accommodate an ever-changing herd of boys and Julianne all at once. But none of the boys minded the separation.

The bunkhouse had been the perfect boys' retreat, and Julianne spent her fair share of time over there, as well. The entire downstairs was an open living area where they could do their homework, watch television, play video games and Ping-Pong, and roughhouse without breaking anything important. They even had their own mini-kitchen with a refrigerator, microwave and sink. As growing boys they were starving at all hours, and Molly didn't want them running across the yard to the house in the cold and dark.

Upstairs were two huge bedrooms and adjoining baths. The rooms had twin beds and a set of bunk beds to accommodate up to six foster boys at one time. In addition to Wade and his brothers, there had been other children who came but didn't stay long because they went back to their parents or were adopted by relatives. They rarely had an empty bed back then.

These days there were just the four of them, each having outgrown bunk beds. Molly had redecorated after they all moved out, and each room now had two queen-size beds. Typically the kids all arrived back at the farm at the same time: Christmas Eve. The big house hadn't gotten any larger in the past decade, so the boys found themselves back in the bunkhouse.

Since he was the only one there, Wade could stay in the upstairs guest room of the big house. At least until Christmas when the others arrived. But somehow that felt wrong. Instead, he carried Molly's requested groceries inside the big house, put them away and then locked the back door behind him. He grabbed the rest of his things from the hatch of his SUV and rolled his suitcase over to the bunkhouse.

Anticipating his move, Molly had left the porch light on, and on the mini-kitchen counter was a slice of lemon pound cake wrapped in cellophane and a note welcoming him home.

As he read the note he smiled and set the rest of his groceries beside it. He stashed a small case of water, cream cheese, Sumatran coffee beans and a six-pack of his favorite microbrewed dark ale in the fridge. He left the bagels and a bag of pretzels on the counter beside the cake.

God, it was nice to be home.

His loft apartment in Tribeca was nice—it should be, considering what he paid for it. But it didn't feel like home. With its big glass windows and concrete floors, it was a little too modern in design to feel welcoming. It was chic and functional, which is what he thought he liked when he bought it. But it wasn't until he set foot in this old barn with the battered table-tennis table and ancient two-hundred-pound television that he could truly relax.

Things hadn't changed much in the bunkhouse. The futon where he first made out with Anna Chissom was still in the corner. She'd been his first girlfriend, a shy, quiet redhead who kicked off a long string of auburn-haired women in his life. The latest, of course, was giving him the most grief. But he still wished he could pull Victoria down onto the futon and finish what they'd started outside that bar.

He'd done it intending to get under her skin and punish her for dumping that drink on him. Then he found he liked touching her. Teasing her. He enjoyed the flush upon her creamy fair skin. The soft parting of her lips inviting him to kiss her. She responded to him, whether she wanted to or not, exposing her weakness. Now he just had to take advantage of it. There were worse negotiating tactics. Yet she wasn't the only one suffering. He wanted to feel her mouth against his. And not just so she'd sell him her land.

Wade flopped back onto the couch and eyed his watch. It was only nine-thirty. He didn't normally go to bed until well after eleven, especially on the weekends. He was tempted to pull out his laptop and get some work done but was interrupted by the faint melody of his phone.

It was Brody's ringtone—the dramatic pipe-organ melody of the theme to *The Phantom of the Opera*. It was a long-running family joke, considering his computer-genius brother was pretty much living out the plotline as a scarred recluse. But when you had the kind of life that most of the Eden boys had lived, you developed a pretty thick skin and a dark sense of humor to make it through.

"Hey, Brody," Wade answered.

"Wade." His brother's tone was cautious and, as always, serious.

"No," Wade said, cutting off the next question. "I went out to the property to talk to the owner, but there's a...*complication*."

Brody sighed heavily. "I knew this wouldn't be as easy as you seemed to think."

"I said a complication, not a complete failure, Debbie Downer. It's just not going to be open-and-shut. The owner is reluctant to sell."

"Even at double the price?"

"I offered her half a million and she turned me down flat."

Brody groaned on the line. "Why on earth would she turn that down? Half a million dollars is a lot to just push aside."

"Well, it's partially my fault." And technically, it was. He had the feeling Victoria Sullivan might've sold the land if any of his brothers had shown up at her doorstep. But not Wade. Oh, no. She was bound and determined to get back at him for firing her, even though it was her own doing.

"What did you do?" Brody asked in the same sharp tone he'd always used as a child. Whenever one of the other boys lamented about being punished, those were always the first words out of his mouth. Brody was the one who never got into trouble, who never did anything wrong. He was too worried about being punished, thanks to his abusive father. Brody was always happiest sitting at his computer, whether he was playing games or helping Molly upgrade to the latest financial management software. He never got into trouble.

"I didn't *do* anything. She just doesn't like me. She used to work for me years ago."

"Did you sleep with her?"

Wade couldn't help snorting into the phone at his brother's assumption that this had to be a spurned lover. Compared to the lifestyle of his brother, he supposed he appeared to be a bit of a dog when it came to the ladies. "Then or now?" he teased.

"Either."

"No, I've never slept with her." Despite the fact that he would like to. Very much. He eyed the mostly dry spot on the crotch of his pants and smiled. She was a feisty one, for sure. He was certain they'd have a hell of a time in bed. But if she didn't like him enough to conduct a business deal, she probably didn't like him enough to take her clothes off for him.

Well, at least not yet. He'd seen the passion blazing in her pale blue eyes as he'd pinned her against that wall tonight. She wanted him, all right. But she was too stubborn to give in to it.

"I fired her. For cause, I might add. She still seems to be a little perturbed about that."

"I knew we should've sent Xander. No one can say no to him."

Their brother Xander was a Connecticut congressman. He was smooth, charming, likable and well-spoken. Everything a good politician needed to be. He would be perfect to handle the situation, if he were available. "Well, Xander is busy negotiating the country out of a huge deficit, so you're stuck with me. I can make this happen. I assure you. It just isn't going to get done in a day. She's going to take some convincing."

"What can I do to help it along? Run a background check? See if I can dig up any information on her?"

"That wouldn't hurt, although I doubt you'll come up with anything useful. At least, not anything blackmail worthy. I get the feeling her faux pas at my company was a fluke."

"Maybe there's something in her history you can use to soften her up. It will make me feel like I'm doing something."

Wade could hear the aggravation in his brother's voice. Brody wanted to help, but not much could be done from the supersecure corporate offices of his software empire in Boston. His brother was brilliant, had built a company that rivaled Google and Facebook, but Brody didn't go out in public. The only time anyone saw him was when he came home for Christmas or Easter. The rest of the time it was just he and his secretary, Agnes, on the top floor of his Boston high-rise.

It was a damn shame. If Brody's biological father ever got parole, Wade would make him wish he'd stayed in jail. The kind of bastard who would dump battery acid on his young son's face didn't deserve to see the light of day. Especially not when his son didn't get to see it, either.

"For now, some good intel may be all I need to convince her. She doesn't like me, but if I know what buttons to push, maybe I can change her mind. Look into her company for me and some of her recent projects. I'll send you the basic info to get started. I know she's passionate about her work. That might be all it takes. If I'm right, and this is the right property, once I secure it, there won't be any more trouble. If she holds out, maybe you and I can go out in the dark over the holiday and start digging holes."

"Digging holes in the dark?"

"You said you wanted to help," Wade pointed out, only half joking. If the shovels came out, they had big, big problems.

"Don't let it get to that point, Wade. This isn't a missing time capsule we're looking for here. It's a dead man's body. One that we all share some responsibility for putting into the ground. It absolutely can't be found. Do whatever it takes to fix this. It could ruin all our reputations—maybe even our companies. Who wants to do business with someone involved in the death of—"

"Just stop," Wade interrupted. He didn't even want the words spoken aloud.

"This could kill Dad with his heart condition. I don't want another death on my conscience."

Neither did Wade. It would probably do all that and more. And if it didn't kill Ken, Wade was certain he wouldn't be able to bear the look of disappointment on his father's face. He'd spent his whole life trying to be good enough. For his teenage birth mother, who had dumped him on an old relative. For the foster families that had passed him around like a hot potato. For the Edens, who had treated him like their son. He couldn't, wouldn't disappoint Ken and Molly.

He'd already failed fifteen years ago to protect his

brothers and sister as he should have. Wade wouldn't make that same mistake twice.

"I'll handle it," he promised. "One way or another."

"Welcome to the Garden of Eden Tree Farm. I hope we can help you have a very merry Christmas!"

The moment Tori crossed the threshold into the gift shop among the jingling of bells, Molly Eden greeted her from her post behind the counter. Tori had met the older woman once, at closing, but there had been paperwork to sign and not much time for chitchat.

Today she was determined to change that. Wade thought he could sneak around town and get information on her. Well, two could play at that game. And what better source than his mother? He claimed his family was more important than anything, even money. Spending some quality time with them under the guise of Christmas shopping was the perfect way to do a little digging of her own.

"Oh, Miss Sullivan!" Molly came out from behind the counter with a wide smile that was bookended by rosy cheeks. The woman was tiny and round, with gray-blond hair swept up into a neat bun at the back of her head. In about ten more years, once her hair had gone completely white, she'd make the perfect Mrs. Claus. And judging by her surroundings, Tori was pretty sure that was the plan all along.

"Please call me Tori."

"Only if you call me Molly, dear. We're neighbors, after all." Molly embraced her as though they were lifelong friends instead of acquaintances through real estate.

Tori smiled. She couldn't help it. The woman was

just so damn sweet. How was it that she could raise a sneaky corporate weasel like Wade? "That we are."

She noticed that nothing in the woman's tone or expression conveyed any hint of concern about the fact that Tori lived on her old land. The same was true when they'd met at closing. Neither she nor Ken had seemed bothered at all by it. In fact, Ken had appeared a little relieved. She remembered Ken had commented that they were getting to an age where nearly three hundred acres was a lot of land to deal with. Tori's piece was too rocky and sloped to grow trees. The other two larger plots were the same. No great loss there.

So why did it bother Wade so much that they'd sold it? It made Tori wonder if his parents even knew what he was up to. The burning, childish urge to tattle on him swirled in her gut. It would be so easy. Even a millionaire CEO could be brought down by the wrath of his mama.

But somehow that didn't seem like fighting fair. They hadn't taken the gloves off yet. She'd reserve that tactic until it was absolutely necessary. In the meantime, there wasn't any harm in being neighborly. She wasn't very good at it, since her neighbors typically changed out every few weeks, but she was willing to give it a try.

"So what brings you by today? Do you need a tree?"

"Oh, no," Tori said. "I don't have room for one in my little trailer. When the house is finished, I'll get one for sure. But for now I thought I might pick up one of the lovely fresh pine wreaths you put together. When I was down at Daisy's the other night, the waitress Rose was bragging on your artistic skills."

Molly was beaming with pride as she led Tori over to the display of wreaths. "Rose is such a sweetheart.

She used to date my Xander when they were in high school. I hate that it didn't work out."

They stopped in front of a stone wall covered in about ten different wreaths. There was a variety of sizes, all with decorations of different styles. Tori wasn't really in the market for a wreath, but she would buy one. If she didn't, she'd probably buy a package or two of the homemade fudge by the register, and she certainly didn't need that.

She picked the first one that really caught her eye. "That blue-and-silver wreath is gorgeous. I think I'll take that one."

"That's one of my favorites, too. Let me get the hook to get it down."

Molly headed off across the store, pausing only when the jingling of bells signaled someone else had come in. "Oh, Wade, perfect timing. Could you get that blue wreath down for me?"

Tori snapped her head around to see Wade shaking the snow off his boots on the entryway rug. Today he was wearing a deep red cashmere sweater with a white collared shirt beneath it. It made his shoulders look impossibly wide and strong. After being so close to him last night, she found it wasn't hard to imagine being wrapped in his arms. And being pressed against his chest… Tori shook her head to chase away the unproductive thoughts.

"Sure, Mama," he said without turning her way.

"And I want you to meet Tori Sullivan," Molly continued. "She's the one who bought that little piece of land near the ridge."

At that, Wade stiffened and turned in her direction. He frowned for only a moment, wiping the expression from his face before his mother could see it. He followed her over to the wreath display and, without speaking, lowered the blue-and-silver wreath into his mother's arms.

"Tori, this is my oldest son, Wade. He's in real estate in New York. Perhaps you two run in the same circles. Wade, Tori is an architect. She bought one of our lots, and she's designing a beautiful house to build up there."

"You flatter me," she said, avoiding Wade's gaze until she had to greet him. When she did, there was a polite blankness in his eyes. He was obviously going to pretend they had never met before. She was willing to play along with that for now. "It's nice to meet you, Wade." She held out her hand to him.

"And you, Tori," he said very formally, while managing to emphasize the pronunciation of her first name. It was the first time he'd called her that since he'd shown up at her trailer. Actually, it was the first time he'd ever called her "Tori." When she'd worked for his company, she'd gone by Victoria. She couldn't help but watch his lips as he said her name. There was something oddly seductive about the way his mouth moved that just wasn't there when he called her Miss Sullivan.

When he finally reached out and shook her hand, Tori realized a second too late that touching him was probably a bad idea. She was right. The minute his hand encompassed hers, it was as though she had dipped it into a warm bath. The heat of his soft touch engulfed her, sending a delicious surge of need up her arm that tightened her chest and made it hard to breathe. She found she couldn't pull away from him.

Her body was betraying her, and for what? A chaste, polite handshake?

But then she looked into his dark green eyes and realized it was more than that. He, too, felt the current of desire that traveled through their skin-on-skin contact. Unlike last night, when Wade was prepared and in control of the seduction, this seemed to catch him off guard. For just a brief moment the animosity and arrogance was stripped away, leaving him only with the expression of pure, unadulterated desire. He was fighting the urge to devour her, then and there.

His gaze was so penetrating, it felt like a caress. When his thumb gently stroked the back of her hand, her heart started racing, her breath quick in her throat the way it had been the night before when she thought he might kiss her. The feeling was intense. Too intense for a Christmas store with his mother only a few feet away.

Tori jerked away suddenly, hoping Molly didn't notice the invisible sparks as she rubbed her palm on her jeans to deaden the lingering sensation from his touch. Wade's eyes didn't stray from hers for a few moments, intently searching her as though he were looking into her soul. He turned away only when Molly spoke.

"Tori, I'm going to get this wreath boxed up for you. Do you have a hook to hang it?"

"No," she admitted, sounding oddly out of breath for someone standing still. "Pick whatever onc you think will look the nicest with it, and I'll take that, too."

Molly grinned and dashed off to the other side of the store, leaving Wade and Tori alone.

"What are you doing here?" he asked, his tone unquestionably accusatory, yet low enough for his mother not to hear them.

Tori crossed her arms under her breasts, burying her still-burning hand. "Shopping, obviously."

This time, when his green gaze raked over her, there

was no heat behind it. Just irritation and suspicion. "Did you come here to get back at me for last night?"

"Get back at you for what? You claimed you were just hanging out with some friends. Do you think I came here to tattle on you to your mama?"

"No," he said, although the deep lines of the wary expression on his face gave away his lie.

Tori cracked a wicked grin, knowing she'd easily discovered an Achilles' heel. Of course, any son of a decent family had a soft spot where his mother was concerned. Even the pushy, arrogant sons. She opted to rub it in by parroting the line he'd used on her last night. "I'm here buying some Christmas decorations. If your mama just happens to supply me with some information about you, then great. I like to be well-informed. Especially when going up against a worthy adversary."

"Touché," he said drily before casting a quick glance over his shoulder to see where Molly was.

"I take it Ken and Molly don't know what you're trying to do to me?"

His head snapped back to look at her. *"Do to you?"* he whispered with a touch of incredulity in his voice. "Offering to pay you four times your property value is hardly twisting your arm. But no, they don't know about it, and I'd like to keep it that way. They don't need any more stress."

"If they don't care, why are you so determined to get it back? I don't understand."

A barrier went up inside Wade. Tori could almost feel the steel walls slamming into place. She'd obviously trodden into dangerous territory with him.

"I don't have to explain to you why this land is important to me. All you need to know is that I intend to get it back one way or another."

"So you seem to think."

Tori watched as Wade's hands curled into controlled fists at his side. She couldn't tell whether he wanted to kiss her senseless or bludgeon her with a nearby reindeer statue. But he couldn't do any of those things. Not with Molly nearby. Tori had no doubt he'd give her a piece of his mind the minute he could. She was kind of looking forward to it.

"Wade?" His mother's voice called over the cheerful carols playing in the store.

They both turned to look at his mother, and Tori noticed a curious expression on Molly's face. She seemed...intrigued by their quiet discussion. Tori hoped she hadn't mistaken their subdued animosity for real attraction. Tori wouldn't put it past her to try to fix them up. Yes, there was a current running beneath the surface, but it was pointless to consider what that meant. Fortunately, Wade's living in New York would easily put a damper on anything Molly tried to start up.

"Coming," Wade said before he shot Tori a heated warning glance and turned away. She watched him talk to Molly for a minute, then nod and walk out of the store without another word to her.

Tori let out a deep breath and realized she'd been holding it long enough for her lungs to start burning. Her whole body was tense from bickering with him and—if she was honest with herself—anxious with the need he built inside her with a simple touch. It was an extremely confusing combination.

"Your package is ready, dear."

Tori returned to the counter. "Thank you. I'm sure it will look great. The silver and blue against the shiny aluminum will be perfect."

"It will," she agreed. "What are you doing for Christmas? Do you have any family nearby?"

Tori shook her head. "No. My parents travel a lot. The last time they called, they were in Oregon. I'll probably call and check in with them Christmas Day, but I haven't spent an actual holiday with them in years."

"What about any brothers and sisters? Aunts? Cousins?"

"I'm an only child. And my family moved so much that we never really connected with our extended family."

"Hmph," Molly said thoughtfully, although Tori wasn't exactly sure what that meant. "Would you like to join me by the fireplace for some hot mulled cider?"

"I don't want to take up your time."

"Posh! The store is empty. Business won't pick up until later today, and then just with last-minute folk in a rush. Come on, I'll fix you a cup. I've also got some snickerdoodles I took out of the oven right before you came in."

Unable to turn down the Christmas pied piper, she followed Molly over to the refreshment stand, then to the rocking chairs in front of the fireplace.

"You guys really have a lovely place here. It's like a child's Christmas fantasy."

"Thank you. That's really what we were going for—a treasured holiday tradition as opposed to just a shopping trip. Ken and I have always loved children. We'd hoped to have at least five or six." Tori watched Molly gently finger the rim of her paper cup as she spoke. "When that didn't work out, of course, we started taking in foster kids. Wade was the first child we took in."

"Oh," Tori said, the pieces of her conversations with Wade and the bartender finally clicking into place. That was why he had a different last name from the people he considered his parents. He obviously adored Molly as though she were his biological mother. Perhaps not all of his story was meant to play on her emotions. It was possible he did want to preserve the land that had been a special home for him.

Did that change how she felt about selling her property? No. But it did change a little of how she felt about him.

"I didn't realize Wade was a foster child."

"Yes. Julianne is the only child nature blessed us with. The rest came to us through the Litchfield County Social Services office. We had so many over the years, but Wade, Brody, Xander and Heath were the ones who really became a part of our family. It gave us a lot of joy to give a home to children who really needed one. We'd hoped that one day we would be able to turn the farm over to one of them, but that probably won't happen. We raised them to dream big, and they did. Unfortunately, none of them dreamed of being a Christmas tree farmer."

Tori took a bite of one of the warm cookies and nearly moaned with pleasure. The cinnamon, sugar and butter were a divine combination. She'd honestly never had a cookie this good before. "Oh, Molly, this cookie is wonderful. I couldn't have expected anything less with everything you have here. I never had a Christmas tree growing up, but I always imagined buying one at a place like this."

"You've never had a Christmas tree?" Molly looked appalled.

"No. My family liked to travel. My mom homeschooled me so we could move from one town to the next every few weeks. The camper wasn't much bigger than the one I have now, so no real room for a tree. Sometimes, on Christmas morning, my parents would get up really early and decorate one of the nearby trees in the RV park where we were staying."

"Christmas in a camper." Tori could see the wheels turning in Molly's head. "Then I suppose a huge turkey with all the trimmings and homemade pies were out of the question."

Tori chuckled. "Not once in my life have I ever had that. My parents are hippies, really, so they were more into tofu and organic vegetables when I was young. And, yes, even if she'd wanted to cook a turkey, my mom didn't have the room or the equipment. Sometimes we'd eat at a Cracker Barrel when my dad got nostalgic for home-cooked food."

At that, Molly paled beside her. The rosy cheeks had vanished as though Tori had just told her there was no Santa Claus. "You're coming over to our place Monday night for Christmas Eve dinner."

Tori's eyes widened in surprise. "Oh, no," she insisted. Wade would think she'd deliberately done this. He'd make her miserable, glaring accusingly at her across the table all night. "I couldn't possibly intrude on your family dinner."

"Nonsense. Come up to the big house Monday night around five. We'll eat about six, but I want you to get there in time to meet everyone."

"Everyone?" What had Tori gotten herself into?

"It's just me and Ken and the kids. You'll get to meet my other boys. Brody will come up from Boston. He runs a software company. Xander is a congressman, so he's flying back from D.C. Heath, my youngest, will be up from Manhattan. He owns an advertising agency. And my daughter, Julianne, will be home from Long Island. She has a sculpting studio and art gallery in the Hamptons. I'm so excited. I only get them all together once a year. Christmas is a big deal for our family."

Holy crap. Molly made them sound wonderful, but Tori wondered if she wasn't wandering into a trap. How many of them knew about Wade's plans? Would she have his four siblings staring her down, as well? Tori didn't know if she could refuse three powerful CEOs and a congressman if they ganged up on her. She couldn't help imagining herself being slipped a roofie in her eggnog, waking up hog-tied in the basement and being forced to sign over her property.

"Really, thank you, but I already have plans." It wasn't technically a lie. She had planned to eat chicken soup and peanut butter and jelly sandwiches while watching old Christmas movies on DVD. Not good plans, but plans. Hopefully it was enough to appease the older woman.

Molly arched an elegant eyebrow at her. "I have seen your camper, dear. It's really lovely, but I can't imagine you putting together much more than a peanut butter sandwich and a can of soup in there."

Tori smiled. "How did you know what I was having?"

"Oh, Lordy," Molly wailed, dramatically getting up from her chair. "You're coming over for dinner, and that's final."

Tori trailed behind her, tossing her cup and napkin into the trash. She had to admit the idea of some real, home-cooked holiday food was tempting. But she would pay for it later. Wade would see to that. She could see that he got his stubbornness from his mother. The determined glint in Molly's light green eyes left no room for negotiation. Surely Wade would understand his mother was a force of nature.

"Can I bring anything?" Tori had no clue what she could possibly contribute, but her mother had raised her to at least be polite enough to offer.

Molly tried to hide her smile behind her hand and then shook her head. "Not at all. I'll have everything we need. Just bring your darling self, and we'll be waiting for you."

Tori nodded and walked to the cash register to pay for her wreath. She had no doubt Wade would be waiting for her Monday night. Armed and ready for battle.

Four

Tori couldn't make herself go inside the Edens' house. She felt stupid. It was the most unintimidating place she'd ever seen. The old white two-story home was lit with clear icicle lights, and each shutter-framed window had a wreath and candle gracing it. The two short columns that flanked the three stairs leading up to the front door were wrapped with garland and more lights. She could hear Christmas music and laughter from inside. Golden light shone through the downstairs windows and onto the snow.

It was beautiful. Welcoming. The kind of house you wanted to go caroling to because you knew the owners would give you hot cocoa and cookies.

But there was no walking up the steps. Instead, she stood there freezing, clutching the potted poinsettia she'd brought as a hostess gift.

This was a mistake. She just knew it. Tori had spent

the past few hours pacing in her Airstream, trying to think of a way to get out of coming tonight. And when she wasn't pacing, she was looking around at her empty trailer, considering whether she really preferred to watch sentimental old black-and-white Christmas movies and feast alone on peanut butter and chicken soup.

It was Christmas Eve, a day of family and celebration and community. Unfortunately, she wasn't quick to make friends, and small towns were notoriously hard to crack. The only people she knew in Cornwall were her real-estate lawyer, who was apparently best buddies with her enemy; Rose, the waitress at Daisy's diner; and Wade and Molly. That made for a fairly unmerry Christmas this year if she turned down this invitation.

She just couldn't have two miserable Christmases in a row. Last year she'd hoped to spend it with her boyfriend, Ryan. They both traveled so much with their work, but it had seemed that meeting for the holidays in Colorado would be possible. Instead, he'd canceled at the last second, leaving her with a whopping bill for a winter bungalow for one.

Later she discovered he'd never had any intention of coming. He was married with three kids. Ryan was going to be home with his family no matter what he told her. Dating Tori had been perfect for him because she was always moving around and never pressuring him for more. Their relationship was sustained by phone calls, emails and long weekends together. When she'd mentioned moving permanently to Connecticut, only a few hours from his home near Boston, he panicked and broke it off. Finding out about his whole other life had been just the icing on that miserable cake.

He hadn't been the first womanizer to steal her heart and probably wouldn't be the last. She just had a soft spot for smooth, seductive liars. She confused their calculated moves for cultivated charm, but whatever the label, the relationships didn't end well. Slick and likable, they seduced you with words to get what they wanted, then they walked away, uncaring of the shambles they left behind.

Unfortunately, Wade was one of those men, and despite her better judgment, she could feel the attraction building inside her. She wanted him, even as she plotted and planned to make him suffer for the way he'd treated her. She simply couldn't get her brain and her body on the same page. Would having dinner with his family at Christmas make the situation better or worse?

She supposed that all depended on how he reacted to her being there. Perhaps the best way to make him suffer would be to have a good time tonight. Not let him get to her, by rousing either her anger or her desire for him. Having an excellent meal with the enemy was far better than a subpar meal feeling virtuous and lonely.

"I will have a good time," she said out loud, her breath creating a soft cloud of fog in the cold.

"Of course you will. But if you keep standing out here, you're going to get frostbite."

Tori whipped her head around and saw a man standing in the snow a few feet away from her with an armful of firewood. He looked as if he was in his late twenties, tall and strongly built, with short, light brown hair and a wide disarming smile. Her heart was still racing with surprise when she shook her head and laughed. "You scared the daylights out of me."

"Sorry," he said, although his mischievous expression did not lead her to believe it. "You must be Miss Sullivan."

"Tori, yes," she said, shifting the plant in her arms

so she could reach out to shake his hand. "Which one are you?"

"Heath. I'm the baby, if that helps."

The tall muscular man in front of her hardly qualified as a baby. He held the heavy logs in one arm to shake her hand as though they were made of Styrofoam.

Then a thought struck her. Heath knew who she was and was expecting her. Did Wade know she was coming? "Did your mother tell you I was coming to dinner?"

"She told me when I was peeling potatoes on KP."

"Does Wade know?"

"Nope," Heath said with a wicked gleam of pleasure in his eyes. "What's the fun in that?"

Tori's lips twisted in concern. She wanted to see the expression of surprise and irritation on Wade's face when she walked in, unannounced, to his family Christmas party. Apparently so did Heath. But it still felt like a bit of a trap. "Am I walking into the lion's den here?"

Heath shrugged. "Eh, they're fun lions. They'll play with you before they eat you. Come on, let's go in. I'm freezing out here, and the sooner we get in there, the sooner I get pie."

There was no avoiding it now, despite Heath's assurance that she would be eaten. Hopefully she could get some of this famous pie first. Tori let the youngest Eden boy usher her up the stairs, and he held the door open.

"Look what I found outside!" he announced.

Tori had barely recovered from the sudden rush of warmth and light when she was struck with five sets of eyes. She clutched the plant tightly in her hands and tried to gather some holiday cheer in her expression. It probably ended up coming out a little pained.

Molly and a younger woman who looked very much like her looked up from their napkin folding at the large dining room table. Standing in the living room talking were Ken and another of the boys. This one looked vaguely familiar and a bit like Heath, actually. Another, younger man watched her from his crouch in front of the fireplace. Their expressions varied. Curiosity, cheer, surprise and even a touch of anxiety from the one tending to the fire.

But Wade was nowhere in sight.

"Oh, Tori, you came," Molly said, rounding the dining room table to greet her.

"She was just standing in the snow. What did you tell her about us, Ma?" Heath broke away from Tori's side to carry the wood over to the brother by the fireplace.

"You hush," Molly chided and accepted the poinsettia Tori offered. "This is beautiful. Thank you. I told you that you didn't need to bring anything, dear."

"You told me I didn't need to bring any food," Tori corrected with a smile for her warm welcome.

"You're very sweet. Merry Christmas to you." Molly leaned in to give her a big hug. "Ken," she said as she pulled away, "could you introduce her to everyone while I find a place for this and check on the turkey?"

"Sure thing." The tall, lean frame of Ken Eden ambled toward her, a friendly smile on his face. "Hey there, Miss Sullivan. Merry Christmas."

"Merry Christmas to you, too. And call me Tori, please."

Ken nodded. "Now, you met Heath. He's the youngest and most troublesome of the group."

"I heard that!" a voice shouted from the general direction of the fireplace.

"He also has excellent hearing. This is Xander."

"Xander Langston," Tori said, reaching out to shake the man's hand. Molly had mentioned one of her sons was a politician, but Tori didn't connect the pieces until she saw the man she recognized from television news and advertisements. She'd had no idea Xander Langston was also one of the "Eden boys" until she saw him standing by the couch.

Xander smiled, greeting her with a polished finesse that practicing politics must have perfected. "Welcome, Tori. Sounds like you've heard my name before. Are you a registered voter?" he asked with a touch of humor in his light hazel eyes that let her know he was trying to be funny.

"Not here. My previous residence was a PO box in Philadelphia, but I'll be changing that."

"Excellent. I hope spending time with my family doesn't negatively influence your vote."

"Stop campaigning, Xander." The young woman from the dining room came over, shoving the congressman aside with her shoulder. "Sorry, he has trouble turning it off. I'm Julianne."

"This is my baby girl," Ken said, his blue eyes brightening at the sight of his daughter. "She's the most talented artist you'll ever meet."

"Daddy," she chided in a tone very much like her mother's. "I'm glad you could join us tonight, Tori. We need some more estrogen in this house."

Tori shook her hand. The Edens' only daughter was quite beautiful and looked very much like she imagined Molly had appeared when she was younger. She had long golden-blond hair, light green eyes and a smile that lit up the room. A person's eyes just naturally went to her.

"Brody, quit playing with the fireplace and come meet our guest."

The last of the brothers put down the fireplace poker and made his way over. There was a reluctance in his movements that made Tori wonder if this brother was a part of Wade's plot. He'd made a point of mentioning that all of the children wanted the land back. The others didn't seem to look at her or treat her differently than any other dinner guest.

Then she saw it. As he stepped into the shimmering light of the Christmas tree, the previously darkencd side of his face was illuminated. Tori sucked in a surprised breath and stiffened her whole body to keep from reacting inappropriately. Almost the entire left side of Brody's face was horribly scarred; the skin puckered and twisted into a horrible mask. She couldn't even imagine what kind of injury would leave a mark like that.

She noticed that Brody had deliberately hesitated at the edge of the group, almost giving her time to react and process everything before he greeted her. He'd apparently lived with this, and people's reactions, for quite some time. She felt the sudden urge to put him at ease. As quickly as she could, Tori made eye contact and smiled. "It's nice to meet you, Brody."

He reached out and shook her hand, nodding gently to himself. "Nice of you to come," he said, the corners of his mouth curving up in subdued welcome. The unmarred side of his face was quite handsome. She could tell that if he really, truly smiled, it would be very charming. He had beautiful dark blue eyes with thick coal-black lashes that his injury hadn't touched. His gaze was initially wary, perhaps anxious at meeting someone new, but the smile eventually made its way into his sapphire depths.

Julianne frowned, looking around the living room. "Where's Wade?"

"Bringing in the last of the Christmas presents from Brody's car. How exactly did I get saddled with this job on my own? What are all of you doin—"

Wade stopped in front of the Christmas tree, his arms overflowing with brightly wrapped packages. His gaze zeroed in on Tori in the crowd of his family members. Her hair must have made her stand out. For a moment, a confused mix of emotions played across his eyes. There was a flash of anger, irritation, concern, surprise... Then his gaze flicked over to his father, and Wade's jaw tightened to hold in whatever words Tori's sudden appearance brought to his mind.

"Wade, have you met our new neighbor?" Ken seemed oblivious to his son's consternation.

"Yes, I have." Wade lowered the presents to the floor, leaving them beside the small mountain of gifts that was already arranged there. He dusted his hands off on his jeans and pushed the sleeves of his hunter-green sweater up the strong bulge of his muscled fore-arms. He took a deep breath, cast a few meaningful glances to his siblings and walked over to the group. "Mama introduced us in the shop a couple days ago. I didn't realize you were coming to dinner tonight." Wade speared her with a sharp, accusing gaze.

Tori straightened and put on a polite smile. He was unhappy about her being here. Good. He shouldn't be the only one who got to run around town with a smug grin on his face. "Yes, Molly insisted I come tonight so I wouldn't spend Christmas alone. She's very sweet."

"And stubborn," Heath added with a grin.

"Glad you could join us tonight," Ken said, with a reassuring hand to her shoulder. "Dinner should be ready soon."

From there, the group seemed to disperse. Julianne and Ken disappeared into the kitchen to help Molly. Brody and Heath went back to building the world's greatest fire. Xander made noises about presents in his car and slipped out the back door where Wade had just come in. It left Tori and Wade alone in the entryway, surrounded by twinkling lights and Bing Crosby crooning in the background.

Wade watched her intensely for a moment, letting the pressure of his anger out while no one was watching. His face had grown a bit red from the strain of holding it in for so long. He quickly threw a glance over his shoulder for witnesses before he spoke. "May I take your coat?" The words were stilted. Formal. As they'd been Saturday in the gift shop.

Nodding, Tori stuffed her gloves into her pockets and slipped out of her jacket. Wade took it from her and walked a few feet to the closet. She watched him slip the coat onto a hanger, meticulously straightening it as he spoke. "What the hell do you think you're doing?" His voice was extremely low, almost a hiss.

"Having Christmas dinner," Tori retorted. "Your mother invited me, and there was no telling the woman no."

Wade turned toward her, his brow furrowed. He was still irritated, but some of the red blotches were fading from his neck. He had to know there was no arguing with Molly Eden. She was a force of nature. "You could've had the decency to fake the swine flu and cancel."

Tori crossed her arms over her chest. "It's Christmas

Eve. So sue me if I'd rather spend it with other people than sit alone in my trailer. It was a nice invitation, and I accepted it. You can stand there and believe it's part of my supersecret plan to undermine your dastardly plot. And maybe it is. But there's nothing you can do about it except smile and eat some turkey, unless you want to make a scene and ruin your mother's holiday."

Wade thrust her coat into the closet and shut the door as forcefully as he could without audibly slamming it. He turned to her with venom in his dark eyes. "I told you my family is the most important thing in the world to me. It's the reason I'm willing to pay you more than anyone in their right mind would pay for that land. To preserve my family. You can come here and have dinner. But you'd damn well better know that I won't sit back and let you toy with any of them."

"I'm not out to manipulate people like you are, Wade. I have no intention of doing anything to your family."

"You'd better hope you're right."

"Or what?" Tori challenged.

Wade opened his mouth to answer, but his gaze moved over her shoulder to someone behind her. His defensive posture melted away, his expression softening.

Then Tori heard Heath's amusement-laced voice behind her. "Hey, you guys are standing under the mistletoe."

"Mistletoe?" Molly came running from the kitchen, a gleam of excitement in her eyes.

Wade and Tori both looked above their heads and back at each other with a touch of dismay. Dangling from the ceiling was a small sprig of green leaves tied with a festive red ribbon. What the hell was mistletoe doing in the house? Everyone here was related. If not by blood, by circumstance. His mother never hung mistletoe....

Then it hit him. She'd invited Tori to dinner. She'd hung mistletoe. Molly was plotting. The woman had five children in their late twenties or early thirties and not the slightest forecast of weddings and grandbabies in her future. She must have gotten it in her head that Tori would be perfect for one of her boys. Maybe even him. What was she thinking?

By now, the entire family had piled back into the living room to watch.

"Mama," Wade complained. "Why did you hang this stuff? It's silly."

"It's tradition," Molly countered. "This is the first year I've been able to hang it, so you bet your sweet bippy you're going to play along and make me happy."

Wade swallowed the lump in his throat and turned from his family to look at Tori. She looked even more anxious than he felt. She was stiff, her light blue eyes wide with shock from the unexpected declaration. Her cheeks were slightly flushed. He didn't know if it was from their argument or the embarrassment of kissing him like this.

Two seconds earlier they'd been fighting, and now he had to kiss her in front of his entire family. Several times over the past few days he'd fantasized about doing just that. Running his hands through the silken fire of her hair. Halting the flow of poisonous words from her mouth by kissing her into silence.

But not now. Not like this. Not in front of everyone.

"If you don't do it, I will," Heath offered from the

back. Julianne threw an irritated elbow into his ribs, doubling him over. "Ow, Jules!"

That made Wade frown. He sure as hell wouldn't let Heath anywhere near Tori or the mistletoe. He'd punch his brother in the jaw for even thinking about kissing Tori.

He'd worry about what that meant later.

"Just hurry up and get it over with."

Tori's voice distracted him from his brother's taunt. He frowned at the redhead. Even though the sensible thing to do would be to give her a quick peck and move on, he didn't like her attitude. Never in his life had a woman asked him to "hurry up and get it over with." It made him want to pull her into his arms and kiss her breathless. He wanted her to eat her words.

But doing that in front of his family was dangerous. Brody would worry that he'd let sex distract him from their goal. Molly would start knitting booties. He needed to just kiss her so they could have dinner and send Tori on her way.

"Kiss her!" someone shouted. He wasn't sure who.

Wade took a step forward, Tori's whole body tensing as he did. Leaning in to her, he didn't hesitate to bring his lips to hers. He had every intention of giving her the kind of kiss appropriate for a stranger caught in this awkward ritual. But the moment his skin touched hers, it was just like before. The handshake in the gift shop had nearly thrown him for a loop. Touching her so innocently had sent his blood boiling, and he hadn't been able to make himself pull away.

Just like now.

Tori's mouth was soft and more welcoming than he'd expected. There was no tight-lipped resignation. Instead, she leaned in to him just slightly, tasting like the honey she'd put in his tea a few days earlier. The gesture was enough to coax him into closing his eyes and deepening the kiss. His right hand slipped up to caress her cheek.

The surge of desire that ran through his body urged him forward, keeping him from pulling back the way his brain knew he needed to. In the back of his mind he registered that Tori wasn't pulling away, either. There was something stronger than both of them holding them in place. A tingle of electricity danced across the palm of his hand where he touched her. He wanted to wrap his arms around her. He wanted to forget about their circumstances and press his body against hers.

A loud wolf whistle from one of his brothers startled both of them out of it. As if receiving an unexpected slap, Wade jerked back. Tori did the same. He looked at her, a little startled by his reaction to her. The intensity had completely caught him off guard. Judging by the wide-eyed expression on Tori's face, she was equally confused by what had just happened.

Glancing behind her, he saw that his whole family stood with mixed expressions on their faces. A few were surprised, Brody was irritated, Heath was amused. Only his mother was grinning, a smug satisfaction in her eyes. Wade could tell she was picking out the perfect color of pastel yarn at that very moment.

"Well," Ken said, breaking the awkward silence. "I think it's time to carve this bird. Everyone finish up and make your drinks."

The family scattered again, Molly reluctantly returning to her duties and leaving Wade and Tori alone. He looked back to her, and his chest suddenly felt tight and uncomfortable. The white collared shirt under his sweater was choking him. He was unpleasantly warm, despite being on the opposite side of the room from the fireplace.

Maybe it had nothing to do with his clothes. It was her. She looked more beautiful than she ever had. Her pale skin was flushed a rosy pink. Her lips were moist and slightly parted. The light blue of her eyes seemed darker around the edges than before. Maybe it was the dark blue of her scoop-neck sweater that drew out the color. It highlighted the long column of her neck and the delicate line of her collarbones. Between them, a small cameo hung on a gold chain. It was the ivory silhouette of a woman set against a blue background that reminded him of his mother's Wedgwood.

Wade wanted to sweep the necklace aside and plant kisses in the hollow of her throat. He wanted to know how her skin would taste and smell. He sucked in a deep breath to draw in her scent. It was a smoky mix of sweet flowers, like honeysuckle, and the herbal undertone of burning incense. It was surprisingly seductive.

"What was that?" Tori's voice was small and without the biting tone she normally hurled at him.

"Just a kiss," he answered, dismissing the powerful feeling that had set fire running through his veins when they touched. He wasn't ready to let her know how it had affected him. How she affected him. That would put him at a distinct disadvantage in their negotiations.

Her blue eyes searched his face for a moment before she sighed and looked away. There was a touch of disappointment in her expression as though she'd expected him to acknowledge it was more than that. She nodded softly and took a step away from him. "I'm going to wash my hands before dinner."

Wade pointed out the small half bath beneath the stairs and watched her walk away. The sweater was enticing, but more so were the charcoal-gray skirt and knee-high leather boots she wore with it. There was a sway to her hips when she walked that was deliciously outlined by the fit of the skirt, and the slit in the back offered him a momentary flash of thigh with each step. It made him wish the bathroom were farther away so he could continue to watch her walk.

Brody stepped into the path of his view just as she pulled the door closed behind her. A frown lined his brother's face as he thrust a mug of mulled cider into Wade's hand. "Here. There's no whiskey in it. I figured you were being dumb enough without alcohol."

Wade scowled at his brother but accepted the drink. "You worry too much. It's all part of my plan," he lied, hoping it sounded like forethought on his part. "I'm softening her up. Then, when you dig up some good information on her I can use, she'll be putty in my hands."

Heath came past them to put his own coat into the closet. "Hey, Wade, I thought you were supposed to be buying Tori's land, not checking her for tonsillitis."

"Both of you just cool it. I know what I'm doing."

Brody's dark blue gaze narrowed at him. Wade often wondered if his brother's personality would be different if he had been born into better circumstances. Would he be less serious? More open to life?

"Try not to scowl at her, Brody. Make her feel welcome, more at ease. It will help. You said you wanted to do something. Here's your chance."

Brody sighed. "I know. I just wasn't prepared to see her walk in. I wish Mama had told me she was coming. She knows I don't like those kinds of surprises."

Wade nodded. "Neither do I." He knew his brother didn't like to meet new people. It was a painful ritual he had to repeat every time someone came face-to-face with him for the first time. "How did she do?"

"Better than most. She didn't run screaming or anything. Although, I need to tell Julianne not to sit her across from me at the table. I'm sure it wouldn't help her appetite to look at me the whole time."

Wade sighed and took a sip of his cider. "Stop it. No self-flagellation during the holidays. Would you rather she sits across from me?"

"Hmm," Brody said thoughtfully. "You two might end up playing footsie at this rate. Maybe across from Xander or Heath."

"Dinner is ready," Molly announced from the entryway to the kitchen. "Is everyone ready?"

The bathroom door opened and Tori came out much more composed than when she went in. Wade watched her paint a smile on her face and curl her hands into fists before she took a few steps toward the dining room. The kiss seemed to have thrown her for a loop. He was glad. Perhaps keeping her off balance was the best thing to do. Kill her with kindness. Use any information Brody came up with to charm her. Being nice might confuse her, make her like him and his family. Maybe then she could understand how important buying the land back was to him.

"Wade, I've put you here," Julianne said, indicating a chair on the far side of the table.

He nodded and made his way over. His sister smiled wickedly at him as she seated Tori next to him and Brody to her left, his good side facing the guest. The rest of the family took their places.

The table was laid with a red-and-gold tablecloth that was barely visible beneath the edge-to-edge casserole dishes, platters and bowls. In the center were thick red

pillar candles, poinsettias and golden ribbons that sparkled in the light. As always, Molly had outdone herself.

As tradition dictated, they stood at the table and held
hands. Wade reached out and took Tori's hand, trying
hard to focus on his father's words instead of how her
touch affected him.

"I'm thankful that all of us are back together again.
It's been a tough year for everyone," Ken began. "But
certainly not the worst we've ever had. We're fight-
ers. We have each been blessed with perseverance and
drive and have been brought together for a reason. May
we each have a glorious and prosperous New Year and
may we each find ourselves back here again next year,
blessed in life, love and happiness."

Wade felt Tori gently squeeze his hand. A lump
formed in his throat. She understood. At least, she understood his family. She could never truly understand
what he was dealing with. He doubted she had such
dark secrets buried in her past. Few people did.

Ken smiled. "Merry Christmas, everyone. Let's eat."

Five

Tori was glad she hadn't chickened out after that kiss. She had stood in the bathroom for longer than necessary and toyed with the idea of trying to climb out the tiny window. Reason and hunger trumped her flight reflex, and for that she was grateful. She was stuffed almost as full as the turkey had been before the feasting started. She'd had no idea what a real Christmas dinner was like—one cooked without chafing fuel or charcoal briquettes—until now. There had been mashed potatoes and chestnut-oyster bread stuffing covered in gravy. Maple-glazed carrots. Hot yeast rolls. Then dessert. Good Lord. She'd never known pumpkin pie could melt on your tongue like that.

Everyone had been very friendly, engaging her in their conversations, including Wade. There was a lot of family banter, laughter and tall tales. Tori supposed this was what it was like to have a large family. Growing up as an only child, she'd always longed for a home with a family like this. She'd imagined holidays with merriment and shared stories from childhood.

Tori had sometimes thought that when she married and built her home she'd want to have a lot of children. Four. Maybe five, like the Edens. When things fell apart with Ryan after two years, she'd decided to go ahead and build her dream house anyway. Hopefully love and children would follow. But at the rate she was going, the dreams of that large family were dwindling away. She might end up living in that big house alone.

Perhaps that was why every attempt to start drawing up an architectural design had failed. Even her pen knew there was no point in a home without lively discussion or shared memories to be made there.

Tori turned to listen to Heath as he very animatedly talked about one of his obnoxious advertising clients. They were all such great storytellers. After hearing Ken talk, she knew where the children had learned their skills.

It was a welcome distraction from the night's wildly swirling undercurrents. Having Wade only a few inches away all night had been its own form of torture. She couldn't help but be hyperaware of him. For one thing, he was like a radiator. She could feel the heat of his body penetrating her sweater. Tori tended to run cold, and it took everything she had not to curl against his side and lean into his warmth.

They also kept touching one another. First, holding hands during the blessing before dinner. Then passing food around the table. Without fail their fingers would brush or their shoulders would bump. Innocent, meaningless touches that sent a jolt through her body each time. And the kiss certainly hadn't helped. Whenever her mind drifted away from dinner, it would go back to the moment under the mistletoe.

She hadn't expected anything like that. Wade had had a look on his face as though he were being marched to the guillotine. Clenched jaw, blank eyes. He hadn't wanted to kiss her. And yet, once he did…everything changed. And it really did feel as if everything was different. In less than a minute the way she thought about Wade, the way she looked at him, the way she perceived him shifted on its axis.

Tori dragged her fork through the streaks of whipped cream left on her dessert plate and pondered the kiss. There was a tenderness in his touch that surprised her. A need thrummed through the glide of his fingertips across her skin. It made her want to wrap her arms around his neck and pull him close. Wade! Of all the people to make her react like that… A part of her wished she had found herself under the mistletoe with any of the other brothers. They were all handsome and successful. She could do worse, even considering scowling Brody.

But it had to be Wade, the one she was determined to keep her defenses up against. He was out to push her aside and get what he wanted at any price. She had to remember that.

But somehow that kiss had put a dent in her armor. Sitting so close to him during dinner, Tori couldn't help but wonder if he knew it. He'd made it clear that first night that he would do whatever it took to change her mind, including seducing her. But the mistletoe kiss wasn't planned. And she got the feeling from his reaction that it wasn't just a scheme.

So what was that kiss all about? He'd blown off her question when she asked. She didn't know why. It was more than just a kiss. More than his ruthless drive. At least, it felt that way to her. Maybe it was just her old attraction to him coloring her impressions.

Tori glanced at Wade beside her. He was watching her. He was facing Heath as his brother talked, but his gaze had strayed to her. There was no anger or animosity in his green eyes. Only desire swirling with the flicker of candlelight. His eyes invited her closer. Dared her to stand under the mistletoe with him again.

No, she had been right. It had been more than just a simple kiss.

Taking a deep breath, Tori turned away and found herself facing Brody. He stiffened when he noticed her move toward him. She could tell he was extremely uncomfortable with her there. While almost everyone else at the table was relaxed and chatting, Brody was board straight in his seat and quiet. He wouldn't look at her, but every now and again his gaze would stray to her, then nervously back to the others at the table.

She hoped she wasn't the cause of his discomfort. Tori would hate it if his holiday was ruined because of her surprise arrival. Why had they seated him beside her if he would be miserable? She didn't know what she could do to make it better. Speaking to him made it worse. So she shifted back toward Wade and felt Brody subtly relax into his chair.

"Can we open a present tonight?" Julianne asked as she got up from the table with a stack of dessert plates she had collected.

"You know the rules," Molly chided. "Only Tori gets her present tonight."

Tori was in the process of standing with her own dish when she paused, hearing her name. "What?"

"Why does Tori get to open her gift?" Heath asked.

"Not once in eighteen years have you ever let one of us open a gift early."

"Stop whining, Heath," Ken said. "Tori is getting her present tonight because she won't be here in the morning when we do gifts."

Tori frowned and pushed in her chair. "No more, please. Having me over for dinner was kind enough, really."

Molly shook her head. "It's too late. If you don't take it, it will be a waste." She turned on her heel and headed into the kitchen, ending the argument.

The next few minutes were a blur of activity. Tori was shooed from the kitchen but watched the activity with interest for a while. Everyone took on a task. Not just the women as she had expected. Wade and Brody pushed up their sleeves and started washing and drying pans. Ken brought in dishes from the dining room. Julianne loaded the dishwasher. Xander loaded plastic containers with extra food. Heath bagged the trash and carried it outside. Molly watched over the process like a tiny drill sergeant.

Feeling useless, Tori went to sit in front of the fireplace. Brody and Heath's fire was quite excellent, and it warmed her back. The old house was beautiful, but a touch drafty, and being near the blaze was a prime spot.

Looking around, she found the same decorating enthusiasm from the gift shop carried over into the house. The fireplace and railing up the stairs were draped in garland. There were candles and poinsettias and other sparkly things everywhere. The tree was the grand centerpiece of the living room. She had expected a tree decorated with coordinating ribbons and glass globes, but this was a family tree. There was a mishmash of ornaments and pieces made with felt, clothespins and glitter glue. Crafts from the children's younger days. Multicolored lights. A shiny gold star on the top. It was perfect.

The rest of the room was equally interesting. There were built-in bookcases filled with leather-bound books, knickknacks and a million picture frames. It was a fascinating thing to Tori. Her family was minimalist out of necessity. They had a strict policy that if they didn't use something for six months, it was gone. And if it didn't serve more than one function, there was no sense in getting it at all.

Tori was distracted by footsteps on the dark hardwood floor. What should've taken at least an hour in the kitchen was done in less than ten minutes. The family poured back into the living room far earlier than Tori had expected.

They all held mugs of cider. Wade had two, one of which he handed to her as he sat down on the stone hearth beside her. She took it with a touch of hesitation. "Did you put something in this?" she asked quietly enough for only him to hear.

He smiled widely, his dangerous charm making it obvious that he could have if he wanted to. "No. Just cider."

With no real choice but to believe him, she sipped the drink. It was warm with cinnamon and caramel undertones. It tasted just the way Christmas should. Not the slightest hint of any chemicals.

"Ken," Molly urged, "go get Tori's gift from the shop, would you, please?"

"I'll get it, Dad." Wade leaped up and beat his father out the door.

Tori sat anxiously awaiting what he was bringing her. He returned a few minutes later with a tiny potted Christmas tree. It was about two feet tall, and it was decorated with tiny balls of birdseed that looked like ornaments, and strands of cranberries and popcorn threaded around it like garland. It was adorably festive and just the right size for her Airstream.

"Is that really for me?" she asked, wishing she had brought something else with the poinsettia. It didn't seem like enough for all their kindness.

"Absolutely," Molly said, beaming with the excitement of gift-giving. "Anyone else would've gotten a larger tree."

Wade approached her with the tree in his arms. "When Mama mentioned you'd never had a Christmas tree, the entire family was rightfully appalled. Everyone needs a Christmas tree, as far as the Edens are concerned." Wade set the tree on the small end table beside her. "This balsam fir is alive and well-potted, so when it's warmer you can plant it somewhere. The decorations are for the birds, quite literally. You can set the tree outside after Christmas, and they'll happily eat up all the decorations so you don't have to find a place to store them."

Tori couldn't help the look of surprise on her face. The gift itself was thoughtful enough, but there was also an attention to detail that she appreciated. These people knew nothing about her, and yet they'd chosen the most perfect present. She didn't know what to say, so she just reached out to touch the ornaments and admire her tree instead of the man who brought it to her.

"It's beautiful," she finally got out. "Thank you for the tree. And for having me to dinner. You may have single-handedly salvaged my holiday."

Wade smiled, and Tori's breath caught in her throat. He'd never smiled at her that way. There was always a challenge, a hard edge of negotiation in his expression, even when he was trying to charm her. Tonight, for the holiday, he seemed to have put that aside. Now his smile was just pure joy. It lit up his face, making him more breathtakingly handsome than he'd ever been.

She swallowed hard and took a sip of her cider to distract herself. Wade sat down beside her again and took up his own mug. Tori held her breath, just knowing that the rapid pound of her heartbeat was loud enough for him to hear sitting so close.

Fortunately, someone suggested Julianne play some carols on the ancient-looking upright piano in the corner. That would be loud enough to muffle the sound. Heath goaded his sister until she took her place at the bench and started playing. She began with "The First Noel," and everyone sat quietly listening to her play.

Tori was relieved to have some time without having to maintain a conversation with someone. She wasn't an introvert, per se, but she did spend a lot of time alone. She'd gotten a little rusty at basic small talk. Eating dinner had taken up a lot of that time until now. Lifting her mug, she happily sipped her mulled cider and listened to the music.

"You may want to leave before too long," Wade suggested.

Tori turned to him with a frown curling her mouth down. Just when she thought they'd called a truce. "Are you ready to be rid of me already?"

"No," he said, turning to the piano and leaning toward her. "But you should know we're hard-core on tradition around here. Once Julianne plays a couple songs, a group of grown men is going to watch *How the Grinch Stole Christmas* on an old VHS tape. Then

Dad will read 'A Visit from Saint Nicholas' to all of us before bed."

Tori smiled. She could hardly imagine a room of powerful CEOs watching cartoons. "It sounds sweet. Are there footie pajamas involved?"

"No, thankfully they don't make them in my size. When we were kids, yeah, it was cute. Now it's just getting old and sad, but we haven't provided the requisite grandchildren to pass on the tradition."

"Mmm…" she murmured, taking the last sip of her cider as the final notes of Julianne's song rang out. "I'd better go, then."

"I'll walk you out. My mom is loading you down with leftovers, so I'll carry your tree."

Tori arched an eyebrow at Wade but didn't argue. As she rose, Molly got up as well, and the two women headed into the kitchen where Tori disposed of her mug in the sink. Wade was right: Molly had packed a bag full of containers to feed her for a few days. Molly gave Tori a big hug, thanked her for coming and walked her to the door.

Tori was careful to avoid the mistletoe this time as she grabbed her coat and flung it over her arm. She waved good-night to everyone, then headed out the door with Wade behind her.

They crunched through the snow to where she'd parked her truck without saying a word. She unlocked the passenger door and set the leftovers on the floorboard. Wade put the tree on the bench, and Tori fastened it into place with the seat belt. "That should hold it steady," she said, tossing her bulky jacket inside and slamming the heavy door closed.

Wade was standing beside her, leaning casually against the truck. She expected him to go back into the house—he didn't even have his coat on—but he stayed firmly in place. His green eyes were black in the dark night, fixed on her face. The intensity of his gaze made her skin flush and a tingle run down the length of her spine.

"That wasn't so bad, was it?" she teased, unsure what else to say with him watching her so closely.

"No, it wasn't. I rather enjoyed it. I hope you had a good time. My family seems to like you."

"I did have a good time. They seem like really great people."

"They are. I would do anything to protect them."

Tori felt the mood shift. He wasn't just talking about Christmas dinner anymore. She'd hoped they could shelve this argument for at least one night.

"I know there's a part of you that thinks I'm the big bad wolf out to steal your property. The fact of the matter is that without getting lawyers involved and doing some fairly ugly things that would hurt my parents and their reputation, I can't take this land from you. And I can't force you to sell it. But I hope that meeting my family tonight helps you understand where I'm coming from and how important this is to me. So you know that I've been telling you the truth the whole time."

Wade took a step forward, invading her space. If he was deliberately trying to use his size to intimidate her, his plan was backfiring. She was anything but intimidated. When he was that close, she was thoroughly turned on and extremely distracted from the conversation.

"I need you..." he began, wrapping a gentle hand around her upper arm. Tori couldn't help leaning in to him, her brain short-circuiting with his touch and his words. "...to believe me, Tori."

Tori sighed, an expression of disappointment wrinkling her delicate nose. "Wade, what difference does it make if I believe you or not? You want my land. I don't want to sell it to you. It's a fairly cut-and-dried scenario."

Wade shrugged. "Nothing is that simple. Years of experience have taught me that there is always room to negotiate. Everyone has a pressure point. For some people, it's a dollar amount. That's obviously not the case with you or we would've resolved this the first day. I didn't plan for you to be here tonight, but maybe some good can come of it. Perhaps you have a soft spot for family that would help you understand. I don't want to be the bad guy. I like you, Tori. You're spunky. And beautiful when you aren't pointing a gun at me."

He watched Tori's eyes widen and her mouth softly part at his compliment. "You're just flattering me to get your way," she accused, shrugging off his hand.

"I won't lie to you. I do want the land. But I also want to get to know you better. And for you to like me. I'd like to ask you out to dinner sometime. A nice romantic dinner without my family's prying eyes watching our every move. The perfect scenario ends with both of us achieving everything we want."

"How do you know anything about what I want?"

Wade looked into Tori's eyes. They reflected a confusion he could sense in every inch of her tense body language. She wanted him. She despised him. He was walking a fine line between the two sides. He decided to push her until her desire won the battle. He leaned in and gently brushed a strand of red hair out of her face, barely grazing her forehead and cheek with his fingertips. Tori sucked in a ragged breath when he touched her. He spoke low, almost like a lover's whisper. "Maybe I don't. So tell me, what do you want, Tori?"

She swallowed hard but didn't pull away from him. "I want…" Her voice trailed away as though she couldn't find the right words. "I didn't think you'd stoop so low as to try to romance the land out from under me," she replied, choosing to ignore his question. "As if you even could."

So she was onto him. That might make the seduction harder, but not impossible. "You doubt my abilities?" He grinned a wide, mischievous smile at her and pulled back to give her some room to breathe. He'd rattled her enough.

"No, but perhaps you underestimate my ability to resist you. Tell me, what was that kiss about?"

That was a damn good question. What *was* that kiss about? Tori was the last woman he needed to be attracted to, but his reaction to her was undeniable. Stupid, but undeniable. At best, he could try to use their attraction to tip the scales in his favor. "I told you already. I'm after the win-win scenario."

"I'm not going to sell you my land, Wade. If that's all tonight was about, all that kiss was about, then you can take your Christmas tree and go back inside."

Tori shifted her boots in the snow and crossed her arms under her breasts. The act of defiance did little to discourage the thoughts about her running through his mind. It had only focused his brain on the perky orbs of her breasts that pressed against her chenille sweater and threatened to erupt over the top of her scoop neckline.

It made his mouth water to think about gliding his hands over the soft fabric and kneading her supple flesh. He had the fierce urge to run his tongue along her collarbone and the crest of her breasts.

When he tore his gaze away and looked her in the eye again, he knew he'd been caught in the act. Her eyes widened, and he was struck by what a gorgeous shade of blue they were. Her eyes were a lovely shade of light blue that reminded him of the ice-blue eyes of his friend's Siberian husky. Cool, wary and penetrating. They were also sparkling with the hint of a desire she didn't want to acknowledge. She dropped her hands back to her sides to ruin the display she created.

"Actually, no. That isn't all that it's about." He didn't elaborate, but the pointed way he watched her lips as she tentatively licked them should have spelled it out for her.

Whether it was due to the cold or to his blatant admiration, her creamy cheeks turned a rosy pink and her breath came out rapidly in foglike bursts. He wondered if that was how she would look when she was flushed and breathless from his passionate caresses.

He hadn't been lying when he said he wanted her to like him. That he wanted to ask her out to dinner sometime. When they argued, his blood boiled with irritation and arousal all at once. Wade liked a challenge. Tori was certainly that.

Sure, he intended to get that land back one way or another, but that was a separate issue. Business versus pleasure. He wished she could see the difference, but the women he'd known had a tendency to tangle issues together into an impossible knot. Tori was no different where this was concerned.

Initially he'd thought that indulging in their undeniable connection would complicate the issue. But kissing her in the foyer had changed everything. Denying the electricity between them might actually make their problems worse. He was certainly getting cranky returning to his bunkhouse room every night, alone, with Tori on his mind. Tonight he would have to share the room with Brody and listen to his opinion on the matter.

That wouldn't help the tension building up, either. Perhaps if he and Tori blew off a little steam together, the situation wouldn't seem quite so dire. On her end, at least. On his end, it was most certainly dire, no matter how much pent-up sexual frustration taunted him.

His perfect solution would be to get the land back, offer her enough money that she could buy land that was even better for her needs, and have her in his bed for a while. There didn't have to be a bad guy in this story if she would be open-minded to the options. He wasn't above abusing their sexual chemistry to get his way—if they happened to end up in bed together, so be it.

And at the moment, he wished it would happen sooner rather than later.

"This is also about the chemistry between us." Wade took another step toward her and she didn't back away. His hand went to her face, tipping her chin up to look at him. Even in heeled boots, she had to strain to look him in the eye this close. "I'm not the only one to feel it, am I?"

Tori gave just a subtle shake of her head. He could detect it only by his hand against her smooth skin. "I feel it," she whispered.

She stepped closer until their bodies were nearly touching. He was suddenly aware of the scent of her perfume again, an alluring earthy and floral mix. It made his whole body tighten with anticipation of touching her the way he'd wanted to earlier but couldn't. Now he was free to act without the eyes of his family and their obnoxious critiques.

Wade didn't need any more of an invitation. He dived into her, capturing her lips and cupping her upturned face in his hands. She was soft and open to him.

He felt her hands press against his chest, not to push him away, but to feel him through the thick wool of his sweater. Wade moaned against her mouth as her silky tongue glided along his own. It sent a sharp barb of pleasure through his body, urging him to take more than he should tonight. His hands fell from her face to slip around her waist. He tugged her to him, relishing the feel of her soft body against his hard angles.

Without pulling away, he inched them backward through the snow until her back was pressed against the cold metal of her truck door. She gasped but didn't resist it. In fact, it seemed to light a fire in her. When his mouth left hers to finally taste the hollow of her throat, Tori wrapped her arms around his neck, her silky stocking-clad leg sliding up the outside of his thigh to hook around his hip and draw him in.

The throbbing of his groin pressing into her was almost as uncomfortable as the needling cold on his exposed skin. His hot lips scorched across her frosty throat in a delicious contrast. It wasn't until her pebble-hard nipples pressed into his chest that reality intruded. He was practically devouring her in twenty-degree weather, and neither of them had on a coat.

Forcing himself to pull away, he took one last gentle kiss and backed off. Wade sucked in a large breath of painfully icy air to kill his arousal. He couldn't walk back into the house like this. He grabbed her upper arms and pulled her away from the frigid metal siding of her truck. "I'm sorry," he said. "You've got to be freezing. I didn't think about that at the time."

"To the contrary," she said, her lips swollen and her

cheeks still red. "I'm feeling quite warm for some reason." She smiled sheepishly and brushed a long strand of red hair behind her ear.

Damn. He'd forgotten to touch her hair. He'd ached to do that from the first moment he saw it.

"You don't have a coat on, either," she said. "You'd better get back inside or you'll spend your Christmas Day sick instead of with your family. You don't want to miss the Grinch."

Wade smiled and shook his head. "I'm certain they'll wait for me, whether I want them to or not." There were unnecessary words swirling in his gut that he had the urge to say before he left. They probably wouldn't help the situation, but he couldn't keep them inside. "I want you to know that all this doesn't have anything to do with the land."

Tori stood on her toes to press a soft goodbye kiss to his lips. "I know," she whispered faintly against his mouth.

He had to force his hands into fists buried deep in his pant pockets to keep from reaching for her again.

"I'm glad this one wasn't in front of your whole family," she said with a grin. Before he could respond, Tori turned and ran around to the other side of the truck. "Merry Christmas, Wade." She climbed inside and the engine roared to life.

Tori gave a quick wave as she turned her truck and pulled away from the Garden of Eden. Wade watched her disappear into the darkness, and then ran his hand through his hair.

"Merry Christmas, Tori."

Six

Thursday night, Tori sat in her favorite seat at the counter of Daisy's Diner. Now that the holiday had passed and the leftovers Molly forced on her were all eaten, it was back to her usual haunt.

Over the past few weeks she'd made her first friend in the waitress who handled the counter there. Her name tag said "Rosalyn," but she told Tori to just call her Rose. Rose was off on Wednesday nights, but any other day of the week Tori would be at Daisy's for dinner.

"Hey there, Tori. What will it be tonight?" Rose asked, leaning casually against the countertop.

Her eyes barely glanced at the menu before she made her decision. "How about the chicken pot pie and some hot tea?"

Rose smiled. "You got it." She spun from the counter and disappeared into the back, returning a few minutes later with a teacup and a small kettle of hot water. "I'm surprised you didn't starve over the holiday with us closed," Rose said with a smile.

"I was able to depend on the kindness of strangers," Tori admitted. "The Edens invited me over for dinner."

Rose perked up in quite a peculiar way. "The Edens, huh? Are they *all* in town for Christmas?"

"Yes. At least they were. I met all of them on Christmas Eve. Some of them may have left by now."

The waitress nodded, a hint of disappointment in her dark brown eyes. She turned and Tori followed Rose's line of sight to where her son was sitting alone in a corner booth. The little boy was eight or nine, and whenever Tori came in, he was doing homework or playing his handheld video games while Rose worked.

"I always had a soft spot for Xander. We dated on and off in high school before he left for college. He had a smile that would make my heart just melt. Very charming. It's no wonder he's a politician. He has a way with people."

Tori nodded in agreement. "He was very nice. I was more worried about Wade, though. He's been giving me some trouble."

"Worried? Why? My sister went to high school with him." A sly grin spread across Rose's face. "A lot of women in this town wouldn't mind Wade Mitchell giving them trouble. Some say he's the pick of the litter."

Tori chuckled, a hint of bitterness beneath it. "Well, those people would say differently if they had something he wanted. He's very persistent and downright irritating when he doesn't get his way."

"What could you possibly have that he wants? You just got here."

"He wants my land."

Rose frowned. "The land you just bought?"

She nodded and sipped her tea. "It belonged to his family and he wants to buy it back."

"I don't know why he'd want it. None of the kids have ever shown much interest in the farm. But I'll tell you, if I had to have someone causing me trouble, I'd take an Eden boy in a heartbeat. At least you'd have something nice to look at while you suffered."

That was certainly true. All the Eden boys were attractive. Even Brody, if you could look past the scars and the attitude. If given her choice of the lot, the decision wouldn't be difficult. Wade was certainly her type: dark hair, soulful eyes, a wicked smile... Unfortunately, the magnificent view was a distraction she couldn't afford. "As nice as that all sounds, he's becoming a major pain in my—"

"Well, speak of the devil." Rose straightened immediately and started fidgeting with her dark brown ponytail. Tori turned in her seat and found Wade there, hanging up his coat on a rack by the door. She turned back before he could see her, hoping he wouldn't notice her. Unfortunately, Rose was strutting around so conspicuously in front of her that he was certain to look her way eventually.

"Hey, Rosie," Wade said, sitting down at the counter a few seats away. "How've you been?"

Rose slid down the counter as if she'd been pulled in by his tractor beam. "Good. How about you?"

"Busy. How's your dad doing these days?"

Tori watched the smile fade from Rose's face. "He's okay. I'm sure he's bored out of his skull, but twenty-three hours a day in a cell will do that to you."

Wade straightened in surprise. Apparently he hadn't kept up with the latest Cornwall gossip. Even Tori knew that Rose's dad had gone to jail last year. She didn't know what for, exactly, but it didn't sound as though he would be getting out anytime soon.

"Oh, I hadn't heard he was, uh… I'm sorry. *Um*…do you guys have the pot roast special tonight?"

Rose smiled again and let the uncomfortable subject drop. "That's only on Mondays. But we've got the sliced roast beef with mushroom gravy and mashed potatoes. It's almost as good."

"That'll do. And a lemon-lime soda, please."

"You bet." Rose shot Tori a wink and disappeared into the kitchen.

Alone at the counter with him, Tori couldn't decide if she should shrink into herself and hope she became invisible or sit up tall and dare him to say something to her. She hadn't seen him since Christmas Eve. Since they kissed. And now she didn't quite know how to act. Was he still the enemy? Her body didn't think so, but her brain disagreed. He could be exploiting their natural attraction to get his way. She would have to err on the side of caution and continue under the assumption he was the enemy, kisses or no, until he stopped asking to buy her land. She couldn't trust his motives.

And yet she didn't want to fight with him anymore. It was all too confusing.

She opted for a happy medium, quietly sipping her tea and waiting for her dinner to arrive. Tori focused so intently on it that she noticed only a familiar heat, and when she looked up, Wade was on the stool beside her. She hadn't even realized he'd moved.

"Hello, Tori."

She turned in her seat to look at him. He was wearing dark tailored jeans and a black cashmere sweater that fit his broad shoulders beautifully. She itched to reach out and brush the soft fabric as an excuse to touch him again.

"Wade," she responded simply. She was afraid she'd give away too much if she said anything more.

Wade smiled broadly, undeterred by her cool reception. He took the drink Rose offered him before she disappeared into the kitchen again, leaving Tori high and dry. He took a sip before he spoke. "Do you eat here a lot?"

"Most nights. You've seen my kitchen." She was certain her confusion was etched on her face, but there was nothing she could do about it. "You're awfully friendly tonight."

"Why wouldn't I be? The last time I saw you, we made out against the side of your truck."

Tori's cheeks lit up as bright as her hair. "Don't say it like that," she said, wishing her pot pie would come and give her something to focus on instead of her memories of making out with Wade. She couldn't think of anything else with his scent so close, tempting her to do it again.

Wade grinned and she was glad she was sitting down and didn't have to worry about her knees giving out from under her. She wished she didn't amuse him so much. If he smiled less and sat farther away, she might not be fighting this pointless attraction to the man she was trying very hard not to like. A man she *shouldn't* like, considering he fired her, made her lose her apartment and was hell-bent on taking away her second chance at settling down.

It was that stupid smile that did it.

"Okay," he agreed, leaning in to whisper the words softly in her ear. "The last time I saw you, I drank in your lips like a sweet wine I couldn't get enough of."

Rose approached at that moment, heard Wade's low words, then immediately spun on her heel and vanished. Tori knew she'd hear more about that later, but she could hardly care with Wade's deep voice vibrating through her. A shiver ran down Tori's spine when he spoke, and gooseflesh drew up all over her skin. His warm breath on her neck took her back to the snow, to the truck, to the kisses she couldn't forget. Why did he have this power over her? "I s-suppose that's a better way to put it," she stuttered. "And yet you haven't darkened my doorstep since then."

"I wanted to, believe me. But I had to put in the family time. We only get together once a year. The last of them left today, so I'm free to begin harassing you again."

Honestly, she'd felt his presence even with him gone. The past few days he'd plagued her thoughts, overrun her dreams and disrupted her focus. Memories of his kisses lingered. She was on edge thinking he might show up any minute to continue his petition to buy the land. Or better yet, to pick up where they'd left off. He might as well have been sitting in her camper since Monday night.

"Why did you stay behind when the others left?" she said, pushing the thoughts of his touch out of her mind.

"A few things needed my attention," he said.

She swallowed hard. "Like what?"

"Like you." His lips curled in a smug grin. He knew he was pushing all the right buttons. "So how long have you been here in Cornwall?"

The change in discussion nearly gave her whiplash, but the topic was thankfully a safe one. "Two months. I had been looking at this area for a while before that but hadn't found any land that suited the house I want to build."

"Shouldn't an architect build a house to suit the land, not the other way around?"

"Perhaps." She shrugged. "But this is going to be my one and only home. The place where I live for the rest of my life. I've been thinking about what I want for years, and I finally have the money and time to make it happen. That plot of land is perfect for what I envision. I refuse to settle."

"Understandable. How are the plans coming for the house?"

Tori's lips twisted with concern before she spoke. "Not as quickly as I'd like. But you can't rush perfection. I hope to have the blueprints finalized this week and break ground before the end of January."

Wade's eyes widened almost imperceptibly and his brow furrowed with thoughts he didn't choose to share. "Why Cornwall? You're not from around here, are you?"

"No and yes. I'm not from anywhere. My parents and I traveled my whole life. But I came to visit this area on a long weekend while I was working in Philadelphia, and I fell in love with it."

Wade was listening intently, and it bothered her. The conversation seemed innocent enough. What was his angle? He couldn't really care. Was he just making small talk or was he trying to get information he could use against her later? Maybe he'd try to stall her building permits and frustrate her into selling.

"I've lived around here my whole life."

"Cornwall?"

"Not exactly. Here and there in Litchfield County. I bounced around through a lot of different foster homes at first. I came to Cornwall when I was ten and stayed here until I went off to Yale."

"Is that where you met Stanton?" Alex Stanton had been Wade's business partner when she first went to work for him.

"Yes. We started our own company together after college, and then after you left, we decided to split up and focus on different types of projects. He wanted to branch out, go nationwide and, eventually, international. I wanted to focus on Manhattan, so I've been on my own a few years now."

"Now the two of you can make money twice as fast."

"Precisely the idea behind our dastardly plan."

Damned if she didn't smile at him. He had a way of making her like him no matter how badly she didn't want to. He was only a few days into his petition and he had already managed to charm her. He'd kissed her. How long could she hold out against this? How long until he tired and gave up?

"So, tell me about some of your green innovations. I've been hoping to add more into my projects."

At that, Tori outright frowned. He really was taking every available angle to butter her up. "Really?"

"Yes, really. I've been investing heavily in a couple of green companies over the past few years. They're really making some great strides in products that are earth friendly and, I hope soon, affordable for consumers. I think more people will use them when the price isn't so intimidating."

That surprised her. When you're in the business of renovating and reselling buildings, every penny spent cuts into the profit. She never expected him to be the kind who would invest in green products. But she was glad he did. She wished more people would. "I agree.

That's why I try to get as much exposure for my work as possible. I want to increase interest and demand, which will hopefully make some of these innovations mainstream and drive down the price."

"It's hard to do. My folks have managed to run an organic farm without the crippling prices breaking their profit margin, but it's taken decades to perfect it."

Tori's brows shot up over her teacup. "The tree farm is organic?"

"For the past twenty years."

Wade was full of good surprises tonight. She wouldn't admit it to anyone, but she was actually enjoying her conversation with him. It felt almost like a fun, casual first date.

Did she just use the word date?

"I've been looking at some of your recent projects online. You really do great work. The building in Philadelphia is stunning."

Tori blushed again. If he was playing her, he was good at it. She couldn't help but believe him. Her latest project really was incredible. Her best apart from her own house, which was going to be her greatest work. "Thank you. It's almost done. The ribbon cutting is scheduled for just after the New Year."

"I wish we hadn't lost you at our company. Your talents would've been put to good use."

It sounded like a compliment, but this time it rubbed her the wrong way. Tori was about to say something rude about how he shouldn't have fired her, but Rose returned then, placing a piping-hot dish of chicken pot pie on the counter in front of her. It was the perfect opportunity for her to focus on something else.

The pie had a golden flaky crust that Tori yearned to bust open with her fork. Typically, she'd leaned toward club sandwiches and grilled chicken plates, but dinner with the Edens had been a gateway meal. Now she was on a personal mission to make up for twenty-eight years of home-cooking deprivation.

"That smells great," he said, leaning closer to her and inhaling the enticing aroma. "Don't let me stop you from enjoying your meal."

Tori opened her mouth to argue with him about etiquette, but Rose came by with his plate, too. Now she couldn't even refuse out of politeness.

"Perfect," he said, eyeing his roast beef. "Now we can eat together. Not exactly what I envisioned for our first date, but it will do."

"Date?" Tori's head snapped up from her plate. The man must be reading her mind. It was the only answer.

"I told you I wanted to take you out to dinner," he said before popping a bite of beef into his mouth and swallowing. "I was thinking more of wine and candlelight, but we can save that for our second date."

"We're dating now?" It was news to her. News that made her heart flutter momentarily in her chest as though she were a teenager.

Wade shrugged. "Why label it? We're just enjoying each other's company and getting to know one another. What are you doing tomorrow night?"

Tori paused with a bite of chicken and vegetables in midair. "Why?"

Dropping his fork to his plate, Wade spun on his stool to face her. His brow was furrowed with irritation, but the light in his green eyes indicated it was more exasperation than anything else. "Why must you make everything so difficult? It's a simple question. Do you have plans Friday night or not?"

"No." It was the truth. She worked during the day

on the blueprints for the house, fielding calls and holding virtual meetings on other projects, but most of her
evenings were spent reading or messing around on her
computer until she got sleepy.

"Well, you do now. I'm going to take you out on a
proper dinner date."

Wade had to admit this was the first time he'd ever
dressed in an Armani suit, gotten into his BMW and
driven to a trailer to pick up a woman for dinner. As he
climbed out of the SUV, he was pleased that the sunny
day, while cold, had managed to melt most of the snow
and reveal the well-packed gravel of her temporary
driveway. A couple more warm days and he might be
able to find the turtle-shaped rock on her property that
served as a makeshift headstone.

He had tried to talk himself into canceling this date
several times today. He was attracted to Tori, but he
could suppress that urge if he needed to. Asking her out
had very little to do with his desire for her. As much
as he didn't like the idea, getting close to Tori was the
best way to soften her up. She'd gone from a hellcat to
a kitten after spending time with his family. The information Brody had supplied him with about her business
had made her putty in his hands. He was confident that
a date or two would wear her down.

It had to. If Tori intended to break ground on the
house in a few weeks' time, he had to hurry. There
wasn't time to finesse this situation. He had to win
Tori over one way or another, and this seemed to be
the quickest way. She was attracted to him. If the past
was any indication, that might be enough to influence
her decision.

It was sleazy. Underhanded. And absolutely necessary. He couldn't fail his family.

As he made his way to her front door, he enjoyed feeling the crunch of gravel against the soles of his dress shoes. He'd opted not to wear his snow boots and was hoping Tori had done the same. The knee-high boots she'd worn at Christmas were nice, but he was a self-proclaimed ankle guy. Just another reason for him to despise the cold and ice of New England winters. His favorite part of the female body was tucked away until spring.

He had his fingers crossed that she would step out of that Airstream in one of her sexy pairs of heels. Back when she'd worked for him, he could always count on finding her near the copier or in the break room wearing an attractive yet professional outfit and a pair of luscious heels. It had been the highlight of his day.

He gave a quick rap on the aluminum door and waited for her to answer. A moment later it swung open, and he stepped back to hold it for her. Cling to it was more like it.

The elevated camper gave him a prime view of a pair of black patent leather pumps with a strap around each delicate ankle. His heart almost skipped a beat as his gaze traveled up the length of her calves to the dark red bandage dress that clung to her round, full hips. The neckline was off the shoulder, and dipped low to give a tantalizing yet tasteful view of her breasts.

Tori smiled and slipped into a black full-length wool coat before stepping down to join him. Her thick auburn hair was swept up into a twist, exposing the long, pale line of her neck and sparkling ruby earrings. Her pale eyes looked mysterious and exotic lined in black with a smoky shadow.

She was, in a word, breathtaking.

He reached out a hand to help her down the stairs and then pushed the door shut behind her. "You look beautiful," he said.

"Thank you," Tori replied. The blush of her cheeks was made even more evident by the powerful red of her dress peeking out from under her coat. "You look very nice, too. I don't think I've seen you in a suit since we worked together."

Wade smiled and held out his arm to lead her to the passenger side of his car. "I wear them all the time in real life. On the farm, I'd just get pine sap on it. More rugged attire is required out here, as you know."

Tori eased into the heated leather seat and pulled her legs in. "Yes, these heels aren't very practical in the country."

"That's a damn shame," Wade said as he slammed her door closed. He then got in on his side.

Tori waited until they were on the highway before she spoke again. "So where are we going?"

"A little French place I know on the west side. It's a far cry from Daisy's Diner, I have to tell you."

"Wait, I think I've heard of that place. Incredible food, but almost impossible to get in?"

"That's the place."

"How did you get reservations? You just asked me out last night. It's Friday, one of the busiest nights. I've heard people can wait months for a table."

Wade turned to her with his cockiest smile. "I know people."

"Oh, that's very impressive," she mocked.

"I went to high school with the executive chef. We've stayed good friends over the years. Whenever I'm in town, all I have to do is call and I've got a table held for me."

"That must go over well with all the women you take there."

Wade tried not to make a face, but he couldn't help it. She made him sound like a tomcat running around west Connecticut. "I'm usually alone or with one of my brothers," he said. "I think this is the first date I've ever taken there. I'm usually not in Cornwall long enough to romance anyone."

Tori nodded and turned to glance out the window at the rapidly darkening sky. "So when do you head back to the big bad city?"

"I don't know," Wade admitted.

And he didn't know. His plan had been to secure the land, spend Christmas with his family and hop the next plane to Jamaica. He should be gone by now, but that hadn't panned out. All his brothers and Julianne had returned to their respective homes. And he was still there. Without the land. And without a ticket to a warm tropical locale.

When all this was over, he was going to demand a vacation on Brody's private Caribbean island. He owed Wade after all the grief he'd served him the past few days.

"Don't you have a business to get back to?"

"Not until after the New Year. My company shuts down for two weeks so my employees can enjoy the holidays."

"Was it your intention to spend those two weeks here, badgering me?"

"No. By now I'd intended to be on a beach, soaking in the sun and badgering a waitress for another drink."

Tori turned to him. "So you'll stay in Cornwall until you wear me down, right?"

Wade met her gaze momentarily before turning back to the road. "Yes."

"And what if I deliberately stalled just to keep you around?"

Wade slowed the SUV to turn into the parking lot of the restaurant. For a packed night, there weren't many cars, but the dining room was small and didn't have many tables. Or a menu, for that matter. They served a series of tasting courses, chef's choice. Wade pulled into a spot and turned off the car.

Unbuckling his seat belt, he pivoted to face her. "If you're really interested in keeping me around, there are better ways to go about it."

"Like what?" she asked. The challenge lighted her eyes like sparkling hunks of aquamarine.

"Like making wild, passionate love to me until I can't bear to leave your side."

Tori's mouth dropped open. Her lips moved in vain for a moment, but there were no words. He seemed to have that effect on her, and he had to admit he liked it. Wade grinned wickedly and climbed from the car. He came around and opened the door for her, taking her hand as she slid from the seat.

They walked to the restaurant with his arm around her waist. He liked the feel of her body against his side. She fit perfectly there, and he needed only to turn his head toward her to breathe in the floral scent of her shampoo. It made him want to spread the strands across a silky pillowcase and bury his face in them. Soon. Hopefully.

Just as they opened the door, he leaned in and whispered, "And I hope you'll put that new plan into place tonight after dessert."

The sounds of the restaurant eclipsed any response she might have cobbled together. He focused instead on greeting the hostess, the executive chef's wife, and following her to an intimate table for two by the fireplace. Wade helped Tori out of her coat, then handed both their jackets over to the hostess to be checked.

Moments later their server, Richard, arrived with two glasses of white wine. After welcoming them and introducing himself, he placed the glasses on the table, adding, "We're starting tonight with an '83 sauvignon blanc and a tasting of caviar and white asparagus."

A second server swooped in behind Richard with their first plates, and then both of them disappeared into the kitchen.

"I hope you're hungry," Wade said, admiring the artistry of their first dish. "There's nine more courses."

They'd need every bit of spare room to eat all the food and wine presented to them. There was a *fois gras* terrine, butter-poached lobster, potatoes with black truffles, lamb, sorbet and the most delicate white chocolate mousse with cherries he'd ever put into his mouth. The food and wine flowed as easily as their conversation.

Wade had been concerned at first that their usual antagonistic banter might ruin the evening. As much as fighting with Tori aroused him, he wanted tonight to be about something else. The more she got to know him, the more she seemed to open up to him. The information Brody had been able to uncover about Tori had proved fairly useful so far. Talking about her work and her passion for environmental causes had opened a door to him.

Tonight the romantic atmosphere and the multiple courses of wine seemed to help her relax and enjoy herself. After about the third course, he could see the tension ease from her shoulders and a lazy pleasure settle into her eyes. She laughed and flirted, smiled and watched him over her glass with warmth in her gaze. He liked this side of Tori just as much as, if not more than, her fiery red side.

They talked about their work and their college experiences. Tori shared details about her travels as a child and all the things she'd seen. Wade had to admit he was a touch jealous that she had seen so many things at such a young age. When he was young, he was poor. And now that he was no longer poor, he was too busy to travel.

In turn she asked him a lot about his high school years and growing up with brothers and sisters. They had lived quite different lives.

Before he knew it, he looked up and found they were the only customers left in the restaurant. There was only the sultry music playing in the background and the crackling of the fireplace beside them. Even the servers seemed to blend into the background, well-trained not to interfere with their customers' romantic evenings.

"Did you say you never went to prom?"

Tori looked up from her last half-eaten plate. "No prom. No high school graduation. None of the normal stuff."

"Do you like to dance?"

She hesitated a moment before she answered. "I don't know. I've never actually danced with a man before. I mean, I went to a few nightclubs in college, but not real dancing. There's never really been the opportunity. No school dances, no family weddings…"

Wade frowned and eyed the area just beside their table. "That is a travesty." He stood, placing his napkin in his seat, and reached out for Tori's hand. "Come here."

Despite a flash of wariness in her eyes, Tori didn't argue with his demand, and he was glad. Instead, she rose gracefully from her chair and took the few steps over to the open area that was the perfect dance floor for two.

Wade pulled her into his arms, giving her time to adjust to the proper stance before pressing her body against his own and rocking in gentle time with the music. At first she was stiff in his arms. He worried that it was him, but her glance kept nervously shifting down to her feet. She was uncomfortable not knowing how to dance.

"I don't think I'm very good at this," she said, worrying her lip with her teeth.

"Just relax," he cooed into her ear. "No one is watching. It's only you and me." Wade splayed his hand across her lower back, pressing her into him and guiding her movements. "Close your eyes and feel the music. Feel the movement."

Tori closed her eyes, her body relaxing after a few moments. Then she leaned in and placed her head on his shoulder. Wade reveled in the feel of her in his arms, closing his own eyes to block out everything but the experience of holding her.

Her skin was like satin against his. The soft curves of her body fit into each hard ridge of his own. He could feel the crush of her breasts against the wall of his chest and the rapidly beating heart behind it. The rhythm of it matched the pounding in his own rib cage. The blood had started rushing in his veins the moment he touched her. Every nerve in his body was tingling with arousal and anxiety.

Despite all the complications and reasons he shouldn't want Tori, he did. He wanted her very badly. And he was fairly certain she felt the same way.

Tori shifted in his arms, and he opened his eyes to see her pull away just enough to look him in the eye.

"I'm ready," she said.

"For what?"

The corners of her red lips curled up in a seductive smile. "To make you never want to leave my side again."

Seven

Tori had never seen a man pay a check so quickly. A wad of large bills was tossed onto the table, and he grasped her hand to lead her out of the restaurant. They paused only long enough to collect their coats, and then they were back on the road.

Whereas on the way to the restaurant his engine had purred, now the German motor roared and devoured the highway ahead of them. The speed only fueled the desire burning inside her. Its flames licked at her skin, flushing her pink and melting her core into a pool of liquid need. She wasn't exactly sure where they were going, but she didn't care. She just wanted to get there fast.

Her left hand crept across the gap between them and planted itself firmly on his thigh. Her fingers rubbed over the soft material of his suit, his muscles tensing beneath her grip. The speedometer surged in response, and the reaction urged her on. She stroked his leg, inching ever higher.

When she glanced up at Wade, his face was rock hard, his jaw locked and his eyes burrowing into the road. His knuckles were white as they gripped the leather steering wheel. He was fighting hard for control. So far, he seemed to have it managed.

That made Tori want to push him. The road was deserted and dark. With a wicked smile, she moved her hand higher, dipping between his thighs. She found the firm heat of him struggling against the confines of his pants. Wade jerked and groaned at her touch, but the SUV remained steady and in control as they traveled.

With curious fingertips she explored him. She gently stroked his length and swallowed hard when he extended beyond her expectations. She wet her lips in anticipation and clamped her thighs tightly together to quell the ache building inside her. She wanted him so badly. Even back when she was his employee, she'd fantasized about this. At least before…

No. She wasn't going to ruin tonight with thoughts about the past. She'd always wanted a taste of Wade Mitchell, and tonight she was going to have it. When she spied the apple-shaped sign of the tree farm, a rush of relief washed over her. They were almost there.

As the SUV's tires met the gravel of the driveway, Tori palmed his fly with one last firm stroke. Wade growled low, whipping the car to a stop. They'd parked in front of a building that looked like a barn, but without the hayloft, large swinging doors and livestock. Thank goodness they weren't heading to the big house. As much as she wanted him, she just couldn't… Not there with Ken and Molly so close by.

The engine went quiet. Wade stretched his hands to

relax the tense muscles and turned in his seat. His gaze dropped to her hand, which was still touching him, and shifted back up to meet hers. "I've got to get you in the house before I'm forced to make love to you in the backseat like a teenage boy."

Instead of responding, Tori gave him another firm squeeze. Wade's hand grabbed her wrist and tugged her away before she could move again. "No, seriously," he said, his eyes closed. "It's not very comfortable back there."

"Okay," Tori agreed with a grin. "But only because having sex in a bedroom without wheels is a rare treat for me." With a laugh, she climbed out of the SUV, too anxious to wait for him to open her door. He met her around the other side and took her hand, leading her to the front door.

Once inside the building, Wade locked the dead bolt behind them and swept her into his arms. His mouth crushed hers, devouring her with an enthusiasm her body had been craving since their fourth course. Tori let her purse fall to the ground and wrapped her arms around his neck. She was glad she'd chosen to wear these heels, because they brought his mouth closer to hers and aligned their bodies perfectly. His erection pressed into her lower belly, and she tilted her hips to grind against it. A growl vibrated across her lips, followed by the glide of his tongue along hers.

Wade's hands moved up her back until they reached her zipper. A hum ran along her spine to the base as it glided down and exposed her back to the cool air. His fingers delved beneath the fabric to caress her skin and undo the snaps of her strapless bra.

As much as she hated to break away from him, she knew she needed to if she wanted to feel her bare skin on his. Tori pressed against his chest until his lips left hers. His warm hands cupped her shoulders, pushing her dress down until it pooled around her ankles with her bra. Now she was wearing only her lace panties, sheer thigh-high stockings and heels. She could feel his eyes on her, drinking in every inch of her body. Tori thought she would feel self-conscious, but the fire in his eyes was undeniable. He wanted her. There might be other layers of conflict between them, but his desire was genuine.

To tempt him, she reached behind her head to pull out the few pins that held her hair in the twist. Her breasts reached out to him as she moved, the tight nipples aching for his touch. His gaze went to them, his tongue darting across his lower lip as he watched. Instead of reaching for her, he tugged down his tie and threw it to the ground.

Once the pins were removed, the thick red curls fell down over her bare shoulders. She gently shook her head and stepped out of her dress.

"God, you're beautiful," he said, his voice a hoarse whisper. "Come here."

Tori closed the gap between them. Her palms ran over his chest and up to his shoulders to slip his jacket off. It fell to the floor beside his tie, and Tori made quick work of the dress shirt buttons.

When Wade shrugged out of his shirt, Tori's breath caught in her throat. His chest was broad and chiseled, with each muscle well-defined. A dark sprinkle of chest hair trailed down to his stomach. Her gaze followed the line of it down, but before she could reach for his belt, he reached for her wrist and tugged her to him. She slammed into his chest, her nipples pressing against the firm, tan skin she'd just been admiring.

His mouth found hers again and then traveled down her throat. He nipped at her skin with his teeth, soothing it with his lips and tongue. Wade buried his hands in her hair, rubbing the strands between his fingertips. She closed her eyes and just focused on the sensations he coaxed.

Wade's hand slid down her back, caressed a round cheek through the lace of her panties, then continued along the back of her thigh. He tugged her leg up around his hip, then wrapped his arm around her waist. With his mouth still on her throat, he lifted her off the ground, hooking her other leg around him.

Clinging to his shoulders, Tori squealed at the sudden movement. Then with a laugh she threw her head back, arching her spine and offering her breasts to him. He accepted, taking one nipple into his mouth as he walked them slowly through the large open room. The tug of pleasure shot straight to her center, and Tori groaned loudly. She thought she remembered him saying his brothers had left, but she didn't know that for sure. She hoped no one else was here, but frankly she didn't care. She needed him now.

"Bed?" she whispered.

His lips parted with her flesh only long enough to say, "Upstairs."

Tori glanced at the staircase behind them. They'd been moving toward it since he picked her up. He began to carry her up the stairs, but she shook her head. "Too far," she gasped between ragged breaths. "Right here."

"On the stairs?"

"Yes, now."

Wade didn't argue. He eased her onto one of the steps, the plush carpeting meeting her bare skin. She leaned back onto her elbows, sprawled across the steps as he pulled away to look at her. His breath was rapid, his chest rising and falling as if he'd been running a marathon. His gaze slowly traveled up her body until it met her eyes. The green depths were almost penetrating.

He didn't look away as he unfastened his belt and eased down his own pants and briefs. Tori caught only a quick glance of his magnificent body and the flash of foil in his palm before he was crouched down, kneeling on a step between her leather-wrapped ankles. He lifted one leg and planted a kiss on her ankle, then on her inner calf and knee. He placed a searing kiss on her inner thigh just above the lace band of her stocking. Tori's leg quivered in his hands, his hot breath near torture on her exposed center. His fingertips glided across her panties, hooking around the edge before tugging them down her legs and tossing them to the bottom step.

Tori let out a heavy sigh as his body moved back up to cover her own. His blazing-hot skin glided deliciously across hers. The man was as hot-blooded as they came, like a furnace. He picked up where he'd left off, placing a kiss on her hip bone, then on her belly. The evening stubble on his chin scratched and tickled her delicate skin. His mouth moved over her stomach to the valley between her breasts. Braced on his elbows, he took his time teasing each nipple into fierce, throbbing peaks with his tongue.

She could feel the brush of his arousal along her inner thigh. Her whole body ached to have him inside her, but Wade didn't appear to be in the same hurry she was. "Wade, please," she said, her hands tugging impatiently on his upper arms.

He pulled away for just a moment, quickly sheathing

himself in latex and moving back between her thighs. This time he covered her completely, and she was glad. She'd quickly become accustomed to his warmth, and losing it, even for a few moments, had left her shivering. Now that he was back where he belonged, Tori tilted her head to look him in the eyes. Wade dipped down to kiss her again. As his tongue slowly penetrated her, so did the rest of him. He surged forward. Inch by inch he filled her. Tori held her breath and eased her legs open farther to accept all of him.

When at last he was buried deep inside her, Wade stilled. His lips parted from hers so he could suck in a ragged breath. "Victoria," he murmured against her lips, "you feel so incredible."

His words were nearly as sexy as the almost pained expression on his face as he said them. Tori drew her stocking-clad legs up and wrapped them around his waist. That movement alone was enough to draw a hiss from his lips. She placed a hand on each side of his face. Feeling the rough stubble in her palms, she drew him down for another soft, brief kiss. "Love me," she said.

A flash of challenge lit in his eyes. Pulling back, he thrust into her again without breaking their visual connection. This time it was Tori who cried out. Before she could recover, he moved again and again. The desire that had been building inside her for the past few hours was now a constant throb of pleasure. The ache of it increased with their every movement.

Everything else faded away but that feeling. There was no land to be bought. No lost job. No animosity between them. Not even the burn of the rug on their elbows or the bite of the stair across her back registered. There was only their frenzied drive to fulfill the need.

Tori clung to him, panting and whispering words of

encouragement in his ear. "Yes," she repeated, the pressure building inside reaching the critical point. "Yes, Wade, yes!" Tori cried out as the wave of her climax crashed over her. Her body trembled against his as he quickened his pace and found his own release. The roar was almost deafening as he poured everything he had into her, then collapsed.

Tori held him to her, the sweat of their bare skin mingling together, until their rapid breaths finally slowed. It was only then, when the passionate fog had lifted, that she could find the strength to speak again.

"Let's go find a real bed," she said.

Wade woke up to the delicious smell of coffee and bacon. He smiled, shifted and rolled over, expecting to see the other side of the bed empty. Instead he found himself looking at Tori's bare back.

Molly.

Wade flopped back against his pillows in disgust. The movement was enough to wake Tori. She tugged the sheets modestly over her breasts and sat up, a touch disoriented. When she turned to look at Wade, he was struck by how beautiful she looked, tousled. Her red hair was wild, her lips swollen from a night of kisses. She looked like a woman who had been thoroughly and completely loved the night before.

And he'd be inclined to pick up where they left off if he didn't think his mother was downstairs.

"Good morning," he said.

"Morning," she said with a yawn and a long, feline stretch that accentuated the bare curve of her back. Then her delicate nose wrinkled and her brow furrowed. "Are you cooking something?" she asked.

"No."

"But I—" Tori brought her hand up to her mouth. "Molly isn't downstairs, is she? My panties are…" She lifted the sheet, then quickly brought it back down. "Oh, no. They're still on the stairs."

Wade sat up and shook his head. "Don't worry about all that. I'm not a teenager anymore. And if I know my mother, she's probably pleased as punch to find our clothes strewn across the living room. She knew I was taking you out to dinner last night."

"Are you sure she won't be upset?"

"Extremely. The woman hung mistletoe. She knows exactly what she's doing."

"And what's that?"

Wade swallowed hard and swung his legs out over the edge of the bed. "Working on grandchildren."

He pulled on a pair of his pajama pants from his luggage, turning his back to Tori to hide the laugh her wide, panicked eyes brought on.

"I, uh, I—I mean…"

"Relax. I'm sure the next generation of Edens has yet to be spawned. I'll go run her off."

Wade opened the bedroom door and slipped down the stairs to the ground floor. His mother was nowhere to be found, but she'd certainly been in the bunkhouse. Their clothes from the living room floor—not the panties, thankfully—had been picked up and neatly laid over the arm of the couch. The coffeepot was on and dripping the last of a fresh pot. There was a pitcher of orange juice and a foil-wrapped casserole dish on the counter. In the center of the breakfast table was a vase filled with some of the greenhouse-grown roses left over from the pine centerpieces she sold in the shop.

"Is it safe?"

Wade turned to find Tori standing a few steps from

the bottom of the staircase, a blanket wrapped around her like a toga.

"Yes, she's gone. She brought us breakfast."

Tori stooped down at the bottom of the stairs, snatching up her panties. She found her purse by the front door and stuffed the panties inside to hide the evidence in case someone came back. "Breakfast?"

"Yes, are you hungry?"

She smiled sheepishly. "After the meal last night I thought I might never eat again. But I did manage to work up quite an appetite."

That was for sure. After they made it upstairs, they'd taken a shower together, starting another round of love-making they finished in the bed.

"Would you like coffee or orange juice?"

"Juice," she said, reaching for her red dress. "This seems like a little much for breakfast, but I didn't plan for an overnight trip."

"Upstairs in the bedroom drawer are some shirts you're welcome to try on. They'll be big, but it's better than a cocktail dress. And under the sink are some extra toiletries that Molly keeps here in case one of us forgets something. There should be a new toothbrush and anything else you might need."

Tori nodded and slunk back toward the stairs. "That's great. I'll be right back."

By the time she came back downstairs in an oversize Yale alumni sweatshirt, Wade had made them both a plate with breakfast casserole and diced fruit that Molly had left in the fridge. He handed her a glass of orange juice as she sat down at the table.

"This looks wonderful. Molly really didn't have to go to all this trouble."

Wade sat down with a mug of coffee and shook his head. "She lives for this. Don't let her fool you."

Tori took a few bites, quietly eating and avoiding making eye contact with Wade. He wasn't sure if the typical morning after had been made more awkward, or less, by his mother's culinary interference.

"How are you this morning?" he asked.

Tori brushed her loose hair behind her ear and took a sip of juice before she answered. "Honestly, I'm a little weirded out that your mother knows we slept together, and I'm still trying to process that fact myself."

"Do you regret last night?"

"No," she said. "But sex always changes things. I'm not quite sure what's going to happen from here."

"I believe we go out on another date."

Tori frowned. "I don't know if I'm ready for that. Three dates in a week. With a man who wants my land and fired me from my first real job."

"That still bothers you, doesn't it?"

"Yes," she admitted. "Despite what you believe, I didn't do anything wrong. I didn't so much as shake that guy's hand, much less handle anything else. I was so naive. And when you fired me, it felt like I'd lost everything. My apartment, my confidence in my abilities. Even a little of my trust in men."

Now it was Wade's turn to frown. "I damaged your ability to trust men?"

Tori shrugged. "In a way. More me not being able to trust that I know what I'm doing in a relationship. I had been attracted to you. You were the boss, and I knew it was a bad idea, but I couldn't help it. Sometimes I wondered if the feeling was mutual. Those couple of nights that we worked late together, I thought I'd felt a spark of something."

"You did. I wanted very badly to ask you out, but I wasn't sure if it would be appropriate, since you worked for me."

Tori sighed and sat back in her chair. "I'm glad I didn't imagine that. One afternoon I remember asking your assistant, Lauren, what she thought, since I figured she knew you best. She said I was way off. That I wasn't your type at all. Then you fired me, and I figured I must've been imagining things."

Hearing the name of his former admin was like finding a missing piece to an old mental puzzle. "Lauren," he said.

"Yes. What about her?"

"What else did she tell you about me and my tastes?"

Tori paused for a second and turned to look at him. "You don't think…?"

"She made it all up," he said with certainty. Something about Tori's ethics violation had always troubled him, but he could never put his finger on what, aside from him not wanting to believe she could do it. There had been a real connection between them. That was probably why the idea of her with another man was more painful than it should've been. "Lauren is the one who told me she saw you having an intimate dinner with one of our suppliers. The next day you started making recommendations… The timing was too suspicious."

"He had a superior product. He didn't have to seduce me for an endorsement. But why would she say that about me when it wasn't true?"

With that piece in place, the entire picture became painfully clear. "I am so sorry," he said, shaking his head. "This was all my fault."

"How? If Lauren did it, why are you to blame?"

Wade had ended up firing Lauren only a few months after Tori. She'd seemed sweet at first. After Tori left, she developed some extremely suggestive behaviors. She made it no secret she wanted Wade, although he wasn't interested at all. After catching her being rude on the phone to Julianne, thinking she was a girlfriend and not his sister, he had to let her go. She was an efficient employee, but she was letting a misplaced territoriality compromise her performance.

"She must've been jealous of you. I don't know why I didn't connect this before. I asked her one afternoon if she could help me find out what kind of flowers you liked. I was going to send some to your home and ask if you'd like to have dinner."

"I never got any flowers," Tori replied.

"I never got to send them. Lauren showed up with her story about you the next day. It never occurred to me that she was jealous enough of you to sabotage your whole career like that, but that has to be it. Not long after you left, Lauren made it quite obvious that she was interested in me. I'm sorry I didn't believe you."

Tori nodded and glanced down at the remains of her breakfast. "There was no way to prove it either way. You did what you had to do."

"I feel horrible. I want to make it up to you somehow."

"That's not necessary," she said. "I know I've given you a lot of grief over it, but look at where I am now. It might have been a rocky transition, but things turned out the way they were meant to. If I had continued to work for you, I'd probably still be there, making you money, but I never would've gone for my dream. When I lost my job, I took the chance to start my own company, and it was the best thing I could've done. When

I think of it that way, I don't know…maybe I should be thanking you."

"Yet you've been angry with me all this time?"

"I was hurt because you didn't believe me. It was easy to blame you for the upheaval in my life that came after it. The truth is probably that I wasn't ready to settle down in one place yet. I was just rebelling from my parents. Who knows, if you hadn't fired me, I might've quit a few weeks later and started wandering again."

"What made you ready to settle down now? Here?"

"I started doing genealogy a few years back as a way to connect with my roots. My parents were so nomadic I never really met any extended family or knew where we came from. A little digging uncovered that my father's family was from this area, a few generations back. Cornwall was where they settled after migrating to America from Ireland."

She took a sip of juice before continuing. "I came up here on a whim once, when I had a free weekend away from the project in Philadelphia. I just drove around, mostly. But then I spied this beautiful wooded area and I pulled over and started walking around. For the first time in my life, I felt like I was home. Like I'd spiritually dropped anchor. I wanted to stay here. So I started looking for land to buy. I couldn't have found a more perfect piece of property than the one your parents were offering. I snatched it up and started hatching plans to build my dream house."

Seeing the excitement light up Tori's face, Wade felt smacked in the gut with guilt. She longed for a connection to her family and a chance to build a real home. And he wanted her to. He felt crappy for keeping her from that dream. But he couldn't risk the body being found, even for her dreams. "And once again, I've charged into your life and tried to ruin it all."

She chuckled softly but didn't contradict him. "Life should never be boring."

Wade watched a touch of sadness creep into her eyes. Sadness that he knew he was partially responsible for. It made him want to sweep her into his arms and kiss her until she was too wrapped up in them to be distressed. He wanted to distract her with something so fantastic she wouldn't think about the past for at least a few days.

"I want to take you to New York."

She looked up, startled by the sudden change in topic. "New York? Why?"

"I want to make amends for the past and take you someplace as exciting and beautiful as you are. I want to spend New Year's Eve with you in Times Square."

"Are you kidding me?" She laughed. "I'd pretty much prefer to be anywhere over freezing to death in a mad crush of people in Times Square. I'll be happy to watch the ball drop via my television, though thank you for asking me."

Wade smiled and reached across the table to take her hand. "We're going to New York. Pack your bags because I'm picking you up Monday morning. We're going to see a show. We're going to eat some great food. And when that ball drops, you and I are going to be right there to watch it."

Tori squirmed but didn't pull away. "I don't know, Wade. As nice as that sounds, I don't want to spend my night outside in the cold with a million other people. I'd rather spend it alone with you."

Wade smiled; a plan was forming in his head that would satisfy both their desires. "Who said anything about being outside?"

Eight

"Oh. My. Dear. Lord."

Wade tipped the bellhop and followed Tori's voice into the penthouse suite's master bedroom. He found her standing in front of the wall of windows that lined the room from floor to ceiling. The view overlooked Times Square and the hustle and bustle of the theater district. He'd had this exact view in mind when he renovated this building. His architect had designed this suite, and these windows, for the precise experience Wade had planned for tonight.

"This is amazing. You can see everything from here. How did you get us a room like this on such short notice?"

"Easy," he said, sneaking up behind her to wrap his arms around her waist and tug her against him. "I just called and asked for it. Although it helps when you know the owner and renovated the hotel."

"Ah…" she said, curling into his warmth. "I should've known better than to think you'd be down there with the crowds tonight. Look how many people are already standing around and there's hours to go."

"I've done that before," he said, biting at her earlobe. "When I was younger and poorer. It was fun. But I'd much rather watch the ball drop tonight with your naked body pressed against this glass."

Tori responded by arching her back and pressing her hips into his throbbing desire. He growled against her neck. "And the best part is that these windows are one-way glass."

"Nobody can see in, even at night with the lights on?"

"Correct." Wade's hand snaked across her stomach and up to caress one firm breast through the silky fabric of her blouse. Tori gasped softly when his thumb brushed over the hard peak of her nipple. "No one can see me do this, even if they were right on the other side of the window."

"That should prove interesting," she whispered, near purring.

"Indeed," Wade said, undoing the top button of her shirt. "We have all night to test our theory." He moved down for the second button. Then the doorbell rang.

Blast. He'd ordered room service, hadn't he? It seemed like a good idea at the time. He just hadn't realized how much driving in the car with her would turn him on. Maybe it was the memories of their drive home from the restaurant that had made it hard to focus on the road.…

Tori pulled away, smiling when she saw the pained expression on his face. "Sorry. Are we expecting someone?"

"Dinner."

She arched an eyebrow and breezed past him to the front door of the suite. "You mean you aren't taking me out somewhere?"

"On New Year's Eve? In the theater district? No, sorry. You said you didn't like the crowds, and there's no way to avoid them tonight unless we dine in."

Tori opened the door, and a man rolled in a cart covered in silver domes. He pushed the cart over to the dining room table and transferred the platters, unveiling them one by one. There was lobster, prime rib, herb-roasted potatoes, haricots verts and a platter of plump red strawberries with a bowl of chocolate fondue in the center. Last of all he placed on the table an ice bucket containing a bottle of champagne, and two glasses.

Wade tipped the server. The man thanked him before disappearing just as quickly as he'd arrived.

"This is quite a spread you've ordered. You've done nothing but feed me indulgent food since we met."

"Nothing?" he asked with a mischievous grin.

"Okay, well, it's not all you've done, but we certainly haven't worked off all these calories, either. I'm going to grow out of my clothes."

"Well…" Wade approached her and continued undoing the buttons of her blouse where he'd left off. "We'd better remedy that, right away."

By the time they got around to dinner, it was nearly cold, but salvageable. The only warm food remaining was the ramekin of chocolate fondue, which was heated by a candle to keep it fluid for dipping. It didn't matter. Tori had worked up a huge appetite and wasn't feeling very particular.

"The festivities will be starting soon, and the view

in the dining room isn't as grand. How do you feel about a picnic here in the bedroom?" Wade asked as Tori slipped into the bathroom.

"Sounds great. Is it safe to say we're staying in for the night?"

"That was the plan."

"Okay," she called, eyeing her wardrobe bag hanging beside her in the bathroom. Wade hadn't really told her what they were going to be doing, so she'd packed a variety of clothing. Unzipping the bag a few inches, she spied the beaded neckline of the dress she'd been dying to wear.

It was a fully beaded midnight-blue gown with a halter neckline and a slit up the side that went almost to her hip. It had been an impulse purchase. Tori rarely bought things like that because her storage space was at a premium in the Airstream. She'd simply had to own the dress and figured she'd worry later about what she would wear it to. She'd packed it for their trip thinking they might go someplace fancy. But why not wear it tonight?

She was spending New Year's Eve in a glamorous penthouse overlooking Times Square. She was about to dine on lobster and champagne with a handsome date. The dress would be perfectly suited for a night like this if they were in a chic restaurant or at a party in a grand ballroom. It should be just as suitable for a private dinner for two.

With a giggle of girlish excitement, she fully unzipped the bag and slipped into the gown. The indulgent purchase had been sealed the moment she'd first tried it on. It fitted as though it were made just for her, hugging each curve. Tori reapplied her lipstick, ran her fingers through her hair and went back into the bedroom.

Wade had carried the food into the master bedroom and spread out a blanket for a picnic on the floor by the window. He had slipped back into his trousers but left off the dress shirt. It was thrown across a chair in the living room the last time she saw it, but Tori was glad he'd left it off. Wade had a magnificent chest, and she couldn't spend enough time admiring the hard lines and the dark curls of his chest hair. Unfortunately she hadn't found a reason for him to just stay shirtless all the time.

He was kneeling on the blanket, pouring flutes of champagne, when he looked up at her—and froze. His jaw fell open, and his gaze took in every inch of her body. He licked his lips before he spoke. "You did hear me say we were staying in, right?"

"Yes," she said with a smile. "But I felt like dressing up a little bit for the occasion." Tori held out her arms and spun around for effect. "Do you like it?"

He swallowed hard. "Very much."

"Is it too much for a picnic on the floor?"

"Not at all." He reached out his hand and helped her down onto the blanket. "Looking that beautiful, you can do whatever the hell you like."

Tori blushed. She felt beautiful in this dress, but hearing him say it made her all the happier that she'd decided to put it on, impractical as it was. She settled down beside him, curling her legs to the side and spreading the gown out around her.

Wade handed her a glass of champagne and held up his own for a toast. "To...letting go of the past and embracing a new year and new beginnings."

It was the perfect toast for them in so many ways. Over the past week it did seem as though they had come so far. There was a time in her life when the mention of his name would've sent her into a rampage. Now, sitting across from him, she felt that everything had changed. Thoughts of Wade brought on tingly, warm sensations and a nervous, excited feeling in her stomach.

Tori clinked her glass flute to his. "To new beginnings," she echoed. And that was really what she wanted. A fresh start. Knowing the truth about the circumstances around her firing made the past, the past. She could finally set down the grudge she'd held all these years, and she was glad. She didn't want that dark cloud hanging over their relationship.

Relationship.

Is that what this had become? Things had moved so quickly, but it certainly felt like something more than a fling. But a relationship required more than just attraction and compatibility. It also required trust. She wasn't sure that she had much left. Wade had damaged it pretty badly. Whatever ability she'd regained after several years had been shattered by Ryan. Was trusting a man even possible? And trusting a man like Wade Mitchell? That seemed out of the question. Even with their past resolved, he still wanted her property. That hadn't changed.

Taking a sip of her champagne, she realized how badly she wanted to trust him. This had started out as a game between them. A battle of wills to see who would crack under pleasure, so to speak. But now...she feared it was her. Wade seemed as though he'd put the game behind them, as she had, but she couldn't know for sure. She wanted something more between them. Tori wanted to build her dream house. And if she was honest with herself, she wanted Wade living in it with her.

The thought made her champagne hard to swallow.

How had she made that kind of leap in just a few short days? Maybe it wasn't much of a leap. She'd wanted him years ago. Fantasized about more. Perhaps that was why his supposed betrayal hurt her so badly. The feelings had remained, buried under her anger and rushing to the surface the moment the barricades were brushed away.

"I'm starving," Wade said, oblivious to the thoughts running through her mind.

She forced the champagne down her throat to respond. "Me, too." Better for her to focus on food than on her dangerous thoughts.

Wade made them both plates, and they sat eating quietly. They'd spent so much time together in the car on the drive down that they were clearly out of small talk. That left only serious discussions. She wasn't sure either of them was ready for that.

Tori was biting into a chocolate-coated strawberry when Wade set aside his plate and looked down at his watch. "It's getting close to midnight," he said. "We don't want to miss it. I'll pour more champagne."

Tori nodded and accepted his hand to stand up. She went to the window. The dim lights in the bedroom suite allowed her to see everything outside. The lights and activity in the square were stunning. It was amazing that so many people could be in one place at one time. Crowds were gathered around stages where musicians performed for broadcast specials. The sound was probably deafening, yet not a peep made it through to their room. She had seen this scene on television every year, but somehow looking down on it was a completely new experience.

As was the warmth at her bare back as Wade came up behind her. He brought an arm around her to hold out her refilled glass of champagne. On a nearby table, he'd set down the platter of strawberries and chocolate.

His hands gently swept her hair over one shoulder. His lips seared a trail across her bare skin, sending a shiver of anticipation down her spine. It didn't matter how many times she'd had him, she wanted more. Her need almost seemed to get worse, like an escalating addiction. Her body reacted in an instant to his touch. Her breasts tightened within the confines of her gown. Her belly clenched with need.

Wade's fingertips sought out the clasp of her dress at her neck. With a snap it came undone. The fabric slipped over her skin, gliding to the ground with the heavy thump of beads. Tori kicked the dress aside and placed her drink on the table with the fruit. He followed suit, obviously needing both of his hands for what he had planned.

Grasping her by the waist, he turned her to face him. "We've still got a few minutes," he said. "Plenty of time for some dessert."

Without his powerful green gaze leaving hers, he plucked a strawberry from the platter and dipped it in chocolate. He held the fruit in front of her lips, but before she could bite into it, he dropped it to her collarbone. He dragged the berry down her throat to the hollow between her breasts. It left a warm trail of chocolate in its wake. The plump, red fruit circled one breast, teasing at her aching nipple, then traveled to the other. Nearly devoid of chocolate now, the strawberry made its way back to her lips.

She took a bite, the sweet juice instantly filling her mouth. Tori chewed and swallowed as Wade patiently held the rest of the berry for her to finish it. "Don't you want any?" she asked.

"No," he said with a wicked grin. "I prefer the chocolate." Wade set the rest of the berry aside and leaned in to kiss her. His lips tasted of champagne. He buried his fingers in her hair and moaned against her mouth. Tori drank him in, feeling a touch light-headed from his kisses and the alcohol.

When he did pull away, it was to clean up the mess he'd made. He bent Tori back over his arm, and she offered up her throat and breasts to him. He started with her neck, tasting and teasing her with his tongue as he licked every drop of chocolate from her skin. The scalding heat of his lips moved down her chest, following the berry's path to curl around each breast. He bathed each nipple, coaxing it into painfully hard peaks, then biting gently until she cried out.

By now, Tori was certain the chocolate was long gone, but Wade was nothing if not thorough. He traveled back up to her lips and murmured against them, "It's almost time. I don't want you to miss seeing it."

He spun Tori in his arms until she was facing the window and the chaotic scene below. She felt oddly exposed, standing completely naked in front of the glass. It was an exhilarating feeling. Dangerous, yet safe, since no one could see her. Firm hands pressed at her back until she bent forward and braced her hands against the glass. Wade's palm glided leisurely down her spine. He gripped her hips, tugging her bottom back against his hard desire.

"One minute to go. Let's see if you can last that long." Wade sought out her moist center with his fingers. They glided expertly over her, coaxing the building tension of release deep inside.

Tori's fingers clutched uselessly at the glass, but it was all she could do. In front of her there was nothing but the lights of the cityscape, as though they were making love on the roof. She gasped as a finger penetrated her, her muscles tightening around him. A wave of pleasure rocked her, but it wasn't enough. "Wade," she said, an edge of desperation creeping into her voice.

"Fifteen seconds." He leaned over her and placed a burning kiss between her shoulder blades.

Tori glanced over her shoulder and saw him kick aside his trousers. Soon. Thank goodness. She needed him now. All of him. "Ten, nine, eight," she whispered as the numbers began counting down, the building pressure of her orgasm certain to beat the clock. "Seven, six, five."

His fingers glided over her moist flesh, taking her closer to the edge. "Four, three, two, one," Wade said, thrusting inside her at the stroke of midnight.

The infamous ball dropped to the base, the number of the New Year lighting up, but Tori hardly gave it a glance before closing her eyes and absorbing the pleasurable impact on her body. He barely moved in her before she came undone. As the cheers and shouts rang out in the city below, Tori heard only her own cries.

Wade filled her, pushed her, thrilled her and touched her as no man ever had before. He took her to a place she hadn't known existed, and she wanted to stay there with him in this moment forever.

"Oh, Wade," she gasped as the last throbs of pleasure dissipated.

Wade's arms snaked around her waist, tugging her up until her bare back pressed against his chest. "I could make love to you all night and never have enough."

"There's quite a few hours left," she teased, breathless.

"Is that a challenge?" he asked, thrusting hard into her.

Tori laughed and tightened her muscles around him. "Absolutely."

In one quick move Wade pulled away and swept Tori up into his arms. She squealed in surprise, but before she could recover, he dropped her, bouncing, to the bed.

He was back over her in an instant, driving into her body with renewed fervor. The laughter died in her throat as the pleasure began coursing through her veins once again. This time when her release came, so did his. He groaned low against her neck and lost himself inside her body.

Tori cradled him against her as his trembling arms and legs threatened to give way beneath him. After he caught his breath, she tipped his chin up so he could look at her. There was a green fire blazing in his eyes, and she was pleased she was responsible for it. She brought her lips to his, this kiss tender and meaningful.

"Happy New Year, Wade."

The rest of the champagne was forgotten, the strawberries abandoned. Wade didn't care. He had his red-haired beauty in his arms, and that was all he wanted. For the first time in months—hell, years—Wade felt at peace. It was possible that he'd never felt like this. The world was stable on its axis. Tori had done that. The woman whose spirit he had been determined to crush so he could get what he wanted.

Now, with her head resting on his chest and the flaming silk of her hair sprawled over her shoulders and his stomach, he knew he couldn't go through with it. His plan to seduce her had backfired.

The implications were dire. It made him almost sick to his stomach to think of what it might mean for his family. If the body was ever uncovered, it would ruin everything. But that was his mistake. His price to pay. Not Tori's.

There had to be another way. He'd figure something out. He always did.

"Wade, are you still awake?"

"Yes."

Tori rolled off his chest and looked at him. "What was this trip about, really?"

Wade frowned. "What do you mean?"

"The hotel, the food, the champagne—that's a lot of effort just to make up for the whole job thing."

He supposed it might seem that way, but he didn't mind. Having money and powerful connections allowed him the luxury of doing things for people when he wanted to. "You're worth the effort."

"You are, too, you know."

Wade had the sudden urge to climb out of bed and go get a drink, but Tori had her arms clasped around him like steel manacles. He swallowed hard. "You're just supposed to say thank you."

"Thank you." Tori held him in place with her icy blue eyes. "What happened to you, Wade?"

He knew what she meant without her elaborating. He was surprised. Few people ever bothered to ask him about his life before the Edens, so he didn't tell the story very often. Those who mattered in his life already knew. Except Tori. She mattered. More than he ever wanted or expected her to.

"A person doesn't become such an overachiever, so driven to prove himself, without a reason," she pressed. "You don't have to do things to impress me. I don't need ten-course French dinners and penthouses in Manhattan to want to spend time with you. What are you trying to prove? And to whom?"

With a sigh Wade let his head drop back against the

pillows. If he had to talk about it, at least it was dark and he didn't have to look at her. "For a long time I thought I was trying to be a good son for the Edens. To repay them for taking me in and helping me turn my life around. All the good it did me, since they wouldn't accept my money when I tried to give it to them. Then I wondered if maybe I wasn't trying to prove to…those who left…that I was worth keeping."

"Like your mother?"

"Yes. And others. My mother was still in high school when she got pregnant. I wasn't exactly part of her plans. So, after she had me, she played at being a mom for a while. When that didn't work out, she took me over to her aunt's house. What was supposed to be a couple hours of babysitting turned into seven years. She just never came back."

Wade could hear Tori's breath catch in her throat. He didn't want her pity. That was why he never told anyone about this. He'd rather people saw him as the strong, powerful businessman. That was the point, wasn't it? To keep this part hidden? And yet he wanted to tell her everything now that he'd started talking. He wanted to let Tori in.

"My aunt never married and wasn't particularly interested in having children, but it wasn't bad with her. I didn't know any different. When she died of breast cancer and my mother was still off the grid, I ended up in the foster system. She had never terminated her parental rights, so I couldn't be adopted even if someone had wanted to. I doubt anyone but the Edens would have. I bounced around a lot. I was an angry child. Rebellious. A trouble starter. I had a lot of crap to work through for a ten-year-old, but it was how I coped. I guess it was easier to push people away than to get close to someone who would eventually cast me aside. But the Edens didn't fall for that game. They wouldn't let me push them away. They believed in me. So I changed my tactic to be the best man I could possibly be."

"And now you're successful, powerful and have a family that loves you."

"And you know what that got me?" he said, a bitter edge creeping into his voice.

"What?"

"A mother showing up on my doorstep with her hand out."

"What did you do?"

"Well, as you said, I'm always out to prove myself, so I did what I felt I should. I gave her a lump sum of cash and bought her a house as far from New York as I could get—in San Diego. And I made her sign a contract agreeing to never contact me or anyone in my family again, or she'd have to repay me for everything."

Tori's grip on him tightened ever so slightly. "And she agreed to that?"

Wade had not been there for the contract negotiation, but his lawyer told him she couldn't sign fast enough. There was a part of him that had hoped she wouldn't. That she had changed and wanted to get to know the son she'd abandoned. He'd been a fool for even entertaining that fantasy. "Without hesitating. So in the end, my money and my success didn't prove anything to anyone."

"What about to yourself?"

Especially not to himself. No one else on earth was able to see inside him and know what he was truly like the way he could. Strip away the money and the suits and what was he left with? When things were important, truly important, he failed.

He couldn't protect his family the way he should have. If he had done his job, Heath never would've had to do what no thirteen-year-old boy should have to do. Julianne wouldn't have to carry those dark memories with her. His parents wouldn't be secretly selling off pieces of the farm to stay afloat. No success in business could make up for that kind of personal failure.

"Is that even possible?" he asked. "Can someone like me ever reach the point where they've achieved enough? How would I know when I've expunged my sins? There's always the opportunity to disappoint myself. Or someone else."

"You haven't disappointed me."

Wade chuckled. "I haven't, now? Well, considering I fired you erroneously, harassed you mercilessly and want to take your land away from you, I imagine you have very low standards."

Tori sat up on one elbow and looked down at him. "I don't have low standards. I think I'm just better at seeing past the bull."

"And where did you learn that skill? Traipsing across America studying the human condition?"

"Something like that," she admitted. "Attending the school of life has its perks and its pitfalls. I think never building real relationships handicapped me when I grew older. I was too trusting because I'd never had the opportunity to be hurt. I didn't build relationships, like you, but because I couldn't. We were gone too quickly. I was naive."

"You?"

"Yes." She smiled. "I wasn't always so cynical. The

real world brought that. What life didn't teach me, my ex-boyfriend did."

She hadn't mentioned much about her past relationships, but Wade picked up on the pained tone in her voice. The darkness couldn't veil that. "What did he do?"

Tori sighed and shrugged. "Like I said, I was too trusting. He took advantage of the fact that I was always moving. I wasn't going to pressure him for marriage or a commitment, even after years together, because I wasn't in that place."

Wade could tell where this was going. "He was married."

"With three kids. Living happily outside Boston. When I told him I was thinking of buying land in Connecticut, he came unglued."

"And that was the last man you dated?"

Tori nodded.

Wade already felt like crap for the way things had gone down between him and Tori. Knowing she was trying to recover her trust in men when he showed up, scheming to manipulate her, made it that much worse. She deserved more than just a luxurious weekend in Manhattan. She deserved a week in Paris. Or better yet, for him to go away and leave her life and her plans alone.

"Tori," he started, not quite sure at first what he was going to say. "I'm sorry."

"For what?"

Wade swallowed the lump in his throat. He had so many feelings swirling in his gut. So many things he wanted to say to her. But he couldn't put them into words. Wouldn't. At least not until after he'd dealt with the situation that had brought him here in the first place. Whether he intended it or not, Tori could get hurt. And he didn't want to say or do anything now that might make the pain that much sharper.

"For everything," he whispered.

Nine

Tori strolled into Daisy's Diner a few days later with a bounce in her step and a smile on her face that wouldn't fade away. Her trip to New York with Wade had been wonderful. Magical. Romantic. Everything she'd hoped for and more than she'd dreamed it could be. They'd strolled through the city, window-shopping and sight-seeing. They went to a show. They talked and spent hours in each other's arms. And then it was time to come home.

Back to Connecticut—and reality. She hadn't seen Wade since they'd returned to Cornwall. They both had things to do. She was certain he would have to return to his life in Manhattan soon, although he hadn't mentioned it and she hadn't asked. He had a business to run. And she had a house to build. But they'd opted to meet here tonight for dinner.

"Hey, there," Rose said as Tori walked past her usual seat. "No counter service today?"

"No." She smiled. "I have a date tonight, so I thought a booth might be better."

"Oh, really." Rose poured a mug of hot water for Tori's tea and came out from behind the counter with two menus tucked under her arm. She sat across from Tori in the corner booth she'd selected. "Spill it," she demanded, pushing the hot water over to her customer.

Tori began fidgeting with the mug, knowing her cheeks were probably as red as her hair now. "Wade is meeting me here."

"Wade Mitchell? The man who was making you crazy a week ago?"

"The same."

Rose flung her dark ponytail back over her shoulder and leaned in closer. "So, you wanna tell me what happened between then and now?"

Tori could barely explain it. Everything had changed. Even the past, if that were possible. "It feels like the world has shifted."

Rose sat back against the padded pleather of the booth, her brown eyes wide. "You're in love with him."

"What?" Tori perked up at her friend's bold assessment. "No, no. That's silly. It's only been a few days."

Rose crossed her arms over her chest and refused to budge on the subject. "I can assure you, with the Eden boys, a few days is all it takes."

The words were like a fist to her gut. The truth barreling into her at fifty miles an hour. She was in love with him.

"I...I like him a lot," she countered, even as her mind raced with a different version of the facts. "We have a good time together. But it's nothing more than that. He's leaving to go home shortly, so it would be stupid of me to go and fall in love with him."

Rose nodded mechanically, clearly disbelieving every word of Tori's argument. Tori understood. She didn't believe her own words, either. And they were sensible. She shouldn't be in love with Wade. He *was* leaving. They *weren't* serious. She couldn't trust him because he still wanted her land. None of that added up to a fairy-tale romance. Just another disaster waiting to happen like before.

She wished someone would tell her heart that.

The heart in question started pounding madly in her chest when she looked up and spied Wade coming in the entrance. "He's here," she whispered.

Rose dutifully got up and flashed a smile to Wade on her way back to the counter. "What can I get you to drink tonight?"

"Coffee, thanks," Wade said. "It's freezing out there." He slipped out of his jacket and tossed it into the booth before sliding in where Rose had been sitting.

Wade looked so handsome tonight. He was wearing a dark blue collared shirt with thin gray pinstripes. His skin was freshly shaved and slightly pink from the sting of the icy wind outside. Tori wanted to reach out and touch his face. She wanted to breathe in his cologne. Some of her clothing had come home smelling like him after their trip. She hadn't been able to make herself go to the Laundromat to wash them yet.

Tori suddenly felt like a shy, smitten teenager sitting with him. Her realization of love only a minute before left her feeling vulnerable even though there was no way he could know how she felt. She certainly wasn't about to tell him. She had barely come to terms with it herself, although sitting on the edge of her bed sniffing a sweater should've been her first clue.

"How are you?" he asked.

Tori smiled, although it felt nervous and forced to her. She hoped it didn't look that way. "Good. You?"

"Good," he said. Wade looked down at the menu and began thoroughly studying it without elaborating.

Tori winced and hid her face with her own menu. Did he notice? Things felt weird when they'd never felt weird before. It was all her doing. She needed to act normal. This was the same man she'd spent a good part of the past week with. Naked. After that, dinner in the local restaurant should be no big deal. She just had to relax.

Rose came back with the coffee; she took their orders and the menus. Now neither of them had anything to hide behind. Once Rose disappeared into the kitchen, Tori took a deep breath. "I had a nice time in New York. Thank you for taking me. You know you didn't have to go to that much trouble."

"No trouble at all. I had a great time, too. I'm glad we were able to go. It was certainly more exciting than spending New Year's Eve here with my folks. They never even make it up to midnight. As kids, we used to stay up in the bunkhouse and watch Dick Clark on television after they went to bed."

"It must be strange to stay up here this long without the others. Are you heading back to New York soon?" Tori almost didn't want to know how much time she had left, but she had to ask.

Wade nodded. "In a couple days. I still have a few things to take care of before I go back."

"That's right. You still haven't bought my land," she said with a weak smile. She'd enjoyed the past few days without the topic coming up. "Time is a-ticking on that."

He glanced down at his mug and took a sip. "I guess I'm not going to worry too much about that anymore."

Tori's brow shot up in surprise. She didn't hide it well at all. "What?"

"You don't want to sell it to me. I can't make you. I don't know what I could offer to change your mind, so there's no point in fighting over it anymore."

What should've been a victorious moment didn't feel quite how she'd expected. Going up against Wade, she'd always secretly thought she would lose. One way or another he would wear her down. And now, although he'd named her the victor, it didn't seem as if she'd won. After the past few days, a part of her didn't want to beat him. The thought had crossed Tori's mind that if he'd stay, she'd consider selling it to him. She wanted to build a home, not just a house. Somehow having Wade there with her was an integral piece of her design.

Selling him the land would make him happy. She wanted him to be happy. She could find another piece of land, but replacing Wade's place in her heart felt nearly impossible.

And yet, she felt a tug of hope deep inside. If he no longer wanted her property, maybe she could have both him and the land. She'd known trusting Wade would be an issue as long as he had this ulterior motive. If that was gone, what could that mean? Had he really given up wanting the land or did he care too much about her to hurt her like that? He hadn't said anything about how he felt for her. If he was going back to New York and life as usual, he probably felt nothing at all but had just run out of time.

She'd be left with no reason to hate him when it was all over.

"I'd like to spend the last few days with you before I go."

She hadn't expected that at all. If he wasn't just romancing the property away from her, maybe there was more here than she'd thought. With a sigh of dismay, Tori shook her head. Wade always seemed to want the things she couldn't give. "I have to leave tomorrow. I'm going to Philadelphia for a few days. They're having the ribbon-cutting ceremony on my building down there on Saturday afternoon. I've got to wrap up all the loose ends. I probably won't be back until the seventh or eighth."

"Oh." Wade's expression was curious. A hint of disappointment mixed in with something else she couldn't put her finger on. She could almost see his mind spinning. She remembered that expression from watching him at his desk when she worked with him.

"You could come with me," she suggested.

He looked at her and shook his head. "I can't. I'll need to be back in Manhattan before that."

"I guess I'll have to catch up with you in the city sometime. Or the next time you're up this way."

Wade nodded, his expression guarded. He must've realized, as she had, that this would be their last date. Their last night together. "Do you have another project coming up that you'll be traveling to soon?"

"Not for a few months. I'm going to Vermont for a while this summer to design a ski lodge. Until then, I'll be here, working on building my house."

"Do you have the final plans drawn up yet?"

Yes and no. She had twenty plans completed, but for some reason her clarity about what she wanted had become muddled over the holidays. "I have to make a few final decisions. That's all. I should be able to get the contractors in place to break ground in the next few weeks."

Wade's green eyes widened just a touch at her words, but Rose brought their plates and the expression vanished. "I should give you Troy Caldwell's number. He's got a great building team that does excellent work."

Tori nodded and tried to focus on her food. She'd heard Caldwell was the guy to work with around here. She just hadn't gotten around to speaking with him before the holidays. It seemed that once she got back from Philadelphia, she'd have plenty of time. Wade would be long gone.

The rest of the meal was spent discussing the neutral topics of local electricians and concrete companies. Every now and again Tori would look up to find Wade watching her. There was a hesitation in his voice, a touch of worry lining his eyes. She wasn't certain she was the cause of it, though. He seemed a million miles away tonight. Maybe the stresses of being away from work were distracting him.

Tori was absentmindedly drawing the design for the front of her home across her plate with her fork and leftover ketchup when Wade's voice startled her. It seemed he wasn't the only one distracted this evening.

"Would you like to come back to the bunkhouse for some dessert? Molly baked a really nice chocolate cream cheese Bundt cake this morning."

His words were asking her if she'd like to join him for dessert, but the intensity of his gaze promised more than that. He wanted to have her in his arms one last time before they parted ways.

Tori knew she should say no. It would be so much easier if she just walked away now. She could take her land, her dignity and what was left of her heart back to her Airstream.

Instead, she found herself meeting his gaze and nodding yes. She wasn't quite ready to say goodbye to Wade.

Yet.

They'd spent another incredible night together. He hated to wake her up that morning but knew she had a schedule to keep. He would rather have lain in bed all day with her ear pressed to his heart and her hair strewed across his chest. He had to admit he'd gotten used to having her there when he woke up—grumpy face, wild hair and all.

But he had to.

After they'd reluctantly gotten out of bed, Wade made his way downstairs. Molly hadn't sneaked in with breakfast today, so Wade made coffee and toasted bagels while Tori showered.

They ate quietly together. There was an awkwardness in the air. For all intents and purposes, their relationship was over. They'd had their last date, their last chance to make love and this was their final breakfast.

Unlike other relationships that ended in angry fireworks or bitter barbs, their relationship would die quietly, because it was the practical thing to do. Neither of them really wanted to say goodbye, but neither was willing to say or do anything to change it. This needed to be the end.

When they were finished, he walked her out to her truck. They loitered at the door, so many unspoken things lingering between them. But Wade wouldn't say what he wanted to. Not until he'd finished what he came here for. And to do that, Tori needed to go to

Philadelphia. If he was successful, maybe he'd call her. Or maybe he'd be smart and just let this whole thing go. If she ever found out the truth about his past, it would be over anyway.

But that didn't mean he didn't want one last embrace. He wrapped his arms around Tori, hugging her tight to his chest. She clung just as fiercely to him, letting go only when he pulled away for their last kiss. He pressed his lips to hers, losing himself in the soft feel of her. There was no heat in the kiss. Just…goodbye.

When he stepped back, Tori quickly slipped on her sunglasses and climbed into the truck. He thought he saw the glint of tears in her eyes for a moment, but it could've been the morning sun blinding her.

"Goodbye, Wade," she said, slamming the truck door closed before he could respond. The engine roared to life, and he watched the truck disappear down the road to the highway.

It was over. And he didn't like it at all. But now it was time to put his plan into action.

If there was one thing Wade knew for certain, it was that he could call Heath at any hour, with any number of crazy requests, and his younger brother would be up for it. Brody second-guessed everything. Xander worried about how things might look. But Heath… He was the impulsive brother, and that was exactly what Wade needed. He headed back inside the bunkhouse to get his phone.

"Hey there, big brother," Heath answered. "What's happening?"

"You busy tomorrow?" Wade cut to the chase. His brother knew him well enough not to take offense. Neither of them usually had the time to waste on pleasantries.

"I don't have to be. What do you need?"

"You, a high-quality metal detector and a large plastic tarp."

"What, no shovels?" Heath joked.

"Dad has those. And the backhoe if we need it."

He'd been using the backhoe that day fifteen years ago as part of his chores on the farm. When he needed to bury the body, it seemed like the quickest and easiest thing to use, since he was working alone. No one would think twice about him driving it around the property. But the grave wasn't really that deep. He hadn't taken the time to bury the body seven or eight feet as he should have.

With Heath's help they could probably skip it this time. "We'll definitely need the metal detector. The snow has mostly melted, so it should be easier, but I still have fifteen years working against me on this. You up for an unorthodox treasure hunt?"

"Sure, yeah," Heath said without hesitation. "Whatever we have to do. I mean, hell, it's my ass if this all goes down wrong. You bet I'll help however I can to keep this a secret. I take it the plan to buy the land didn't work out."

"Nope. This is plan B."

Brody would've lectured him about the failure of plan A, but Heath always rolled with the punches. "What's plan B, exactly?"

"Find the body and move it back onto the family land while she's out of town. Can you come up tomorrow?"

"I can. I'll make some calls and dig up a good metal detector tonight, then leave in the morning."

Tori should have felt excited. There were hundreds of people gathered around the new arts-and-sciences center she'd designed. The press was there, snapping pictures and filming pieces for the nightly news. The mayor had personally shaken her hand and told her she'd done a beautiful job. This was huge exposure for her business.

But she wasn't excited. She was…lonely. This was a big moment for her, and she had no one to share it with. She pasted the smile back on her face for the photos and fought the tears that threatened to ruin the moment.

She wanted to share all of this with Wade. She wanted him standing next to her, beaming with pride. And yet he wasn't there. Why? Because of a stupid piece of land.

That's what it had become to her. She had imagined that it would be a magical thing to own a piece of the earth and make her mark on it by building her dream house. But the reality was much different. Even before Wade had shown up and started throwing money around, she'd begun to have her doubts. She'd dug in her heels only because he wanted something she had.

But he'd changed his mind. Wade wasn't going to fight her for it anymore. Why? Maybe for the same reason she no longer wanted to keep it. If this land was the only thing standing between them, he could have it.

The mayor cut the ribbon, and the crowd cheered amid the blinding flash of cameras. The dignitaries stepped back and the front doors were held open for everyone to go inside. There would be folks wandering around all afternoon sipping champagne, eating appetizers and talking about the virtues of green architecture as though they understood it.

As she watched the crowd file in, she knew she should go in with them. Answer questions. Do interviews. But she hadn't felt so desperate to get out of a place in her whole life.

If she left now, she could be home in a few hours. Wade should still be at the farm. And then she could tell him.

Tell him what? That she loved him? That he could have the land because it was nothing but dirt and rock without him in her life? Maybe. If she could work up the nerve.

Turning away from the building, Tori headed for the parking lot and her truck. She had a few hours' drive to figure out what she wanted to say. But she knew she had to go to Wade. Now.

It was probably thirty degrees outside, but Wade was sweating as though it were summertime. They hadn't even started seriously digging yet. That was probably why. They hadn't found what he was looking for so they could start digging. The afternoon had not gone as well as he'd hoped. The snow had melted, revealing a landscape just as confusing as before. No turtle-shaped rocks. No crooked trees like he remembered. Maybe his memory was faulty. Maybe he'd just been a freaked-out kid that night and the whole incident had gotten scrambled in his mind. He wished someone had gone out there with him.

They'd taken to just running the metal detector over every inch of the property. Periodically, they'd get a hit and they'd dig furiously into the frozen ground, only to find an old quarter or a screw. Heath would move on with the metal detector and Wade would stomp the ground back into place. There was another snowstorm in the forecast for tomorrow. By the time Tori returned, the evidence of their search would be buried for a few weeks and hopefully undetectable.

The sun had set not too long ago, and the darkness was making their job even harder than the rock-hard dirt. Heath had turned on the headlight on one of the four-wheelers, and they both carried flashlights, but they were getting discouraged.

"Wade, I don't see any rocks that look like a turtle. Not even if I scrunch my eyes up and look sideways."

"I know." Wade sighed. Maybe this whole plan was a bad idea. Even if they could find the right place, moving a fifteen-year-old corpse couldn't be easy. It's not as if he would be in one piece anymore.

"I'm not getting much with the metal detector. You're sure he still had that ring on when you buried him?"

"Yes." Wade remembered the large gold ring with the black stone in the center. How could he forget it? He'd had an imprint of it punched into his face once. "I remember because I thought about taking it off so no one could identify him. But I didn't know what to do with it. I decided it was better to just leave it on, since he would've taken it with him when he left."

"I guess that was a good idea. We'd never find him without it."

"I'm beginning to think we won't find him even with it." Wade looked across the dark landscape of Tori's property. The rocky ridge where she planned to build the house was off to the back. There was no way he could've buried anything there, even with the backhoe. Maybe the construction crew that would build her house wouldn't find anything. Maybe, despite his failures, this secret would stay buried.

"Are you sure it's on her plot and not one of the others?" Heath asked.

At this point, Wade couldn't afford to consider that possibility. To know he'd wasted all this time on the wrong property? And if there was one thing he knew, it was that the owner of the largest plot, a large commercial development company, wasn't going to sell for any amount of money. Brody had done some research, and they were building a small resort retreat. They'd already started working out there.

"No, I'm not sure," Wade admitted through gritted teeth. "But I swear I didn't go that far. This area looks right. It's got to be right."

Heath nodded and started swinging the metal detector over a different segment of land.

"Let's load up and call it a night. We can try again in the morning before it starts to snow."

They each grabbed their shovels and equipment and had started walking back to their four-wheelers when they were suddenly bathed in bright white lights. Headlights.

Wade froze in place like a deer. He clutched his incriminating tools tighter in his fists. Who was it? He couldn't tell. They were blinded, unable to see anything but the bright white orbs aimed in their direction.

Was it the sheriff? No. He wasn't that lucky. He knew the sheriff and could talk his way out of this. The lights were way too high for a patrol car. It was a truck. An older truck, judging by the loud rumble of the engine.

An old truck.

Wade swallowed hard. She couldn't be back already. Not this soon. The ribbon-cutting ceremony was today. Tori would've had to drive straight back after it ended to be here already. She said Monday or Tuesday at the earliest. Why would she have rushed home again?

The answer was on the tip of his tongue, but he didn't even want to think it, much less say it. The way she'd looked at him last night had been different. Something had changed. He'd tried to deny it at dinner, and when he made love to her. He told himself it was just because they both knew it was the end for them.

Wade was a fool to ignore the truth. Tori had fallen in love with him. He couldn't be certain, but maybe she'd decided to come home early before he returned to New York so she could see him again. Or maybe she'd gotten brave enough to tell him how she felt.

And instead she'd caught him red-handed on her property with a shovel and a metal detector. Damn.

Heath leaned in to him, finally daring to move. "Are they just going to watch us or get out of the truck? You think they're calling the cops?"

Wade shook his head. "I doubt it. I think it's Tori."

"Oh, man," Heath said. "I thought she wasn't coming back for a couple of days. What are you going to tell her? You can't tell her the truth."

That was a great question. He'd have to think of something, because the truth was completely off the table. "I have no idea. But you just get on your four-wheeler and go, okay? She and I need to talk alone."

"I'm not going to leave you out here. Doesn't she have a shotgun?"

Wade had forgotten about the shotgun. Hopefully it was locked in the Airstream and not with her in the truck. "Yes, you are. Seriously. I'll be okay. Go, now. It's better that way."

Heath shrugged and turned away from the light to go to his ATV. He loaded his things, cranked the engine and disappeared into the trees. It wasn't until he was gone that Wade heard the truck's engine die. The lights stayed on when the heavy door clicked open.

Wade still couldn't see, but he could hear boots crunching on the gravel. Then a woman's silhouette appeared between him and the truck's headlights. He'd know those curves anywhere.

Tori stopped a few feet away. He was about to say something to explain himself when she suddenly charged forward. Her hand reared back to slap him, and he was going to let her. His hands were full. What was he going to do? Swing a shovel at her? He deserved it, anyway.

Instead, she hesitated for a moment and her hand finally fell back to her side. Tori took a step back, her breath ragged in the darkness. He could finally make out her features in the light. Her eyes were wide, her jaw clenched tight. "You bastard!" she said. "All this time. All those nights we spent together were a lie. You were just using me. Lulling me into complacency so you could slip in and get what you wanted."

"Tori, it wasn't like that." Wade tossed the shovel onto the ground and reached for her, but she took another step back.

"Don't you dare. Don't you try to smooth everything over with your charming lies. I've fallen for enough of those already. I can't believe this." Tori buried her fingers in her hair and clutched her skull. She turned from him and started pacing through the yard like a caged lioness. "I can't believe I let myself trust you when I knew you were the last person I could trust."

"I'm sorry, I—"

"That night in the diner was especially well done," she continued, her sharp tone leaning toward the sarcastic and bitter. "Letting me believe that I'd won. That you had given up trying to take the land from me. And I just ate it up. Watched you with love-stricken doe eyes and sucked up all the crap you threw my way."

"That wasn't a lie. I don't want to take your land. I knew I would hate myself for doing that to you. I couldn't."

"So, what? You decided you'd just wait until I left and steal what you really wanted? Save yourself the trouble and the half-million-dollar expense?"

Wade looked down at the ground, the expression on his face too guilty to be washed out by the bright lamps shining on him. "You don't understand."

"No, I don't understand. And maybe I would, but you've wrapped everything up in a web of lies so thick I couldn't see the truth even if it was right in front of me. What is it that you're after, Wade? It's obviously not the land and your family legacy, as you said before. What do I have on this property that is so valuable to you? What could be so damn important that you would ruin everything…" Her voice trailed off.

Tori's voice trembled at the end, and it made his chest ache to hear her like that. He'd never wanted to hurt her. He'd spent his whole life trying to care for and protect the important people in his life. Why would he want to hurt her? He wanted so badly to tell Tori the truth. But that secret wasn't just his to protect. He couldn't betray his family, even for her. He'd failed his brothers and sister once. Wade absolutely could not do that to them again. No matter how he might feel about Tori. "I can't tell you that. I want to. Believe me, I do. But I can't."

Tori chuckled bitterly and crossed her arms defensively over her chest. "Of course you can't tell me. I can't believe I trusted you. That I let myself fall… *No.*" She corrected herself with a firm shake of her head. "The only thing I fell for was your sob story about family. I'm not about to do that twice."

"Tori, please." Wade reached for her, but she moved out of the way.

She held out her hand for him to keep his distance. "You don't get to touch me anymore." Turning on her heel, she marched back toward her truck. She killed the lights, slammed the door and headed for her trailer.

Wade took a few steps to follow her. He wanted to talk to her. To help her understand.

"You know," she said, "when I was in Philadelphia today, I had started to think that maybe this land wasn't so important after all. I can build a house here, but if the things that make it a home are…somewhere else… what is the point? It seemed so vital for you to preserve your family legacy. So I decided you should. I got in my truck as soon as the ceremony was over, and I came home to tell you that I wanted to sell you the land. And some other things that aren't relevant anymore."

Wade closed his eyes, her words hitting him hard in the gut. She'd trusted him. She cared enough about him to give him the one thing he wanted. And he had ruined it by sneaking behind her back and trying to steal the gift before she could give it. He was an impatient ass, and there were no words in his defense.

"Can I ask one thing? Maybe this is a question you can actually answer."

Wade looked up at her. She was standing on the metal stairs and gripping the door handle with white-knuckled intensity. The patio light illuminated the shimmer in her blue eyes as she watched him. Just the slightest thing could send those tears spilling down her cheeks, but she fought to hold on.

"I'll answer if I can."

"Was all of this just about the land to you? The dinners, the trip to New York, the chocolate-covered strawberries... I know at first it was a game of wits for both of us, but along the way it changed for me. I'd hoped it changed for you, too. Was it all just an attempt to charm me into giving you what you wanted, or did any of that mean something to you?"

Yes, it meant something. He wanted to yell it. He wanted to scoop her up into his arms and kiss her until she couldn't be angry with him anymore. But her furrowed brow and glassy eyes made him wonder if the truth would make things better or worse. Would it hurt her more to know that what they had had was special and he'd ruined it? Or to believe that it all had been a game?

"Tori, I—"

"Wait," she interrupted. "Forget I asked. I think I'd rather not know the truth. Goodbye, Wade."

Wade saw one of the tears escape down her cheek as she opened the door and disappeared inside.

Ten

"You look like hell."

Wade looked up from his desk to see Heath standing in the doorway of his office. He had to admit he wasn't surprised by the impromptu arrival of his youngest brother. He'd been dodging calls, texts and emails from his siblings for over a week. He'd canceled dinner plans at Brody's place. Before too long, he'd figured, they'd send someone to track him down. Since Heath lived and worked in Manhattan, too, he was the obvious stuckee.

Wade looked down at his watch. "Eight days, thirteen hours and forty-two minutes. That means Linda in accounting wins the office pool."

"Very funny," Heath said, coming into the office and shutting the door behind him. "What's going on with you lately? You've been too quiet."

Wade shrugged. "I've been busy. Work always picks

up after the holidays, and it takes a while for everyone to get back into the swing of things."

"Uh-huh." Heath wandered over to the minibar and pulled out a soda from the stash. "Do the other people you say that to actually believe you?"

With a heavy sigh, Wade sank back into his leather executive chair. "No one else ever bothers to ask how I am, so I haven't gotten much practice in yet."

"Tell the truth. How are you?"

"I'm fine."

Heath sat in one of Wade's guest chairs and propped his feet up on the edge of the large mahogany desk. He scrutinized Wade with his hazel gaze as he casually sipped his drink. "Brody was right," he said after a few silent moments.

Wade frowned at his brother. "Brody was right about what? I haven't even spoken to him since I had to cancel our dinner plans."

"Doesn't matter. He was still right. You're in love."

The declaration sent Wade bolt upright in his chair. What did Brody know about being in love? The man was a hermit. "That's ridiculous."

Heath shook his head. "She loves you, too, you know."

"Since when did my entire family become psychic?"

"Mama saw her at the grocery store. Said she was an absolute mess. She's not sure what went on between you two, but she's very unhappy about it."

"I don't date to please Mama. She needs to focus her matchmaking skills on you for a change."

"She shouldn't waste her time," he said with a wide grin. "I'm already married."

"You're hilarious. Keep telling that story and she'll move on to demanding those grandchildren she wants."

Heath shuddered in his seat and took a large swig of soda to wash away the bitter aftertaste of Wade's suggestion. "The point is that she's miserable. You're miserable."

"I'm not miserable."

"You're not Jolly Old Saint Nick, either. You've been avoiding everyone. You've got bags under your eyes large enough to store loose change. Your tie doesn't even match your shirt, man. You're obviously not sleeping."

Wade looked down at the blue shirt and green plaid tie he was wearing. He could've sworn he'd reached for the blue striped one. Must've grabbed the wrong tie and not noticed. Not sleeping for a few days would do that to a guy, he supposed. "I've got new neighbors. They've been louder than usual, and after a few weeks at the farm, I got used to the quiet."

"And it has absolutely nothing to do with the red-head whose heart you broke last week?"

Heath just wasn't about to let this go. Wade knew that if he didn't say something soon, Heath was liable to put him in a headlock and knuckle his scalp until he confessed.

Wade opted to answer the question without really answering it. "She's better off without me."

"Isn't that for her to decide?"

Wade shrugged. "It doesn't matter. She hates me."

"I doubt that. She was just hurt. Your betrayal was that much worse because she let herself fall in love with you."

"She didn't say that."

"Why on earth would she? Anyway, she didn't need to say it. We both know why she rushed home from

Philadelphia. And even if she does hate you now, that doesn't change anything. *You're* still in love with *her*."

Wade's chest started to ache at the mere thought. The pain had plagued him since the door of Tori's Airstream slammed shut in his face. It had woken him up the few times he had managed to fall asleep. He'd started popping antacids. He'd even done a Google search for "heart attack symptoms" to make sure he wasn't dying. As best he could tell, he wasn't on death's door. He was just in love with a woman who hated him.

"She's never going to forgive me for lying to her. And I can't tell her the truth about what we were looking for. I can't just go to her and tell her I love her and that she's just got to trust me."

"You know, fifteen years ago our lives took an unexpected turn. For the most part we've been able to carry on with our lives. Sure, we remember. Our consciences are burdened with it. We worry we handled it wrong and made a bigger mess of the situation. We pray that no one ever finds out what happened. But for more than twenty-three hours out of every day, I can live my life like it never happened. Can you?"

"Usually. Until I found out Dad sold the land."

"But before that...were you happy?"

Happy was a funny word. Wade didn't like using it. "I was content. 'Happy' sounds like puppies and rainbows. I was pleased with how my life was going."

"And now?"

"And now...I guess, to use your words, I'm miserable."

"We've decided you should tell her the truth."

Wade's brow shot up at his brother's words. "We? Did you all hold some secret council meeting without me?"

"Yes," he said, very matter-of-factly. "Via Skype. We talked it over and decided that you shouldn't give up your chance at real happiness just to protect us."

Wade almost laughed for a moment before he realized Heath wasn't kidding. They had no idea what they were asking him to do. He'd spent his whole life trying to protect them. Trying to make up for that night. He couldn't just flip-flop because they said it was okay. It wasn't okay. "I'm not going to expose everyone, including myself, just for a woman."

"She's not just any woman, Wade. She's the woman you love. Do you want to marry her?"

The image of Tori in an ivory lace gown instantly sprang into his mind. Her red-gold hair was pulled back into an elegant twist. Her peaches-and-cream skin rosy from excitement and champagne. He'd never even thought about it before, and yet the vision of her in his mind was so real that he couldn't push it aside. "If she'd have me."

"Then you can tell her. After the wedding."

Wade opened his mouth, then realized what they had in mind. If he married Tori, he could tell her everything and she couldn't be compelled to testify against them.

"She's not going to marry me unless I tell her the truth. And I can't tell her the truth unless she marries me. So, really, I get nowhere with this."

Heath shrugged. "I disagree. When I came in the door, you were 'fine.' Now you're a man in love who wants to get married. I think you're way ahead. Now you just have to go tell her."

"Yeah, sure. Tori, I love you and I want to marry you. And once you marry me, I can tell you all about how I buried some guy on your property and I'm afraid you'll dig him up while building your dream house."

"Those aren't the words I'd recommend. But if you show up there, tell her you love her, offer her a ring to prove you're serious and explain where you're coming from with all this, I think she'll understand."

Wade frowned at his brother, then turned back to stare at his desk blotter. He'd lain in bed night after night replaying those last moments with Tori. If he'd said or done something else, might it have ended differently? Sometimes the door slammed in his face just the way it had happened. But once, Tori had listened to his words. She'd forgiven him. And that was the time he'd imagined telling her the truth.

He wanted so badly to go back and have another try. Heath insisted he still had a chance to turn things around. He had permission to tell her what she wanted to know, but he wasn't sure if it would make a difference. Could Tori really trust him enough? What if it was too little, too late? Was it possible she was still in love with him after everything that had happened between them?

Wade closed his eyes and pictured Tori as she'd been Friday morning before she left for Philadelphia. Her pale blue eyes were wary, but the love he saw there was undeniable. Maybe he hadn't lost his chance yet. God, he hoped so. He couldn't function like this for much longer. He'd have a real heart attack before too long from the stress and the copious amounts of caffeine he was drinking to compensate for lost sleep.

He had to give it a shot. The gaping hole in his chest begged him to at least try. If she turned him down, he would not have lost anything he hadn't already given away.

Heath looked at his brother. His expression was about as serious as it ever got. "This will work out."

He sure as hell hoped so.

"You always were the optimist in the family." Wade rolled his chair up to the desk with a new fire to put his plan into action. "Okay, Mr. Advertising Executive, direct me to the most environmentally conscious jeweler on the market."

"I should've known—" Heath grinned "—that you would pick the only woman on earth able to resist the little blue box. Let me call one of my guys who handles most of our jewelry accounts. But be warned—odds are it won't be local. You might have to wait a couple days."

Absolutely not. He would be in Connecticut tomorrow, come hell or high water. "That's unacceptable," he said.

"Well, then, get ready to get on a plane."

Wade nodded and rang his admin to clear his calendar for the rest of today and tomorrow. He'd fly to the ends of the earth to get Tori back.

"It's crap. All crap." Tori ripped the sheet of paper off the pad, then crumpled her latest blueprint into a ball and tossed it into the overflowing wastepaper basket. It had to be the hundredth design she'd sketched in the past week, but she hated them all. Even the ones she'd been really happy with before Wade came into her life.

Now everything felt wrong.

Maybe this whole settling-down thing was just a bad idea. Maybe her mother was right when she said that they had a wandering spirit that shied away from the tethers of the typical American dream. A month ago it had seemed like a great plan. She had been bursting with ideas. Fantasizing about her new closet with room for more than five pairs of shoes. Just the thought of a full-size kitchen and an actual living room with a couch and big-screen television was enough to get her blood pumping with excitement.

Now the only thing that set her heart to racing was Wade. And he was long gone, along with the piece of her he'd taken with him.

Tori cussed and flung her pencil across the Airstream. It bounced off her cabinet door and rolled toward the bathroom. She watched it move across the floor, stopping at the butt of her shotgun, which was leaning against the door frame.

It brought to mind the first day he'd shown up on her property. His charming smile. His infuriating arrogance. The way she'd threatened to shoot him. How was she supposed to carry on with her plans when even the sight of her shotgun brought memories of him to mind? Living on his parents' old property would guarantee that she could never get away from Wade Mitchell.

But Tori didn't want to get away from him. She wanted the charming liar back in her arms. She sat staring blankly at her notepad, thinking about what had happened. Since he left, replaying the scene in her mind had given her some clarity. It had allowed her to focus on the words she'd refused to listen to in her anger.

Whatever it was he wanted was important. The land itself had no real value to him, just whatever was on it. Given she didn't even know what it was, it wasn't something she would ever miss. A part of her understood his reasoning. If he could take or move what he needed, Tori could keep her land and they could both be happy. Maybe even happy together.

If only she hadn't decided to come home early.

Tori looked back down at her fresh sheet of paper. The blank squares were taunting her. Picking up a new pencil, she took a deep breath and tried something different. How would she design a house for both her and Wade to live in?

She started with his office. It had an entire wall of windows that opened up on a view of the valley below like the ones overlooking Times Square in their hotel suite. On the opposite wall were floor-to-ceiling bookshelves. A see-through fireplace connected his office to the great room. Both spaces would have twelve-foot ceilings and huge panes of glass. One panel would slide out to let them onto the deck. She sketched in a hot tub where they could sit together in the evenings, talk and drink wine.

Wine... Tori started sketching a dream kitchen with a staircase that led down into a wine cellar. Her pencil moved feverishly now, the rooms flowing together perfectly. Nearly an hour passed before she sat back and looked at the design.

This was the house she wanted. The one with Wade in it. Her gaze moved over the second-story guest bedroom that was right off the master suite. It would be perfect for a nursery. She could just see the ivory-and-green wallpaper, the mobile over the crib. The sunlight that streamed in would provide the perfect amount of natural light. Wade could sit in the rocking chair and read bedtime stories....

That was the thought that brought the tears to her eyes that she'd fought for days.

Tori grasped the corner of the sketch, ready to rip it off and trash it with the others, but she just couldn't. This was the house she wanted.

The rumbling sound of a car pulling onto her property pulled her attention away from the design. Unable to see from her seat, she got up and walked over to the window.

The corner of a red hood with a BMW logo nearly sent her heart into her throat. She stumbled back against the sink, gripping the counter to keep her knees from giving out under her. Wade had returned to New York a week ago. Why was he here now? To apologize? To offer her more money? Her mind raced with different options, but she shook each one aside. The only way to know for sure was to go out there and find out.

Glancing to her right, she picked up the shotgun and went to the door. She was in love with him, but she was still angry and hurt by what he'd done. He needed to know that.

Tori swung open the door and stepped down into the snow. A snowstorm had blown through the day after she came home, blanketing the property in white and making it impossible for her to look around and search for clues about what he was after.

When she turned, Wade was standing near the hood of his SUV, his arms raised in surrender. In one hand was a bundle of tulips wrapped in florist paper. "Don't shoot," he said with the smile she'd missed.

She raised the gun and studied his face. He looked older, more tired than she remembered. Hopefully he'd had as bad a week as she had. Knowing he might have suffered without her helped soothe her pride a bit. "What do you want?"

"I came here to make you an offer."

It took everything Tori had not to pull the trigger and cover his body in painful welts. An offer? Here she was, designing their home, decorating their damn nursery, and he came here focused on the same old agenda.

"You're too late," she said. "I wouldn't sell you this

land for every dime you have. Flowers won't help, either."

Wade nodded. A flicker of amusement in his eyes
sent a flame of irritation through her veins. "That's
fine. I'm not here to buy the land."

Tori frowned. "If you don't want my land, what do
you want, Wade?"

"I want you."

The intensity in his expression was undeniable. His
green eyes were burrowing into her. It made it hard to
breathe. He wanted her. *Her.* Not the land. Not what
was hidden on it. Her. Her heart leaped in her chest
for a moment, but she refused to so much as blink on
the exterior. She wasn't going to let him off that easily.
"I'm not interested in any more dinner dates. All I got
out of that was indigestion and rug burn."

A smile curled Wade's lips. Instinctively she wanted
to smile back, but she wouldn't.

"That's okay," he said. "I'm not here to ask you on
a date. I'm here to tell you that I'm in love with you."

Tori's hands started trembling, the shotgun unsteady
in her grasp. She stood there with her mouth open but
without words as Wade came closer.

"Let's just set this down, shall we?" He eased the
gun from her hands and laid it in the snow a few feet
away. "I'd rather not have our love story turn into one
of those tragic tales." Wade handed her the bouquet of
tulips. They were her favorite flower. She hadn't ever
told him that.

"How did you know?" she asked.

"Brody is a genius. You can find out almost anything
with a computer. I've waited seven years to give you
those flowers." He put his hands on her upper arms,
gently rubbing her skin to warm her. "I've been mis-

erable since we fought. I can't get that night out of my head. I can't sleep. All I can see is the look on your face when you walked away, and it breaks my heart. I'd give anything to see you smile again. Today, and every day of the rest of my life."

If the mention of love wasn't enough, he was making sounds like he wanted to...to...

"I want to tell you the truth. Every bit of it. But it's not just my secret to keep. There are others who could get hurt if the story were to be made public. But I can tell you this much... I was once very young and very stupid. When faced with something no child should have to handle, I made the wrong decision. I believe the evidence of that night is somewhere on your property. I've been doing everything I can think of to make sure no one ever finds it. I've done some things in the past few weeks that I'm not proud of. But I did what I felt I had to do to protect my family. You know how important they are to me. I would protect them with my life, just as I would protect yours. And for now I have to continue to protect their secret, just as I would protect a secret of yours."

Tori could see the pain in Wade's expression. His past was eating at him, gnawing at his gut on a daily basis. She was amazed that she hadn't noticed it before now, but maybe he just kept it too well hidden. He was letting down walls for her. Because she wanted him to. Even if he couldn't tell her everything, he was making the effort. And she could appreciate that. If she could be certain of nothing else, she knew that Wade would do anything for the people he loved. And if he loved her as he said he did, she would be just as fiercely protected.

The sense of security and stability that washed over her in that moment was unprecedented. A lifetime of moving from place to place had never provided it. Even buying this land hadn't provided it. But she'd found it in allowing herself to trust Wade and be protected by him.

"One day, I hope to be able to tell you the rest of the story. And that you'll hear everything I've done and trust me when I say that, right or wrong, I only ever had the best of intentions. I pray for your understanding because you are a beautiful, intelligent woman and I adore you. You make me happy just lying in bed listening to you breathe. I want to wake up every morning to your messy hair and pouty face. And I want to do it here, in Connecticut, in the house you designed."

Tori gasped. "You'd move here?"

He nodded. "I would. There isn't much I can do in the office that I can't do from here with teleconferences and virtual meetings. I might have to go to the city from time to time, but when I do, I want to take you with me. I don't think I like the idea of traveling without my wife."

"But I—" Tori started, then stopped. She watched as Wade eased down onto one knee in the snow. Reaching into his coat pocket, he pulled out a small wooden box wrapped in a gold ribbon. "Wade…" she said, disbelieving. The flowers slipped from her fingers to the snow.

"Victoria Sullivan," he began, unwrapping the bow. He eased open the hinge and held the box up to her. "Would you do me the honor of being my wife?"

Tori glanced down at the engagement ring in his hands. The nearly two carat round diamond was set in a multirow pave diamond band of platinum. It sparkled so brightly with the sunlight reflecting off the snow that she was almost blinded. She had stood in the snow very nearly dumbstruck for the past few minutes, but now she knew she had to find the right thing to say. And it should be easy, since she'd been screaming it in her head since he knelt in the snow.

"Yes," she said, tears pooling in her eyes from the light and the emotions ready to spill out of her.

Wade stood back up, slipping the ring onto her finger. It fit perfectly.

She tore her eyes away from the ring to look up at the man who would soon be her husband. "I love you," she said.

"And I love you." He leaned down to kiss her, almost the official sealing of the deal he'd come here to offer her.

Tori melted into his arms, losing herself in the feeling of being with the man she thought she'd lost forever. Her blood instantly began to heat with the desire he easily stirred in her. Just when she was ready to tug him into the Airstream and make love to her fiancé for the first time, he pulled away and looked down at her with a smug grin.

"Do you have any idea how hard it was to find the perfect diamond for you?"

Tori frowned. "Am I that picky?"

"I don't know if you are, but I certainly am. It had to be perfect. So perfect, I was willing to fly to San Francisco and back to buy it from a jeweler there. This ring is from an environmentally conscious and well-regulated Canadian diamond mine. Certified conflict-free. The band is made of recycled platinum. Hell, the ring box is even made from Rimu wood, whatever that is."

Tori grinned. Wade could have marched right into Tiffany's, bought any ring he wanted, and she would've said yes. But he didn't. He traveled all the way to the West Coast and back to get the ring he knew she would want. That was more precious than the large, flawless stone in the center.

"Rimu is a sustainable wood from New Zealand. And I love it. There isn't a more beautiful and perfect ring in all the world. Absolutely perfect."

"Like you," he said.

Rising on tiptoe, she kissed him again. "Now, let's go inside and get you out of those wet pants."

Wade's brow shot up at her suggestion. He glanced down at the wet knees of his trousers, then back at the Airstream behind him. "Okay, but after that, you need to get back to work designing that house."

"Why?"

"Because," he said, "I'm afraid if I make love to you the way I want to, we're going to roll this sucker down the hill and into a ditch. I need a house. Without wheels. ASAP."

"I'll do my best," Tori said. Taking his hand in hers, she led him over to the Airstream. "Until then," she said, laughing, "if this trailer's a rockin'..."

Epilogue

Two months later

"**R**emind me again why we're hiding eggs? In the dark?" Tori looked across the silver, moon-illuminated yard at Wade and Brody. They were both chucking the plastic Easter eggs under bushes and behind tree trunks.

Brody straightened and shrugged. "It's tradition. Like watching the Grinch at Christmas. Don't question our methods."

"But there aren't any children to find them."

"It doesn't matter," he explained. "For as long as I have lived on this farm, Wade and I have hidden Easter eggs for the younger kids. I swear to you, if Julianne and Heath wake up and there are no eggs to find, bunny heads will roll."

"You know, when Wade first told me about this, I

thought he meant the Edens hosted a community egg hunt here on the farm. I didn't realize I'd be out in the middle of the night hiding candy for your twenty-seven-year-old brother."

"It's good practice," Wade replied with a wink. "If Mama has her way, there will be grandkids hunting here in no time."

"Yeah, well," she muttered, "I don't know why all the pressure is on me when there are four other kids in this family. We need to get Brody a girl."

"Ha, ha," Brody said flatly. "You're funny. Why don't you get me a unicorn and a time machine while you're at it? Then I can go back to the nineties and gouge my father with the unicorn horn before he could ruin my chances of ever dating."

Tori shook her head and put an egg under the steps of the front porch. Over the past few months she'd gotten to know Wade's family better, including the grumpy and serious Brody. She found that he wasn't really that grumpy or that serious. He had a marshmallow center under that hard-candy shell. It made her want to help other people see though his defenses, as well.

"How do you expect to meet women if you never go out in public?" Wade teased. "Have one ordered on the internet and delivered to your office?"

Brody chucked an egg at Wade. The plastic shell separated on impact with his chest, sending candy scattering across the grass. "I imagine the shipping would be outrageous on that, so no. I have a woman in my life, thank you very much."

Wade retaliated with his own egg. Brody ducked and his egg missed, hitting the tree behind him and flying open. "Agnes doesn't count. She's your fiftysomething secretary. And she's married with grandchildren."

"Don't I know it," Brody complained. "She started making noises a few weeks ago about her anniversary coming up in the fall. She says she wants to take some time off for it."

"That's nice. Are they going on a trip to celebrate?" Tori asked.

"Yes," Brody responded with a heavy sigh. "It's a milestone year. Apparently they've booked a three-week Mediterranean cruise."

"That sounds wonderfully romantic," she said.

Brody shook his head, unconvinced. "Not for me."

"Agnes is Brody's connection to the outside world," Wade explained. "Without her, he's helpless as a babe."

"I am not helpless. There are just some things that I can't do from my office. Or that are easier to have her handle. Like picking up my dry cleaning."

Tori couldn't imagine living in Brody's world without contact with other people. From what Wade had told her, he had a housekeeper who worked at his home during the day while he was gone, but she always left before he got back. And he had his secretary. Aside from family visits, that was it. He lived in seclusion. "What are you going to do when she goes?"

"I don't know," Brody said. He put the last of his eggs in the curled-up nest of the garden hose. "I've been trying not to think about it. I've got months before I have to make a decision."

"I'm sure you can hire a temp from a local agency to come in while she's gone."

Brody frowned at her. "I don't like new people."

"I'm new, and you like me."

"That's because I realized Wade was hopelessly in love and there was no getting rid of you."

Wade came up behind Tori and wrapped his arms

around her waist. She curled against him, seeking out his warmth in the chilly night air.

"You have to keep yourself open to the opportunities around you," he said to his brother. "You never know what you might find. Great things can show up where you least expect them."

Brody looked at the two of them and shook his head. "People in love are disgusting."

"Disgustingly happy," Wade countered, placing a warm kiss just under Tori's earlobe. The touch sent a shiver down her spine that made her want to dump her basket of eggs and drag him back to the Airstream.

"Happily ever after," she agreed.

* * * * *

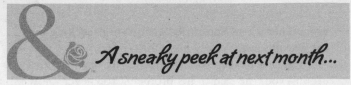

Desire™

PASSIONATE AND DRAMATIC LOVE STORIES

My wish list for next month's titles...

In stores from 15th March 2013:

2 stories in each book - only £5.49!

☐ The King Next Door – Maureen Child
& Bedroom Diplomacy – Michelle Celmer

☐ A Real Cowboy – Sarah M. Anderson
& Marriage with Benefits – Kat Cantrell

☐ All He Really Needs – Emily McKay
& A Tricky Proposition – Cat Schield

Available at WHSmith, Tesco, Asda, Eason, Amazon and Apple

Just can't wait?

Visit us Online

You can buy our books online a month before they hit the shops! **www.millsandboon.co.uk**

0313/51

Special Offers

Every month we put together collections and longer reads written by your favourite authors.

Here are some of next month's highlights— and don't miss our fabulous discount online!

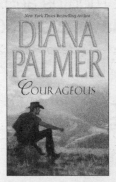

On sale 5th April

On sale 15th March

On sale 5th April

Save 20% on all Special Releases

Find out more at
www.millsandboon.co.uk/specialreleases

Visit us Online

0413/ST/MB410

Join the Mills & Boon Book Club

Subscribe to **Desire™** today for 3, 6 or 12 months and you could **save over £30!**

We'll also treat you to these fabulous extras:

 FREE L'Occitane gift set worth £10

 FREE home delivery

 Books up to 2 months ahead of the shops

Bonus books, exclusive offers... and much more!

Subscribe now at
www.millsandboon.co.uk/subscribeme

Save over £30 – find out more at
www.millsandboon.co.uk/subscribeme

SUBS/OFFER/D

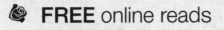

Mills & Boon® Online

Discover more romance at
www.millsandboon.co.uk

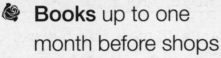

- **FREE** online reads
- **Books** up to one
  month before shops
- **Browse our books**
  before you buy

  ...and much more!

For exclusive competitions and instant updates:

 Like us on **facebook.com/romancehq**

 Follow us on **twitter.com/millsandboonuk**

 Join us on **community.millsandboon.co.uk**

Visit us Online   Sign up for our FREE eNewsletter at
www.millsandboon.co.uk

WEB/M&B/RTL4

The World of Mills & Boon®

There's a Mills & Boon® series that's perfect for you. We publish ten series and, with new titles every month, you never have to wait long for your favourite to come along.

Blaze.
Scorching hot, sexy reads
4 new stories every month

By Request
Relive the romance with the best of the best
9 new stories every month

Cherish™
Romance to melt the heart every time
12 new stories every month

Desire™
Passionate and dramatic love stories
8 new stories every month

Visit us Online

Try something new with our Book Club offer
www.millsandboon.co.uk/freebookoffer

M&B/WORLD2

What will you treat yourself to next?

Ignite your imagination, step into the past...
6 new stories every month

INTRIGUE...

Breathtaking romantic suspense
Up to 8 new stories every month

Captivating medical drama – with heart
6 new stories every month

MODERN™

International affairs, seduction & passion guaranteed
9 new stories every month

n o c t u r n e™

Deliciously wicked paranormal romance
Up to 4 new stories every month

RIVA™

Live life to the full – give in to temptation
3 new stories every month available exclusively via our Book Club

You can also buy Mills & Boon eBooks at
www.millsandboon.co.uk

Visit us Online

M&B/WORLD2